W9-BZB-917

BLACK GOLD

#6 (Anita Richmond)

Anita Richmond Bunkley

BLACK GOLD

A DUTTON BOOK

DUTTON

Published by the Penguin Group
Penguin Books USA Inc., 375 Hudson Street, New York, New York 10014, U.S.A.
Penguin Books Ltd, 27 Wrights Lane, London W8 5TZ, England
Penguin Books Australia Ltd, Ringwood, Victoria, Australia
Penguin Books Canada Ltd, 10 Alcorn Avenue, Toronto, Ontario, Canada M4V 3B2
Penguin Books (N.Z.) Ltd, 182–190 Wairau Road, Auckland 10, New Zealand

Penguin Books Ltd, Registered Offices:
Harmondsworth, Middlesex, England

First published by Dutton, an imprint of Dutton Signet,
a division of Penguin Books USA Inc.
Distributed in Canada by McClelland & Stewart Inc.

First Printing, February, 1994
1 3 5 7 9 10 8 6 4 2

LIBRARY OF CONGRESS CATALOGING IN PUBLICATION DATA
Bunkley, Anita R. (Anita Richmond)
Black gold / Anita Richmond Bunkley.
p. cm.
ISBN 0-525-93752-8
1. Petroleum industry and trade—Texas—Fiction. 2. Afro-American families—Texas—Fiction. 3. Texas—History—1846–1950—Fiction. 4. Family—Texas—Fiction. I. Title.
PS3552.U4715B53 1994
813'.54—dc20 *93-30611*
CIP

Printed in the United States of America
Set in Janson and Caslon Openface

Designed by Steven N. Stathakis

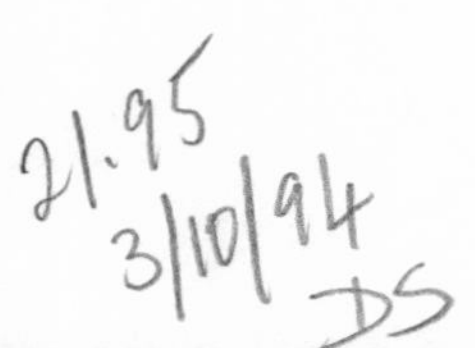

This book is dedicated in love and gratitude
to my parents,
Clifford and Virginia Richmond

ACKNOWLEDGMENTS

I would like to acknowledge and thank the following individuals for their assistance:

Attorney Louis A. Bedford, Jr., Dallas, Texas
Bruce Bell, Houston, Texas
Silvia Childer, Limestone County Historical Museum, Groesbeck, Texas
John Chronic, Sastex Exploration, Houston, Texas
Velma Harrison, Mexia, Texas
Mary Lou Kirvin, Dallas, Texas
Dorothy McBay, Mexia, Texas
Patricia Prather, Houston, Texas
Mary Shelby, Mexia, Texas
J. S. Stubbs, Blair-Stubbs Funeral Home, Mexia, Texas
Margie Walker, Houston, Texas
Carla Wilkins, Gibbs Memorial Library, Mexia, Texas

Prologue

1891 Fort Worth, Texas

Even though Ed Brannon was deaf in one ear, the baby's cries woke him up. He didn't know what time it was, or how much longer it would stay dark, but he knew he had to get himself down to the train station by daybreak. He swung his feet to the floor and listened for a moment, hoping Leela would go back to sleep. She didn't. The infant wailed and squirmed in her basket at the foot of his bed until the tired father leaned down and put his finger in her mouth. As his two-month-old daughter tugged on his thumb, Ed slipped on his pants and groped for his work shoes with his other hand. No need to wake Grandma so early, he thought, forcing his sock-clad feet into the regulation boots the Missouri, Kansas & Texas Railroad made him wear.

From the looks of his heavy, reinforced shoes a person would have thought he laid track or cleaned the yards like the other Negroes. But he was a dining-car cook and had to clomp his way through the tiny kitchen area with a leaden step. The MK&T issued him two cook's uniforms and a tall baker's hat, and the boots were included, so he didn't complain.

As Leela dozed off, Ed eased his thumb from her mouth and lit the thick candle atop the overturned packing crate he used as a bedside table. The flame sputtered, illuminating the shabby room, infusing his daughter's copper-colored hair with golden points of light. The finely spun hair fanned out around her plump, brown face in a fuzzy ring of tangled curls. Stiff, dark lashes rested on her dimpled cheeks, which rose and fell in a furious sucking motion that Ed knew would continue until she woke herself up again or Grandma got up to feed her.

Two days off ain't enough, he thought as he ran a comb through his close-cropped hair and splashed cold water over his creased bronze face. He had hoped to stay longer in Fort Worth before shoving off again on his route that took him to Galveston. Two weeks on the rail, four days at home: that was the schedule he longed for. But Ed Brannon worked whatever shift they gave him, cooked any kind of food the white folks wanted, slept night after night in a cramped four-foot crawl space above the galley and never complained. He had been a cook for almost two years and wanted no other job.

Tucked away in his tiny kitchen, Ed chopped onions, boiled greens, and fried chicken while humming to the hypnotic clatter of iron wheels grinding over track, exchanging dirty jokes with the other black men who worked his route. Leaving home had never bothered him before, but since his wife, Mabel, had died two months ago, it was becoming harder and harder to leave Leela behind. He hoped this trip would be a smooth one, getting him back to his baby girl as soon as possible.

Pulling a blue work shirt over his bulging forearms, Ed looked into the basket again and met Leela's wide-awake stare. She was just lying there, sucking her thumb, looking at him as if she knew he was leaving. Ed felt his chest tighten as he picked his baby up, ignoring her damp bottom and sour smell.

"I'll be back before you even know I'm gone," he comforted her. "Don't you fret, now. This here job's gonna let me give you everything a pretty girl ever wanted. Everything. You hear me, Leela?" He kissed the top of her perfectly shaped head and closed his eyes for a moment. "Gotta move you back inta Grandma's room, baby," he murmured. "Time for your pa to go to work." He held her to the rough cotton of his shirt for a moment, then placed her back into the oval-shaped basket which served as her cradle. "Come on now," he said to Leela as he carried the basket into the next room. "Let's wake Grandma up."

Grandma Ekiti lay on her low straw-filled mattress, her small mouth gaping wide open, her gruntlike snores echoing through the tiny room. Thin damp sheets were twisted around her scrawny, naked body, and her head remained wrapped in an elaborately folded piece of brightly colored cloth.

Ed detested his African mother-in-law, who still wore tribal markings and preferred to cook over an open fire even though his two-room shanty had the best wood-burning stove available in Fort Worth. The toothless old woman talked in jumbled, broken English and only spoke to her son-in-law when he addressed her directly. Ed had steered clear of Grandma Ekiti while Mabel was alive, leaving the spirit-calling soothsayer alone with her voodoo rituals and around-the-clock incantations. Now she blamed him for his wife's demise, and Ed had even caught her placing a figure sewn of black snakeskin under his bed. When he ran her out of his room, she fled into their neighbor's house, telling them Mabel Brannon died because her husband followed the iron snake and coveted it.

To hear Grandma Ekiti's version, his wife had died of loneliness. In fact, she died of a massive infection from the unsanitary and primitive way in which Grandma Ekiti had delivered her only grandchild. Ed was disgusted with the old woman's open hostility, but strained to tolerate her: he had no one else to care for Leela.

"When you're older," he told Leela, setting the basket on the floor next to the snoring woman, "I'll take you with me. And you'll eat sugar cakes and drink lemonade while I whittle a doll on every trip. I've got just the place in my kitchen where you can ride."

Several hours later, Ed found himself rolling through the deep piney woods of McLennan County. The trip from Fort Worth to Galveston could take four days or a full week, depending on how long the train stayed in cities like Waco, Temple or Bastrop. On this particular Saturday in July, just as the train rolled to a halt at the Waco depot, Mr. Collins, Ed's boss, gave him and the other cook, Zep, an unusual leave from the train.

An important U.S. postal shipment, delayed somewhere along the line, was en route to meet their train at Waco. Might take as long as twenty-four hours to get the cargo on board, Mr. Collins told them, so the passengers would be rerouted and the cooks were free until five o'clock the next morning.

Ed, who always slept on the train and never ventured far from the depot of any city, looked forward to finishing a doll he was whittling for Leela. But Zep Taylor, who had a passel of cousins in Waco, ripped off his apron and turned his gleaming white teeth on Ed. "Boy, get your overnight bag," he bellowed. "I'm gonna show you my hometown!"

The thick leafy forests of McLennan County were ten degrees cooler than the depot at Waco. Bird Dog's Lodge was so far off the traveled road only a man who grew up in this thicket could find it. The narrow path to Zep's cousin's place wound eerily through the dense trees right up to a low square cabin no bigger than two railway cars hooked together. The pungent smell of mesquite wood smoldering in an open pit burned the back of Ed's throat. He inhaled deeply, savoring the biting odor. Zep pressed two bits on the wagon driver and hopped down to the ground.

"Come on, Ed. We havin' us a good time tonight."

Ed shook his head and laughed as the short fat man sprang toward the cabin. Zep moved so fast and so lightly that it was hard to believe he was carrying around at least two hundred pounds. It sometimes got awfully crowded in the galley with the two of them trying to cook and serve at the same time.

"You ain't come close ta paradise, 'til you sink yo' teeth inta Cousin Bird Dog's ribs. Think you can cook, Junior? Bird Dog's barbecue be so good make you wanna slap yo' momma for not cookin' better." Zep's laughter echoed through the tall pines.

"I'm shore nuf hungry, Zep. You better be tellin' the truth."

They hurried past several high-sided wagons and a few saddled horses standing in the clearing. Zep slammed both hands against the heavy cabin door and watched it swing open as his short bulky figure blocked the sun.

"You niggers ain't gonna start this Saturday night without me," he boomed into the smoke-filled room.

Ed, feeling like an outsider, remained directly behind Zep, hidden from view.

A short, startled silence followed before cries of welcome and taunts of familiar recognition rose up.

"Man, where you come from?"

"Zep Taylor! Get yo' black ass in here."

"Lawd, if it ain't Fryin' Pan Joe. How you get the boss man let you off on a Saturday night?"

Zep bounced into the room, leaving Ed at the door. Men in soiled work clothes and cowboy hats jumped to shake his hand, slap him on the back and, within seconds, set him up with a jar of corn liquor.

"Git on in here, Ed," Zep hollered back at his friend. "Don't be goin' shy on me, now. These here is my kin . . . all of 'em." He turned back to the small crowd of men and added, "This is Ed. The guy I tol' you cooks on the train with me. We got 'til five tomorrow mornin', and I tol' him I's gonna show him how the folks in Waco have a good time on a Saturday night."

The men motioned for Ed to come in, take a seat, have a snort of whiskey and join the usual gathering of Taylors, near Taylors, or close friends who might as well be Taylors who filled Bird Dog's Lodge every Saturday night.

Someone shoved a chair up to a long table in the center of the room, and Ed squeezed between Zep and a scar-faced man whose teeth had rotted off at the gums.

"This here's my cousin, Bird Dog," Zep said, watching the owner of the cabin pour Ed's drink into a cracked jar.

"Where you from?" Bird Dog asked.

"Fort Worth."

"Been on the train long?"

"Close ta two years."

"A real railroad man, huh?"

"Seems that way."

"First time stepping off at Waco?"

"Yep. Zep talked me into it this time."

"This is home to Zep, you know?" Bird Dog picked at his gums with the tip of a pocketknife. "You got family?"

At this question Ed hedged, still unsettled by Mabel's recent death. "A baby girl back home . . ." he started.

Zep interceded and added in a low voice, "Just lost his wife a few months ago."

An embarrassed silence that lasted less than ten seconds followed. Then Bird Dog fingered the scar running from his left eye to his chin, laughed and told the men, "The girls be 'round later. Maybe we can help him chase those blues away."

At this news they all cheered and poured themselves another round of drinks.

The cool dark cabin rocked with a kinship and unspoken familiarity that Ed had never experienced. The rough-looking, hard-drinking, gambling, cursing men passed the next three hours trading tales about women, horses and white folks. They complained about misfortunes and bragged about their luck. They cursed the heat and praised the recent rains that made fishing so good up around Aquilla River. They openly cheated at cards and laughed when caught, brandishing their pistols as they argued a hand. And they swilled corn liquor until they all were breathing fire.

When the light faded, someone lit low-hanging kerosene lamps, and Ed was too drunk to remember he had come in hungry.

The pain gripping the top of Ed Brannon's head was not as bad as the foul taste settled at the back of his throat. He had fallen asleep with his good ear to the table and woke to the silence of a room filled with people. Ed lifted his head and looked around. He could see through a haze of gray-blue smoke that the girls had, indeed, arrived.

There must have been close to thirty people in the cabin, ten or twelve of them women. A boy who looked to be about fourteen years old forced a wailing tune from his big harmonica while a pencil-thin lady in a purple dress sang. The twosome belted blues from atop a rickety table. A space had been cleared for dancing. The scattering of couples bumped and ground their bodies into the song, clutching the good times at Bird Dog's Lodge.

"Decided to join the party?"

Ed had smelled the woman standing behind him even before she spoke. He filled his nostrils with her jasmine scent as he turned in his chair to answer.

"I shore have," he told her, lifting his face to hers.

She wore a white dress with a red paper rose pinned on her shoulder. She seemed tall, or maybe it was because he was sitting down, but Ed sensed a largeness about her. She tilted her pale, square jaw upward in a slightly haughty manner and her thick brown hair fell over one eye. Just as Ed started to stand, Zep appeared out of the crowd and clasped him on the shoulder.

"Boy, I thought we'd lost you! Gotta do better 'n that to keep up with the Taylors. I see you met my second, or maybe it's third, cousin, Hattie Logan."

Ed pushed himself to his feet.

"Hattie Wilder," the woman corrected.

"Why you still using that man's name?" Zep asked, mopping sweat from his ebony face with the back of his hand. "Been gone seven years. You's still Hattie Logan 'round here."

Ed shook her hand and smiled. "Pleased to meet you."

Zep wrapped his big arms around Hattie and told Ed, "Better let Hattie get you some o' Bird Dog's ribs if you's plannin' on lastin' the night. The party's just got started." Then he bolted off to grab a pretty girl in a polka-dot dress and pulled her onto the dance floor.

"You hungry?" Hattie asked as she sized Ed up.

"Starved."

"Bird Dog's barbecue will fix you up. Be right back."

Ed followed Hattie's big hips with his eyes as she crossed the room and entered the kitchen. She wasn't exactly pretty, but she had a real presence about her. She kind of overwhelmed a man, cut out a space in the room for herself. He had never favored light-skinned women, but this one was different somehow . . . not like any woman he'd ever seen in Fort Worth.

The music heated up; the harmonica player and the singer stepped down; and a trio of men playing the banjo, the tambourine, and something that closely resembled a washboard took over. The choppy, erratic rhythm they feverishly pounded out brought the revelers to their feet. They shouted, stomped, clapped, whistled and threw themselves into a spirited hoedown. Without enough women to go around, men danced with each other in a frenzied hustle, tossing hats to the floor as they let themselves go.

"I call it the Bird Dog Shuffle." Hattie laughed as she set a plate of ribs in front of Ed. "You ain't never gonna see this dance nowhere but right here. At Bird Dog's."

Ed laughed at that and took advantage of her closeness to look into her eyes. She stared right back, lips slightly parted, her pink tongue pressing against small white teeth, and she even brushed her heavy breast against his arm as she reached to place a glass of dark liquid on the table.

She settled across from him and watched as he ate.

"Good, ain't it?"

"Never had better, and I've ate a lot of ribs in a lot of towns."

"You been a lot of places?"

"Yeah," Ed mumbled as he sucked on a bone. "I work the MK and T with Zep."

"I ain't never been out of McLennan County," Hattie confessed, not particularly ashamed or proud. Just stating the fact. "My husband, Benny Wilder, went to Carson City but wouldn't take me with him."

"Why Carson City?" Ed asked.

"Oh . . . he had some wild idea 'bout strikin' it rich in a silver mine. Now ain't that the most outlandish kinda thinking you ever heard? And from a man who never dirtied his hands to even plant a cotton field."

"Still there?"

"Reckon so. Ain't heard nuthin' from him in seven years. Kinda believe he's down in a mine shaft somewheres, either dead or darn close to it. Good riddance, I told him when he struck outta here."

Ed did not know what to say. She didn't seem sorry or angry or even upset. She appeared smugly content with Benny's absence.

"You and Benny got kids?" he managed to ask.

"One boy . . . call him T.J., but his name's Thomas Jacob." Now Hattie's demeanor did change. She softened around the eyes and her mouth pooched forward in thought. "Only thing bad about Benny leavin' town was the sorry way he left his son. Here," she said, shaking her head as if to clear away the memories. "You need something to wash that down." She shoved the amber-colored drink toward Ed.

"I don't know," he stuttered. "Maybe I better go easy on the whiskey. Gotta be back on the train by five in the morning."

"Don't worry," Hattie reassured him. "This is what we call

Johnny-mash: half lemonade, half sour mash. Won't ever give you a headache. Try it."

She's got all the answers, Ed thought as he gulped the sour-sweet liquid and watched her over the rim of the tumbler. Her dark eyes, framed by thick arched brows, pierced him. He felt hooked, connected, drawn into this woman, and he made up his mind right then to get as close to her as she'd let him. They sat together, Ed eating ribs and polishing off another glass of Johnny-mash while Hattie told him anecdotes about every person in the room.

By midnight, Ed had convinced himself that he was glad he was not a Taylor. He could never have lived up to their expectations of drink, dance, food, and gambling and did not want to try. The party blasted its way through the night, edging into early morning hours when Ed stepped outside for air. He was not at all surprised that Hattie Logan Wilder followed him into the yard.

"You ain't used to all this carryin' on, are you?" Her deep husky voice stirred him. "I could tell when I saw you with your head on the table, you ain't like most the men here at Bird Dog's."

"Been laying kinda low, I guess," Ed admitted. "I lost my wife a few months back and all I been doin' is workin' and sleepin'. But I'm glad Zep brought me out," he hurried to add.

The dense forest around them rattled with night life as frogs, lizards, raccoons and rabbits scurried through the thick underbrush.

"You come here often?" Ed finally asked.

"Yeah . . ." Hattie drew out her response as if she considered lying. "Most every Saturday night for the past couple years. Nuthin' else to do 'round here."

Ed could feel the dizzy pleasure of the Johnny-mash swirl through his head. He hoped Hattie had told him the truth about this stuff. He dreaded a hangover tomorrow.

"You live nearby?" he asked, feigning disinterest, hoping she would rise to his bait. After all, it had been two months since Mabel died and some time alone with a woman would be easy to take. Especially time with a woman like Hattie.

" 'Bout fifteen minutes out the highway," she answered. "Wanna ride over to my place? Or you gotta stay with Zep?"

Ed slipped his arm around Hattie's thick waist. "I ain't gotta do nuthin', 'cept be on the train by five o'clock tomorrow morning."

Within minutes, they started off in Hattie's crude wagon, which consisted of two thick rounds sawed from a hardy oak tree, a wide plank stretched between them, held together with a small pine sapling that served as an axle. It bumped its way down the dark highway toward a splintered lean-to she called home.

"My daddy picked cotton here in slavery times and built this house up to the barn a long time ago. When he died, old lady Fritz let me stay on. I do day's work for her. She don't pay mucha nuthin', but me and T.J. manage." Hattie's mule stopped at the front door.

Ed helped her down and followed her into the pitch-black shelter, waiting as she lit an oil lamp hanging in the center of the open space. He was pleasantly surprised at what he saw.

The large open area, divided with low half-walls, had three distinct rooms. The sleeping area was dominated by a beautiful old bed with turned posts and a thick white quilt. A squat potbellied stove and a washtub for bathing sat off in the cook room, and a smaller space was filled with a cord of wood and washing pots. At the rear, a door opened directly into the barn.

On the floor in the sleeping area, a small form stirred.

"T.J.," Hattie hissed in a loud whisper. "Git up, boy." She leaned down and shook the fair-skinned boy awake. He sat up, rubbed his eyes and stared at his mother in a confused unwillingness to budge. "Git up, boy." Hattie pulled him by his shoulder. "Go on out back to sleep. Go on now," she urged as the boy, who looked to be ten or eleven, jumped up and fled out the back door into the barn.

"He most always sleeps out back up in the loft. He got a place back there with all his things. You know how boys be," she said as she turned the lamp lower. "Just crept in here 'cause I was gone."

A table and two chairs stood in the center of the cooking area and Hattie reached into a tall crate that served as her pantry and pulled out a bottle. She set it on the table with two tin cups.

"Have a taste of my dandelion wine. Made it myself." For the first time since he met her, Ed noticed a hint of joy, maybe even a little bragging. "Come on, sit down over here."

He sat, allowing her to fill his cup. He drank, wondering how it would set on top of corn liquor and Johnny-mash. It seemed to set all right.

"Nice," he told her. "Real nice."

Hattie's pale face loomed closer; her scent thickened and settled over him. Ed knew she was talking, but had no sense of what she was saying. Her lips moved in slow motion and she smiled once or twice, refilled his cup, then let her hand fall onto his arm.

Ed began to empty his pockets and Hattie said nothing as he placed a dollar bill, a comb, a small white card and a key in a pile in front of him. She reached over and picked up the card.

"Edward Carey Brannon," she read aloud. "That you?"

"Yeah," Ed mumbled, hoping he wasn't getting sick. "That's my railroad pass card. Can't get on the train without it." He took it from her and placed it back on the pile. "Now, don't you let me miss my train."

"You not gonna miss a thing," she murmured, "but you are lookin' kinda tired." He heard her voice through a swimming blur of yellow light and shadows. "Come lay down over here for a while. I ain't gonna let you miss your train."

He nodded, groping for the back of his chair as he stood and stumbled to her bed. Falling onto it, he groaned with relief, letting the room turn in circles while Hattie pulled off all his clothes. Within seconds, her warm naked body slid down next to his.

Ed fought the demon whiskey until it seeped from his brain, then pulled Hattie's face toward his. He kissed her like a thirsty man drinking water, drowning in the scent of her, the feel of her, the taste of her pale smooth skin. She kissed him back with equal hunger, drove her painted fingernails into his spine and thrust her pelvis against him in a raging quest that welded them together.

The room spun with passion as they caressed and scratched, moaned and clutched, twisted their bodies into a smoldering tangle of hungry flesh which neither wanted to unravel. Ed wrapped his hands around Hattie's huge breasts and sucked. He sucked and groaned and buried his face in the damp soft mounds that threatened to suffocate him. Gasping for tiny bits of air, he explored Hattie's body with his lips.

Hattie's hunger was as intense as his, and the generous body she offered him shimmered pliantly under his work-worn hands. He massaged the soft skin of her thighs and buttocks, finally easing himself above her. She arched her back, begging for him, and with a blinding thrust he entered her. Hattie's moan became a high-pitched scream, but Ed pumped away, tuning her out, determined not to break his frenetic rhythm. She urged him on, meeting each thrust with a vigorous pull that made his senses reel. They rocked along, clinging to each other, until Ed stiffened and shuddered to a climax that nearly collapsed the bed. Hattie threw back her head and laughed. Strangely. As if she had a secret to cherish. Her laughter echoed through the open room, bounced off the bleak walls, and seeped into the barn next door.

The MK&T's engine 4-6-0 pulled out of the Waco depot at exactly five o'clock. The two-hundred-ton locomotive gathered speed as its huge spoked wheels scraped steel tracks and steam soared thickly to the heavens.

By the time they got to Temple, Ed Brannon had already posted a letter in the mail car to Hattie, was flipping hotcakes over a flat iron skillet and was whistling in spite of a dull headache that throbbed just behind his left ear. He couldn't stop smiling and resolved to buy Hattie something special at the next stop. He had found himself a woman to come back to.

"Ham and eggs in compartment seven!" Zep bellowed into the kitchen as he swung his wide body through the narrow space outside the galley. "Better fire up the oven for more biscuits, too!" He poked his head into Ed's domain and flashed a toothy smile. "Man, I's shore glad you made it. Next time don't be leaving yo' pass card behind. Lucky I got you back on the train. Ita been a long haul without you."

"Ham and eggs comin' up!" Ed replied, grinning at his friend. "Biscuits on the way!" He pushed his greasy iron skillet to one side and picked up a sulfur match to light the oven. "You the one to blame if I'da missed my train—you the one introduced me to your cousin."

Zep winked at Ed and stepped a little closer. "Something, ain't she? That Hattie's some kind o' woman." He smiled broadly at his friend, not having the heart to tell him how many railroaders his cousin had entertained. Why throw cold water on good memories?

"Gonna get her a bottle of some good-smelling perfume when we pull into Houston tomorrow. What you think? Think she'd like that?" Ed asked as he leaned down and struck the match.

"Sure she'd like that," Zep said, frowning at the absentminded way Ed was standing, holding on to the lighted match.

"Watch out there," he cautioned as Ed bent over, but his friend had his bad ear toward the doorway and couldn't understand what was said. Zep hollered again, "Be careful there, Ed," just as a flash of blue-white fire roared from the open stove burner into Ed's face and ignited his stiff baker's hat.

"Oh my God. My God! Get out of there!" Zep reached over to grab the cook by the jacket to pull him out of the galley, but long yellow flames stung his hands and he jerked back screaming in horror. "Ed! Ed! Yo' hat's on fire." Forced to stand back, he saw the fire quickly engulf Ed's jacket and trousers and rip through an open five-pound tin of lard. The hot grease splattered all over the galley and shot into the doorway, hitting Zep.

Zep jumped back, screaming for help as he watched the tiny space boil into a thundering inferno while his good friend writhed in torment on the floor. By the time two of the porters got to the scene, Ed Brannon lay in a crumpled, smoking mass. The pungent smell of his blackened flesh filled the car.

Within an hour, the conductor of the MK&T turned Ed's charred body over to the Negro undertaker who served the black community outside Bastrop, then blasted his whistle and steamed down the tracks toward Houston.

CHAPTER ONE

1906 MEXIA, TEXAS

Effie Alexander wiped her hands on the ruffled edge of her green-and-white apron and picked up a scattering of paper patterns, satin ribbon, and buttons before carefully placing a big chocolate cake in the center of her table. The tiny woman pushed wisps of gray hair from her face and smiled with satisfaction that the frosting hadn't melted, despite the ungodly heat of her kitchen. The temperature had soared close to ninety degrees and it was only the beginning of May.

She looked the table over, nodded in satisfaction, then turned and called over her shoulder, "Josephine . . . Leela . . . y'all get Parker and come on now. Everything's ready."

Effie hummed to herself as she waited for the children and smoothed a wrinkle from the middle of her lace tablecloth.

The young man, who entered first, bent his head at the doorway to be sure he cleared it, then moved to take his usual seat next to his mother. Effie placed a hand on his starched cotton shirt and said,

"Parker, sit at the head of the table since yo' poppa's not here. You be the man of the house tonight." Parker dutifully circled the table, eased down into his father's ladder-back chair and stretched his long legs out before him.

"Leela, you're the birthday girl so you sit here across from Parker. Josephine, you're over there," Effie finished, beaming over their heads. "I wish Bert coulda made it home," she added, knowing how much her husband loved her chocolate cake.

She struck a big match and lit the fifteen candles atop her niece's birthday cake, then sat back to watch her blow them out. Effie saw her deceased brother's bronze coloring, dark eyes and wide bright smile whenever she looked at Leela. She even had Ed's lyrical voice and a few of his mannerisms, like the way she asked a question, boldly and directly, over and over until the answer made sense to her. In the six months she'd been in Mexia, Leela had nearly questioned Aunt Effie to death. The girl was almost as curious as Parker.

When Grandma Ekiti died, leaving Leela all alone, Effie Alexander had fallen to her knees in thankfulness that the word had gotten to her and she was able to take her brother's child to raise.

Now Effie held her breath as Leela made her secret wish and blew out all fifteen tiny points of fire on the first try.

"You see that?" Effie said excitedly. "All Leela's wishes gonna come true. That's a sign she's supposed to be here, that everything's gonna work out fine."

"Josephine," Effie urged. "Tell your cousin happy birthday."

Josephine shifted uncomfortably in her chair and raised pale, colorless eyes at Leela.

"Happy birthday, Cousin Leela," she mumbled.

Leela turned toward her aunt and whispered, "I never had a birthday party before. Grandma said that coming one year closer to the end of your life was no reason to have a celebration." Tears welled up in the girl's large brown eyes. "I'm so glad I'm here with you and not back there in the . . ." Unable to finish her sentence, Leela lowered her chin and smeared tears from her face with the back of one hand.

"Now, now," Effie said as she picked up the knife and turned the cake around on its milk glass plate. "There's no reason for tears. We celebrating. Celebrating you comin' to live with us and all the happy years you gonna see here in Mexia." She cut a thick slice and laid it on a small dish. "Since you's the guest of honor, you get the first piece. Josephine, you spoon out the ice cream," Effie urged, hoping to get her sullen daughter into a more tolerable mood.

She had hoped the two girls, with less than a year between them, would get along more like sisters. But since Leela had been with them it was obvious Josephine disdained such a thought, making no overtures of friendship whatsoever.

Josephine splashed a spoonful of ice cream onto Leela's plate. Most of it landed on the lace tablecloth. Effie sighed, shaking her head as she ignored Josephine's grating behavior.

"Parker, pour some lemonade in Leela's glass," she said.

"Why's Poppa not here?" Parker asked, a frown turning his brown eyes into narrow slits as he handed Leela her drink.

"Your poppa's got a real big job to finish for Mr. Green. He's making new iron fencing to go around the old cemetery west of town. Gonna be pretty late gettin' home. Soon as you finish, I want you to carry his supper down to him at the smithy. He'd just keep workin' with no food, lessen I send some over."

"Poppa's never home at night anymore," Parker grumbled, polishing off the last piece of cake from his plate. "I think he works too hard for Mr. Green."

"A man can never work too hard," Effie cautioned. "Be thankful you got a poppa who worries about you and is willing to sacrifice his time for your future. Just be a little more grateful," she said, hoping her words were reaching Josephine also. Her daughter's behavior was becoming more irritating each day.

When everyone had finished, Effie went to the sink and plunked down the dirty dishes. "Parker, you better get along now. Take yo' poppa's dinner on over to him. It's gettin' late."

Parker got up and remained standing at the table, his hands on the back of his chair. "I know, Momma." He stood quietly for a moment, hesitating, as if he wanted to say more. Then he picked up his father's dinner pail and turned to Leela. "Come on, Leela. Walk with me. I'm gonna stop by the *Banner* on my way back home. You can watch the presses run."

"What's Mr. Foreman doing working so late on a Friday night?" Effie's displeasure was evident.

"A special edition's coming out in the morning. About that trial that just finished over in Tarrant County. You know, Momma. Those white men who lynched that preacher. We just got news the jury let all three of those men go. Scot-free. It's a shame, a damn shame."

"Watch your mouth, son." Effie dried a plate as she watched Parker pull on his hat, then added rather sternly, "and be careful. You hear?" Her voice rose. "You and that newspaper! Sometimes I wish you focused in on some other type of work in this town. No telling what that kind of news is gonna stir up 'round here." She shook out her towel and hung it across the front of the stove, dismissing the children with a wave of her hand. "Josephine? You not going along?"

Josephine got up from the table and roughly pushed her chair up against it. Her face flushed pink as she spoke. "No. Why should I interfere? I wasn't invited." Then she glared at Leela and stomped out of the room.

"That girl!" Effie snapped. "I don't know what I'm gonna do with her."

"Leave her alone, Momma. She'll come around."

Leela and Parker left the house through the front door and started down Palestine Street toward the smithy.

Tonight, as Leela tried to keep up with Parker's long, determined stride, she felt a twinge of excitement to be going to the *Banner*, especially to watch a special edition being printed. She hoped Parker would let her do something, even if he only let her help bundle up the papers for morning delivery. She took double steps to stay alongside him.

"Aunt Effie really doesn't want you to work for the *Banner*, does she?"

"You already picked up on that, huh?" Parker replied as he slowed a bit to let her catch up. "She just worries too much," he answered. "I don't know why . . . all I'm doing is writing the truth."

"Are you ever afraid you'll write something and make somebody mad . . . real mad at you?"

"Nope," he said curtly and defiantly. "As long as it's true I'll write it." He stopped under the last gas lamp on Titus Street and looked seriously down at Leela. "I'm going to be the publisher of my own newspaper someday. Then, no one can tell me what I can print.

I know I can't change much in Mexia, but I'm going to leave here and change myself. I just want to finish my last school term here and go East to work, maybe go to college if I can get the money together."

"Where in the East?" Leela knew little of colleges for Negroes, let alone where such places might be.

"Howard University in Washington, D.C., for one. You know . . . the capital of the United States. Surely you've studied that much." His tone seemed to rise in exaggerated importance.

"Of course, I know about Washington, D.C. Where else?"

"There are grand schools in Boston, New York, Chicago, Ohio . . . any number of places where colored can go." Parker's tone was intently serious as he outlined his plans to leave Mexia.

"I never want to leave Mexia." Leela was adamant. "I have a family now, a real family. I don't ever want to be alone again."

"What do mean, alone? You lived with your grandmother, didn't you?" He slowed a little to let Leela catch up.

"Yes, but sometimes she'd go away in the night," Leela began. "She'd be gone for two or three days."

"Where'd she go?" Parker asked, wanting to know more, hoping Leela wouldn't get upset.

"I asked her just that," Leela replied wistfully. "I said, 'What is it you look for, Grandma?' You know what she told me?" Leela stopped walking and turned toward Parker. "She said, 'The part of me that's missing, baby. What else I need to find?' "

"That's all?" Parker raised his eyebrows in puzzlement.

"That's all. And I never asked again."

"Well," Parker went on, "you'll soon begin to feel as I do. You'll want to leave this place. Just wait and see."

"I don't think so, Parker," Leela replied as memories of the hollow aching loneliness of her childhood flitted through her mind. "I plan to stay right here where I've got family."

Soon the smell of burning wood and forged iron signaled their arrival at the blacksmith's shed at the end of the unpaved street. The wide door stood open and Leela could see Uncle Bert hammering away, sparks flying as he coaxed a long bar of iron into shape. Steam rushed forth and obscured her vision when he plunged the piece into water.

"Wait here," Parker cautioned. "I'll just run this in and we can get on over to the *Banner*."

Uncle Bert lifted his head from his work and waved at Leela as he took the dinner pail from his son.

A short three blocks later, Leela and Parker entered the glass doors of the *Banner*. Mr. Foreman smiled, nodded his head, but did not leave his station beside the noisy press.

Leela inhaled and looked around. There was something about the smell of ink and paper that excited her. She liked the immediacy of the whole operation. In fact, she had come to like most everything about Parker's work and Mr. Foreman didn't mind her being around the place.

When the press came to a halt, he moved toward them. "Glad you came down, Parker." The publisher of the only colored paper in the county removed his glasses and wiped his eyes. "Hello, Leela," he added.

Parker took off his jacket and threw it across a nearby chair. "How does it look?" He stooped to pick up a copy and read the headline aloud. "Negroes in Tarrant County Protest Jury's Decision." He absently handed the paper to Leela as he headed toward the back of the office. "Real good job, Mr. Foreman. The headlines ought to get folks' attention. How many more do we need to run?"

"We've nearly got enough papers now," he replied. "Just need to get 'em bundled up and ready for pickup in the morning. Bring me some twine from the closet."

"Can I help, Mr. Foreman?" Leela asked, already rolling up the sleeve of her blouse. She was thrilled to be in the center of a three-county protest, so far from the isolated life she had led with her grandmother. For Leela this was the most exciting thing that had ever happened to her, besides finding a family to call her own. When Aunt Effie had insisted she call herself Leela Alexander, though no legal papers were ever drawn, that had suited Leela just fine. Life in Mexia was all she'd ever dreamed of and for the first time she felt hopeful about her future.

"Leela, I know your aunt would have my hide if I let you dirty yourself with all this fresh print around here. Bundling papers gonna leave your hands black. That's man's work, child. You just sit down over there and keep us company." He turned to Parker. "Tom

Walker, from out Comanche Crossing way, is gonna come by and get some papers to carry over to Freestone County. Said he'd be here 'round seven."

"Mr. Foreman, please!" Leela walked up to the publisher and planted herself directly in front of him. "There's a lot I could do if you'd let me. I don't care about getting dirty. Let me help bundle the papers."

Foreman chuckled and wiped his nose with his handkerchief, then caught the ball of twine Parker tossed over to him. "Here." The newspaperman gave it to Leela. "Why don't you start cutting us some lengths to tie up these papers?" He handed her a pair of scissors. "Parker, better get to inking that press again. I don't want to be here all night."

"You know, Mr. Foreman," Leela started as she stretched the twine out on the table, "I could come in after school on Monday if you need some more help. I could sit right here at the front desk and take money from the people who come in to buy a paper. I could add it all up at the week's end, kinda keep track of things, you know?"

"I'll bet you could do just that. You're a real smart gal, Leela. We'll see. We'll see. Right now let's get this finished. Your aunt might have something to say about you taking on a real job over here." He came up behind Leela and patted her on the shoulder.

The three worked intently for nearly an hour. Parker and Mr. Foreman printed fifty more copies, bundled papers for Tom Walker to pick up and were about to lock up for the night when the sound of voices outside interrupted them. Mr. Foreman quickly raised the paper shade covering the big plate-glass window and put his hand to his face to see better.

"There's a crowd gatherin'," Foreman noted, straightening up to give Parker an anxious glance. "Don't like the looks of who's out there."

Parker came up behind Foreman while indicating with his hand that Leela stay away from the window, but she could see over their shoulders that six white men were standing on the sidewalk.

"You darkies better stop printing lies about decent white folks!" The deep angry voice frightened Leela and she shrank down in her chair as if it would shield her. "If you don't," the voice continued, "somebody's gonna be sorry. Real sorry."

"What do they want?" Leela hissed as more voices joined in to start up a chant.

"Print the truth or get out of town! Print the truth!" the crowd yelled.

Parker and Mr. Foreman stepped back from the window just as a rock came hurtling through. Shattered glass sprayed the room. Leela ducked under the desk. Mr. Foreman yanked the door open and stood, glowering, in front of the crowd.

"We only print the truth," Foreman yelled back. "Get on away from here and let us alone. Go on, get away from here, if you don't I'm . . ." Before he could finish his sentence, another rock was hurled through the already-broken window.

Parker grabbed the rock and angrily threw it back into the crowd, not caring where it landed. Leela saw the big stone thud into the dust near a man's left foot. A roar came up from the mob.

"You'll pay for this, you black bastard!" someone screamed above the chanting. "This rag of lies gonna be burnt down to the ground. You'll pay for hitting a white man. The sheriff's gonna be 'round soon. We gonna run all you darkies out of town."

The mob began to pull back and Foreman came into the office.

"Parker, take Leela and get out the back. Now! That was Ed Smith out there, the sheriff's cousin. Go on . . . get on home before Sheriff Thompson shows up."

"I can't leave you here. This could turn ugly. Nobody was hurt. It's the *Banner*'s window was broken. We oughta be chasing them down."

"You know damn well things don't work that way. You and your cousin get on home. I can settle this with the sheriff. I know how to handle him."

Parker protested. "I'm not afraid . . ."

"You better be, son, 'cause we could have real trouble over this tonight."

Parker grabbed his jacket and pulled Leela by the arm. "Come on."

In frightened obedience, Leela followed Parker out the back door, into the alley and together they plunged into thorny bushes lining the shortcut back to his house.

"Don't say a thing about this to Momma," Parker warned as he pushed weeds from their path and stepped onto Palestine Street. "You hear, Leela? Not a word."

Too afraid to say anything, Leela nodded and slowed her pace to match Parker's. He knows how to handle this, Leela told herself, feeling slightly better. He was a serious newsman and most folks respected him. So what if he was only seventeen? He already acted like a man.

They stepped onto the dark porch. "Go straight to your room and go to bed," Parker ordered. "And don't say a word to Josephine."

The lamps were turned low when they entered the house, and Parker fairly shoved Leela into her room and made his way through the kitchen, where he mumbled good-night to his mother and slipped behind his bedroom door.

In the middle of the night a loud knocking jolted Leela from a restless slumber. She sat up quickly and through the curtained window could see the ill-defined shadow of a man on the front porch. He was banging on the door frame and the darkened windows yelling Parker Alexander's name. Leela clutched her blanket with one hand, too terrified to move. Josephine flung a heavy leg across her cousin and mumbled, "What the devil's going on?"

"Shhh!" Leela hissed. "There's a man at the front door."

Soon Uncle Bert's voice echoed through the small house.

"Sheriff Thompson? What you want?"

The frightened girls slipped from their bed and crept into the hallway. Leela could see her uncle tightening his robe about his wide girth as he lifted the lamp to better illuminate the doorway.

"Send Parker Alexander out," Sheriff Thompson ordered, staring stonily at the man before him.

"What for?" Bert asked.

"You don't be asking the questions around here." The sheriff stepped closer to Bert. "Your boy's in a heap of trouble. Get him out here. Now!"

Bert turned around, not surprised to see Effie, Parker and even Josephine standing in the dim parlor behind him. Leela hung back, shadowed in the hallway, straining to hear what was said. Parker's voice, steady and clear, filtered back to her.

"What do you want with me?"

Leela rose up on tiptoes to see Parker stepping forward as he tucked his shirttail into his pants.

"Were you over at that colored paper tonight, boy?"

"Yes," Parker readily admitted.

"Got a complaint filed against you. Ed Smith's got a broken leg. Says you attacked him with a rock. In front of the paper. What you got to say for yourself?" The sheriff lit a big cigar, then blew smoke over Parker's head.

"He's lying," Parker said resolutely. "I did not attack Ed Smith with a rock."

"Got witnesses say otherwise. Good upstanding witnesses, boy."

Parker glared at the big-hatted man before him and allowed himself to be filled with hate. This setup really stinks, he thought, knowing his words of protest were useless.

"Boy, I'm giving you the chance to come clean. Things might go a bit easier if you do."

Parker could barely keep a smirk of disgust from his face as he stood silently, refusing to speak. Bert gripped his son's arm in fear. "Just tell the man the truth, son. What happened tonight at the *Banner*?"

"Just like I said, Pa. I did not attack Ed Smith." The young man's voice now trembled. He turned slightly to look into his father's eyes. "I didn't do anything to hurt that man."

Leela could see Uncle Bert put his arm around Parker's shoulder. "I believe you, son," he said softly.

"That's all well and good to say," the sheriff started, "but there ain't a witness to back it up. You better come along with me." He reached out to take Parker's arm.

Stifling a scream, Leela burst forth, pushing herself between Parker and her uncle. "I was there," she shouted at the lawman. "I saw exactly what happened."

Effie groped at her niece, trying to pull her back into the parlor by her nightgown.

"Stay out of it, Leela!" Josephine screamed. "Just shut your mouth and be quiet!"

Leela tore free of her aunt and stood, shoulders back, eyes glaring, in front of the sheriff.

"The rock Parker threw landed in the street. It didn't hit that man. It didn't!" Frantically, Leela grabbed Parker's arm. "I saw where it fell, Parker. You never hit that man."

"Leela, shut up!" Josephine shouted again; then she reached over and slapped her cousin in the face. "You stupid bitch! Don't you see what you're doing?"

Effie jerked Josephine back by the shoulders.

Uncle Bert quickly gathered Leela into his arms and pushed her head against his shoulder. "Enough, child. Enough. Stay still, now. Be quiet."

No one spoke for several long seconds, and the chirping of crickets in the violet patch at the end of the yard seemed shrill and disquieting to Leela.

"Better come on quiet now, boy," Sheriff Thompson said gruffly. "Don't be making this more difficult than it has to be." He took out his handcuffs and rattled them noisily.

Uncle Bert nearly squeezed the life from Leela as he held her fast to his chest. She wiped tears on the front of Bert's old robe, and though she could not see Parker being led away, she shuddered convulsively at the sound of the sheriff's big black car pulling away from the yard.

Uncle Bert eased Leela's head from his shoulder. "You dry your eyes and get on back to bed. Effie and I'll figger this out." He reached over and touched Josephine on the cheek. "You too, baby. Go on back to bed. This is something yo' momma and I gotta handle."

Reluctantly, the two girls entered the house and went to the small room they shared in uneasy tolerance.

"Stop all that sniveling! You've made a real mess of things, Leela." Josephine slammed the door shut and pushed Leela onto the bed. "Don't you dare get up, you little nobody. Just sit there and listen."

Defiantly, Leela rolled across the bed and stood on the other side of the room, her back against the open window.

"You sure are stupid," Josephine started in, her voice controlled and frigid. "Interfering in grown-up affairs. Nobody asked you what you saw. If you had kept your mouth shut, Parker would not be in jail. You think you know so much? Well, you've got a lot to learn about how things work around here." She moved slowly toward

Leela. "To tell the sheriff that my brother threw a rock at a white man. Are you crazy? Who do you think you are? Running all over town, acting like you're somebody special . . . different from the rest of us. We know how things work in this town. You don't! You need to go on back where you came from . . . wherever that was!"

Leela took her hand from across her mouth and inhaled deeply, gathering her strength. "I just told the truth. Just like Uncle Bert asked. I didn't mean to . . ."

"Poppa wasn't talking to you! Nobody cares what you saw." By now, Josephine was standing so close to Leela she could almost feel the heat of her cousin's angry breath on her face. "I wish you'd never come here," Josephine finally spat out. "I wish to God my momma had never brought you into this house."

In a sudden movement, Josephine wrapped her icy fingers around Leela's arm and squeezed. Leela winced in pain. "Let me go!"

"You better get your butt down to the *Banner* in the morning and talk Mr. Foreman into getting my brother out of jail. He's the only one Sheriff Thompson might listen to. You better do it, Leela. If you don't, you might as well forget about staying around here."

CHAPTER TWO

By the time Leela awoke the next morning, Josephine had gone. Thankful to be left alone, Leela lay very still and thought about what had happened last night. A sinking feeling washed over her and filled her with dread.

Parker in jail! What would happen to him? Could he be lynched like the preacher he'd written about? She pulled the soft sheet up to her chin and stared at the ceiling.

What had she done? She bet Uncle Bert and Aunt Effie wanted her gone. The thought of angering her aunt and uncle pained Leela and she wished she could undo the damage she had unwittingly committed. Sunlight streamed warmly through the windows and Leela turned on her side to shield her face.

Agitated by the evening's bizarre turn of events, she felt her welcome to Mexia had turned sour. That awful feeling of not belonging began to ease itself over her again. Parker's in jail. Josephine hates me. Uncle Bert and Aunt Effie must think I'm terrible. Tears threatened to spill down her cheeks but she blinked them back. My new family, she thought as she bit her bottom lip. It's all over. Surely they want nothing more to do with me.

For Leela, her newfound security at the Alexander home had disappointingly fractured and begun to slip away. Her dream of living the rest of her life in this happy cocoon had suddenly turned into a nightmare.

In a flash of memory, frightful images from her childhood rushed to the surface: freshly killed chickens, bloody feathers strewn over bare dirt floors, small black snakes tethered to sticks in the yard. Leela could still smell the dank rooms and outbuildings where her grandmother had patted clay into bowls, filled them with legs of the grasshopper, fur of the brown rat, leaves stripped before dawn from the cabbage palm tree. Big iron pots belched dreadful odors as they boiled and simmered over outdoor fires: the musty, sour days of her childhood.

Life for Leela and her grandmother had been complicated and unsettling. Fearful neighbors had forced the old woman and the little girl to move from room to room, shanty to shanty. Suspicious of Grandma Ekiti's vile-smelling concoctions and wizardly incantations, they had bolted their doors in her face. And as the toothless conjurer had slithered off down the road, she pulled Leela along in the dust behind her.

I'll never go back to living like that, Leela vowed. I've got to make Uncle Bert and Aunt Effie understand. She threw back the coverlet and began to pull on her clothes, setting her mind to getting Parker out of jail.

She entered the kitchen to find Aunt Effie at the table, coffee cup in hand, the special edition of the *Banner* spread open.

She looked up and smiled at Leela. "You feeling better this morning?" She reached over and took Leela's hand in hers. "Don't you fret about what happened last night. You didn't do nothin' wrong."

Leela sat down across from her aunt and lowered her eyes. "I never meant to make things worse. I didn't think it out right, I guess."

"Bert went over and talked to the sheriff early this morning. Seems like we can get Parker out if we pay three hundred dollars . . .

something about damages due Ed Smith 'cause of his broken leg."

Leela was horrified. "Three hundred dollars. That's an awful lot of money! And Parker did not break that man's leg. The rock never hit him. It didn't."

"I know, I know," Effie sighed as she spoke. "But we can't do a thing about that. We just gotta manage to find the money. Bert's gone into town to try to find some more work. He'll set things straight. Don't you worry, you hear?" Effie folded the paper and got up. "How about some pancakes? Eat a good breakfast. Put a smile on your face, honey. Things are gonna work out."

"I'm not hungry, Aunt Effie. Really I'm not," Leela protested. "I'm going over to talk to Mr. Foreman."

"That's not a good idea, Leela." Effie reached into her cabinet and took down a heavy mixing bowl. "You better stay away from the paper for a spell. A young girl like you . . . a witness, too. Better keep close to the house until all this is settled."

Leela rose quickly and went to the back door, hand on the screen as she faced her aunt. "I don't want to disrespect you, Aunt Effie, but I've got to go. I've got to help Parker get out of jail."

"And just what do you think you can do? A child like you?"

"I'm not sure just yet, but I've been thinking things over. I need to talk to Mr. Foreman."

Without waiting to hear what Effie had to say, Leela rushed out the door and took the shortcut to the *Banner*.

As she crossed the railroad tracks at the end of Palestine Street, Leela's mind was whirling. All she needed was a horse and a wagon, but where in the world could she get one? Would Mr. Foreman agree to her plan? He was so damned old-fashioned about women doing anything. He must think we're made out of glass, she thought. He's just got to see this my way. Leela rounded a corner and entered Preston Avenue.

Stepping up to the *Banner*, she was not terribly surprised to see the newspaper shuttered and dark. Mr. Foreman had nailed boards over the broken window and tacked a handwritten note to the front door. BE BACK AT NOON, it read.

Leela glanced up and down the street. An hour to wait. She sat down on the wooden stoop and planted her feet on the steps. A young boy came by to get a paper for his father. Leela told him to come back at noon. As she sat there, warming in the sun, she began to think about Parker.

What was he thinking? Did he blame her? The more she thought about it, the worse she felt. Her chest tightened with shame, and she knew she had to see him, let him know just how sorry she was. Leela jumped up and dusted off her skirt, then headed across the tracks toward the center of town.

She arrived at the jail breathless and flushed. The sleepy deputy who greeted her believed her story that she was Parker's sister and showed her to the boy's cell. Keys rattled loudly, stirring Parker from his cot. He looked up to see Leela enter the dark, cramped space.

"What in the world are you doing here?" Parker had a frightened look on his face. Leela rushed over and wrapped her arms around her cousin. He pushed her away to hold her at arm's length. "Why did you come, Leela? Does Momma know you're here?"

"I had to see you, Parker. I just had to. I'm sorry about what I told the sheriff. I didn't know it would make things worse."

"You're not to blame, Leela. What you said made no difference. Who's put this in your head that you caused anything? The sheriff was gonna do what he wanted to last night. Nothing anyone said could have made a difference."

"That's not what Josephine said."

"Don't listen to her." Parker stepped back and let go of Leela's shoulders. "Poppa was here early this morning. He said he's gonna take care of everything. Just burns me up. Three hundred dollars! It's gonna be hard to raise, but Poppa said he would."

"I can help, Parker. If Mr. Foreman will print up a special edition about what happened last night, I could go around and sell them, all through town. I could help raise the money to get you out."

"Stay out of it, Leela. Leave Mr. Foreman alone. He's feeling bad enough about all of this. You can't raise three hundred dollars selling newspapers for a nickel."

"People who know you might pay more than a nickel. You know, like a donation to help . . . help you out. Uncle Bert and Aunt Effie know most everybody in town. I'll bet some white folks would even be willing to help."

"Leela. Don't get yourself all worked up and involved in this. Better leave things to Poppa. He knows what to do." Parker slumped down onto his cot. "I'm sorry I ever took you to the *Banner*." Filled with remorse, he rested his chin on his folded hands. "It was dangerous. I knew it. Momma knew it, too. That's why she was so worried. Guess I should have listened to her. You've got no business tangled up in this. Forget it, Leela."

Leela moved quickly to sit at Parker's side. "No business?" Her voice rose in indignation. "Parker! Don't you know how much I love you and your family? You're the brother I never had. How can I forget it?"

Parker turned and faced his cousin, his misery fully apparent. Leela watched him struggle to keep from crying.

"Leela, it's been great having you live with us. You're more fun than Josephine ever was. You're real smart, too. I know you can do anything you set your mind to, but now I feel like I've let you down."

"How? What do you mean?"

"I knew when I threw that rock that I was asking for trouble . . . deep trouble." He rose and stood at the thick iron bars. "I should have thought about you. My actions got you involved in this mess, and now here you are talking about going out to sell papers. Don't do it, Leela. It's too dangerous. You don't know how ugly things could get." He walked over to her and pulled her to her feet. "Go on home. Promise?"

Leela didn't answer.

"Go on, now. Don't get Momma to worrying about you."

"Time to leave!" The deputy's voice interrupted them. He opened the cell door and scrutinized the two of them.

Leela hugged Parker good-bye, holding him close for a moment. "Don't you worry," she whispered into his ear. "You'll be back home before you know it."

She pulled away, determined to help bring her family back together. She didn't need anyone's permission to get Parker out of jail, she realized as she left.

On the way to the paper she stopped at Watson's Livery and convinced Mr. Watson that her uncle needed a mule and a wagon for the day. Mr. Watson quickly agreed to let Leela take it to him.

He'd been doing business for years with Bert Alexander; in fact, Bert was the only smithy he'd let shoe his horses. Watson didn't even mention money at all.

"I'll settle with your uncle tomorrow," he said, as he helped Leela into the wagon.

When Mr. Foreman arrived at the *Banner*, he admonished Leela for her actions, but seeing how determined she was he relented and printed up a stack of single pages about Parker's arrest and the attack on the *Banner*. It took less than an hour to bundle them and load the back of the wagon.

Mr. Foreman could not help smiling to himself as he watched the girl settle into her seat and pick up the reins. She flashed him a smile as she snapped them sharply above the wiry brown mule she had borrowed.

Guiding the surefooted animal down Preston Street, Leela began her mission. If it takes until nightfall, she told herself, I'll not return home until every last paper has been sold.

A knock at the back door interrupted Effie's sewing, and she sprang to her feet to see who was there.

"Why, Gladys Rolings. Come on in. You been a stranger too long." Effie unlatched the screen. A short, pretty woman stepped into the room.

Though glad to see Effie, she seemed nervous and tense and stood awkwardly in the center of the room before speaking. Opening her worn cloth purse she took out a single sheet of paper.

"Effie," she started, "I been knowing you close to twenty years and when I read this about Parker, I could hardly keep from goin' right down there to the sheriff and give him a piece of my mind. Lockin' up your boy! What's things comin' to 'round here?"

Effie caught her breath. "You read what?" She snatched the paper from her friend and quickly scanned the words. "Where'd you get this?" Her voice remained controlled, but her hands were shaking.

"There's a little redheaded gal trotting all over town, selling the paper for Mr. Foreman. Cutest thing you ever saw. And I'll tell you, Effie, she makes such a case, I paid the girl fifty cents for the copy. You know I'd do what I could for you and your family. A more upstanding boy than Parker Alexander can't be found if you searched three counties."

Effie crushed the single sheet in her hand. "A redheaded girl. About fifteen?"

"Yes. That's her. Smart as a whip. Talks so proper and polite."

"That's my niece, Leela." Effie's voice was tinged with exasperation. "She's been here with us a few months now."

"Shows how long it's been since I come over this way."

Effie stared at the paper. "I never dreamed this was what she had in mind." She sat down at her kitchen table, shaking her head. "We've gotta raise three hundred dollars, Gladys. By noon tomorrow. If not, the sheriff's sending my boy over to the county jail in Groesbeck." She paused as her friend settled into the chair across from her. "And you know if he gets took over to Groesbeck, we ain't never gonna see him again."

Gladys Rolings dabbed at her brow with a pink handkerchief then pushed it back into her purse. She fumbled with her change purse for a moment and gave her friend an earnest look. "Don't you fret, Effie. The word's been spread. You and Bert got a lot of friends in Limestone County." She handed Effie a ball of crumpled bills. "It's only five dollars. All I got to my name. Here, you take it," she persisted, brushing away Effie's hand of protest. "Us colored folks gotta pull together and get this thing with Parker settled."

The room fell silent, filled only with unspoken words of understanding.

Gladys patted Effie's hand, pressing the bills firmly to her friend.

"It's like a nightmare, Gladys. My Parker locked up like this." Effie opened her palm and looked at the money. "You don't know how much this means." Her words were fraught with pain.

"Oh, yes, I do. I lost a brother to a situation like this. Ten years ago, over in McLennan County. It was a lynchin' folks still talk about today. When I let my mind go back to that sight . . . well, Effie, it's somethin' you never forget. If I was you, I'd think about sendin' that boy of yours up north. Ain't nothin' here for him but more trouble, just like he's havin' now."

Gladys shrugged back her shoulders as if throwing off her memories, then stood to leave. She tugged at the frayed cuff of her white cotton blouse as she headed to the door.

Effie rushed to hug her friend, fighting back tears of gratitude. She kissed Gladys on the cheek, unable to say more.

"And Effie," Gladys started as she pushed her purse onto her arm, "we gotta help old man Foreman keep the *Banner* going. How else us colored gonna know what's going on in the world outside Mexia?"

All afternoon friends like Gladys Rolings knocked on Effie's back door. They left a dollar, maybe two, and the local preacher, Reverend Pearson, donated twenty-five dollars to the cause. By the end of the day, when Bert got home, Effie had one hundred sixty-four dollars and twenty-eight cents stuffed into a cracked canning jar.

"I started to say I don't believe it," Bert Alexander began as he fingered the crumpled bills his wife spilled onto the table. "But I believe it, all right. That gal's got spunk . . . and a right smart head on her shoulders. Going around town, stirring folks to do this!" He chuckled and began smoothing out the money. "She not home yet? It's gettin' dark. Maybe I better go see."

Effie placed a hand of caution on her husband's shoulder. "Not right yet. I think she'll be all right. Give it a little more time." Effie smiled at Bert. "You know, my brother, Ed, was a lot like Leela. When he'd set his mind to doing something, nothing anybody could say made a bit of sense to him. He'd just go on and act like nobody ever said a word. Used to anger my momma so." She drew an audible breath and ran her hand over her lips. "Wish he coulda lived to see what a fine daughter he got."

Bert nodded and began to empty the deep pockets of his worn denim jacket. "I think I shoed over a hundred horses today and probably ran three miles of barbed-wire fencing for old man Green." He lowered his voice and added, "I sold that extra bellows that I had 'specially made. Got fifty-two dollars for it." He pulled out his own contribution and put it on the table alongside Effie's money. They counted it together. Three hundred sixteen dollars. More than enough to pay Parker's fine.

An atmosphere of hopeful anticipation filled the tiny house as Bert washed up while Effie hummed to herself and put dinner on the table, though neither was successful in getting Josephine from her room. She refused to come out and eat with them.

"Wish I knew how to get Josephine to act more civil," Effie

worried as she passed the mashed potatoes to Bert. "She's been holed up in that room all afternoon, soon as she heard what Leela was doing. They just don't get along. Seems nothing I do helps that fact."

"They gotta work this out for themselves. You know that." Bert broke open a fat buttermilk biscuit and spread honey inside. "Parker's who we better be worryin' about," he said solemnly, raising tired eyes at Effie. "I'll be at the sheriff's at daybreak and pay him his money first thing. Another day won't pass with my boy locked up like that." His voice was husky with anger. "Many a family done lost a son when things like this come 'round."

"I know, Gladys Rolings was talking 'bout just that this morning." Effie fiddled with the chicken on her plate as if weighing her next words carefully. "You know, Bert, it ain't never gonna be safe for Parker in Mexia. Never again. He's so bullheaded and determined to rile folks up. I know what he's doing is right and he's writing what needs to be told, but I'm afraid something real bad gonna happen to him. Those white folks ain't gonna stop 'til the *Banner*'s shut down and Parker's not gonna stop writing those articles."

As they both sat dwelling on the truth of it, neither heard Leela step onto the back porch where she stood in the shadows, just beyond the screen door, listening to their desperate conversation. She quietly wiped gritty dust from her face as she strained to hear what they said.

Bert didn't look up from his plate as he spoke. "Well, at least we got the money to get the boy out. With Leela spreading the news like she did, we come out all right, didn't we?"

Effie nodded and took a sip of coffee.

"Now," Bert went on, "after we get Parker back home, we gotta rethink all this writing and hell-raising he's been doing." He took a big gulp of lemonade from his glass.

"Tom Walker came by today, gave me seven dollars," Effie began. "Know what he said?"

"What?" Bert asked, finishing off a chicken leg and grabbing another.

"The same thing Gladys Rolings said . . . we oughta get Parker out of town." Effie's words rushed out. She watched Bert carefully as he laid down his chicken leg and wiped his hands on a towel, raising an eyebrow at her.

"Might be some truth in that."

"Tom said he's got a brother living in Chicago who works for that colored paper up there, the *Defender*." Effie put down her fork and clasped her hands together. "Said his brother would be real happy to take Parker in. Let him finish school up there, get him on at the paper."

In the dim shadows of the porch, Leela trembled. Parker leave Mexia! For good! She stepped closer to see her aunt and uncle more clearly. Uncle Bert was now pacing, head lowered, back and forth in front of the stove.

"Tom think he could work that out?"

"He told me not to give it another thought. If you agree, he can get the telephone operator in town to place a call. His brother could meet Parker at the train station in Chicago whenever we say."

Bert scratched his head, then hitched up his pants. "My boy. My boy. He ain't just anybody. He's different. Got a heap of ideas in his head. There's something real special about him. Ain't never seen so much ambition in such a young man." He locked his fingers together and placed his hands under his chin. "There sure ain't no future for him here." Bert went around the table to stand behind Effie and put his hands on the back of her chair. "You go on and get my old trunk from out the shed. Pack Parker's things. I'll go over and tell Tom Walker to make that call to his brother. We puttin' Parker on the train in the mornin'."

At these words Leela slumped back against the wall. They were sending Parker North! Tomorrow! The lump in her throat grew large and throbbing as Leela took in what was happening. It was all falling apart! Her family. She'd be left here with Josephine! She looked dismally at the brown paper bag in her hand. Thirty-four dollars and fifteen cents. That's all she'd collected for Parker. And now it wasn't even needed. As Leela slowly pulled the back door open and stepped into the kitchen, she made up her mind to give the money to Parker. He'd need it up North she was certain.

Parker's train to Chicago didn't pull out until seven o'clock the next evening. Saying good-bye at the station was frightful. Uncle Bert struggled to remain calmly in charge, Effie clung to Parker and cried softly to herself, while Josephine sobbed loudly and actually accused

Leela of running her brother out of town. Leela held her tongue and tolerated Josephine's biting words. She'd deal with her when they got home.

As Leela blinked back tears, she embraced her cousin fiercely and wished him well. If only we'd had time to talk, she thought as she watched him step into the passenger car marked COLORED. She could tell Parker had mixed emotions about going. After all, he was setting off on a great adventure, heading for a big city and a big-time newspaper. She envied him, yet feared for him. What would life be like in Chicago?

"Don't forget to write," Leela yelled above the hissing steam engine. She ran alongside the train as it began to pull away. "Write to me, Parker. Tell me everything that happens." He waved his long arm out the window and blew a kiss to his family. Within minutes the train had disappeared down the track.

The small family rode home silently in their buggy. What was there to say? Parker was safely out of Mexia and they would carry on with their lives.

At home, Leela entered her bedroom and sank down onto the double bed she shared with Josephine. She stared at the floor in disbelief. Parker was gone! The house seemed unusually quiet already.

"I hope you're satisfied," Josephine snapped hatefully as she came into the room and shoved the door shut. "You've ruined everything for my family, you little witch!"

Leela swung around and scowled at her cousin. "Just shut up! I'm sick and tired of you blaming me for everything that goes wrong around here." She got up, placing her fists on her hips as she confronted Josephine. "Did it ever occur to you that Parker might be happy to be going to Chicago?" Josephine didn't answer. "I didn't think so," Leela said in disgust. "You wouldn't know because you don't know what Parker really wants."

"And you do?" Josephine threw back. "How could you know anything about what makes Parker happy?"

"He told me. More than once. He's been dreaming about going North. Going to college. Working for an important paper." Leela moved away from Josephine toward the open window. "I'll miss him, but I'm happy for him. He's going to see things and do things you never even heard of."

"You put that nonsense in his head. He never said a word about leaving Mexia before you showed your face around here."

Leela didn't answer. Why bother? She glared at Josephine and watched as she plopped herself down at the dressing table and began combing her thick, wiry hair. How strange her hair is, Leela noticed again. It was snow white. Without any color at all, really. Just like the rest of her body.

When Leela first met her cousin at the train station, she had been startled by the clarity of Josephine's watery eyes and the translucent appearance of her skin. She was not light-skinned. Not olive. Not even buff-colored. White. Yet with her nappy hair and clearly Negro features she could not be mistaken for a white girl. Not at all.

Aunt Effie had explained that her cousin was albino. A rare occurrence among their race. Leela still didn't understand exactly how it happened, but she knew Josephine used it to her advantage.

Nonchalantly, Josephine rose and slipped off her dress, rolled it into a ball, and stuffed it under the bed. Wearing only her panties, she stood unembarrassed in the center of the room.

"Might be a whole lot better if you were the one leaving town," Josephine began, leaning back over the dresser to look into the mirror. Her ponderous breasts swayed in the eerie, soft light of the tall oil lamp. She opened a square purple box and patted dots of Pompei Rouge on her plump cheeks.

"Well, it's Parker's life and I'm happy for him," Leela managed to say as she shifted her eyes from her cousin's wanton nakedness. In the dim light she appeared luminescent, almost glowing, as if she had drifted in from the spirit world where Grandma Ekiti dwelled—an evil apparition sent to trouble Leela.

"Just stay out of my family's affairs," Josephine snapped; then she took her index finger and rouged her lips. "You're not an Alexander, not really. Keep your nose to yourself, you hear me?" She picked up her hairbrush and shook it at Leela. "Your big mouth is what started this mess."

Gritting her teeth, Leela watched in silence as Josephine put on a blue-and-white middy with matching skirt. "Slipping out again to meet Johnny Ray?" Leela taunted, knowing how much Aunt Effie disliked the dim-witted ragpicker who had recently been run out of town for pulling a knife on a white man.

"What's it to you?" The pale girl dabbed perfume behind each ear. "Jealous? I don't see any boys hankering after you." She pushed past Leela and easily slipped over the windowsill, landing softly on the grass outside. She peered back in at Leela. "And if you tell Poppa I'm out, you'll be sorry. I'll make you wish you'd never set foot in this house."

Leela watched Josephine scurry away in the moonlight and shook her head sadly when Johnny Ray Mosley came out of the bushes and threw a big hairy arm around his girlfriend.

Having sex with Josephine Alexander was as close to having sex with a white girl as Johnny Ray Mosley would ever come. His coal black hands, hardly visible in the dappled shadows beneath the willow, moved with practiced ease into the secret places he knew Josephine loved him to touch. She teased him with feathery fingers, guiding his hard, thick fingers where she wanted them to be. He stroked and probed until she squealed with pleasure as he massaged the pulsing spot. He licked the sprinkling of freckles across the top of her breasts and savored the combination of perspiration and Midnight Waltz perfume that always drove him mad. His long pink tongue made its way over mounds of sweet flesh to curl around her rosy nipples rising stiffly under his chin. As Josephine pressed her naked body more tightly into the barrel-chested young man above her, the zealous farm boy clasped her buttocks firmly with both hands and happily settled in for the ride.

And what a ride it was. Josephine wiggled and snaked beneath his frenetic pumping until she filled Johnny Ray's eyes with tears of joy. He took her as she wanted him to: roughly, without caution, with a fierceness he secretly feared might hurt her. Yet she never winced in pain or tried to get away. The more forcefully he drove his stiff, hungry manhood into her soft, plump flesh, the better she liked it. And she usually begged for more.

Johnny Ray felt no guilt in taking what Josephine so freely offered; there was no better way, that he knew of, to spend a few hours on an unusually hot spring night.

The humid air boiled ten degrees higher and melted the damp grass beneath their sweating bodies. With strong, sure thrusts, he met her rhythm as she pulled him into a blinding swirl.

Johnny Ray didn't let Josephine from beneath his hulking body until dawn was nearly breaking and she pushed him away roughly and said, "That's enough."

Brushing bits of grass from his thick, bushy hair, Johnny Ray rolled over onto his back.

"I've gotta get home," Josephine said, groping around to find her middy. She crouched on her knees and strained to see her companion's face. When he said nothing, she repeated, "I've gotta go." Johnny Ray didn't budge. "You got nothing to say?" Josephine's voice was shrill, biting.

"What's to say?" he finally mumbled, pulling his pants up over his hips.

"You don't care if I gotta leave? Don't you want me to stay? You could act a little more like you cared, Johnny Ray!"

"I do care. You know that."

"Enough to get married?" Josephine scooted over and put her hands on the boy's hairy chest. "Let's get married. Go out to your daddy's farm and live like we want to. Free. Just think, if we were married, we'd be together all the time."

Johnny Ray pushed her hands from his chest and stood up. Frowning down at the naked girl, he said, "Don't start up with that marriage stuff again, Josephine. I done told you I ain't got no hankerin' to get hitched. Not no time soon, anyway."

Stung by that remark, Josephine yanked her middy over her head, clenched her jaws in resentment and thought to herself, We'll just see about that, Johnny Ray.

Chapter Three

Behind the white-columned portico and vine-covered windows of the only brick building on Grayson Avenue lay thirty-six patients in various stages of illness, cared for by a team of nurses and one aging doctor. The elegant structure, centered on five acres of finely manicured lawn divided by curving brick walkways and colorful beds of roses, gardenias, zinnias and petunias, had once been the home of the Howers of Waco, a family whose fortune had been carved from the bustling stockyards west of town. The Howers' wealth soared to such heights, people still referred to them in reverent terms as if they had been royalty.

When George Hower had died five years before, with no heir to manage the sprawling estate, he had willed that his home be converted into a private clinic for families of means. Like the vast majority of such medical facilities in Central Texas, the well-equipped Hower Clinic accepted white patients only, and the handful of Negroes allowed into the exclusive nursing home included two cooks, a gardener, a cleaning woman and a laundress: Hattie Wilder.

It didn't bother Hattie that Negroes were excluded from the clinic: that's just the way things were done. Blacks who needed special care had better have enough money to go up to the Bluitt Sanitarium in Dallas or down to Saint Anthony's in Houston if they were seeking care for conditions like consumption, a weak heart, emphysema or the malaise of emotional disorders often referred to as hysteria.

Today, Hattie Wilder emptied a foul-smelling bedpan into the white porcelain toilet, flushed its putrid contents away and submerged the filthy receptacle into a washtub of sudsy water. An acrid wave of ammonia rose up and burned her eyes. She immediately squeezed them shut and kept scrubbing, swirling hot water with her big white rag like a cook kneading dough in the kitchen. With big strong arms, shoulders tensed in square resistance, Hattie attacked her chores with methodical, staunch resolve.

As she finished off the bedpan, Mose Kerry, the gardener, pushed open the back door to the laundry room and stuck in his head. Sunlight flooded the area. A mild breeze stirred the ammonia-laden air.

"Mornin', Hattie." He tipped his battered straw hat to her. "How you be feeling this beautiful Wednesday morning?"

"Like I be feeling every morning, Mose." Her tone had a touch of irritation. "Worse than some, but better'n most o' the folks in here."

"See they got you hard at it already." He gave her that lopsided grin that Hattie hated.

"Since seven this morning," she said, wishing the simpleminded gardener would leave her alone. He popped into the laundry room every ten minutes for absolutely no other reason than to get her attention. Too old to do his job, so he gonna keep me from doing mine, she thought. "Mose, I got too much work to be shucking around with you." She tried to shoo him away with one hand. "You know this place don't bother me none. I done cleaned up after worse than what they put on me here. Ain't nothing to this job. I be finished by noon."

The gnarled old man grinned and nodded knowingly, disappearing back outside.

In reality, Hattie felt lucky to have this job, but she'd rather die than act like she was grateful. Acting so thankful would please all those haughty nurses. She often told Mose, "They think I oughta be scraping and bowing down to them just 'cause they gonna let me wash their bedpans and clean up their vomit."

When her son, Carey, finished school, she thought, he'd get a real good job, like working at the telegraph office or waiting tables at the Regal Hotel. Then she could leave this place, let him take care of things. Hattie picked up a small paring knife and shaved bits of lye soap into hot water. But this is the way things are now, she admitted, so ain't no good in complaining.

The director of the clinic, Dr. Steiner, was an easygoing liberal-minded man who openly supported better medical treatment for colored, though he was not foolish enough to scuttle his position by letting Negro patients into Hower Clinic. Hattie got along with him all right. He let her work half-days for pay nearly equal to what others got for six or seven hours, and usually left her alone to complete her chores as she saw fit, sometimes even asking her opinion on how the place was run. She liked being talked to as if she had something to say, and liked it even more that he listened. There were not many places where a fifty-one-year-old black woman was treated as if her presence really mattered.

Five minutes after Mose Kerry pulled his head out of the steamy laundry, Edna Sutter, the head nurse, entered. Hattie gritted her teeth and said nothing as the stern-faced woman handed her two more dirty pans.

"The sheets in Mrs. Echols's room need changing right now, and when you finish, better check on Joe Driggs, room seventeen. He's been spitting up blood all morning and his pillows need washing. Don't know what's going on with him," Nurse Sutter mumbled as she turned to leave. "And pull that hair net down in the back, Hattie. You'll have the patients all upset if you don't cover your hair."

"Yes, ma'am," Hattie replied, giving the thick black net a sharp tug to cover the flyaway strands of gray that had escaped the heavy cap. She pulled the dirty pans into her tub of hot water as the door slammed shut, leaving her alone with her work.

It was eight-thirty in the morning and she had already changed Mrs. Echols's bed two times since she started work at seven. Oughta just prop the old woman up on the toilet and let her stay all day,

Hattie thought as she started in on the bedpans. Her raw red hands pulsed with pain as she poured more boiling water into her huge washtub and plunged into the dirty work she had been doing for the past two years.

At ten o'clock, the bedpans were all finished, lined up in a pristine row on the table. Hattie picked up a stack of fresh linen and started on her third round for the day.

"It's about time you got in here" was Hattie's greeting in room six. Widow Jonas pushed herself upright in the bed and scowled. "Nurse Sutter said you'd be here hours ago. Where the devil you been?" The frail woman leaned forward, preparing herself to be lifted. She remained slumped over, staring into the sheets as she continued to complain. "Leaving me here like this. Gal, you ought to be fired."

Hattie made no reply, going about her task of lifting and turning the woman's skeletal frame in order to put clean sheets on the bed. She never paid old lady Jonas any mind. The woman gave everyone hell.

By noon, Hattie had cleaned up every patient and made sure they had fresh water, then headed back to the laundry room. Her feet ached, her ankles had begun to swell, and her eyes still watered painfully from the ammonia she used.

When the shrill whistle blared from the train depot in town, Hattie folded her rags, pulled off her hair net and removed her full white apron. She stood still for a moment, listening for footsteps, then swiftly picked up two bars of lye soap and buried them deep in her pocket. Nurse Sutter entered the room as Hattie threw dirty water out the door.

"Leaving already, Hattie?" The dour woman frowned.

"Yes, ma'am. It's noon. Time for me to quit. You know that." Hattie looked into Nurse Sutter's unsmiling face.

"Dr. Steiner said you won't be here tomorrow?" She asked the question as if doubting what she had been told.

Hattie nodded. "That's right. Gotta take my son, Carey, up to Dallas. He's got his heart set on getting fit for a suit. I told him we'd make the trip in the morning."

"A new suit? You're going to miss a day's work to go have your son fitted for a suit? Seems like you could do that on Saturday." The nurse ran her thumb over her fingernails and pursed her lips in a sour grimace.

Though she didn't want to, Hattie explained. "The man what makes suits up there says he gotta fit Carey tomorrow if he wants the suit for summer. We going over to Limestone County soon and I want my boy looking nice," Hattie finished, hating to tell this woman all of her business just because she'd be off one day.

Nurse Sutter slammed a stack of soiled sheets on the table and blinked her eyes rapidly. "Well, there's a lot of work still here to be done. Three new patients are set to arrive in the morning. It's not a good time for you to be gone."

"Well," Hattie said as she pulled a handkerchief from her frayed brown purse and wiped perspiration from her brow, "I guess the dirty sheets will still be here when I get back day after tomorrow."

"Don't be sassy with me, Hattie," Nurse Sutter ordered through clenched teeth. "You might be able to get away with that kind of talk with the other nurses, but I don't let niggers walk all over me. Your back talk is going to get you fired . . . or worse."

Hattie looked at the woman in silence for a moment, shrugged her sloping shoulders as if she didn't care and left through the back door. As it slammed shut behind her, she started the twelve-block walk toward her home on the other side of town.

Hattie really didn't mind the work. It was the white folks she minded most. If they would just leave her alone, everything would be all right. But some of the nurses, Edna Sutter in particular, pressed her and prodded her to exasperation. Hattie had made up her mind a long time ago not to let them get under her skin. Dr. Steiner had hired her and liked the way she did her work; if Nurse Sutter had a complaint, she'd better take it up with the doctor. Hattie refused to bite her tongue for any of them.

Hattie plodded along, moving steadily and directly toward the small frame house she shared with her son. The thought of going to Dallas in the morning cheered her, as doing anything special with Carey did. He'd been badgering her for weeks about getting this suit made, she mused. If they weren't on that train in the morning, she'd never hear the end of it.

She relaxed, feeling smug that the money for the suit was already saved up: twenty-two dollars it was going to cost. All that Saturday ironing for those picky Reynolds sisters had paid off well for her.

Won't Carey look grand, she thought, in a real man's suit, custom-made just for him? It's time, she had to admit. He was fourteen, now, too big to be wearing those short pants she'd sewed for him since he first started school.

Hattie smiled to herself as she thought about Carey: the gift Ed Brannon had left behind. News of Ed's death in that terrible fire had only become tolerable when Hattie learned she was pregnant. Why that man got taken from me, I'll never understand, Hattie thought bitterly. He was a good man. We could have had a future—he said so in his letter.

Carey was her salvation, the reason she got up in the morning and struggled to keep going. Maybe she did spoil the boy now and then, but why not? He was her world, her heart, her future. Only one more term and he would finish the primary grades. Then on to high school at the Central Academy, the best school for Negroes in the state. Hattie swelled with pride. T.J. hadn't had the chance to get his schooling, but Carey was going to go all the way through.

That child's got a real flair about him, she admitted. When he shows up in a custom-made suit, he's going to be the envy of every colored boy in the ninth grade at Rayther School.

When Hattie reached her house, she went straight to the kitchen, poured herself a small glass of blackberry wine and drank it down in one gulp. She savored the taste of the rich sweet liquid, rolling it around on her tongue. The best I ever made, she decided, starting to pour herself another small amount. But she hesitated, thought better of it, and recorked the bottle, putting it back in the cabinet behind a can of flour.

In the cool shadowy sanctuary of her bedroom, Hattie eased off her heavy black shoes and rubbed the soles of her feet. That walk from the clinic to her house tested her endurance. Things had been simpler when she lived in the country.

Removing her ammonia-smelling work clothes, the tired woman lay down on the bed in her slip. Paper shades on the bedroom windows cut the heat of the day and darkened the room enough to let her rest. She did this every afternoon; stretched out and took a short nap before starting her dinner. Carey would be showing up soon enough. She could see him now, bursting through the back door, throwing his books on the table, flashing that bright smile of his as he asked, as he did every day, "What you cook today, Momma?"

Pushing strands of gray hair out of her eyes, Hattie chuckled to herself, then rolled over on her side and promptly fell asleep.

Not wanting to dirty the spit-shine on his best leather boots, Carey decided against rubbing out the circle with his foot. After gathering up his marbles and pocketing his winnings, he told Pauly Webster, "You wipe that out. If Miss Glass sees we been shooting marbles back here, we're gonna be in trouble."

Without a moment's hesitation, Pauly dropped to his knees in the dust and vigorously scattered the dirt until no trace of the game was left. Three other boys, who knew what was coming, took off toward the schoolhouse on the other side of the yard, leaving Carey and Pauly alone.

"That last play was mine, Carey! It wasn't your turn. You cheated. I gotta have my dime back, you hear?" Pauly whined, slapping his plump hands together to shake off the gritty dirt.

Carey stepped closer, allowing his shadow to fall over the face of his overweight classmate huddled on the ground. "What'd you say? You want your money back? Ha!" He tilted his lean square jaw to the sky and laughed. "You must be crazy, I won it fair and square, got witnesses, too."

"My momma's gonna have my hide if I don't bring home a pound of sugar like she told me." Pauly straightened up to sit on his heels. "Come on, Carey. That last shot was mine. Give me back my money. Now."

"Seems like you shoulda thought about that before you laid your measly dime on the line," Carey admonished triumphantly. "Once money's wagered, it's fair game." He tugged his cap down snugly over his curly black hair and tossed the dime into the air, caught it, and put it back into his pocket. He jangled his pocket, full of change, loving the sound of coins clinking together.

"Stupid!" he went on, clearly enjoying the opportunity to chastise Pauly. "You played, you lost. Ain't no skin off my back your momma's gonna have your hide." He turned to look back toward the school, noticing that the other children had already entered the building. Miss Glass would be out to ring the bell any minute. "Just shut up, Pauly. Act like a man. Stop sniveling and whining like a baby." Carey brushed the lapels of his beige linen jacket and examined the tiny gold ring on his little finger. Well, not really gold, he reminded himself, but he'd shined that brass so much it looked like gold to him.

Pauly craned his neck forward and shouted, "Gimme my money, Carey. Give it back!" Then he suddenly lunged forward and grabbed Carey's legs, pulling the boy down in the dusty yard with him.

"What the hell you think you're doing?" Carey pushed Pauly aside and rolled into a grassy area. Smudges of brown and green marked both sides of his jacket. Kicking wildly at Pauly, Carey managed to land a blow to the boy's stomach. He jumped up and stood glowering down.

"You're gonna be real sorry you did this," Carey threatened, trying to clean off his coat. "You ain't been living 'round here long enough to start changing the rules of the game." He cuffed the boy again with his foot. "Stay out of the game if you're gonna be a sore loser." Pauly clutched his stomach and groaned. He had no wind left to say a word.

Carey frowned and picked up his cap.

"You two! Get inside! Right this minute!" Their teacher's voice shrilled across the school yard. Miss Glass, hair flying, spectacles catching the sun, hurried toward the boys as she continued to yell. "Carey. Pauly. Come in. Now." She stopped midway across the yard and waited.

"Get up!" Carey ordered, then hissed, "You better not say a word about any money." He placed his boot on Pauly's right hand and pressed. The boy struggled to get free. "You gonna keep your mouth shut?"

"All right," Pauly gasped. "All right. Leave me alone and let me up."

Carey relented, turning away from Pauly to saunter off behind Miss Glass.

Once inside the tiny school, he flopped noisily into his seat at the back of the room and rolled his eyes to the ceiling as Pauly passed by. The angry boy sat down two rows from his classmate.

"Damn," Carey muttered under his breath. "My favorite jacket. Ruined." He twisted in his seat and tried to see his back. He knew it was streaked with dust, and if there was anything Carey Logan loathed, it was dirt. He spent a great deal of time on his appearance and avoided all contact with the filthy farm boys who came to school in sweaty flannel shirts and mud-covered overalls. To distance himself from the stench they brought with them, he sat in the last row of desks.

A sorry lot, Carey noted, his eyes coldly sweeping the room. Only the girls were worth speaking to and not many of them. Only Marry Ellen Whatly really deserved a second glance.

He leaned forward and tapped the pretty girl on her arm. She turned quickly, smoothed her dark hair from her forehead and smiled. Carey winked, giving her what he thought was his most seductive expression, and tried to visualize her big breasts without the middy. Marry Ellen giggled, squeezed her eyes shut, and covered her mouth with one hand.

As usual, Miss Glass rapped on her desk with a heavy wooden ruler and brought her fifteen students to attention.

"Boys and girls, before we start our lessons today, I want to announce the winner of our penmanship contest. You all did such a good job. I'm proud of every student in the class. However, we do have one among us whose work is truly exceptional." She turned back to her desk and picked up a sheet of paper which she held up facing the class. The evenly spaced, boldly drawn letters seemed to jump from the page with life.

"Carey Logan"—the teacher's long white teeth dominated her smile—"please come forward."

Carey's eyes flew open. He sat up straight, a childish grin on his smooth olive face. "Me?" he asked, exaggerating his surprise. "I'm the winner?"

"You most certainly are, Carey," Miss Glass replied, almost wishing another student had won. He'd been in so much trouble this term, expelled twice for fighting, reprimanded severely for skipping classes on a fairly regular basis, and she'd even talked to his mother several times about the way he disrupted the class by getting up and leaving when he felt like it. Yet the woman refused to punish the boy, always letting him have his way. A spoiled brat, that's what he is, the teacher decided. But she had to admit he was no dummy and his penmanship had no rival.

Carey constantly created reasons to be center stage, and now, his teacher observed, he truly had one. "Come to the front of the class, Carey. I have a prize for you."

Miss Glass waited as the slim young man stood up. He slipped out of his dirty jacket and straightened the red string tie around his neck. His self-assurance and haughty manner grated on Miss Glass's nerves, yet she had to admit the boy was unusually handsome; he stood out from the other students as if he were white, and he treated them with such arrogant detachment, he might as well have been.

"Carey," she began as he made his way forward, "congratulations on winning first prize in penmanship for this term." She handed the boy a small white box.

"Open it, Carey. What'd you get?" Several of the students prompted.

Carey pulled back his shoulders, annoyed to be caught in his shirtsleeves, but he preferred that to standing up in a dirty jacket. I'm gonna get Pauly Webster good after class, he vowed to himself as he opened the box.

Carefully, Carey removed an elegant fountain pen. Its shiny golden cap caught the light and sparkled. He turned the pen sideways and read the name aloud—"Falcon"—then he gasped in pleasure and rolled the instrument into his palm. "It's beautiful, Miss Glass. Really nice!"

The students clapped enthusiastically, all except Pauly Webster, who sat slumped down in his seat, arms folded tightly across his chest.

"Thank you," Carey said clearly, giving his teacher a heart-melting smile. "This is great." He held it up to show the class, then walked briskly back to his desk.

"You're very welcome, Carey. I just hope you use it well as you continue your schooling," Miss Glass replied, hoping this honor might impress the boy enough to make him stay out of trouble for the rest of the term.

The school was nearly two miles from his house, but Carey knew a shortcut through Farmer Baily's cotton field. He rarely took it because of all the dust he got on himself and because Mr. Baily stayed on the lookout for students who dared tromp through his crops.

Carey had seen the old man waving a long rifle and knew he'd use it, too.

But in his excitement today, Carey ran through the tall rows of blooming cotton plants and made it home in record time.

Hattie looked up from a big black kettle on the stove, surprised to see Carey home so soon.

"Boy, you skip out early, again?" She laid aside her long-handled spoon and scrutinized her son.

"Naw," Carey shot back, "lay off, Ma. I just cut through old man Baily's field." He quickly took off his grass-stained jacket and rolled it into a ball, stuffing it under his books. He wasn't up to an argument with his mother about getting into it with Pauly Webster.

"You know that man don't want you kids on his property. He's mean. Coulda took a shot at you. I told you not to do that, Carey." She picked up her spoon and resumed her stirring. "Someday he gonna take a shot at you."

"Quit worryin', Ma. I can take care of myself." The irritation in his voice was laid on thick. He sighed loudly and thumped his books on the small pine table in the center of the kitchen. "I wanted to get home and show you this." He held the small white box in his hand. "Look, Ma. Look what Miss Glass gave me today." He removed the box top and pulled out the pen.

Hattie leaned closer to examine the instrument. Carey handed it to her and let her feel its expensive weight. "This a mighty fine pen. Miss Glass give it to you, you say?"

"Yeah, Ma. I won it!"

"Don't lie to me, Carey. This pen too good to be givin' to a child. You take this off your teacher's desk?"

Carey snatched the pen from his mother. "Why you gotta think that, Ma? Why?"

The hurt look in his eyes pained Hattie, but she had to be sure. She'd been through three other incidents with her son when he'd boldly taken what he wanted from others and she didn't want any trouble from Miss Glass.

Carey shoved the pen back into its box. "I won it, Ma. The writing contest, remember? I told you about it last week."

Hattie nodded slowly, then reached over and picked up the small glass of blackberry wine she always kept nearby and took a sip. "I just never thought Miss Glass would be givin' away something as fancy as that."

Carey lowered his eyes, hating his mother's accusation. If she'd stop drinking all that homemade wine, maybe she'd remember what I tell her, he thought angrily.

"I'm sorry, baby," Hattie offered, going back to the preparations of their dinner. "You say you won it, that's fine. That's mighty fine, son. Just watch, you gonna go to Central Academy next term. You'll need a fine pen like that when you get there."

"Yeah," Carey mumbled, starting toward the back door.

"Don't go far," Hattie cautioned, keeping her back to her son. "Dinner be ready any minute."

Carey sat on the sagging little porch behind the house, gazing in boredom at the patch of dirt before him. There were no flowers or blooming trees on their place, just this ugly plot covered with fallen tree branches and layers of leaves that had not been raked in the five years he and Hattie had lived there.

He felt like crying. Like putting his head down on his knees to let this anger at his mother flow forth in a hot stream of tears. To accuse him of stealing that pen!

So what if he'd had a little trouble in the past—that was no reason to call him a liar forever. She ain't so perfect herself, he fumed, hating the rush of memories that suddenly emerged: the snatches of drunken conversations he'd heard over the years—at Bird Dog's Lodge, in the early morning hours, as he dozed sleepily in a corner waiting for his mother. He'd heard her laugh off questions about who his daddy was, telling folks she'd entertained too many railroad men to recall exactly who might be her baby's daddy. The shame and embarrassment of Hattie Logan's younger, wilder days in McLennan County seeped into Carey's thoughts.

Pulling his lips between his teeth, Carey squeezed until he felt pain. If she was so worked up about being truthful and acting so fair and square with folks, why wouldn't she tell him who his daddy was?

CHAPTER FOUR

Two weeks after the fitting in Dallas, Mr. Slater, the tailor, personally delivered the pinstripe suit. He told Hattie he was on his way to visit relatives in Temple and didn't mind stopping in Waco to drop off Carey's suit, knowing how much it meant to the young man.

Hattie invited Mr. Slater into her shabby little home, led him to the common room at the back of the house, then went to shake Carey awake.

"Mr. Slater's brought your suit," she told him as he sat up and peered at his mother in the still-dim room. "Get on up and try it on. If it don't fit right, he gotta know now."

Eager to oblige, Carey leapt from the bed, washed quickly, put on the soft wool suit and let the tailor tug and pinch at the loose-fitting fabric with thick fat fingers. His creation fit perfectly.

After accepting a cup of coffee and one of Hattie's soda biscuits, Mr. Slater thanked her for her business and left.

"So much excitement, so early," Hattie muttered, casting an eye at the small round clock she kept in the kitchen. She was already late for work and if Carey didn't hurry he'd miss the first bell at school.

"Go on, Carey. Get out of that suit and put your school clothes on. You gonna be late." She moved toward her bedroom, leaving Carey admiring himself in the cracked mirror hanging in the hallway. "Quit all that preenin', boy," she said gruffly, secretly very pleased at how handsome her son looked. "You can try it on again this evening. T.J.'s coming by on his way back to the farm."

"What's he doing over this way?" Carey shot back quickly, his mood turning suddenly sour.

"Had to see about a few breedin' hogs he's fixin' to buy from old man Williams," Hattie answered, wishing her two boys were not so badly estranged. With eleven years between them, they had little in common, yet in her opinion, that should not matter. Blood brothers they were and always would be, so they ought to try harder to get along.

"He don't do a thing but preach about saving money and how he's squeezing another penny out somebody's pocket." Carey remained fussing with his jacket at the mirror.

"Might be you could learn a few things from your brother. He's managing real good out on that farm. Real fine. Bought another fifty acres last month."

"Who cares?" Carey sneered, his forehead wrinkled deeply. "I don't see him asking me or you to come over there to live, like you said he would. Like some old hermit, he is. Out there in the country all alone. Don't make sense to me." Carey went into his room and brought back a blue tie. He knotted it with an expert flourish. "How's this?" he asked Hattie, dropping the subject of his brother. "Think this looks all right, Ma?"

"You take all that off. You ain't wearing it to school," Hattie ordered, knowing what her son was leading up to. "You not gonna wear that suit 'til we go visit my cousin in Mexia. So don't go gettin' any ideas about wearin' it out the house this mornin'." She wagged a finger at Carey.

"Oh, Ma. Just today. I'll be careful. It'll be like new when I get home. Nothing will happen. Trust me." He went over and put his arm around his mother, cocking his head to one side. "Please, Ma?

Just today?" I'll show those clods how a real man dresses, he thought, excited at the prospect of all the attention he'd get.

Hattie's eyes gave him hope that she was softening. He pressed on. "Anyway, I don't have time to change. I'll be late if I do. You don't want me to be late, do you, Ma?"

"Well, all right. But," she tried to put on a stern face, "if you dirty that suit, don't come complaining to me. I done spent all I saved up on that suit." Hattie started toward her bedroom, but stopped when there was a knock at the door.

"Who the devil?" she said, glancing around. "Mr. Slater musta left something behind." She moved away from Carey and peeped through the big crack in the door frame, then turned back to Carey. "It's your teacher, Miss Glass." She raised both eyebrows in question. Carey shrugged his shoulders and said nothing. Another sharp rap rang out.

The woman Hattie saw when she opened the door was solemn-faced and serious, not on a happy mission. Behind her stood one of her students, a chubby little boy with plump puffy cheeks. He remained cowering behind his teacher.

"Good morning, Miss Glass." Hattie greeted the intimidating teacher as cordially as she could. "What's bringing you over here so early?" She stepped back and indicated that the woman should come in. Miss Glass entered the narrow hallway. The boy stayed outside on the steps.

"Mrs. Logan," Miss Glass started right in, "I've received some distressing news about your son and I need to talk to you about it immediately." She paid no attention to Carey.

"What's this about?" Hattie asked, a tightening pull centering itself in the pit of her stomach. "You care to sit down?" she managed to offer.

"No, thank you. I can't tarry too long. Classes start in half an hour." The teacher took off her gloves as she began. "Mrs. Logan, seems your son has been gambling at school. He's taken quite a bit of money from several students and I'm getting complaints from their parents."

"Gambling?" Hattie's dark eyes widened in surprise. She turned from Miss Glass to Carey, then back to the teacher. "What you mean?"

"Dice, marbles, penny pitching." Miss Glass hesitated before going on, hating to bring this mother such disturbing news, but she'd had enough complaints to warrant this visit. In fact, this conversation was long overdue. "I don't know if you're aware of it, Mrs. Logan, but your son skipped classes yesterday and was run out of a poker game in the back room of the Regal Hotel—my husband works in the kitchen over there. He said the boy's been coming around real often and yesterday he cheated on a hand—caused a big fuss."

"Carey!" Hattie spun around to face her son. "This true what she saying? You been doing these things?" Her mouth hung open as she waited to hear what he had to say.

"Ah, Ma. Wasn't nothing like it sounds. Those kids at school are lying. They wanted to play . . . just didn't know how. All I did was show 'em the play." He lifted his jaw and surveyed the two women as if they were out of their minds. "Wasn't nothing but a few pennies lost. What's the big deal? They played, nobody forced them. We were just having fun."

"From what I've heard," Miss Glass continued, "you took more than a few pennies from a lot of students over the past several months. Robert Sanders's father said the boy lost two dollars and John Finney's missing a small gold ring."

"It ain't gold," Carey said, laughing and holding out his hand. "Look! This look like gold to you? Brass, maybe copper, who knows? But if John told you this ring was gold, he's lying."

"That is not the point, Carey!" Miss Glass's tone rose in exasperation. "It's against school policy to be gambling on the school grounds, and you're intimidating the students into participating."

Now Hattie stepped forward, not liking this attack on her boy. "Just wait a minute, Miss Glass. Carey ain't the kind to go hurtin' anybody. Exactly what do you mean by that?"

Miss Glass didn't answer, just reached over and opened the door. "Pauly, come on in here, please."

The frightened boy stepped inside.

"Show Mrs. Logan your hand."

The boy held up a bandaged left hand.

"Mrs. Webster told me this child has two broken fingers. Pauly says Carey crushed his hand beneath his boot."

"That's a lie!" Carey planted himself directly in front of Pauly.

"It was an accident. Tell her! You shoulda been more careful. We were just horsing around." He leaned closer to his terrified classmate. "It was an accident, wasn't it, Pauly?"

The frightened boy whimpered like a wounded puppy and shrank back toward the door. Miss Glass told him to go back outside.

"Well, Mrs. Logan, I'm truly sorry about all this. Carey's got a lot of potential, but I'm not sure he's headed in the right direction. His bad influence on the other students is too strong to allow him to finish out this term. I discussed the situation with the school director in town and he's agreed with me that Carey must be expelled immediately."

"Expelled?" Hattie's hand flew up to her mouth. "You not gonna let him finish out the term? There's only a few weeks left. Don't be too quick, Miss Glass. Give the boy a chance to straighten up. We'll talk, we can . . ."

"Other than his penmanship," Miss Glass interrupted, "I really have to say that he's not doing well enough in the rest of his subjects to be considered for recommendation to Central."

Hattie's face slackened, and deep lines of disappointment creased her jowls. "You not gonna recommend him to the academy next term?" She put her hand against the wall to steady herself. "Miss Glass, let me talk to Carey. We can settle this restlessness he got right now. Just a passing thing, you understand. He'll do just fine next term. Going on with his studies means a whole lot. He's gonna need more learning to make it. He's bright. He can do the work."

"I never said your son wasn't bright, Mrs. Logan. He's smart enough to do about anything he puts his mind to. Just seems he's put his mind to the wrong kind of learning, that's all."

Without another word the teacher walked stiffly away, leaving Hattie standing in the doorway, her hand to her chest.

Slowly moving back inside, Hattie tried to still the heavy throbbing that raced through her body. She faced Carey, unable to speak for a moment. The tick-tick of her small clock seemed loud and irritating as she waited to hear what Carey had to say.

"Don't listen to that old prune," he began, a flippant edge to his words. "So what if I'm expelled? I was getting sick and tired of sitting around that stuffy old room with all those silly country folks, anyway." He began to sway back and forth as he talked. "Don't worry,

Ma, I got plans. Miss Glass don't decide my future. I got plans bigger than she can even think of."

"Carey," Hattie started, her voice low and controlled, "finishing this term and completing the academy was what you said you was gonna do. You promised to stick with it. Remember?"

"That was ages ago, Ma. Now I can see things better." He walked away from her down the dim hallway into the common room where the kitchen area was. He kept his back to his mother as he poured himself some coffee.

"What things?" she demanded sharply, following Carey down the hall. "What kinda fancy ideas you got?" She sank down at the table. "Colored ain't got a chance for a real job 'round here lessen they got book learning."

"What's a real job, Ma? Huh? Driving a horse and buggy through the country delivering telegrams for the postman? Carrying suitcases for the white folks at the Regal Hotel? Cleaning up after them?" He turned around so suddenly, he spilled coffee on the front of his suit. Glancing down at the stain, he shouted in anger, "Like you do, Ma? Like you do at Hower Clinic?"

Hattie jumped up, crossed the sparsely furnished room and slapped Carey's face. He stared at her in horror. She stared back, watching the bright red print of her palm swell up on her son's fair skin. Never had she hit him. Never. And the shock of it forced more angry words from his throat.

"Leave me alone! I know what I'm doing. I can get by just fine without you." There were tears behind his words, but he'd never let Hattie see them.

"Don't you ever—ever—say a word against what I do," Hattie started in. "I been working two jobs since two weeks after you was born, just to keep us in a house and food on the table. You ever wanted for anything, Carey? Answer me. You ever done without?" There was no response. "No! I sacrificed to bring you up decent and if I had to clean up white folks' shit, so what? You never refused a thing those wages bought."

He rubbed the side of his face and lowered his eyes. "I know. I know," he forced himself to admit. "But I ain't sorry to be through with schooling. All those stupid lessons about Abraham Lincoln and white folks' wars. Who cares?" He picked up a towel and dabbed at the coffee stain. "I'll make more money than you ever dreamed of—my way—big money, Ma, you'll see."

Hattie began to back away, frightened by Carey's defiant attitude. She managed to sit down, the throbbing in her chest growing stronger. "You sound just like Benny Wilder," she mumbled as if to herself. "Benny thought he could thumb his nose at everybody. Talking about making it big. I done heard those words before."

"Benny Wilder!" Carey spat the name at his mother. "Benny Wilder? Why in the devil you gotta go bringing up that man?" He stepped closer to Hattie and stood frowning down at the top of her head, noticing for the first time just how thin and gray her hair had become. "I don't give a damn about my brother's father. If you're so dead set on me telling the truth and doing what's right, why don't you tell me who *my* daddy was?" He clenched his fists and waited.

"Too long ago," Hattie murmured. "Too long ago and too complicated, son. Trust me, you better off not knowing."

"Trust you? Why should I? How many times have I asked you that question?" He paused, an expectant expression coming to the surface as if today his mother might break down and finally give him an answer. She didn't. And the silence that followed filled him with shame. "Nothing changes 'round here, does it?" Carey slammed his fist into his palm.

"I'm going out for a while," he said flatly, shoving his hands into the pockets of his suit, tilting back his head to pull air into his lungs. Carey's words filtered to the ceiling. "No more classes at that stupid little school." Lowering his chin he gave Hattie a forced smile as he told her, "It's a real good feeling, being free. Now I can get on with my life." The young man's tone turned calmly earnest as he disappeared down the hallway. "One day you'll be sorry you didn't trust me, Ma. One day I'm gonna be somebody special, even if you won't tell me who I really am."

Too crushed with disappointment to move, Hattie remained in her kitchen fighting to keep memories of Carey's father from flooding her with pain. If only I could tell him the truth, she lamented. Ed Brannon had been a real decent man, woulda been a good daddy, too. And in the letter he posted on the day of his death he had told Hattie how much he cared for her. Even signed at the end, *All my love, Ed.*

If only the Lord had spared him: we coulda had a decent life raising our son together. Bitterness at losing her final chance for happiness still consumed Hattie, though for nearly fifteen years she'd buried it deeply within the love of her son. Now she allowed her memories to drift back to those weeks after Carey's birth when she'd taken a train ride to Fort Worth.

Baby Carey's shrill cries had filled the near-empty railway car during the long ride north. She had shushed him and nursed him and sung to him the only lullaby she knew—all to no avail. The baby refused to be pacified.

Maybe it was a good thing he'd acted up so badly, she thought for the very first time. His antics had taken her mind off her desperate hope that Ed Brannon's locker at the railway station would contain a little money, even a few dollars, anything to help her raise their son.

Hattie could still feel the weight of the heavy paper she found inside the gray metal box that afternoon. And she could still visualize the delicate ink scrolling all around the edges of the strange-looking paper. Her limited schooling paid off, for she knew the document had value and was not surprised to learn from the attendant at the station what it was—a railroad bond. A bond worth exactly five hundred dollars.

This morning Hattie smiled to herself as she remembered how easy it had been to cash it. The security man felt so bad about Ed's untimely death he had rushed Hattie, pass card in hand, into signing Ed's wife's name. Never did ask her to show any identification. Not knowing Ed's wife's first name, she had signed the bond "Hattie Brannon" and nobody ever questioned her. Never. Not to this day.

I've been lucky about that, she thought, knowing Ed Brannon had had a baby daughter and knowing her crime, if discovered, could have brought time in jail. But keeping this secret so long, she sadly admitted, hadn't made it easy to raise her son.

The overcast sky cleared suddenly, brightening the small dark room. Exhausted from the turmoil of the morning, Hattie pushed herself up from the table and thought for a moment. No need in going over to the clinic, she figured. Too late to even put in part of her day. She'd stew a hen for T.J. He'd most likely stay over for dinner, and he just loved her stewed chicken and dumplings.

Thoughts of her older son's visit put a smile on her face and replaced her worries about Carey.

Seeing his mother's crumbling little house on the edge of town never failed to sadden T.J. From a distance of nearly fifty feet, it emerged splintered and gray, rising from the weed-filled patch of dirt surrounding it. Not much better than where I grew up, he told himself again, vivid memories of that lean-to in the country surging forth. His room in the loft at the top of the barn had been a salvation. Though it was freezing in the winter and stifling hot in the summer, he had loved the solitude he found there.

Living in sparse isolation with his mother, T.J. had kept busy hauling water, chopping wood, doing whatever he could to help his mother and to soften the pain of missing his father.

At the age of eleven he had pretended to be the man of the house, taking care of Hattie until his baby brother arrived. Then everything changed, drastically and horribly, when Hattie sent him to the Powers farm in Limestone County to pick cotton for fifty cents a day. She told him not to come back home: he was old enough to make his own way.

T.J. had cried every night for the first three weeks, but finally accepted his fate, and after eight years of backbreaking work T.J. did get his reward: Stepp Powers named him in a written will as heir to the farm and everything that was on it—the house and furnishings, the horses and cows, the crop of Black Diamonds in the fields.

Though Powers's relatives had tried to refute the legal document, the will held up in court, and at age eighteen T.J. Wilder found himself owning thirty acres of good Texas farmland.

T.J. slapped the reins against the backs of his team of handsome bays and turned sharply onto the gravel lane leading to his mother's house. The high-sided wagon clattered loudly through the rising dust and set the crated hens to cackling noisily in their cages. He squinted against the slanting evening sunlight, holding the reins steady, finally pulling to a halt at Hattie's front door.

"Whoa," he yelled at the restless horses, knowing he'd pushed them pretty hard on this trip. Up to Corsicana, over to Hillsboro, down to Waco, he'd traveled nearly one hundred miles since leaving his farm two days ago. But the trip had been successful. He'd gotten promises from three new greengrocers to accept his Black Diamonds, the firmest, sweetest watermelons grown in Central Texas. Their reputation was rapidly spreading, and now those white grocers and produce brokers who had snubbed him five years ago were demanding first pick of the crop and paying more than acceptable prices.

T.J. tied off the horses and stepped down from the wagon seat, his tall, lanky frame unfolding to its six foot height as he leaned backward to stretch. He took out his big white handkerchief and shook it, then removed his dusty black felt hat and wiped the perspiration from his sunburned forehead. Though the sun was rapidly descending, the temperature still hovered near ninety degrees.

Good weather for growing melons, he thought, stepping up to Hattie's front door, but we gonna need more rain. And soon.

His mother greeted him as he knew she would, a nod of her head, a pat on his shoulder and her usual question, "How you feelin', son?"

T.J. could not remember his mother ever hugging him, kissing him, or holding him close as a child. It just ain't her nature, he told himself, following her into the warm kitchen. Never was where I was concerned. For he'd surely seen her hug and kiss Carey and he struggled inwardly to understand why.

"I'm doing all right," T.J. answered, removing his hat, which he placed carefully on the chair beside him. "Where's Carey?" he asked, watching his mother fussing over her black kettle on the stove. She always stewed a hen when she knew he was coming, and it smelled heavenly to T.J., who got by on simple food: boiled turnip greens; a rabbit now and then; and, when he butchered a hog, salted pork for a spell.

"Carey's stepped out for a minute," Hattie replied, her voice flatly indifferent. "He'll be back right soon. I told him you'd be coming over."

"How's he doing in his studies?" T.J. knew she liked to talk about Carey, and frankly, there was little else they had in common to keep a conversation going.

"He's doing just fine," Hattie lied, unable to face the disgrace her youngest had brought on her that day. "Won a contest for making the best letters in the class. You oughta see the fancy writin' pen his teacher gave him. Musta cost ten dollars. Right fancy it is," she said again.

"Good to hear that, Ma. Good he's taking his lessons so serious. If reading books and writing fancy is what he wants to do, he oughta make out just fine." T.J. forced himself to say such reassuring words to his mother, inwardly resentful that he'd never been inside a schoolroom in his life. Hattie had been content to let him wander around the countryside, ragged and dirty, lonely and confused, while she entertained her friends and drank her dandelion wine, not much caring what he did with his time.

This evening, that creeping jealousy he struggled to keep at bay threatened to inch its way into his soul and fan the fires of resentment he harbored against his half-brother. Everything Carey did was perfect—according to his mother. The boy got whatever he wanted, never said thank you, and never considered the fact that T.J.'s absence had made it easier for her to give Carey all he took for granted.

T.J. swallowed hard and watched as Hattie moved back and forth between the stove and the table. She looked older and more tired than he'd ever noticed before.

"You still having those pains in your chest, Ma?"

"Oh, they come and go, not too regular. Doc Haden gave me some medicine last time I had money to see him. You know those white doctors ain't gonna hardly give us colored the time of day lessen we got cash money up front."

"How much he charge?" T.J. hated the fact that the nearest black doctor was fifty-seven miles away in Mexia.

"Oh," Hattie remarked as she took a pan of rolls from the oven, "he be asking for at least five dollars just for a check-over. More if he gotta do any prescribing. Then there's the cost of the medicine. Doc Steiner at the clinic gives me a break on that, though. He's pretty fair about that."

T.J. stood up and slid his long fingers into the pocket of his faded coat. "Here's ten dollars, Ma. You go on and let that white doctor check you over. You gotta take care of yourself."

Hattie cocked her head to the side for a moment, as if considering whether or not to take the money, then took it from her son and pushed it into the front of her dress. "That's mighty thoughtful, son. I'll do just that. It's a blessing you can help out. Things is pretty tight."

T.J. nodded rather curtly and let his mother put a plateful of steaming chicken down in front of him.

They sat together and ate in awkward silence for a while, speaking now and then about the unusually hot spring weather they were having and how the lack of rain threatened T.J.'s big melon crop. They had nearly finished the plain, heavy meal when Carey suddenly burst through the back door, blood dripping from his forehead, his new suit torn from shoulder to waist.

"Carey!" Hattie dropped her fork, jumped up and stood gripping the edge of the table. "What the devil happened to you?"

Carey didn't answer, moving toward his mother as blood slid down his forehead, over his bruised cheek, onto the collar of his stained white shirt. Hattie grabbed her son by the arm and pushed him onto a chair. "Just sit down. Sit down here, lemme see how bad this is." She snatched up a towel and leaned over Carey, wiping the blood away to examine the wound. "Not so bad, son. Not very deep. Miss Waters next door borrowed my iodine. Lemme run and get it. That'll help clean it out." She quickly left the room, leaving Carey slumped down in his chair.

"How'd that happen?" T.J. asked sternly, as a father might reprimand a son. "What kinda devilment you been into? Coming in here like this." He glared evenly at his younger brother, not at all concerned that he might be in pain. "Just look at yourself," he went on, "like some common hoodlum, fightin' and carryin' on." T.J. pushed his plate of food away and placed both arms on the table. "Why you gotta go and get yourself all beat up? Cause Momma so much hurt? Boy, ain't you got the sense to stay out of trouble?"

"Wasn't my fault," Carey snapped at T.J. "I didn't do nothing wrong. Mule Bledsoe did it. He's a stupid, crazy brute."

"Mule Bledsoe? That old card sharpie? What you doing in company like that?" T.J.'s pointed question went unanswered. "Answer me, boy! What you doing hanging out with the likes of Mule Bledsoe?"

"Just a friendly game of cards." Carey snorted. "Humph! If he'da showed me his hand instead of reaching for the pot nothing woulda happened."

"You out there in the streets gambling? Boy, you oughta be home doing lessons for school. Staying in the streets, missing dinner, you better shape up."

"Shape up, you say? Study my lessons? Guess Ma didn't tell you I don't go to school anymore." Carey watched with satisfaction as his words caught his stern brother by surprise. "Shocked?" Carey threw back his head, laughing as he went on. "That prune-faced teacher came over here this morning and told Ma a pack of lies on me." He shrugged and examined the tear in his jacket. "Mule's gonna pay for doing this. Really pay—in cash dollars."

"Where'd you get those city duds, anyway?" T.J. said bluntly, thinking how ridiculous the fourteen-year-old boy looked in such grown-up attire. "Look just like some Louisiana hustler, all gussied up like that."

"Shut up, T.J.!" Carey was visibly upset. "This is a custom-made suit, especially for me. Ma and I went to Dallas for the fitting."

"What's Ma doing spending money like that for? She don't even have enough to see the doctor. You oughta be ashamed, putting pressure on Ma to waste money like that."

"It was her idea," Carey said smugly. "She saved up for months before she even told me about it." He rocked with laughter at the crestfallen expression that quickly clouded T.J.'s face.

T.J. could hardly believe what his brother had said, but reluctantly admitted to himself that the boy probably told the truth. Wasn't nothing their mother wouldn't do for the spoiled brat. She's got her last dime out of me, he vowed silently, irritated that Carey's smart-ass laughter still echoed through the room.

"So you got yourself turned out of school?" He changed the subject. "This morning?"

"Yep," Carey admitted. "But it's no big deal. Really kinda glad 'cause I got . . ."

"Glad?" T.J. interrupted. "You sorry-ass bast . . ."

"Bastard?" Carey finished his brother's sentence, leaning over the table to lock eyes with him. "Yeah," Carey murmured, "guess that's what I really am. A bastard." He closely examined his half-brother's face. "But you know something, brother? It don't bother me none. None! You hear me. None!" His voice cracked with those words. He slammed his fist on the table, turning over a glass of water. Neither moved to clean it up, letting the clear liquid run off the tabletop to drip slowly onto the floor.

T.J. held his tongue, watching pain wash over Carey's face, knowing there was not a thing he could do about his brother's harsh admission.

"You coulda tried harder to do right and at least finish school." T.J. got up, pacing the floor in agitation. "I had to teach myself to read, write and do figures. I guess sending me over to Limestone County to pick cotton for fifty cents a day made sense to Ma, but dragging that bole sack through the dust from sunup to sundown was hell. Pure hell. Look at my hands, Carey. The scars are still there!"

"That's what you wanted, Ma said so," Carey countered. "You wanted to be a farmer . . . and it worked out for you. You got your own piece of land, ain't you happy?"

"Ma told you what?" T.J. shouted.

"That you run off to learn how to be a farmer, 'cause that's what you wanted to be." Carey pulled back at the sight of his brother's building rage.

"Wasn't nothing like that. Not at all. Guess that was the only decent thing to say. How else could she explain what happened to me?" T.J. shook his head sadly, a bitter grimace on his lips. "Wasn't like that, Carey. After you come along, wasn't 'nuf food around for the both of us. You was just a baby. Ma said she had to take a long train ride and I had to go over to the Powers place, live there and work for my keep 'cause she couldn't take care of me anymore." He paused as he heard Hattie come in the front door. Lowering his voice, he finished, "Next thing I heard, you and Ma were living over here in Waco. She never even sent word she'd moved. I heard it by accident from a traveling railroader."

Carey drummed his fingers nervously on the rough pine table. He didn't want to hear another word. "Cut the sob story, T.J. You got just what you wanted. Go on back to the country and take care of your precious melons. That's where you belong—not here preaching to me."

Hattie entered the room holding a dark brown bottle and a wad of cotton. "Watch your mouth, Carey, I heard what you said. T.J.'s got every right to be here visiting and don't you go running him off." She stood over Carey and began to clean his wound. "Be good as new. Hold still," she cautioned as the raw sting of iodine made Carey flinch. "Good thing ain't no blood on your jacket," she continued, trying to diffuse the angry atmosphere which charged the room with tension. She dabbed Carey's brow and said lightly, "I'll bet Mr. Slater can fix that tear so good nobody'll ever know it was there."

"You think so, Ma?" Carey lowered his chin and fingered the ragged edges of the fabric.

"Yeah," Hattie reassured him, "and it probably won't cost but a few dollars."

T.J. reached down and picked up his hat. Without saying good-bye, he turned on his heel and stalked out of his mother's house.

Chapter Five

"You need to get up out of that bed," Leela told Josephine, bending over her cousin, peering into the new mother's flushed face. A web of small red blotches, blistered and angry, spread from the top of Josephine's forehead, across her nose and disappeared into the neckline of her soiled nightgown, which was so old and worn it no longer had any color at all—rather like the young albino woman who lay drab and pale in the center of her narrow bed. Josephine's matted white hair stuck in clumps to her pillow, and the sour smell of dirty linen, perspiration and the baby's spit-up hung thickly in the air.

At Leela's words, Josephine blinked her light gray eyes, turned a defiant shoulder toward her cousin and refused to speak.

"Your mother won't be visiting for a while," Leela said, backing away from the bed, distancing herself from the unsettling odor. "She stepped in a hole in the garden, turned her ankle this morning. But she sent out some turnip greens, carrots, and potatoes."

Leela shooed a large gray cat off the crude pine table and set the heavy bag of vegetables down.

At two o'clock in the afternoon, the nearly barren cabin was quiet, and it appeared that neither Johnny Ray nor his father, Mister Harry, were anywhere to be seen. A rusty metal dishpan was filled with crusty dishes. A partially eaten rabbit lay covered with flies, and two more cats wandered through the open doorway as if the filthy place were abandoned.

With one foot Leela shoved aside a pile of rags and pulled out a broken chair. She pushed it across the room to the foot of the bed. Looking over at the squirming bundle stuffed under Josephine's arm, Leela wondered if her slovenly cousin had even been out of bed or changed Penny's rancid diaper in the three days since she and Aunt Effie had been there.

"Josephine," Leela said sternly. "Look at me." Her cousin did not move. "You've got to pull yourself together. Get up out of that bed and take care of your children. You can't just sleep your life away."

Josephine settled in on her side, unbuttoned the front of her nightgown and pushed a gorged red nipple between her baby's brown lips.

"You know you're not sick, Josephine. Doc White already told you what to do. Get up. Clean up that bed, eat some decent food. If you don't, you'll never get your strength back."

Leela had vowed three days ago she'd not come back or make one more attempt to reach her sullen cousin. She only came today because Aunt Effie couldn't.

"Your momma's real worried about you. Uncle Bert, too. He said to tell you, if things are so bad you want to come home, it's all right with him. With this new baby, if you can't take care of yourself and Johnny Ray's not going to help, Aunt Effie said for you to come on home, just for a while, until you get your strength back."

Josephine lifted her transparent face to Leela.

"Why don't *you* just go on back home? Coming out here fawning over me. Acting like you really care." She laughed hoarsely. "Tell Momma to leave me alone, too. She's got the daughter she wants in you. What's she want me back home for, anyway?"

"How can you say such a thing?" Leela snapped, half rising from her chair. "Aunt Effie loves you, Josephine. Quit acting so hateful!" Leela rolled her fingers into her palms, squeezing tightly to keep from reaching over to shake the hostile girl. Josephine's twisted jealousy, deep-rooted and unshakable, hadn't waned during the four years she'd lived with Johnny Ray. If anything, her bitter sense of rejection had magnified, grown more contorted, settling deeply within her like a large cancerous sore.

"Your mother is very worried about you," Leela began, unsure her words were even heard. "Why do you torture yourself with the crazy notion that I've done something to turn her against you? I don't even understand how you can say these things to me."

Josephine took a deep breath and glared across the sheets at Leela.

"You think you've fooled them all, don't you? Not only mother," she blurted out, "but Poppa too, and certainly you ruined everything for Parker. Filling him up with your silly talk about college, telling the sheriff he threw that rock. Before you showed up and put a haint on him, he had never talked about leaving Mexia. This is his home. You ruined everything! You made him go away, you witch! You cast some dreadful spell on him and convinced him to leave." Josephine's agitated voice rose to such a shrill pitch, she awakened the baby. The infant wailed loudly, adding her own unhappiness to the tension in the cabin.

Leela opened her mouth to protest, but before she could say a word, Josephine pushed herself up on her knees in the middle of the bed and stretched her neck forward as she railed. "And I've heard that you still go around calling yourself Leela Alexander. That's not your name and you've no right to use it."

"Aunt Effie says I do. And I'll call myself whatever I please. There's not a thing in the world you can do about it, Josephine, so leave it alone, you hear?"

"Another part of your dirty little plot to get closer to Momma, that's all." Josephine gathered the hem of her nightgown into her swollen hands, nervously twisting and knotting the fabric.

Leela stood up, clenching her teeth to keep from shouting, and walked away from the bed.

"You little nobody!" Josephine hurled the words, stopping her cousin in her tracks. "You came to Mexia with nothing. No mother, no father, not even a decent dress to wear to school. And you took everything away from me that you could, including my brother, Parker. And how do I know you're really my cousin? I never heard my mother say a word about having a brother until you showed up out of nowhere." She paused to catch her breath and wipe tears from her fat red cheeks. "Well, now I've got more than you'll ever have. My own house, my own husband . . ."

"Johnny Ray never married you. He's not really your husband," Leela bluntly interrupted.

"I have my own kids," Josephine continued, her chest heaving with agitation as she plunged on. "I can do as I please and I don't have to play second fiddle to you anymore."

"You never did, Josephine," Leela said, her anger giving way to pity for her cousin. "I feel sorry for you. But don't say I forced you into this so-called marriage. This was your own doing. And if you've made a mistake, you ought to admit it and move back home like your poppa wants."

"You must be crazy. Go back to what? I've got everything I want right here. Just leave me alone, hear me? Go tell Momma I'm doing just fine." She slumped down in her bed, exhausted, and pulled the sheet up to her neck.

Leela moaned lowly in exasperation and looked around the filthy room.

"Where's Oliver?" she asked, suddenly worried about Josephine's state of mind. "Did he go with Johnny Ray?"

The three-year-old boy was usually toddling around somewhere, but today Leela had not seen him.

Josephine scooted closer to the center of her dirty bed and rolled her eyes to the ceiling.

"Where's Oliver?" Leela asked again, wondering if the girl even remembered she had another child.

"Outside," Josephine snapped. "Didn't you see him? I told him to stay by the door."

Leela went quickly to the entrance and looked across the yard. Stacks of rotting lumber, pieces of broken-down wagon, rusty metal farm tools and dangerous bundles of barbed-wire fencing filled the half-acre lot. It was a far cry from the farm Josephine had bragged about to her family.

Stepping over a rusted-out washtub with a hole in the bottom, Leela circled the weathered log structure and carefully pulled aside a thorny stand of blackberry bushes that bordered the east side of the property. There, seated near a shallow mud puddle, Josephine's son pushed handfuls of sticky black dirt into his mouth, his pants, his small wooden bucket.

"Oliver," Leela called as she approached the mud-smeared child. "Why don't you come back in with me? We'll cook a pot of beans together."

At the mention of food, Oliver jumped up, threw his stick to the ground and followed Leela into the house.

It was nearly five o'clock when Leela served Oliver his bowl of beans with a big wedge of cornbread and sweet turnip greens. He fed himself with his tiny fingers, then toddled off chasing a cat. After bathing Penny and changing Josephine's sheets, Leela decided it was time to head home. But there was one more thing she had to do, and she was glad she had saved this for last.

"I got a letter from Parker yesterday," she started.

Josephine pushed the sleeping baby away and sat up, pulling her faded wrapper closed over her huge milk-filled breasts.

"Why are you just now telling me? See how hateful you can be? What did he say?" she snapped, her dull eyes finally coming alive.

"Good news," Leela answered, hoping Parker's letter might be a way to bridge the awful distance between them and shake her cousin out of her miserable state.

Leela unfolded the brittle white paper and read:

"November 1, 1910
Chicago, Illinois

Dear Cousin Leela,

The most extraordinary good news has come my way. Though I am still very much aching for Texas and unused to this cold northern weather, it seems as if I may soon be moving even farther east, though I doubt the winters in Washington, D.C. could possibly be any colder or longer than the past four I've suffered through here.

The journalism scholarship I wrote you about last summer has finally been awarded, and it is my good fortune to be one of the recipients. I'll be leaving Chicago for Howard University at the beginning of the new year and can hardly contain my excitement at the move, yet, as I'm sure you can understand, I am somewhat fearful of starting over again in a strange new town. My work here at the *Defender* has prepared me for my studies, and it is because of Mr. Abbot's encouragement and references that I have been chosen to go to Howard. He's told me of many opportunities in the newspaper business once I've finished the university, and I do believe my dream of coming back to Texas and running my own paper will happen one day.

My mother's recent letter told me I'm now an uncle again. Please tell Josephine to write. I've stopped writing to her directly, for she never answers my letters. What ever happened after I left? I do not know what I may have done to hurt Josephine and to deserve this silence. I worry about her health and welcome news of her and the children. I'm making a very decent wage here at the *Defender* and want you to give this small amount to my sister with love and hope that she will write soon."

Leela stopped reading, though the letter went on for another page. The rest was not for Josephine's ears. Besides, the sound of a horse-drawn cart rumbling to a stop outside meant Johnny Ray had finally come home.

Hurriedly, Leela folded the letter and put it back in her pocket, went to the bed and handed Josephine the two five-dollar bills Parker had sent.

Her ungrateful cousin said nothing, just took the money and began to fold the bills in half. Before she could tuck them away in the front of her wrapper, Johnny Ray crossed the room in two giant strides and clamped a dirty, rough hand around Josephine's pale wrist.

"What's this?" he asked, wrenching the cash from her hand. "Where'd this money come from?"

"Parker sent it to me," Josephine said, trying to snatch the two bills back. Johnny Ray slapped her painfully across the side of her face and pushed her back onto the bed.

"Nice of your brother to think about us." He jammed the money into his pocket. Focusing bleary eyes on Leela, he went on. "The guardian angel comes again." He laughed and squatted on the floor, pulled a heavy stone jug from beneath the bed and tilted it up to his lips. He gulped loudly while dribbling the dark brown liquid into his mouth. "Even smells like someone cooked 'round here." He reached over and fingered the hem of Leela's dress. "Wonder why my woman can't be more like you . . . all soft and pretty, even knows how to make up a decent meal."

Leela jerked away from Johnny Ray's touch and went to stand by the open door. He remained on the floor, staring straight ahead, his ashy black hands wrapped around the neck of the bottle.

Leela looked at him in disgust. You dim-witted bully, she thought. You're nothing but brutish trash. Knowing he could be volatile when angered she retreated outside and stood looking in.

"I am leaving, Josephine," Leela said, trying to control the anger in her voice. "But remember what I told you, if things get too bad, you can always come home."

Leela knew her parting words would anger Johnny Ray and probably give him reason to beat Josephine again. But what the devil? Leela thought as she guided her buggy toward home. The brute ought to know Josephine's family was worried and did not take her situation lightly.

When Josephine had defied her parents to sneak out with Johnny Ray, Leela had known a disaster was in the making. Slipping off, night after night, with an overgrown boy who collected rags for a living, who could not read or write, and who spent the little money he earned on bags of candy from Newtons' General Store. What did she expect?

The situation on the Mosley farm saddened Aunt Effie most of all. She told Leela, on more than one occasion, "I raised my daughter to do better than this."

Back home, Leela went into her room to read, again, the part of Parker's letter she had not wanted to share with Josephine.

Parker had found his happiness, she thought with a twinge of envy. He was on his way to becoming a newspaper publisher and had finally found the woman who would share his future. Leela shifted into the lamplight and read:

. . . and even though we argued bitterly at first, we soon learned that our differences contributed greatly to our attraction. Her strong opinions and independent spirit remind me of you. Margaret teaches English at a local primary school and has even published articles in the *Amsterdam News* about her work with children in a reading program she has started. Please don't tell my parents yet, but we plan to be married next June. When I depart for Howard, I will have to leave Margaret behind in Chicago until her school term ends. But I hope to bring her to Texas as soon as possible to meet all the family.

I am so happy to learn that you are now working for the *Banner*. Don't fret that Mr. Foreman will only let you collect money and prepare the ledgers. That's progress for him! He'll see soon enough that you can do more. Be patient, Leela, though I know it's awfully hard. Things don't change so fast in Mexia. Up here, women are working at all kinds of jobs. There's even a woman driving a trolley car in Chicago!

Thanks for the copies of the *Banner*. They really help me keep up with home. I've enclosed a copy of a story I wrote in support of the newly formed National Association for the Advancement of Colored People, which will be very instrumental in moving our struggle for civil and political liberty forward. It's all so exciting, Leela. I wish you could come to Washington for a visit when I'm settled. Living in the capital will be an extraordinary experience for me.

Please continue to write. I can't wait for you to meet Margaret. My hopes are that very soon, you too will meet someone as special for you as Margaret is to me. I feel certain that you'll find happiness with a man who will love you and cherish you with the passion and joy you deserve.

Your loving cousin,
Parker

His words brought tears to Leela's eyes. And as she ran her shaking hands over her smooth throbbing breasts, across the satin copper sleekness of her torso, then wedged them between her thighs, her pain eclipsed the joy she felt at reading his letter, and the loneliness she'd kept at bay for so long swept her up like a snowflake in the midst of a blinding winter storm.

The clatter and thump of the noisy press did not distract Leela from her duties at the *Banner*. As she neatly wrote the figures into lined columns in the big ledger, she blocked out the hustle and bustle swirling around her to concentrate on her work.

It had been a very good week. They'd sold two hundred papers, more than had ever been sold before. Mr. Foreman would never say so, but having Leela sitting in the front window did seem to bring the customers in. Male and female.

The men came in, chatted a few minutes with Mr. Foreman if he wasn't too busy, then paid Leela for their papers. Some of them stood around, initiating small talk with her, mumbling and stammering about whatever the headline might be that day. She tried hard not to be rude, politely thanking them for purchasing a copy of the *Banner*, but not in the least bit interested in those who obviously considered themselves potential suitors. In Leela's opinion, none of the local young men, or the old ones either, came close to sparking her interest.

The women came in out of curiosity, shocked to see that old man Foreman had put a woman in charge of his money. Most of them were friendly enough, inquiring about her aunt and uncle, but Leela had no time for their idle banter about the new bolt of flowered chintz or the latest model stove which was now available at Newtons' General Store.

In fact, what Leela liked most about the job was the sense of freedom it gave her. She didn't earn much, only a dollar a day, but it was enough to make her feel special, as if she were talented and important. She would have liked it more if Mr. Foreman let her write a little article now and then. She had presented him with several pieces, but so far he had turned them all down. Today, she waited until nearly five o'clock to approach him one more time.

"I'm not sure this is such a good idea," Mr. Foreman muttered as he finished reading Leela's copy. He removed his glasses, blew on them, and wiped the tiny circles of glass vigorously with his big handkerchief. "Building new wooden sidewalks on the west side of the train station? That's something that oughta be taken up with the city. Putting this in the paper won't do any good."

"But it could, Mr. Foreman," Leela protested. "Don't you see? We live on the west side of Mexia . . . all the colored do. And why do we have to wade through dirt and mud to get to the station when there are broad, clean sidewalks on the east side of the station? Folks have been complaining about this every year during the rainy season." Her words spilled out in excitement.

"That's true, but putting a story in the paper . . . just gonna raise a fuss. The white folks don't care that the colored have to wade through mud to get in and out of the depot." He shrugged in resignation. "Ever since that time my window got smashed I been warned enough times by the sheriff and the mayor. Better be careful about what I print. I can't afford trouble now. Things are going along pretty good."

"Well," Leela countered, "I can change the story around. If the mayor of the city won't put in the sidewalks, why can't we just organize a group of people from the neighborhood and do it? Couldn't be that difficult. Just need some planks and nails, and a few men willing to do the work."

Mr. Foreman shook his head. "Not that easy, little lady. There's permits and building codes. Things like that, I'm sure."

"Has anyone talked to the mayor about the issue?"

"Not that I know of." He shrugged.

"Well, if no one's even brought the subject up, how in the world can you be so sure the city wouldn't be glad to see us take the matter off their hands?" Leela was very disturbed by the publisher's rigid resistance to her idea.

"Don't get yourself involved in city matters, Leela. We're doing fine, our doors are still open. Things been pretty calm for quite a spell now. Don't go stirring up trouble." He dropped Leela's article into the wastepaper basket. "Better finish up those figures," he said, closing the discussion. Then he went back to inking his press.

Leela sat fuming, unable to get her mind back on the task of adding the list of numbers in the ledger. If the Negro grocer or the cook from the Hurdleson Hotel had brought up an idea like hers, Mr. Foreman would have listened. If Parker had written such an article, Mr. Foreman would have praised it and run it on the first page. How dare he dismiss her as if she had no brains at all? He was determined not to take her seriously, she admitted, wondering if hiring her had been just because she was Parker's cousin and he still felt guilty about that incident with Ed Smith.

Leela glanced over her shoulder and watched Mr. Foreman, humming to himself as he loaded paper into the press. She got up and retrieved her story from the trash can, shoving it into the pocket of her skirt.

He's forgotten the whole thing, she thought morosely. As far as he's concerned the matter is dead. Well, I'm not going to let him dismiss me so fast. I'm a citizen of this town. I've got the right to make a suggestion.

At the end of the afternoon, Leela closed her books, pulled a shawl around her shoulders to block the sudden November chill, and told Mr. Foreman good-bye. Instead of heading west toward Aunt Effie's house on Palestine Street, she turned onto Titus and headed south toward the smithy.

Uncle Bert was glad to see his niece, though surprised she had come so late in the day.

"Something you need, Leela?" he asked, pulling off his worn leather gloves. "Ain't nothing wrong at the house, is it?"

"No," Leela said smiling. "I just want your opinion on something." She sat down on an overturned crate and pulled the article from her pocket. "Listen to this, Uncle Bert. Then tell me what you think."

Bert grinned, remembering the bill for sixteen dollars he'd gotten from Watson's Livery the last time Leela set out with a notion to get something done. He listened intently as Leela read her piece.

"What do you think? Couldn't we get a few carpenters and some donated planks and replace all that rotted-out walkway?"

"Probably so." Bert scratched his chin. "Guess we been waiting for the city to do something . . . ain't no reason we can't lay some boards ourselves." He stepped closer to Leela, feeling proud of her, happy to claim her as kin. "That's a right smart idea you got, young lady. What can I do to help?"

By noon the next day Leela and Uncle Bert had posted handwritten notices recruiting men and materials all through the Negro neighborhood. The volunteers were asked to show up on the west side of the railway station at six in the morning on Saturday. By Friday night it was clear that nearly every able-bodied man who owned a hammer or a saw was planning to participate in the project.

It took less than five hours to complete the job, and afterward, Aunt Effie and her friends served ham and biscuits to the hungry men, their wives, and all the children hanging around the station. The event created an air of festivity, and everyone remarked how nice it would be to finally get on the train wearing dry, clean shoes.

The mayor showed up and thanked everyone for such a dedicated effort to improve the city. He even sat down to eat biscuits and ham, joking and shaking hands.

Mr. Foreman came by late in the day, looked around and nodded to Leela, but had nothing to say, good or bad, about either the sidewalks or her involvement.

On Monday morning, when Leela showed up at the *Banner* for work, she was not surprised that the publisher treated her coldly, speaking stiffly and politely as if she were a stranger. Leela ignored his quirky manner and went about her work as usual—selling papers, documenting the books, chatting with folks who dropped by to comment on the success of the sidewalk project. Leela's spirits soared all day and she truly felt proud that she had helped change her town for the better. But her flush of happiness spiraled to an end at five o'clock, when Mr. Foreman informed her he would have to let her go.

"Why?" Leela wanted to know. "The *Banner*'s doing great. More people than ever are buying it."

"That's true," the publisher admitted, "but I been thinking things over. Seems a young lady like you oughta concern herself more with getting married and raising a family. It's not good, you being so interested in men's affairs. Not good."

"Men's affairs? Wanting to walk from the street into the depot without sinking into mud is men's affairs?" Her eyes grew wider with each word. She could hardly keep from screaming at the man.

"Well," he hesitated, "yes. It is the business of the city fathers. They'd have taken care of it in time." He handed her a small yellow envelope. "Anyway, it's finished. Here's your pay, Leela. You were a hard worker, I gotta say that, but maybe it's better you run along home. Looks like a storm is about to kick up."

Leela snatched the envelope from his hand and left.

The misty rain quickly turned into a downpour, but Leela didn't care. As she trudged along, Mr. Foreman's words burned her ears. Get married! Have a bunch of children! That's all he thinks a woman can do! She skirted a big puddle, unable to keep water from seeping into the tops of her shoes.

Agitated and angry, Leela thought about her predicament. Yes, she did want a husband one day. And children, too. But she also wanted her independence and a sense of control about her future. Was all that impossible? Did she expect too much?

A home of her own. A man to love her. Children. My dreams are no different from Josephine's, she admitted, her cousin's spiteful words suddenly coming to mind. Parker is happy. Josephine has convinced herself she is, too. When will my time come?

Though secure and protected by her aunt and uncle, Leela knew, at nineteen, it was time to start a life of her own. But how, and where, would her future take shape? Her mind flitted over the dismal prospective suitors who had come to the *Banner*. There was no one in this town she would marry.

Stopping at the corner, Leela focused on the yellow lights at the end of the street, pulled her soaking wet shawl more closely around her body, and turned onto Palestine Street, headed toward home.

Chapter Six

After five straight days of picking cotton, building fences, herding cattle, scrubbing floors or frying chickens and washing dishes in white people's kitchens, the tired souls who stumbled into Bird Dog's Lodge on a Friday night wanted to laugh for a while, forget about their troubles, and spend time with familiar folk sucking pickled pig feet while sipping corn liquor. The thick cabin door was open to all members, friends, and long-time acquaintances of any blood-connected Taylor who came through McLennan County. The lively joint rocked along from Friday afternoon straight through Sunday night and was governed by a few simple rules:

A man could keep his gun, but it had to be holstered. No knives allowed at all. He could dance with any woman in the place, if she'd let him, but if he wanted more than a dance, he'd have to take it someplace else. Families were welcome but Bird Dog had his limits:

The young uns could come in 'til nightfall; after that, adults only allowed.

The back room of the lodge was closed to women, boys who hadn't made sixteen, and any man who couldn't prove he had at least two dollars. Bird Dog provided the dice and the cards. Any man who cared to could inspect them.

From Friday to Sunday the scar-faced man rolled out barrels of biscuits, tubs of chitlins, racks of bone-suckin' ribs, and all the watermelon anyone wanted. He placed a Bright Leaf cigar box on the top of a crate and expected everyone to drop in at least a quarter.

"Where you think you goin', boy?" The man at the door lifted a thick, muscular arm riddled with fat pulsing veins which ran from beneath the rolled-up sleeve of a red flannel shirt. Bird Dog paid Stony ten dollars a weekend to keep the riffraff out of his lodge.

Stony deliberately blocked the stranger's entrance and blew cigarette smoke across the man's head.

"Off-limits," he said, squinting as he spoke. "Ain't no action in here for you."

The stranger sniffed loudly, kind of snorted, then slowly eased two slim fingers into the watch pocket of his pinstriped vest and took out a fold of bills. He peeled off several, which he proffered to Stony.

"Might want to reconsider," he said, holding the money under the guard's nose.

"Can't buy your way into this one," Stony replied icily. A lot of cash was floating around inside and he didn't want any trouble. "Better clear out. This here's a closed game. Stakes is high . . . regulars only."

The newcomer tilted back his head. The gas lamp at the doorway illuminated his face beneath the brim of his stylish fedora.

"Lemme talk to Bird Dog." The stranger's voice was controlled, confident, softly insistent.

"I already told you . . . closed game." Stony did not like the man's tone and moved one hand toward the thirty-eight nestled in his low-hanging holster. The pitch-black night spread out eerily beyond the door. "Don't start no trouble, now. Better get moving. I can't disturb Bird Dog, he's busy. He sets the rules, I enforce 'em."

Stony waited, tensing his jaw as he watched the younger man's face.

"I ain't goin' no place 'til I talk to Bird Dog. Take my word on it, tough guy. Bird Dog won't keep me out."

Stony sized the man up quickly. Expensive well-tailored gray-and-white pinstriped suit, silk cravat, a hat he knew must have cost fifty dollars, and the flash of a gold stickpin at his neck. Gold rings on both hands. The odd combination of boyish good looks and costly attire sent a signal of roguish importance.

"Wait here," he mumbled. "Stay right where you are. I'll see if Bird Dog wants to talk to you."

Stony backed away, eased over to Bird Dog and whispered in the old man's ear. Immediately, Bird Dog stood and walked to the door. He looked at the stranger.

"You wanna see me?" Bird Dog asked.

"Understand there's some action here tonight. I'd like a cut-in on the roll."

"Sorry. Game closed to regulars." Bird Dog's response was brusque.

"Taylors only?" the stranger asked, his finely turned mouth showing a hint of a smile.

"That's right." Bird Dog hesitated. "I know you?" he asked, leaning closer. "Take off that hat. Lemme see yo' face. Ain't too many crappies I don't know."

The young gambler slowly took off his gray felt hat and ran a pale hand over his thick dark hair to slick it back into place.

"How old are you?" Bird Dog asked.

"Eighteen," the young man said.

"Where you from?"

" 'Round here. Not too far up the road." The stranger lifted his pale square jaw in an almost haughty manner.

A big smile split Bird Dog's face and exposed a mouth without teeth, gums flaming red and smooth. "You Hattie's boy?" He asked as he decided. "You Carey, ain't you? Cousin Hattie's baby boy."

"That's right," Carey Logan said, allowing himself to be grasped on the shoulder by this cousin he had not seen in nearly four years.

"Chile, where you been? Last time I saw you, you was wearin' short pants. Yo' momma's been in and out of here, crying 'bout you runnin' off since the day you disappeared. She been stayin' back at her old place on the Fritz farm. Probably show up sometime tonight."

At this news Carey tensed, then shrugged it off and made no comment.

"Where you been all this time, boy?" Bird Dog went on.

Carey twirled his soft hat on one finger, leaned back against the wall. "Here and there. Mostly in Dallas, Fort Worth, even been across the border to Oklahoma City."

"You shore growed up. I'da thought you less than eighteen, though. And what you doin' with that choke of bills? Looks like a mighty lot of cash."

"Guess you could say I found my calling, Cousin Bird Dog. I ran into a streak of luck that doesn't seem to have an end. Lemme in tonight. Lemme show you what I can do." He flashed an engaging smile at his mother's blood kin and pulled back his shoulders. Bird Dog quickly led him past the tiny dance floor to a door at the back of the kitchen.

"No dice," Jah-Jah called, as the ivory cubes hit the back wall and spun beyond the white chalk line defining the boundaries of the shaky craps table. "No dice," he repeated, scooping up the chancy squares. "Pin Stripe comin' out."

The five men huddled over the waist-high table tossed their bets on the line. Jah-Jah leaned under the smoky oil lamp and, with a three-fingered hand, whisked crumpled bills into his multipocketed apron.

Carey watched Bird Dog's youngest brother sit back, balance himself securely on his three-legged stool, and prepare to call another game. Jah-Jah, who had lost the better part of one hand to the rage of a drunken farmer, never placed bets. He served as the houseman: holding the money, paying off the winners, crushing disagreements with the wave of his switchblade. He was the only person allowed to carry a knife in the Bird Dog Lodge.

"Comin' out now. Place yo' bets," the caller yelled for the last time.

Carey rolled the dice between warm dry palms and calmly looked the players over. He knew all five men, was probably related to them all through some distant connection and was easily twenty years younger than each one. They were old men with yellow, watery eyes. Lined, weather-beaten faces. Dirty gray mustaches stained brown from cigarette butts clamped between edgy teeth for too many games of chance. They stood, leaning anxiously over the table, blood rushing to their heads, anticipating the combination this newcomer would toss.

"We gonna see what Joy-Boy can do," Buck Bladsom said, separating several bills from the wad of green he kept strapped inside his leg. His gambling usually ran for three days straight, and by Monday morning he'd be broke again, looking to sell off a half-broken mustang to some cowboy passing through. "Come on with it, Joy-Boy," he chided. "Let's see what kinda action you got."

Carey let the dice fly.

"It's a natural," Jah-Jah called as those betting against the young shooter groaned. "What's your pleasure, Pin Stripe? Let it ride or pick it up?"

"Let it ride," Carey answered, no emotion on his face. He stood in silence as the bettors mumbled and threw more cash on the table. He laid two more twenties on the line. "One more time," he begged the dice as a surge of luck tensed his tall, thin frame. He turned the small cubes loose. They settled in two sets of four.

"Boxcars," Jah-Jah called, scraping up the wagers. Carey saw the six-inch blade sheathed in leather beneath the caller's arm. "One more time. Let's see can he boxcar again."

Jimmy Silvers, considered a young man at thirty-seven, tossed a five-dollar bill to the table. "Luck don't last as long as a good lie," he grumbled and turned his wrinkled face up to meet Carey's unreadable eyes.

Carey's dry hands warmed but did not sweat. He knew moisture from his palms could cause the dice to swell, make them fall unevenly and ruin his lucky streak. He blew on his hands and shot the ivory cubes to the table.

Out of the corner of his eye, Carey saw Duke Taylor set his lips into a grim line and squint his bloodshot eyes nearly closed. Known to cheat at poker and beat his Apache wife, Duke had spent five years on a chain gang in West Texas for killing a man over a two-dollar bet.

If there's going to be trouble tonight, Carey thought, Duke's the one to start it. My plans are laid out as tight as kernels on an ear of corn and Duke Taylor had better not get in my way.

Three passes slid by before Carey sevened out. Jimmy Silvers cursed the sixteen dollars he lost, but Jah-Jah silenced the man's complaints with a frown and a lift of his arm. The next four players came out on twos and threes, and the dice were soon curled, once again, in Carey's cool hands.

Dirty bills flew across chalky lines, changing hands so quickly no one noticed when Carey straightened his left arm and released his own lucky dice from the crook in his elbow. He clasped the warm cubes that slid into his left palm, juggled Jah-Jah's dice into the wide French cuff on his right sleeve, then smiled for the first time that evening and settled in for the play.

The young gambler held the dice for three more passes, breaking tense silence with smug laughter when his come-out roll came back every time. And as his winnings piled up, so did the tension at the table, until Carey flipped the house dice back into his palm and pulled a seven. He reluctantly passed the roll.

From his spot in the shadows, Bird Dog watched the action wind down as Carey relinquished the dice. From his table, which was set off from the players, Bird Dog called out, "Pick up your winnings, Cousin Carey. Come have a drink on me."

Carey broke away from the circle and eased his tall frame into a chair at his cousin's table.

"You always that lucky?"

"Usually," Carey replied, running his hands over the smooth lines in his vest.

"You shore got a way with them ivory squares." Bird Dog shook his head in amazement as he spoke.

"Comes kinda natural, I guess," Carey admitted, smiling across the table at his white-haired cousin, satisfied anew with his unfailing ability to turn a game to his favor. "Guess I got a system . . . never worry about the other guy. Concentrate on the feel of the dice." What he didn't tell Bird Dog was he knew he could win with any man's dice, but sometimes, just for the thrill of getting over, he'd try his lucky switch.

"How much time you spend in Dallas?" Bird Dog asked.

"Close to a year," Carey answered, laying out the crumpled bills, stacking them neatly on the table. He loved the feel of old, worn twenty-dollar bills. He hadn't had much experience with fifties and hundreds, but itched to go for the bigger stakes. Soft green currency had a distinctive smell; he recognized it immediately when entering a room and the scent of it stirred him into action no matter where he was.

"First place I went when I left here was Dallas. Got real lucky up there," Carey began. "Ran into a man who needed some help running numbers on the south side of town. Fell in with him, and he brought me in on a few craps games he ran in the back of his meat market. Sure was scary back there, rolling craps with a side of beef hanging over my head. Only thing good was he kept the place cool."

"Wasn't Kid Adams, was it?"

"Yes, it sure was," Carey answered slowly, wondering if he should have lied.

"Kid and I worked a few cattle auctions together," Bird Dog said. "He'd sort 'em, I'd get 'em to the ring. When the bidding was over, we'd switch the bulls before delivering 'em to the ranches." The memory of his youthful escapade put a grin on the old man's face. "Kid would take the best ones to slaughter for his market and I'd hightail it to the next town, lay low 'til the fuss settled down. Then, he'd meet up with me and we'd auction off another couple a head again." He tilted back in his chair in thought. "Worked for a while, but we had to keep moving. Didn't suit me too much . . . runnin' with Kid. I left after a time and came back here where the action was more my style."

Bird Dog pulled his tobacco pouch from his shirt pocket and set it on the table. "What made you leave Dallas?" He watched Carey closely as he spoke.

"I guess I was getting tired of being on the road. Wanted to find a place where I could stay put for a while. Only reason I came in here was to let you know I was back and to see what the action was like."

"Kinda young, ain't you, to be taking this gambling so serious?" Bird Dog gulped a shot of whiskey and poured another one. "Boy, you ain't hardly got shoulders enough to fill out that pricey suit you wearing. Carrying bundles of money and rolling dice like you been at it half as long as I been around."

"It's what I do best," Carey said matter-of-factly. And he knew in his soul, in that part of himself beyond the tangle of his thoughts, from a voice that whispered the truth, that it was more than just luck that kept him winning at craps and he coveted this talent intensely. He could manipulate the dice to fall as he wanted—not every time, that was certain, but with the odds so much in his favor, he usually tripled his stake. "And it's all I plan on doing," he went on. "Why should I sweat and work like a slave on the white man's dole when I can make a living tossing craps?"

"Could be a dangerous life you steppin' into," Bird Dog cautioned. "Bet Kid Adams showed you a trick or two." He shook a generous amount of tobacco into the small piece of paper stretched between two fingers. "Ever notice how Kid shoots craps?"

"What do you mean?" Carey asked calmly.

"Just like you," the older man replied. "You know, changing hands from right to left in the middle of a play. Ain't never seen a man other than Kid shoot from both hands and win."

"Just keeps things moving, I guess," Carey hedged. "I can write with both hands, too."

"That so?" Bird Dog smiled. "Ain't too many fellas can do that either." He twisted up the cigarette with a flick of his fingers and sealed it with a lick, then leaned forward to light it from the smoky kerosene lamp. "Time to pull in another keg of firewater," he decided, rising to head toward his kitchen. When he pulled the door open, he remained in the doorway looking with interest straight through the kitchen into the outer room. He turned back to Carey. "Come over here, boy."

Carey stopped fiddling with his stack of money and raised his eyebrows at Bird Dog. "What'd you say?"

"Come on over here a minute. Somebody out front you oughta see." He motioned for Carey to get up, stepping aside to let his cousin peer past him into the near-empty party room on the other side of the kitchen. "There's yo' momma," he told Carey. "Told you she'd most likely be in tonight."

Carey watched in silence, his eyes on the aging woman sitting alone at a table, hunched over a jar of corn liquor.

"Go on out and speak to yo' momma, cousin. She been waiting a long time to see you, lemme tell you the truth." Then Bird Dog slipped into the kitchen to set up another barrel of liquor.

Carey stepped closer, remaining in the shadows at the edge of the bar. She looked so tired, he thought sadly, so broken and old.

How many nights had she spent at that table? How many railroaders passing through had heard that sob story she always told about Benny Wilder running off? Carey's eyes flitted to the dark corner at the end of the tiny dance floor, the cold little sanctuary where he had slept many a night away. Music blaring, couples stepping all over him, his mother laughing and having the time of her life. Carey's hands began to sweat.

Hattie shifted her bulky frame to settle more comfortably in her chair and looked up. Just one more taste, then I'm heading home, she thought, wondering where the woman who poured drinks had gone. Hattie's eyes swept the room just as Carey moved into the light. The sight of him shocked her so, she spilled her drink as she jumped to her feet.

"Carey!" She held on to the table for support. "It's you! Carey! You back!" Her drunken words boomed in welcome.

Carey remained on the opposite side of the table, not at all sure what to say. It pained him to see his mother in such a disheveled condition, yet the resentment he still harbored for not knowing who his father was, fueled by the bitter reminder that she considered him a failure, prevented him from greeting his mother.

He could still see the blank look on her face when he told her four years ago he was leaving McLennan County. T.J.'s wagon had hardly cleared the yard. The bandage on his forehead was still seeping blood. And he had had enough preaching and warnings to last him a lifetime. Wasn't any use staying around.

It still hurt Carey that his mother never said good-bye. Shutting herself up in her room while he packed. Making no attempt to stop him.

"How you feeling, Ma?" He relented and touched her lightly on the arm, then pulled out a chair and sat down.

Hattie eased into her seat. "Fair to middlin', son. Just so happy to see you, that's all." She absently picked up her jar to take a drink, saw that it was empty, then placed it back down on the table. "When you get back?"

"Yesterday."

"Yesterday?" A crestfallen expression emerged. "Back for good?"

"Naw," Carey said quickly, "on my way east—New Orleans. Just cut through here to relax for a spell."

"You coulda stopped by to see me first, Carey. Shocking me so, running into you like this, like we ain't even kin. I wish you'da come 'round to see me."

Carey let himself be pulled into the emotional exchange he knew was coming. "What for?" He waited, not really expecting her to reply. "Your last words to me were 'You'll be sorry.' Remember saying that, Ma? You were glad to see me go."

"You know that ain't true." Hattie reached out and covered her boy's hand with hers. He pulled it from beneath her moist palm. "Those was words spoke in the heat of argument. It was bad news all around that day: you being put out of school, that awful beatin' you got, your new suit all tore up. Was too much pain that day. Whatever I mighta said came out wrong. It come down hard on me, that's all. Wasn't no need for running off like you did."

"Wasn't no need for me to stay either," he shot back. "No need at all." He sat up straight, shifting to let the dull yellow light better illuminate his mother's puffy face. He stroked the lapels of his expensive suit, suddenly changing the subject. "Like this suit, Ma?" Not waiting for her reply, he went on. "Got four more. Four different colors. All made especially for me." He watched the expression on Hattie's face turn guarded and wary. "You said I'd never amount to a thing if I left McLennan County. Remember? Well, what you got to say now, Ma?" He pulled his roll of bills from his pocket and riffled them under his mother's nose. "I ain't doing so poorly, you see?"

Hattie shrank back at the sting of his words. "Guess ain't much I can say to that," she murmured in defeat.

"That's right! Ain't nothing you can say about a thing I do." He stood. "I got business to take care of, Ma. Why don't you get on back home? It's late." He threw several bills on the table. "Take it, Ma. You look like you need it. Go on, take the money and go on home."

Hattie hesitated only a moment, then gingerly picked up the money. "You coming home tonight?" A tinge of hope colored her voice.

Shouts from the men at the craps table in the back room shattered the silence following her question.

"You gonna come back home?" Hattie probed.

"Maybe" was all Carey could manage. "Don't badger me, Ma. Not now. I told you I got business." He turned on his heel and strode out of the room, leaving his mother staring sadly at the empty jar in her hands.

As the game resumed, Carey pushed thoughts of his mother aside. The dice burned his palms now, the importance of winning even greater than before. He'd show her. He'd show all of them, he vowed, humored by the way Duke Taylor kept looking at his rings. Yes, these are really gold, he wanted to tell the withered hustler. Real gold. No brass or copper for me anymore. And as he took a deep breath to clear his head, Carey pulled the cold unruffled mask of a seasoned gambler over his face and connected spiritually with the dice.

Under Bird Dog's watchful eye, he quickly abandoned his two-hand switch, and still, the dice came back to him time after time after time.

Late into the night, Buck, Duke, Jimmy Silvers and the others grumbled lowly and left the back room. When the door slammed shut behind the last man, the sun was breaking orange over the tops of tall pines and roosters behind the lodge were starting to crow.

Carey lovingly counted his winnings, eyes shiny and clear as if he'd had eight hours of sleep. Bird Dog shook his head in disbelief and began to extinguish brass lamps sputtering light through blackened chimneys scattered throughout the room.

"Got it in yo' fingers, don't you?" Bird Dog said, walking from table to table, his back to his cousin.

"What?" Carey asked.

"That feel for the dice not every man has. I'll have to give it to you, boy. Ain't seen a better performance, not even on the stage at the Fort Worth Palace."

Carey considered the older man's words. "You got a point, Bird Dog. I guess I could call myself an actor of sorts." Smoky back rooms and abandoned warehouses are my stages, he thought. Half-drunk, small-time hustlers and greedy stupid farmers like these, the bit players in my dramas.

With his sharply cut features, pale yellow skin, cap of dark wavy hair that curved into ringlets around a boyish face, Carey knew he made as strikingly handsome an appearance as any legitimate actor on the stage.

"That's where I'm headed, cousin. Over to Louisiana, where professionals play for high stakes and I'm up against men who live the game. Day and night. Around the clock." His voice drifted off.

"You think that's the life for you, huh?" Bird Dog shoved the dirty lamps onto a shelf.

"Yeah . . . where the pretty women are and a man's got action all the time. Like the Chalmette Hotel in New Orleans."

The stale-smelling room was eerily silent.

"Glad to see you finished up using just one hand," Bird Dog finally said, the words dripping off his tongue like sap seeping from a pine.

"Felt lucky that way," Carey threw back, a slight edge to his voice. "Depends on my mood, you know?" If I can just swing a few more games like this one, he thought, I'll soon have my stake to head east. But he didn't like Bird Dog's warning. A few well-placed words in Duke Taylor's ear could ruin this little gold mine he'd stumbled upon.

"Coming back next Friday?" Bird Dog asked.

"If Stony'll let me in." Carey laughed.

"Don't worry 'bout him," the white-haired man said evenly. "You's family, remember? You always welcome here."

Chapter Seven

Leela's bitterness toward Mr. Foreman dissipated over the next few weeks. After venting to Uncle Bert and Aunt Effie her disappointment and outrage at being so curtly and unfairly terminated, she reluctantly settled into the stark realization that the publisher had presented her with a challenge: if her hopes of doing meaningful, interesting work were never to be realized, then she'd better think seriously about just what she planned to do with her life, which she felt was rapidly slipping away.

Aunt Effie had suggested that Leela enroll in Wiley College, the up-and-coming black school over in Upshur County, but the term had already started, and she'd have to wait until next fall.

Leaving the state to continue her studies had also been discussed, but Leela had no enthusiasm for such an idea, not wanting to strike out on her own in some strange, unfriendly city. Leaving Texas was really beyond consideration, though Parker continued to invite her to Washington every time he wrote.

The truth was, Leela had no desire to be permanently separated from her aunt and uncle. She loved them dearly and, with them, had found the only place she would ever call home. Creating a home of her own near them was what Leela really believed would bring her happiness. After all, she thought, it won't be long before Parker returns to Texas, and when he does, we'll all be together again. She'd even have a new cousin when he and Margaret got married.

As the winter days slipped past, Leela fell into a lethargic, almost lazy, manner and moped around the house at a loss. Aunt Effie tried to help by giving Leela errands to run: delivering dresses she'd sewn or picking up fabric over in Groesbeck, the county seat. She doled out bits of motherly advice to her niece, trying to ease her sense of confusion. Once, when Leela stood too long with the flat iron smoking on the padded board, Effie had gently broken into the girl's deep thoughts, saying, "Don't press too hard, child. Might conjure up something all wrong for you." And Leela burned with shame that her aunt seemed to know exactly what the problem was, though she could barely make sense of it herself.

Leela fought the temptation to sink more deeply into thoughts of what she believed would be a hopeless, lonely future. Too many times in one day, she would stand before the big window at the front of the house watching people pass by.

Are all of these people happy? she would wonder. Do they each have someone to love? Someone to hurry home to? Someone to hold them close when the world decides to turn cold and unfriendly? Am I the only girl in this town feeling so desperately alone? These strangers all seem to have a purpose, somewhere to go, and here I stand, just floating through life, growing older every day.

And when the chime of the clock or the bark of a stray dog would shatter Leela's contemplation, she would turn away from the window and return to her chores, wondering if love, romantic love, was to be in her future at all.

Late at night, alone in her bed, she would force herself to think of *him*, whoever *he* might turn out to be. Of course she imagined him to be handsome, intelligent and very romantic, and eager to protect her from danger.

When will I meet him and where? Will I ever? Or will I always feel so disconnected and isolated from the kind of love in my dreams?

With both Parker and Josephine gone and Uncle Bert on the road much of the time, the house now seemed eerily void of conversation, though Aunt Effie bubbled about as usual, reassuring Leela, almost every day, that things were as they should be and she ought not be in such a hurry to grow up. Look at your cousin, Josephine, she would say sadly. She was in just too much of a hurry. Now you don't want to wind up in a fix like that. Now do you?

Everything in time, she would say, patting Leela's hand. What you need to be happy will reveal itself at the right time and not before.

And in the bleak period leading from winter into spring Uncle Bert stayed out on the road, calling on farmers who had horses for him to shoe. Leela kept busy helping her aunt with her dressmaking business, looking forward to making deliveries in town.

On a blustery Friday morning in May, Leela woke up to the sound of voices in the kitchen. That was not unusual, for Aunt Effie often had a fitting with a customer very early. But what was unusual was the sound of the voices. The person Aunt Effie was fitting was definitely a man.

Leela crept from her bed, pulling her heavy robe around her shoulders, and stood in the darkened hallway where she could see into the kitchen. The man standing there in his neatly creased trousers and his clean white undershirt was the most strikingly handsome man she had ever seen.

He appeared mature, perhaps as old as thirty. And at first glance one might have mistaken him for a white man, but Leela could see he was not. Though his bare arms, held stiffly out from his sides, were so pale they looked like wax, his hands and face were deeply tanned; the skin burnished nearly to a shine. His sharply chiseled square jaw and "good" black hair, which he wore slicked back with pomade, came together to create an air of importance.

If he is not important, Leela mused, surely he will be one day. With his head erect, shoulders back, he looked like a soldier standing at attention in a military parade. And when he did speak, his voice was low and respectful, as if he had taken the time to think about each word.

He faced the darkened hallway yet could not see her. Leela slowly, eagerly, scrutinized this stranger as he stood in the middle of Effie's sewing room, white cotton draped across magnificent shoulders, a paper pattern pinned to his chest. Leela remained silent, watching Effie pin and tuck the fabric, chattering all the time about the awful rainy spell that had just passed. He spoke very little, nodding in agreement, seeming to enjoy Effie's cheerful banter, yet looking somewhat ill at ease under the nimble fingers of the tiny seamstress.

Leela leaned back against the wall, exhaling the nervous tension that held her body rigid, and gazed with intense curiosity at the man in her aunt's kitchen. She was captivated. Shamefully wondering if his legs and other parts of his body looked as pale and waxy as did his bare arms, she giggled under her hand and slipped back into her room.

Aunt Effie was the first one to bring up the man's visit. Leela did not have to ask. As soon as she appeared in the kitchen, Aunt Effie bubbled forth with everything she knew about her newest customer, Thomas Jacob Wilder.

"A very wealthy man," Effie said as she fried a thick slice of ham at the stove. "Very seldom comes to town. Owns about three hundred acres, just six miles west of town. And you know what, the place even has a name. *Rioluces*. Just like some big plantation in Mississippi or Georgia."

"Have you ever been there?" Leela asked, pleased that her aunt had so much information. The wave of curiosity sweeping over her created a tingling sensation in the center of her chest.

"No, but I heard about it long ago. I remember that place used to have a river running through it that folks say covered up a big pool of oil. Nothing ever came of it. I been living around here all my life and that tale's been told about almost everybody's farm." Effie turned the gas off under her frying pan. "Leela," she went on, her voice dropping into a conspiratorial whisper, "now don't take this wrong. I'm not suggesting a thing, but we women gotta look out for ourselves. He's a bachelor. Never been married. Lives out there with a slew of field hands and a Mexican housekeeper named Juana. He told me this himself." Effie set a plate of ham and eggs down on the table in front of Leela. "I think Mr. Wilder's about the nicest man I've met in these parts in a very long time."

Leela only nodded and began to pick at her breakfast.

It took very little effort on Leela's part to snag the job of delivering Mr. Wilder's finished shirts. Leela convinced her aunt that she could easily make the trip to his place and back before noon. No reason to worry, Leela had said, she knew the road well. The turnoff was just past Josephine and Johnny Ray's place.

As Leela put the package of white shirts into her buggy, she fought to keep a smile from forming on her lips. She was excited to be going to Rioluces—the most-talked-about farm, owned by the most-talked-about farmer in the county. And she was anxious to see Mr. Wilder again. She had thought of little else for the past three weeks, her daydreams elevating her to the exalted position of mistress of Rioluces. She pictured herself being adored by the handsome Mr. Wilder, surrounded by beautiful children, with a cadre of servants to help manage the place, and of course, wearing the most elegant dresses, which she would have gone to Chicago to purchase.

As Leela guided her buggy off the main road, she strained to see through the tangle of juniper and hawthorn crowding the lane, itching to catch a glimpse of Rioluces.

A gleaming white gate appeared at the end of the lane. Eight feet tall, it spiraled up in tiers of fancy wrought iron to end in a huge letter R scrolled at the top. Beyond the gate a white gravel road led up to a two-story house, a huge square structure flanked by two extended one-story wings which appeared to have been recently added. Freshly painted, windows framed with gingerbread trim, following the trend of the big houses in town, it was completely surrounded by vibrant beds of red salvia, purple iris and golden marigolds. The wooden structure faced the tangled road in pristine elegance: an oasis in the middle of the dense Texas backwoods. The fields behind the house bloomed white with cotton, spread out green with corn and shimmered with row after row of melon vines rolling on and on as far as she could see. By the time Leela got to the gate, a young man had run up to pull it open for her.

"Can I help you, ma'm?" He stepped back and took off his tattered straw hat.

"I have a delivery for Mr. Wilder. I'm Leela Alexander. The niece of the seamstress."

"Oh, yes. Pass on in, ma'am. Just go on around back and knock. Juana, the housekeeper, will take care of it."

Leela turned in, guiding her buggy around the house as she surveyed the property. Just as beautiful as I've been told, she thought, even more curious to see inside. She hoped the housekeeper would not just take the package and dismiss her.

Juana was gracious and warm, quickly ushering Leela into the parlor to wait for Mr. Wilder. Leela looked around.

The heavily carved furniture crowded the small dark room. There were no family portraits on the walls, no watercolors of flowers to break the monotonous dull brown wallpaper, no vases of roses on the small ornate tables. Even the window coverings were drab coarse cotton that looked like they were near to falling apart. The shabby carpet was worn in spots, unraveled completely at the doorway. It was obvious that Rioluces was in need of a woman's touch and the lord of the manor was in need of a wife.

Leela jumped slightly when Mr. Wilder appeared. Pausing awkwardly in the doorway, he looked down at his visitor.

"You've brought the shirts I ordered from Mrs. Alexander?" His plain, direct manner seemed at odds with the nearly exotic combination of tanned skin, dark hair and deep brown eyes. Leela sat very still and blinked at him. He seemed even taller and more imposing than he had in Aunt Effie's kitchen. But now she was close enough to see his high cheekbones, strong chin and the graceful arch of his thick dark brows, and she was immediately drawn to him.

"Yes." She stood and held the soft package out to him. "I'm Leela. Mrs. Alexander's niece. My uncle would have brought the package out but he's not in town and . . ." She stopped her stammering and bit her lip. How foolish of me, she thought, going on about why I came. There's no reason to explain.

"Well, I shore do appreciate you making the trip, ma'am, but I could have picked them up on my next visit to town."

"Aunt Effie prides herself on giving her customers what they ordered on the day it was promised. She's real funny that way," Leela went on, wanting to delay her dismissal, to spend just a few more minutes in the presence of this man who many said owned more land than any other Negro in Limestone County. "She said to tell you, if the shirts don't fit quite right, you're to bring them back immediately . . . if there's anything wrong, she'll . . ."

"Oh, I'm certain they'll do fine," Wilder interrupted. "Your aunt has a fine reputation. I'd been needing some things made. It was good of Mr. Foreman at the *Banner* to tell me about her."

"Do you know Mr. Foreman?" The mention of the man's name brought back all the bad feelings she'd worked so hard to forget.

"I've done some business with him. Placed some ads for the sale of cattle. Things like that." His words had a mild, even tone. His face showed no expression.

"I'm surprised I never saw you at the *Banner*," Leela volunteered, glad to have a reason to extend their conversation. "I used to work there." She watched Mr. Wilder's face closely. Only his eyebrows moved.

"Did you now?" His words did seem tinged with interest.

Leela stepped closer and went on. "Oh, yes. I was in charge of his books. Very interesting place to work."

"But you're no longer employed there?" T.J. Wilder turned to put the package of shirts on the heavy sideboard just inside the doorway.

"No." Leela started thinking rapidly as she wove her story. "My aunt really needed me to help her with her dressmaking. You see, her husband . . . my uncle, has been out of town quite a bit." She liked the way he was listening to her and the way his presence made her feel. "So I quit my job at the *Banner* to give my aunt a hand. Family comes first, don't you agree, Mr. Wilder?"

T.J. Wilder looked at her blankly and said nothing for a moment, then slightly shrugged his shoulders and changed the subject.

"Well, I do appreciate you going to the trouble to bring my shirts out, Miss Alexander. I don't get to town very much." His manner was courteous and direct. When he stepped back into the hallway, Leela knew it was time to go. She looked him directly in the eye.

"You should come to town more often, Mr. Wilder. Mexia's not so bad. Not really."

He smiled at the invitation and Leela felt herself blushing. She took a deep breath to clear her head.

"I'm sure it's not," he agreed, seeming to enjoy the small talk. "But I think it's much nicer here in the country." He lowered his eyes and started through the house toward the kitchen. Leela followed him closely, observing the way his hair curled slightly over the back of his collar.

"Juana," he called to his housekeeper, "would you make sure Miss Alexander gets a cool drink before she heads back to town?" Then he opened the back screen door and turned. His look was one of curious regard, the hint of a frown creased his brow. "Tell your aunt I've need of a blue serge suit. If she can get the fabric, I'd appreciate it." His face softened and he managed a bit of a smile. "You be careful on the trip back to town, miss. I'm mighty grateful for you bringing out my shirts."

As he ambled across the yard toward the barn, Leela watched him, memorizing the way he swung his arms and kind of leaned to one side. The flutter in her chest started up again, and Leela knew she had found the man who could drive away her loneliness to give her the security and happiness she'd been dreaming of so long.

The very next day, Leela took the train to the county seat of Groesbeck and purchased a bolt of dark blue serge. It sat on the shelf in Aunt Effie's kitchen for nearly a month before T.J. Wilder came around. And when he did, Leela did not stay in the hallway. She did not watch the handsome farmer from the shadows. She not only assisted Effie with the fitting of his suit, she convinced the soft-spoken farmer to stay for a glass of lemonade when all the cutting and pinning was finished. Effie neatly disappeared into her garden, leaving the two alone, and crossed her fingers.

Over the next three months Leela saw Thomas Jacob Wilder every Thursday evening and Sunday afternoon. He asked her to call him T.J. Sometimes they strolled over to Mildred's Cafe for ice cream; other times they sat on the porch swing and talked.

Though painfully shy and self-conscious, he would open up in spurts of conversation, telling her a rush of information, then fall silent. He talked about the weather, the crops and the land, finally revealing the much-discussed story of how he came to own three hundred forty acres of land.

"You know, my ma did the best she could. Only reason she sent me over to the Powers place was 'cause she thought I'd be better off. I was eleven years old and scared to death when I got there. All I had was the clothes on my back, didn't even have a pair of shoes."

Leela could see that talking about his past caused T.J. great pain. "You don't see your mother very often, do you?" Leela prompted, wanting to know more about her suitor.

"More now than before," he replied. "When I was first sent away, I studied every night on why my ma would give me over like that to strange white people. But a child can't figger things out like a grown man. Now I understand it better."

"Well, it seems coming to Limestone County was your good fortune. Who would have thought Mr. Powers would leave his land to you?"

"Old man Powers wasn't so bad." T.J.'s face softened with the memory. "He had a no-good son, think his name was Billy, run off with a Mexican singer. Powers was so hurt by that he come out to the quarters and woke me up. I was about sixteen then—been on the place five years. Powers told me, 'Boy, I think you got more sense than my own flesh and blood. I'm gonna make you a farmer.' And he moved me into his house."

"Did the other cotton pickers hate you? It must have looked strange to them, seeing you favored by the boss."

"We was working too hard to think much about it, but when the old man died and the will was read, then all hell broke loose for a spell." T.J. chuckled, rather to himself, then quoted Stepp Powers's will from memory for Leela.

" 'When the Missus and I pass on, this farm kin go to T.J. Wilder, the black boy who works here. He kin have all thirty acres as long as he farms it: Stepp Powers 1896.'

"And that's how I got started," he continued, giving the ground a prod with his booted foot. They swayed back and forth as evening shadows spread slowly over the porch. "At eighteen, I had thirty acres, three mules, four hogs, a mangy brown dog, and a twenty-dollar gold piece. I sold off one mule, butchered two hogs and sold the meat, bought another cow, and laced that gold piece into the ankle of my boot. Still got it with me today. Never can tell when a man's gonna need raw cash to get out of a tight spot."

Leela looked over at T.J., enthralled with the story and liking the sober, hardworking farmer more each minute.

"And how did you wind up with so much land?"

"Well, over the years I just kept buying up pieces of land adjoining my place that nobody wanted. Lucked up when a banker man in town who bought my melons come out to the farm one day. He said he'd loan me money to expand, all I had to do was sign the papers. Wesley Sparks. He's been a true believer in my farm. If he hadn't loaned me the money, I never could have put my farm together like I did."

Leela placed her hand on T.J.'s knee. "Not many colored would be so favored."

"Yep," T.J. admitted, "was a blessing, him loaning me that money. It's taken me close to ten years, but now I think I got the place just about how I want it."

"You must be proud," Leela offered, doubting anyone had ever said such a thing to this man of few words.

"Guess you could say that," he admitted. Then he reached over and took Leela's hand in his. She felt his warm dry hands tighten around her small fingers. "I'd be even more proud if I had a wife . . . and a son." His eyes fastened on hers and he did not flinch. He looked at Leela as if the answer to his unasked question had to come tonight, at that very moment, for he'd never have the nerve to ask again.

Leela placed her free hand on his shoulder and turned more fully toward him. "If you are asking me to be your wife, Mr. Wilder, the answer is yes."

He pulled her hand to his lips and kissed the back of her fingers, then leaned over and kissed her on the cheek. Then, in a very clumsy manner, he rose and stood over Leela. Bowing slightly, he backed toward the steps and said, "Well, you've made me real happy, Miss Leela. But I wish you'd call me T.J." He straightened his broad shoulders and lifted his chin. "I better be going on home. Looks like I got a lot of getting ready to do."

Leela laughed aloud and stood, pressing her breasts very near to his chest. She could feel the fright and nervous tension coursing through his body. It's decided, she thought. I'm going to be his wife. And once I've settled into my new home, no one will ever make me leave.

Boldly she reached up and placed both hands on either side of T.J.'s face and pulled his lips to hers. His kiss was soft, gentle, almost brotherly, but the scent of tobacco and shaving cologne was unsettling. The sensuous smell stirred her deeply. She moved closer to let her breasts rub softly across his chest, smiling up at her husband-to-be as their kiss came to an end.

"You're right, T.J.," she murmured, her lips remaining near to touching his chin, "there'll be a lot to do before the wedding."

Chapter Eight

The sweltering days of August melted away. September arrived with a snap of cold weather that lasted only a week; then the temperature soared so high again, old-timers laughed and said that Cedar Creek was about to boil over and scorch the cotton fields. It stayed that way for the remainder of the month, but folks took the heat in stride, knowing Texas weather could change its mind faster than a bird could pull a worm from the ground.

Throughout it all, Leela and Effie consumed themselves with preparations for the upcoming wedding. Leela's exquisite gown of white lace, threaded with rows of tiny seed pearls, had been finished weeks ago and hung in her room under a clean white sheet, along with her veil and crisp white gloves.

Even Josephine had come around, acting rather civil, and agreed, after much urging by both Leela and her mother, to be a part of the ceremony. It was decided she'd wear pale blue organdy. The three women traveled to Dallas looking for fabric for Josephine's dress, then took the train to Groesbeck to find just the right shoes to match it. The rare family outing made Leela hopeful that she and Josephine might overcome their uneasy estrangement.

Uncle Bert was delighted about the upcoming nuptials. He cracked open his coffee can of savings and hired a cook from nearby Corsicana to prepare a three-tier cake. All of the members of Bethlehem Primitive Baptist Church were invited.

On October 1, fifteen days before the wedding, handwritten invitations were delivered all through town and a notice was even posted on the front door of the church. Leela Alexander was said to be the most fortunate girl in Limestone County to have snagged T.J. Wilder. Leela thought so, too.

The Sunday before they were to become man and wife, Leela and T.J. took a ride in his buggy. They drifted along the road, following the Navasota River, thankful that fall had finally descended. A slight wind stirred the crisp dry air and nudged orange and red leaves from the trees. They stopped in a shady place, allowing the horse to water, and sat in the buggy. A strained silence stretched between them: a silence that Leela knew she'd have to break.

"I wish I had known how you really felt about all this," Leela started, determined to have her say. Lately, it seemed T.J. would not initiate any conversation. If Leela prodded, he'd get to talking, but if left alone, he was perfectly happy to sit in silence with her at his side. He's just lived alone too long, Leela rationalized. He'll come out of this after we're married. Especially when children come along.

"Just because I'm not partial to a big to-do in the church doesn't mean I don't want you to have what you want." He sounded confused and sincere.

"It's not me," Leela lied to cover her great disappointment. "Aunt Effie and Uncle Bert really want to do this . . . you know Josephine kind of ran off with Johnny Ray, and now they're enjoying all the preparations. It's more important to them than to me."

"Now, don't start making a fuss," T.J. said quickly. "I never should have said a thing about it. It just seems like your family's spending a whole lot of money." This time his voice was flatly judgmental.

"It's what they want to do," Leela countered, not seeing where he had any right to criticize anything her aunt and uncle wanted to do with their money. They worked hard and enjoyed their life. If they wanted to spend what they worked for on her, it was their business.

"I hate to see money wasted, that's all," T.J. said, leaning forward with his long arms dangling between his knees.

"I would hardly call my wedding a waste of money." She could scarcely hold back the tears. "Isn't that what money is for? To spend on the things that bring pleasure?"

"Maybe for some folks. Not for me." T.J. was matter-of-fact. "Money needs to be used for the land, the crops, or set back for the season when things don't go so well."

"Well, Uncle Bert is not a farmer!" The words shot out before she could stop them. She watched T.J. from the corner of her eye, hoping her remark had not hurt him.

Leela could tell his ideas were fixed and unshakable.

"You'll soon see that there are other things we'll need to spend money on," she rushed to add. "Just wait until we start a family. Would you deny a pretty dress for your daughter in favor of a sack of feed?" She was dead serious and beginning to get a little nervous over T.J.'s overly practical approach to everything. She thought about the dull brown wallpaper and the frayed carpet in his parlor and shuddered.

He looked over at her abruptly; then his face melted into a smile. This rare display of humor caught Leela off-guard.

"May have a point there, Lee." He shook his head slowly and broadened his smile. "You may just have a point."

Leela fluffed out her hair and straightened her skirt, satisfied to have made a little progress. She moved closer, allowing her leg to touch his, and put her hand gently on his knee. He'll come around to seeing things my way, she thought, already visualizing the changes she planned to make at the farm. The first thing he's going to do, she silently vowed, is run a water pipe into the house. No one pumps water outside nowadays. At least no one with the means to do better.

T.J. patted Leela's hand softly, then rose. He walked to the water's edge, pulled himself up to his full height and tore a colorful branch from the tree. So very much alone in the world, she thought.

So very much afraid of letting life show him there is joy to be found in more than the land and the crops. Well, I can show him how, Leela decided as she stepped down to stand beside her future husband. She slipped her arm through his and stood with him as the sun started its descent into the shadowed creek. Once we are married and settled on the farm, things will be different for T.J.

It rained the day of the wedding, not a light autumn mist to wash away the dust of Indian summer, but a gully-washer of a downpour that created a river of mud through town. Still, preparations for the ceremony moved forward and faithful friends of the family scurried around under huge black umbrellas to make sure everything was in order.

Josephine and her children had arrived the night before and settled into Parker's old room. Johnny Ray did not come, and though Effie would never have admitted it, she was secretly happy to have her daughter to herself.

Trays of food and pretty packages arrived all during the morning, and the tiny house became so crowded there was hardly space to squeeze from one room to the next. But as the hours rolled on toward the evening ceremony, the crowd thinned out and people began drifting over to the church. It was finally time for Leela to get dressed.

After checking the last detail on Leela's gown, Effie slipped away and knocked softly on Josephine's door before entering.

"How are you coming along? Need any help with the children?" Effie reached over and picked Penny up from the bed. The plump baby gurgled and waved her tiny hands in the air. Effie held her granddaughter to her breast and rested her lips on top of the infant's head. Her eyes met Josephine's in the big cheval mirror. "You look so pretty in blue," she said with a sigh, feeling very happy that her daughter was here today.

Josephine averted her eyes. "Don't you think this ruffle around the waist makes me look even fatter than I am?" She twisted around, trying to see her rear end. "Maybe we shouldn't have added all this flounce right here." She tugged at the wide lace-edged ruffle circling her waist. "Can you take it off, Momma? We have time. This peplum makes me look huge."

"Don't be silly," Effie started, seeing that Josephine was beginning to panic. "You look fine. This dress suits you just fine, honey. Stop fussing and let me button up your back."

She laid the baby back down on the bed. "Oliver," she said, patting the three-year-old on the shoulder, "you run along and find Grandpa. I'm gonna help your mother get dressed." The boy darted out the door, happy to get out of the room.

"I've been dressing ladies for a long, long time," Effie began as she moved up behind her daughter. "I think I'm a pretty good judge of what flatters and what don't. Take my word for it, Josephine. The way this dress is cut, it actually slims you." She reached out to fasten the top button.

"Stop humoring me, Momma!" Josephine jerked away and began to pull the dress down over her shoulders. "It looks terrible on me and you know it. I'm not going. I won't be seen looking like an overstuffed pillow. Leela will just have to have her wedding without me." She pulled off the dress and threw it across the bed and stood defiantly in her slip, glaring at her mother.

"What's brought this on, Josephine?" Effie's words were calm and low. "We picked out the fabric and the pattern together. You never said a word about not liking the dress. Through all the fittings you never mentioned you didn't like this dress. What's the matter, child?" Effie moved closer to Josephine and peered into her face. She could see the tears gathered in her daughter's eyes, the quivering of her lips. Another small piece of Effie's broken heart shriveled and grew hard as she saw her daughter's pain. "What's really wrong?"

Josephine pulled her lower lip between her even white teeth and stared at her mother, unable to answer.

"I wish you would talk to me, honey. This is not about the dress, now, is it?" Effie reached out to hold her daughter, but Josephine spun away and slumped on the bed, burying her face in the coverlet.

"It's all wrong!" Her words were muffled and filled with anguish. "All this fancy to-do over Leela! I want no part of it. It's all wrong."

Effie sank down on the bed beside Josephine. She gasped at the sight of the dark purple bruises covering the girl's back and shoulders. She placed a cool hand on the angry welts and caressed her daughter's flesh. Her first thought was to ask how this happened, but she pushed it aside, knowing Josephine would only make up some excuse for her condition. Johnny Ray Mosley ought to be horsewhipped, Effie thought.

"I know how you're feeling, baby," she murmured. "You wish this was your wedding, don't you? Well, I gotta admit, this is just what I'da done for you, if you had let me. This coulda been your day." Effie swallowed hard to keep from crying. "But you chose different. It was your life and you chose different. We can't go back and change that, now, can we?" She pulled Josephine up from the bed and wrapped her arms around the sobbing girl, hugging her tightly as she stroked her bruised back. "You're my only daughter. And, sure, I would have loved to do the same for you." Her voice trailed off, the effort to hold back her own tears too great.

"But, Momma," Josephine managed to whisper through her grief, "you know it's not right that Leela got everything." She leaned back and wiped her eyes. "A big wedding, all the attention. A handsome husband! And all that land." Josephine pressed her hands over her face. "And she's beautiful, too! I saw her in her dress! Beautiful!" she shrieked through her fingers.

"Oh, baby." Effie reached over and peeled Josephine's fingers from her face. "You're just as beautiful as your cousin. Look at me!" She took her perfumed hankie and brushed tears from Josephine's plump cheeks. She smiled as she went on. "What kind of talk is that? You're one of the prettiest girls in Mexia."

"Stop it," Josephine screamed as she lurched to her feet and went to stand before the mirror. She looked at her own tear-stained face as she raged. "I'm *not* beautiful and you know it. I'm a freak, Momma. Not black. Not white. Not anything! I don't even belong in this world."

Effie quickly came up behind Josephine and grabbed her by the shoulders. She spun her around as she spoke. "You have no right to say such things, Josephine. You are the most precious thing in the world . . . to me and to your poppa. You are our one and only baby girl, our flesh and blood. You are our life. The Lord made you special. And that's the way you gotta look at it. You need to see the beauty you have and stop this kind of talk. Don't you ever let me hear you say such crazy things again. You'd break your father's heart. He's worked so hard for so many years to give you a good life, gave you everything you ever wanted. You've had it better than most of the white *and* the colored girls in this town. And we gave you love. Don't you ever say different."

Josephine pulled away and turned a miserable face up to Effie. "Well, there was one thing you didn't give me, Momma. The right color. And there's nothing anyone, not you or Poppa, or Parker or even cousin Leela can do to change that now."

Haltingly, Effie turned from Josephine and started to the door, resigned to the fact that she could not reach her daughter. "I see the rain's stopped." She placed her hands to her stomach and took a deep breath. "Dry your eyes, baby. Put on your dress and look beautiful . . . for me . . . for your poppa. Please."

The look Josephine sent her mother nearly melted her heart and Effie knew her daughter's anguish could not be stilled that day. "Let's make the best of it and have a wonderful evening. Maybe the celebration will take your mind off all this turmoil you done built up inside yourself. You only gonna be beautiful when you're ready to be. I can't do more than love you, Josephine. That's all your poor old mother can do."

Mother and daughter stood facing one another, knowing that each spoke the truth in her own way. The sun burst through the tall narrow window and bathed the pair in gold. Finally, Josephine wiped her face with the hem of her slip and picked up the blue ruffled dress. She held it out to Effie and stood silently as her mother helped her slip it on and fastened the long row of pearl buttons running down her back.

No one in Limestone County had seen a more handsome couple. T.J. Wilder stood at the altar in his blue serge suit, his dark hair waved back in smooth glossy ripples from a tanned golden face. He wore white cotton gloves and nervously clenched and unclenched his hands during the entire ceremony. Leela remained very still, a brush of a smile on her lips, standing beside T.J. in calm elegance, her veil cascading in folds of chiffon netting to the floor. A shaft of light, reflected through the stained glass windows of the small country church, caught the threads of gold running through Leela's hair and gave her a regal appearance.

The traditional wedding ceremony, conducted by Reverend William Pearson, lasted less than twenty minutes. At the appropriate time, when Leela turned to hand Josephine her bouquet of white roses, she gave her cousin a broad happy smile. Josephine stared blankly at Leela, pressed her lips together firmly, and did not smile back.

When T.J. bent to kiss his bride, Leela placed both hands around his waist and kissed him back as fiercely as the occasion allowed, then held on to his arm possessively as they walked down the aisle to the opening bars of Mendelssohn's "Wedding March."

Turning into the festively decorated reception room on the east side of the church, the couple remained standing just inside the door, politely greeting their guests.

Leela knew many of the people from attending church with Aunt Effie, while others were local farmers and craftsmen who had done business with Uncle Bert. Some guests had come from as far away as Corsicana to see the woman T.J. Wilder had taken to be his wife.

Thinking everyone had been greeted, Leela pulled T.J. by the arm. "Let's cut the cake now. I'm dying to taste it. Anyway, some folks probably need to leave pretty soon."

"Just a minute," he hedged, not making a move toward the lace-covered table. Instead, he turned back toward the sanctuary and looked around. He nodded at Leela. "My ma's sitting in there. I thought that was her I saw slip in."

"Your mother?" Leela was shocked at T.J.'s casual manner, remembering how convinced he had been that his mother would not show up.

"Yep." He made a motion for Leela to stay where she was while he went back into the church. Leela watched him bend to speak to a heavyset woman dressed completely in black. She turned and looked down the long aisle, her eyes connecting with Leela's. She turned back to T.J., nodded, then let him help her rise.

"Lee," T.J. started as he came nearer, "this here's my ma, Hattie." He fidgeted with the watch chain hanging from his vest pocket. "Hattie Logan," he added, emphasizing the name he knew she now preferred to use.

When he was a boy she was Hattie Wilder, T.J. remembered, thinking that he had never had to introduce his mother before. It wasn't until after Carey was born that she stopped using T.J.'s daddy's name.

"I'm very pleased to meet you," Leela said, holding her hand out to her new mother-in-law. "Welcome to Mexia."

"I been here before," Hattie said bluntly, not accepting Leela's hand. "I got kin living over this way."

"Oh," Leela said, not sure what that meant, and not at all sure she liked this woman. "Well, I'm happy you came. Please, come and meet my family." She caught T.J.'s eye, silently begging for his help, feeling strangely at a loss for words. "My aunt, especially, will be very glad you came."

"Not right now," Hattie begged off, retreating back a few steps. "I just need to have a word with my son." She remained unmoving at the doorway. "A little something I need to ask him," she said, her eyes resting significantly on T.J.

"Of course," Leela said, struggling to keep a light touch to her words, "and when you finish, please come let me introduce you to all my friends and family. You must have something to eat." Leela moved away. A crowd of pretty young girls with satin ribbons in their braided hair gathered around her. She gaily accepted their hugs and kisses as she made her way across the noisy room.

"You coulda shook her hand, Ma. What the devil you come for if you ain't gonna act decent?" T.J.'s embarrassment caused his voice to tremble. He could tell by the way his mother hung on to the door frame she'd had more than one glass of wine before showing up at the church.

"I come to see just what kinda woman you done finally decided to let live out there on the farm with you."

"We're married, Ma. She's my wife." His words were curt and punishing. "Don't you say one thing against Leela. You know nothing about her. She's a good, decent person. From a fine family, too."

"Humph!" Hattie's lips turned down at the corners. "You know what I mean. All these years you been telling me you ain't needed no woman out there. But you hired on that gray-headed Mexican before you even considered asking your poor struggling ma to move in." She opened her purse and took out her handkerchief and began to wipe beads of perspiration from her nose and cheeks. "Now you done replaced her with this gal."

"You sure got a strange way of twisting things, Ma. It wouldn't have been a good idea . . . you living on the farm." He shook his head, trying to gather his thoughts to make himself clear. "I'm married 'cause I want to be. Hope to have a family, you know."

"You got family! What about me?" Tears filled Hattie's eyes and she blinked rapidly until they rolled slowly down her cheeks. "Carey done run off. I'm all alone, trying to hold things together. Old lady Fritz turned me off her place, had to go back to that rotten little shack of a house in Waco. It's falling down around me. You got room enough out there for me." She paused and struggled to catch her breath. "Say what you want, but if I hadn't sent you over to the Powers place to work, you'da never wound up owning the place. Ever think about that? Huh?"

"We been over this too many times, Ma, and now ain't no time to be bringing all that up." T.J. pulled out his watch, checked the time, then snapped it shut. "Just because I never invited you to live at the farm was no reason for you to believe I'd never marry, so don't be layin' no guilt on me now, Ma."

"You know, living by myself since your brother took off ain't been easy. He comes and goes. Never know when he'll disappear. I'm just sayin' it woulda been the proper thing to do if you'da asked me to come out to the farm. All that space you got," she said, again, "we coulda got along." Her indignant manner infuriated T.J.

"Things was best left as they was. I told you to let me know if you needed anything and I never denied you money." He cast a glance around the room. It was getting late; he wanted to leave. All this whoop-de-do. For what? he wondered. He saw that Leela was watching them, nervously fingering her veil. "Come on and have a piece of cake, Ma. Try to be nice to Leela." He took his mother by the elbow and guided her across the room.

Everyone circled the table, anxious to watch Mr. Chester, a photographer from Waco, set up his big box camera. He posed the handsome couple in front of their cake and snapped their picture while everyone clapped excitedly. Then Leela and T.J. cut the first piece, posing once more for the photographer.

From the corner of her eye, Leela saw T.J.'s mother, apart from the crowd, looking the table over carefully. When she picked up a silver spoon and slipped it into her purse, Leela could hardly believe her eyes. She caught her breath when Hattie also boldly deposited Effie's pearl-handled knife into her bag.

You hateful old woman, she thought. No wonder T.J. didn't care if you came to his wedding or not. Hoping no one else had seen the theft, Leela chose not to say anything. At least not right then.

The crowd began to thin. One of the younger girls sat down at a battered upright piano and clumsily hammered out a few lively bars. Leela did manage to introduce Hattie to Aunt Effie and Uncle Bert, then left her new mother-in-law alone. It was clear she had come to the wedding only to see her son; she made no attempt to pretend otherwise.

Josephine was nowhere to be seen. Leela guessed she'd run home to sulk, but hoped her cousin might visit her parents more frequently now, though secretly doubted she would.

Leela accepted a cup of punch from Gladys Rolings, who looked very smart in a new brown suit Effie had sewn for her. After chatting for a moment, she was about to go tell T.J. it might be time to leave, when a hand on Leela's shoulder stopped her.

"You're the bride, I can see."

Leela turned around quickly and found herself looking into the face of the most strikingly attractive man she had ever seen. A younger, more handsome, more flamboyant version of her husband. Her mouth dropped open as she let her eyes sweep unashamedly from his face, down the length of his well-tailored suit, back up to his red silk cravat. In the midst of the simply attired, small-town folks milling around the room, this stranger emerged like an exotic tropical bird, and his effect on Leela was pleasantly disturbing.

"And you are . . . ?" Leela swayed back slightly to more clearly see his face. The flash of his even white teeth, the curve of his beautiful mouth, and the way he had nonchalantly pushed his soft brown hat to the back of his head made Leela tremble slightly. Her eyes remained wide, anticipating his answer.

"If you're Leela Alexander, my brother's bride, then I'm Carey Logan, your new brother-in-law." He grinned dazzlingly, executed an exaggerated bow while removing his hat, and pierced her with eyes that warmed her flesh.

"Carey! Of course." Leela extended her hand for him to shake and did not pull it away when he kissed it instead. How gallant, she thought, as his soft lips brushed her gloved hand. He's probably the flattering rogue T.J. said he is, but so what? There's no harm in being pleasant to a lady. "T.J. told me about you. I'm afraid you caught me off-guard." She let her fingers rest in his palm, knowing she should pull them away. "He said you were living in Dallas. We didn't expect you to come."

Carey chuckled and slowly turned loose her hand, almost reluctantly releasing her touch. "I wouldn't have missed this for the world." When his line of vision caught T.J., who was standing near Hattie across the table, his brilliant smile turned oddly into a deeply puzzled smirk. "I see our ma's here, too." He lifted his jaw and sniffed. "Not surprised she'd make the trip. Just to see T.J., I'm sure."

Leela looked from Carey to her husband and back to his brother, the younger man's words ringing too true. When T.J. approached, Hattie trailing behind, Leela could feel the tension gathering, threatening to explode.

"Carey." T.J. planted himself directly in front of his brother. "What a surprise." His tone was not pleasant and he did not offer to shake hands. "Ma"—he stepped back and let his mother get closer—"why didn't you tell me Carey was coming?"

"Didn't know it myself," Hattie said, a hint of surprise in her voice, too. "When you get in?" she asked.

"Took the six-fifteen straight from Dallas and came right on to the church from the train station. Nice little town, Mexia. I'll have to come back when I've more time to visit." He shifted his gaze from his brother to Leela. "If I'm invited, that is."

Leela smiled. T.J. frowned. Hattie stepped back as if she were leaving.

"So, Ma." Carey stopped her. "You moving in with the newlyweds?" He met Leela's puzzled look and addressed her unasked question. "Bet you can use Ma's help out there at . . . what's that they call your farm, T.J?"

"Rioluces," Leela volunteered, confused by the obvious uneasiness Carey's words were causing.

"Yes, Rioluces. Guess having Ma around is going to be a big help," he baited, watching T.J.'s face.

"Ma won't be moving to the farm," T.J. said coldly. "Leela and I will manage just fine."

"What a shame," Carey continued. "You know," he leaned close to Leela's ear and whispered in a voice loud enough for everyone to hear, "Ma's always wanted to live on T.J.'s farm. I just thought now she was finally going to get her wish."

"Stop it, Carey." T.J. put his hand on his brother's arm. "You better leave now. I don't want trouble. Not tonight."

Carey brushed T.J.'s hand away. "Don't push me, brother. I haven't even got to know my new sister-in-law. What's the hurry? There ain't no rush."

Leela moved to stand behind T.J., unsure just what was going on. When Carey saw her retreating, he relented and put on his hat.

"Maybe you're right. It is getting late." He gestured to Hattie. "You coming, Ma? I got a buggy waiting outside."

When Hattie didn't answer, T.J. took Carey by the arm.

"I'll just walk you to your buggy, Carey. Make sure you get on your way." Carey laughed aloud at this.

"Couldn't make yourself clearer if you tried." He tipped his hat at Leela. "Hope I see you again real soon, Leela. Maybe then we'll have more time to talk."

When T.J. and his brother stepped away, Hattie cornered Leela at the table.

"Don't go getting any fancy ideas about getting between me and my son. He's been wanting me to come to the farm to live for a long time. I just ain't been well enough to make the move."

"Mrs. Logan, I've never discussed it with T.J." Leela paused for a moment. "He's never said a word about you coming to live at Rio-luces." She stammered, feeling trapped, part of a larger web of confusing deceit that had deep roots in this family.

Hattie lowered her voice and said, very seriously, "If you try to turn my son against me, you gonna rue the day you married him. Maybe we ain't been too close in the past, but me and T.J. got a long understanding. Things you know nothing about." For the first time, Hattie touched Leela, putting her black-gloved hand on the young woman's arm. "Don't try to shut me out of T.J.'s life, you hear me? I got rights to live out there, if I want to."

Leela pushed Hattie's hand off her arm. "Don't you dare threaten me! I don't know what is going on, but I know I don't have to listen to this." Leela looked down at Hattie's shabby purse. "And if you think nobody saw you steal that silver, you're mistaken, Mrs. Logan."

Chapter Nine

The wind gathered strength as it moved across the county splaying white-tipped cotton like big paper fans, bending tender stalks of corn to the ground. It whistled shrilly and persistently through the lacy mesquite trees, gusted sporadically over top-heavy oaks, and rattled the thorny rose-covered vines clinging to Leela's bedroom window.

The summer storm that howled and raged its way over Rioluces did not drop much water on the dry, parched land, but did bring enough wind to pull the temperature down. Leela dabbed at her forehead with the edge of her sheet and turned restlessly onto her side. Fast-moving storm clouds produced a pattern of shadows, letting moonlight intermittently illuminate T.J.'s face. Leela peered over at her sleeping husband, not surprised to see him lying flat on his back, hands folded across his chest, in the exact position he had assumed when he first lay down.

T.J. prided himself on his ability to fall asleep immediately after retiring. His pattern was broken only if he needed his wife—for that was how he approached making love—as an intimate encounter brought forth out of need. Leela knew how he felt and never turned away, though his perfunctory coupling left her empty, disappointed, and lying awake long after he fell asleep.

Leela's eyes slowly traced T.J.'s rugged profile, noticing for the first time that the sharp edge to his jaw had softened slightly. His deeply tanned face held a network of creases, yet they did not give an appearance of aging. At thirty-three, T.J. looked no older or younger than Leela supposed he should; most Texas farmers had skin as weathered and burnished as his.

T.J.'s devotion to Rioluces was unyielding, and the land gave forth a bountiful harvest, providing the couple with a very good life. T.J. pushed himself unmercifully—in blinding summer heat and treacherous freezing rain, rising before dawn, laboring alongside his help, traveling endless miles of back roads to secure buyers for his produce. And as sundown neared, he would stumble into the house, sometimes nodding off to sleep in the big tin tub Leela filled with scalding water for him to wash away the grime of his labor. Lately, he'd been coughing and complaining about pains in his chest, but Leela could not convince him to see a doctor. Immediately after supper the oil lamps would be extinguished, bringing another exhausting day to a close.

Leela had quickly adapted to the cyclical nature of their days, accepting that T.J.'s driving ambition to make Rioluces ever more prosperous was the single most important thing in his life. After two years and eight months of marriage she knew her husband would never change and accepted his unspoken love and pride in her as genuine.

In the still, dark hours before dawn, Leela assured herself, again, that things were as they should be, though T.J.'s clumsy, gentle lovemaking had stripped away any illusion that their marriage would evolve into the passionate union she had anticipated.

Eleven months into the marriage, when their son, Kenny, was born, T.J. had gifted Leela with a string of real pearls and said, "I love you," for the first time since the wedding. Not discouraged by her husband's limited ability to express himself, Leela drew contentment from the security of her marriage, in living on land that belonged to them, and from the joy her baby boy brought her.

The wind died down shortly before daybreak, and Leela drifted into a hazy half-sleep. Suddenly, a loud thump, immediately followed by a piercing howl, brought her and T.J. fully awake.

"He's fallen again," Leela murmured, almost to herself as she threw back the sheet and sat up.

"I'll get him." T.J. stopped her, placing a hand on his wife's shoulder. "Ain't gonna take many more spills like that 'fore the boy learns how to stay in a bed." He pulled on his pants and shuffled out of the room.

Lying back on her pillow Leela could hear T.J. comforting their son.

"So-so, little man," he said lowly. "Done spilled yourself on the floor again, huh?"

Leela smiled to herself, knowing Kenny, at twenty-one months, was not taking very well to this recent separation. But T.J. had been adamant; it was time the boy got used to sleeping alone in his own bed, in his own room.

"So-so," he continued to soothe the child, "get on back to sleep. You going out on the wagon with me tomorrow, ain't ya?"

"Um-hum," the child mumbled sleepily.

"All right then, little man, you better close those eyes. Daybreak be here soon."

The house fell silent and Leela knew T.J. would remain beside his son, unwilling to leave until the boy had fallen asleep again. T.J.'s patient, easygoing manner had created a strong bond between himself and his son. As soon as the child could balance himself, T.J. had propped him up on the tall produce wagons, taking him wherever he went.

Daybreak came quickly, and as the sky lightened beyond the darkened rooms, T.J. rose from his bed, threw cold water on his face, then went to the barn to hitch up his wagons. Leela stoked the fire in her big iron stove, rushed to cook breakfast while packing a basket of cold chicken and boiled eggs, keeping one eye on Kenny, who was determined to dress himself.

The sun was full up when the wagon pulled away. Kenny turned and waved good-bye to his mother. Leela waved back, vigorously shaking her handkerchief in the air, and remained at the front door until the dust had settled in the road.

During the quiet morning hours, Leela went about her chores: washing dishes, ironing linens, putting up five quarts of tomatoes, scrubbing thick black mud from the back porch steps. These were the times when resentment crept in. T.J. could have kept Juana on to help me, she thought, still irritated that he had dismissed the woman who had worked mainly for room and board. But T.J. held firm, saying, "No need for spending good money on wages for her when I've got a wife, now, is there?"

His miserly ways infuriated Leela. The crops were bringing record prices, yet T.J. acted as if they were starving. The first day of their married life he had given her enough money to change the wallpaper and the carpet in the shabby front rooms, but had balked at her demand for an inside water faucet. It had taken nearly two months of persistent convincing before he had relented and installed the line from the pump. After that, T.J. had generally left Leela alone to do the work he felt was hers and kept himself busy in the fields and the barn.

After Leela finished her chores, she went to her small oak dresser and took out the letter from Parker that had come yesterday. Glad to have time alone to read it more carefully, she stepped onto the shady porch and sank down onto her wicker chair. She could almost hear Parker's voice as she read:

> June 2, 1913
> Washington, D.C.
>
> Dear Cousin Leela,
> I hope my letter finds you, your husband, and baby Kenny in good health. It's difficult to believe you've been married nearly three years and I've been away from Mexia nearly seven. It would be grand to return to see my new cousin, but I doubt I will be granted time from my job very soon. Jobs are scarce and it is not good to even think of leaving this one. I'm very happy in my work.

I only wish Josephine could find a little happiness. What I've learned of her situation is not good, I'm afraid. Mother told me of her problems with that brute she continues to stay with—why I do not know. Sometimes I think of coming home just to speak directly to Josephine. If I thought my presence would change things, I'd gladly give up my job here to help my sister.

But I must congratulate you, Leela, on your wonderful son and successful marriage. From your letters, it seems all is going extremely well for you and T.J. I was somewhat concerned that you'd find living so far from town not to your liking. After your work at the *Banner* and involvement with the town folk, I doubted you'd be able to take the isolation of the Wilder place. The only time I met T.J. Wilder was when I traveled to his farm to help him compose a notice about the sale of his Black Diamond melons. He seemed rather reserved, soft-spoken, but perhaps he was lonely—staying so far from town.

At any rate, you've changed his life, I'm sure. How could he not change with someone as full of life and curiosity as you are?

My job at the paper goes well. There is so much news in this town, there's hardly time to finish one article before I'm directly back into another. At the moment I've been writing about the definite shift of Negro support from the Republican party to Woodrow Wilson and the Democrats. Though skepticism runs high, many believe Wilson will hold to his pledge of seeing justice done for all colored people, in all matters. We'll see. Yet it seems as if the prospect of war in Europe may overshadow our problems here at home.

Let me close before I bore you with my political rambling. I'll continue to send you copies of my articles when they're printed. Give my love to all the family and write soon. Your letters bring Margaret and me closer to you.

Your loving cousin,
Parker

Letting the brittle paper fall onto her lap, Leela put her head back and closed her eyes. Such talk about happiness, she thought. Josephine . . . me . . . T.J. How do we measure our happiness? And is it really all that important? She thought not as she remembered the pile of laundry waiting for her, waist-high, in the washroom. Leela took a deep breath, slowly pushed herself up from her chair, and started to go back in.

A movement at the edge of the forest caught her eye. She stopped, stepped to the end of the porch railing and watched a man emerge from the thick stand of pines fronting the east side of the property. Frightened, Leela moved into the shady spot where the clematis grew thick and leafy. With T.J. gone for the day, the two hired hands, who most always were around, had been given work to do on the far side of the acreage, over by Cedar Creek. She was virtually alone on the farm.

A tall, thin man wearing a wide-brimmed hat started toward the house. He was limping, grasping his arm, favoring his right side. Leela's mind whirled with options: should she step right out and make her presence known or go quickly inside and lock the doors and windows?

Curiosity kept her from moving, and by the time a panic began to rise in her chest, the man was already within hearing distance.

"What do you want?" Leela called out, walking into the sunlight that bathed her steep limestone steps.

The man made no reply. He gripped his left elbow with his right hand, looked up to see where the voice had come from, then lowered his head and came closer.

"Who are you looking for?" Leela asked, wishing he would stop where he was and tell her his business.

"Leela?" The man straightened up and took off his hat. "It's me, Carey. T.J.'s brother. Don't tell me you've forgotten me already."

Leela gripped the banister and leaned forward. "Why so it is!" She rushed down the steps and stopped at the sight of the blood-soaked rag on Carey's left arm. "You're hurt!" She looked into his mud-streaked face, which shone with perspiration. "What happened? How did you get here?" She saw no wagon, horse, or buggy in the area. Had he come to Rioluces on foot? Without waiting for his reply, Leela pressed her shoulder next to his, allowing him to put his good arm across her back as she led her brother-in-law up the steps. "Be careful," she cautioned, guiding him into the kitchen. He slumped down at the long trestle table.

Carey sighed loudly and squeezed his fingers more firmly over the bloody rag knotted over the upper part of his left arm.

"Not the way I'd a liked to present myself," he began, lifting his chin to focus on Leela. "But wasn't no place else to come."

Leela busied herself gathering a basin of fresh water, clean rags and a wad of cotton. "What happened?" she asked as Carey let her peel away the sodden handkerchief and examine the long gash in his flesh.

"A miscalculation," he answered. A rueful smile appeared. "Didn't follow my usual gut feelings about a situation and . . . well, this is the price I had to pay."

Shocked at his nonchalant manner, Leela wondered if such miscalculations had happened before. "Hold still," she cautioned, settling his wounded arm more securely on the table. As she leaned over him to put the water basin beneath his elbow, she felt Carey's warm breath on her neck and flushed hotly.

Carey remained quiet as Leela bathed the wound, allowing his gaze to travel from her bright auburn hair, across the swell of her delicate cheekbones, to linger a moment too long on her feathery dark lashes.

Leela swabbed at the gash, trying to ignore her brother-in-law's blatant assessment.

"Where did you come from?" She spoke rather quickly to gain control, upset at the nervous tremble of her fingers. "Where have you been?" she rushed on. "It's been nearly three years since the wedding."

"Where have I been?" he repeated, a cool mocking tone to his words. "Oh, I've been over in McLennan County for a spell. Not that far away, really." He looked around the room and for the first time inquired about his brother. "T.J. hard at work in the fields?"

Leela finished cleaning the four-inch gash and began to wind a wide strip of gauze over it. "Well," she started, "your brother's gone over to Hillsboro. Took our boy, Kenny, with him." She watched Carey's face at the mention of his nephew.

"That so? Ma told me about the boy. Now I'll get the chance to see him. When they coming back?" He examined Leela's handiwork and nodded, then rolled his bloodstained shirtsleeve down over the bulky cotton gauze.

"By dusk, I'm sure. T.J. knows better than to keep the boy out all night."

"Well, well." Carey stretched his legs and leaned back. "My good fortune to come along just now. Gives us time to get acquainted."

"That's a very bad cut you've got there," Leela said, choosing to ignore Carey's invitation. "Probably lost a lot of blood." She rinsed out her basin and gathered her supplies. "There's a cot out there on the side porch," she went on, pointing toward the door at the side of the room. "Why don't you lie down? It's quiet, you can rest. You want some water? Something to eat?"

He shook his head. "No, but I am a bit weary. I hitched a ride into Mexia, but I walked out here from town."

"That's six miles!" Leela remarked, wondering why Carey had made such a trek, not knowing how welcome he'd find himself on his older brother's farm. He could have gone to a doctor in town.

"Yeah." Carey rose and started to the side door, his white shirt sticking wetly to his back. "Quite a ways from civilization, aren't you?" He turned at the doorway to address Leela directly. "How do you stand it out here?" His eyes swept down Leela's plain dress to her heavy work shoes, then back up to the apron tied around her narrow waist. "A pretty woman like you ought to live in the city. This place would drive me crazy."

Suddenly Leela wanted him out of her kitchen. How dare he say such things to her? "I love this place, Carey. Your brother and I are very happy. Living on the land brings us a great sense of peace."

"Peace?" Carey laughed and raised his good shoulder. "I ain't had no peace since I was fourteen years old. Maybe it's a good thing I came out here." Then he stumbled out the screen door and fell heavily onto the cot.

Leela stood staring after him, trying to compose herself. Why in the world does he bother me so? she wondered. There was no reason to feel so edgy. After all, he was family . . . just T.J.'s brother.

Carey slept soundly in the shady spot on the porch throughout the afternoon. Leela sat by her parlor window and kept busy darning linens. As she pulled her needle in and out, through the fabric, she began to wonder how T.J. would react to his brother's presence on the farm. Since Carey's appearance at the wedding reception, his name had been spoken no more than half a dozen times. There's certainly no love lost between the two of them, she surmised, glancing once again at the gate at the end of the road.

It was close to five o'clock when T.J. entered the yard, balancing a sleepy boy on his knee as he urged his tired horses into the barn. When Leela rushed in behind him, he turned and gave her a rare smile.

"Don't go fussing over the boy. He's a little wore out, but he's doing fine."

Leela stood at the side of the wagon, looking up. "It's not Kenny I'm worried about," she told T.J. as she helped him lift the sleepy boy down. She held her son to her chest and let him put his weary head onto her shoulder.

"What's going on?" T.J. asked, starting to unhitch the horses.

"Your brother, Carey. He's here."

"Carey? Here? Where?" T.J. stopped, hand in midair, and frowned darkly at Leela.

"On the side porch. Asleep." Leela pushed Kenny up higher on her shoulder.

"What's he want?" T.J. was already moving swiftly toward the house. "Why's he showing up here?" T.J. turned back to Leela, who was hurrying to catch up. "How long he been here? Where's his horse?"

"He came out of the woods. Early in the day." Leela took two steps to each of T.J.'s long strides.

"Come out of the woods? Walking?" T.J. spoke to his wife as if she were crazy. "Carey don't walk no place. Something strange is goin' on."

Leela grabbed T.J.'s arm and stopped him. "He's hurt. A deep cut all down his arm." She raised her eyebrows in question and shrugged her shoulders. "I cleaned it up as best I could, but I think he needs to see a doctor. Never really said how it happened."

T.J. tore around the side of the house and burst onto the porch. Leela slowly entered the back door and took Kenny to his room.

The brothers' loud voices filtered into the house and frightened Leela. She strained to gather bits and pieces of their conversation, anxious about T.J.'s bitter reaction to his brother's unexpected arrival.

"You didn't learn your lesson when Mule Bledsoe busted your forehead open?" T.J.'s voice was harsh and accusing.

"Wasn't like that at all, T.J.," Carey threw back. "I just walked into a deal gone sour over some corn whiskey Claude Varnet's trying to unload in a hurry. An accident, just like I said."

"Why didn't you run home to Ma? Seems like that's a fair piece closer than my place."

"Naw," Carey reacted sharply, "was better I cleared out of the county for a spell. Anyways, Ma don't need to know about this. You know how nervous she's been lately."

"Nervous?" T.J. almost laughed. "Don't you mean drunk?"

"Don't you say that about Ma, T.J." Carey's voice grew high-pitched and defensive. "She's got problems, I know . . ."

"And you're right there at the root of 'em, Carey. You think I like to see how Ma's going down? Every time I get over to Waco to see her, she don't do nothing but bring up how lonely she is and how she don't know where you are. Next thing I know she's got a bottle on the table. Why? Because you running in and out of her life and keeping her worried 'bout what kinda trouble you're in sets her off. Next time you take off—stay away! You're what turns Ma to drink. You and what you're doing!" T.J.'s words boomed through the house.

Leela decided to let Kenny sleep and put him down on his tiny, narrow bed. Then she went into the kitchen to start dinner. The brothers raged on, dragging up the past that brought both of them such pain.

"Don't act so smug, T.J. If you hada let Ma come live here, she'da been a lot better off."

"I've discussed that for the last time—with you and with her. I see her right often—at least she knows where to find me! That's more than she can say about you!"

"Still can't face the truth, can you, T.J.? You know if Ma had never sent you over here, you'da never wound up owning this place." Carey laughed and pressed his point. "You owe her, T.J. More than I do."

"Two days," T.J. said sternly, as if giving the younger man a sentence. "You can stay here two days, that's it, then I want you to clear on out. Go back to Dallas, or wherever it is you do your fancy living."

"My arm's pretty bad off, brother. Might need a little more time." Silence followed that remark. Leela stood at the stove holding her breath, listening to crickets chirping in the grass. "You wouldn't send me off in this condition, would you?" Carey challenged his brother.

"A week, Carey," T.J. shot back. "You get yourself healed up in a week. Then I want you on your way."

CHAPTER TEN

Leela persuaded T.J. to clean out the storage room behind the black iron stove so that his brother could stay there during his illness. Having resigned himself to having Carey around for a while, T.J. pulled the cot in off the side porch and gave up a shirt and a clean pair of pants to his injured brother. Then he went back to his work in the fields, going about his business day after day in stoic silence, refusing to discuss the situation any further.

Carey's wound did not heal in a week. It festered and filled up with foul yellow pus; his arm turned purple and doubled in size. Leela tended the ugly gash as best she could, but grew frightened when Carey burned with fever for three days straight and slept so soundly he could not be awakened. T.J. relented and sent into Mexia for Doc White, grumbling the whole time about how Carey was going to pay him back: the doctor charged T.J. five dollars.

It took four more days for Carey's fever to abate and another week for his angry flesh to calm down. By the time he was well enough to eat a decent meal, Leela had become very attached to her patient.

"There's plenty more on the stove if you want some," she said, smiling across the table at Carey. "Glad to see your appetite is back."

Laying down his spoon, Carey turned his drawn face toward her. "This is fine," he replied, pushing the empty bowl toward the center of the table, "mighty fine. I'm feeling much better already." He pulled his left arm across his chest and closely examined the fresh bandage Leela had put on it that morning. "You really know how to take care of a man, don't you?" His gentle words flowed evenly, almost caressing Leela. "I want to thank you, Leela, for all you've done. If it had been up to T.J. I'da probably been left by the side of the road."

"Don't say that, Carey!" Leela's tone was sharp. "That's not true. T.J. is family, he'd never do such a thing." The unyielding expression on Carey's face spurred Leela to reach across the table and take hold of his hand. "I know the two of you have had problems in the past. Haven't most brothers? Don't hold on to a grudge. T.J. might not say much, but I know what he's thinking."

"And what might that be?" Carey asked, leaning closer to Leela, still holding her fingers in the palm of his hand.

"He's relieved that you're getting better." Leela gently pulled her hand away. "You could have died. The doctor wasn't even sure you'd make it."

Carey pushed his chair back from the table and stood. "I'm tougher than I look. Take more than a knifing to put me away." He went to the kitchen window and casually leaned against the frame.

Leela followed his every move. Memories of the feel of his hot flesh under her fingers and the sight of his smooth hairless chest surged forth in unsettling waves. At the height of his fever, she had undressed him and bathed him with cold water and touched every part of his firm lean body. Now his casual manner, the way he almost posed his every move, stirred Leela in a way she wished would go away, though she found it disturbingly pleasant.

"Bringing in the melons, I see." Carey supported his injured arm with his right hand and remained at the window, his elegant profile to Leela, watching the field hands in the distance loading large striped melons onto long flat drays. "T.J.'s kingdom," he said absently. "Seems my brother's got everything a man could ever want."

The wistful edge to his words plunged into Leela's heart.

"More land than even he ever dreamed of owning," Carey continued. "A bountiful crop. A handsome son." He cast Leela a glance and connected with her, staring openly at her full red lips. "And certainly the most beautiful wife in the county."

Heat rose from the center of Leela's chest, and she suddenly felt light-headed, distracted. It's only a compliment, she reasoned, unsure if she dared make a reply. Taking shallow breaths while staring at Carey, Leela let him go on.

"You're too pretty to be stuck out here. Too smart, too." He gave her a dazzling smile, his smooth olive skin dimpled on one cheek. "You think I didn't notice? First time I saw you at the church back then, I knew you were smarter than my brother."

"How?" Leela's words came out in a whisper.

"How?" He thought a minute. "You had enough sense not to interfere." He winked at her and laughed aloud when Leela's eyes widened in surprise. "And you made me feel welcome that day. I kinda crashed the party 'cause I knew T.J. wasn't particular about my coming, but I had to see who he'd taken to be his wife. I never figgered he'd found somebody like you."

He's actually flirting with me in his brother's house, Leela observed, struggling to keep a passive face. He's a rogue, all right—she remembered T.J.'s words—but God he's a charmer, that's for sure.

The more she looked at him, the more she thought of the great differences between the brothers. T.J. had never told her she was beautiful, had never really looked deeply into her eyes, and certainly had never winked at her or told her he thought she was smart.

Abruptly, Leela rose and began to clear away the cups and bowls from the table. Carey came around behind her, standing very near. "You know, I've only been here once before, when I was about twelve years old. Why don't you show me around the place, Leela? T.J.'s too busy to be bothered and I'd really like to see the farm."

T.J. helped his mother out of the buggy and gave her his arm as they climbed the steep steps. A white hot sun blazed down on them and cast their long shadows over the deep shady porch. Hattie leaned heavily against her son, breathing loudly, wiping her face with a flowered handkerchief as she muttered complaints about the weather.

"Too damn hot. Been the hottest summer in twenty years. I'm getting too old to go through many more like this."

T.J. opened the front door, stepping back to let Hattie enter first. "Now don't go saying things like that, Ma. This July ain't no hotter'n last. Come on to the kitchen, have a glass of water."

Removing his sweat-stained hat, T.J. helped his mother to the long trestle table, then held on to the back of her chair as she settled her bulky frame. Hattie let out a sigh that sounded more like a groan, looked down, then stuffed her handkerchief into her purse and glanced around the room. "Where's Carey? He ain't gone, is he? He still here?"

T.J. turned his hat around with one hand, nodded slowly, lips clamped together. "Yep," he finally muttered, "still here. Don't do a thing but sit around the house and take up space. Goes off with the boy now and then, draws pictures. All kinds of pictures. Strangest thing how a grown man can spend his time in such foolishness." T.J. lifted his hands in resignation and shook his head. "But Kenny's sure taking a liking to his uncle."

Hattie pulled off her black straw hat and laid it on the table next to her purse. "You should of sent word to me that Carey been here all this time. I been wondering where he went off to. You coulda sent word, T.J." Hattie's accusatory words stung her son. "Six weeks he been here before you thought to let me know. Humph! That ain't no way to treat yo' momma."

"He come out of it all right. Anyway, he made me promise not to send for you . . ." T.J. began.

"That's real hurtful," she interrupted, straightening the white lace collar at her throat. "I coulda come over and nursed him. I nurse white folks all day long. Why wouldn't he want me here?"

The stage for another argument with his mother was now set, but T.J. refused to be baited this time. "Leela handled everything fine. Doc White came out. Wasn't no need really, Ma, for you to make the trip. Now if things hadn't turned out like they did, well . . . maybe then . . ." He drifted out of the conversation as Leela and Kenny entered the back door. Trailing them, a colorful spray of flaming Indian brush in one hand, was Carey, his immaculate white cotton shirt open to midchest, his dark hair tousled around his handsome face.

"So here you are." Hattie smiled broadly at the sight of her favorite son, stretching her thick arms up to give him an embrace. Dutifully, Carey bent down and kissed Hattie on the cheek.

"Well, well. What you doing here, Ma?"

"T.J. came and got me. I know all about what happened." She nodded at Leela, then absently asked, "Think I could have a glass of water? It's stifling hot in here."

"Of course," Leela said, crossing the room to her inside faucet. As she let the water run a moment to cool, she prayed this visit from Hattie would be short. In the past three years, Hattie had visited the farm only three times. And each time had been disastrous. All she did was drink the homemade wine she brought along with her and complain about being mistreated by her sons. Leela had bit her tongue, tolerating her mother-in-law, while keeping a sharp eye on her valuables.

Leela placed the glass of water in front of Hattie, took Kenny by the hand and started from the room. "You need a bath, young man. Then you can visit with Grandma." She turned to T.J. "Your ma's staying for supper, isn't she?"

T.J. looked to Hattie, who shrugged her shoulders and mumbled, "It depends."

As soon as Leela had left the room, Hattie unleashed her hurt on Carey. "Gettin' all cut up. Then not sending for me to care for you. You my boy! How you think that made me feel? You just put me out of your life, huh? Ain't got no more use for yo' momma, huh? Well, if that's the way you want it, don't come crying back to me when you broke and can't get a meal in town. Maybe I just won't answer my door."

Carey shot an angry glance at his brother, then turned on Hattie. "Why you gotta put it like that? Stop twisting everything up your way. Leela did a fine job of bringing me through. Wasn't nearly so bad as you think." He rolled up his sleeve and bared his left arm to show her the jagged red scar still struggling to heal. "See? It's pretty much closed up. I'm feeling right normal."

"Then when you comin' home?"

Carey circled the table and sat across from Hattie. "Don't know as I am, Ma." He squinted up at T.J. "I kinda like being here . . . for right now."

"I'll bet you do! Laying up, doing nothing, letting your brother's wife amuse you."

"Shut up, Ma. What'd you come out here for if all you gonna do is talk like that?" Carey shifted uncomfortably in his chair.

"I come to see you." Hattie's eyes began to fill with tears. "How you think I felt, learning so late what happened?"

Carey dropped his head into his hands and threaded his fingers through his hair. "Ease up, why don't you, Ma? I'm twenty-one years old. I been taking care of myself since I was fourteen. Stop treating me like a child." He raised his head, face lined with torment. "What do you want from me, Ma. What?"

"It's too late to talk about what I want. You just go your merry way, not considering how I feel. Now why you so concerned about what I want?"

Knowing he could never reason with Hattie, Carey let his face go slack, then said flatly, "Why don't you just go on back home?"

Hattie turned to T.J. "You hear how disrespectful your brother can be?" Tears now rolled down her puffy, pale cheeks. "I don't deserve no talk like that." She sniffed loudly and raised her palms in question. "T.J., you gonna let him stay? After what he just said to me?"

T.J. pulled on his hat with a sharp impatient tug. "I don't rightly care what he does, Ma. And I ain't got no use for this argument. I got work to do. Melons going to market in the morning. I ain't got time to worry 'bout whether he stays or goes." Without waiting for either to make a reply, T.J. strode out of the room and headed toward the barn.

He can stay 'til I get back from making the greengrocers circuit, T.J. decided, an uneasy tension creeping into his stomach. But when I get back, he's gotta move on. Things ain't so bad between us right now. Guess I'm finally seeing just who Carey is. But if he stays around here much longer, I got a feeling things just might get off track.

Early the next morning, while the house was still and dark, Leela slipped from her bed and entered the kitchen. Without giving much thought to what she was doing, she went about her usual routine:

lighting the tall oil lamps, stoking up the banked fire, pouring flour and water and eggs together to make the biscuits she knew T.J. liked to carry on his trips. When he left the farm to make his circuit, he would be gone for at least a week.

In the heavy canvas satchel he used to carry food, Leela packed two fried chickens, dried beans and salt pork, a pound of cornmeal, and spicy dried beef. If the opportunity presented itself, Leela knew T.J. would eat at the homes of those who bought his produce, but more often than not, he'd have to rely on what she packed in his grub box to carry him through his lonely swing across Limestone County, into Navarro, until he reached the Miller farm in Corsicana. There he'd stay with a black family Leela knew would be happy to replenish his supplies.

As light began to appear at the edges of the horizon, Leela was startled by Hattie's sudden appearance at the door.

"Up already? Good morning, Hattie. How'd you sleep?" Leela's spirits were high and she managed to sound civil in spite of Hattie's behavior last night. Her visits only brought turmoil and guilt, keeping the whole family upset.

"I didn't sleep well at all. Never do outside my own place." She came closer to Leela. "I'll be leaving with T.J. Said he'd take me on back to McLennan County, even though it's not on his way." She rubbed her hands together nervously and licked her lips. "Guess it's best I head on home."

Leela did not respond, relieved that T.J. was taking Hattie away.

"You know, Leela. Having Carey on the place while your husband's on the road don't look so proper to most folks."

Leela spun around and glared at Hattie. "What folks?"

"Decent folks," Hattie said sharply.

"Just what are you trying to say?" My God, Leela thought, this woman never stops with her meddling, hateful talk.

"You might be fooling T.J., but I seen how you look at my Carey. It's as clear as water in the barrel after a heavy rain; you playing up to Carey and that's why he's staying. You and your dirty ways is what's keeping Carey from coming on back home with me."

"My dirty ways?" Leela's voice rose in indignation. "You've got the dirtiest, most twisted mind of anyone I ever met. You better watch your mouth, Hattie. You don't have any reason to start such nasty talk." Leela plunged her hands into her bowl of biscuit dough to keep from slapping the old woman's face. "It's a good thing T.J.'s taking you away. If he wasn't I'd run you off myself."

"You wouldn't dare. T.J. wants me here."

"I don't see him begging you to stay!" Leela threw back, not caring if her words woke both T.J. and Carey. "Keep your nose out of my affairs and don't come back here unless you're going to act like you've got some sense."

"I got enough sense to see there's trouble brewing right under my son's roof, but you got him so blinded he can't see what's going on."

"How dare you!" All of a sudden, Leela started to shake: a weakness filtered from her throat, into her stomach, down her legs. She leaned against the table as she kneaded the dough. "I took care of my husband's brother. I'd do as much for a stranger. You can't make more of it than what it is."

"Well, if Carey's all healed up, why's he still here?" A smirk creased Hattie's fat jowls.

"You'd better not go off spreading lies about me," Leela threatened, shaking a long-handled spoon at her mother-in-law. "If you do, I'll make sure you never set foot on this place again."

"What makes you think you can do that?" Hattie scowled, not liking this back talk at all.

"Just try me, Hattie. You'll see." Leela smiled inwardly, realizing that she could, indeed, influence both T.J. and Carey to keep Hattie away if she set her mind to it. "Don't you dare go flapping that evil, drunken tongue of yours." Leela threw down the spoon, letting it clatter to the floor, then grabbed Hattie by the arm, smearing biscuit dough onto the shocked woman's white chenille robe.

Hattie pulled back. Leela gripped the trembling figure more tightly.

"If you try to ruin my marriage with that foul drunken tongue," Leela warned through clenched teeth, "I'll fix things so you wind up with no family at all."

The usually dreary farmhouse rang with laughter, song, and animated conversation for the seven days T.J. was gone. Never had Leela felt so alive and engaged—so attractive in the eyes of a man.

Carey talked and talked and talked. He told her more than she really wanted to know about his past, yet she never asked him to stop. After living with T.J.'s maddening silence for so long, Leela thrilled at the chance to sit and have a conversation with someone who had something interesting to say.

Carey never tried to smooth out the wrinkles in his past. In fact, Leela suspected at times he tried to enhance them. She thrilled to his adventuresome spirit, excited by the idea of his making his way on his wits and his charm. He delighted in bragging about his flamboyant, sometimes comical escapades—like the time he hopped a train pulling out of Fort Worth and landed in a car filled with slimy fat hogs, or the black silk hat he coveted and won from a fellow gambler, only to learn the man had lice; and he laughed with relish while recalling for Leela the wild poker games carried on behind Ebenezer Missionary Church, right under the preacher's nose. His stories, dramatically re-created for Leela's amusement, left her reeling with laughter or sitting in shock, her mouth hanging open, wondering if Carey's yarns were pure fantasy, spun only to make her smile.

With time on his hands and no responsibilities, Carey sat around drawing pictures of flowers, animals, even the dark storm clouds which gathered every evening. With gentle patience, he held Kenny's tiny fingers around a stick of charcoal and showed the boy how to make his letters.

As the lush hot days of late July rolled past, Carey gave Leela reason to reflect on the dull isolation of her life at Rioluces and stirred an alarming restlessness in her soul.

"Come sit with me while I sketch," Carey said, gathering up his brittle sticks of charcoal from the table. He flashed his most persuasive smile at Leela, as if taunting her to go off with him. "I'm going to make a drawing of the farm. I've been thinking of doing that ever since I got here." He put a sheaf of rolled paper under his arm and picked up an earthenware jug of grape wine. "This will give me inspiration," he remarked, a lighthearted lilt to his words. "Come on, Leela, sit with me. Up in the loft I can get a real good view of the place." He waited for her to say something. "I'm going to make this drawing just for you."

Leela set aside the bowl of potatoes she was peeling and reached down to pull Kenny onto her lap. "No, Carey. You go on," Leela said, her voice husky and low with anxiety. "I've got things right here to keep me busy."

Shrugging his shoulders, Carey left, humming some dance hall ditty to himself as he took his time crossing the yard toward the barn.

Leela moved to the window, her eyes following the handsome man, her heart racing inside her chest, an inner voice telling her to stay where she was. But as soon as Kenny nodded off against her breast, Leela put the boy down in his narrow iron bed and started off across the dusty barnyard without looking back.

From their position high above the property, they sipped warm red wine from heavy tin cups, exhilarated by the sight of the land unfolding in shimmering green rows of cotton, corn and Black Diamond melons as far as they could see. Carey positioned himself on a low bale of hay at the huge loft opening and propped his sketch paper on his knee. Leela stood behind him, fixated on Carey's slim, delicate fingers curled around the small black stick, captivated by the effortless way he brought Rioluces to life.

As Carey concentrated on his drawing, Leela relaxed and sat nearby, absorbing the sun on her face, the peace of the moment. She could feel the wine settling warmly all through her body, enfolding her in a tranquil, languid web. They sat in comfortable silence for nearly an hour until a noisy blue jay fluttering around in the pecan tree shattered the quiet afternoon.

"I'll bet you could make a living at that," Leela remarked as Carey held up the finished picture for her to see.

"Maybe so," Carey answered, his voice vague and soft, "if that's what I wanted to do."

Leela reached to take the drawing. Carey placed his hand on her wrist. His flesh seared hers, sending shivers down Leela's arms. She swallowed hard, raising her eyes to caress his face. As he rose up in front of her, the drawing fluttered to the floor. As he gently pulled her to her feet and guided her into the shadowy space at the back of the loft, she let him put his hand on her waist. And when he pressed her back against the musty-smelling boards, all splintered and raw, thick with spidery webs, she lifted her chin and accepted his lips, which he placed ever so softly over hers.

When Carey released her mouth from his, he kept his lips very near Leela's cheek. She closed her eyes, hoping to disguise her smoldering desire. But the urgent probing of his fingers as they skimmed down the front of Leela's blouse ignited a passion within her that burst to the surface and nearly brought tears to her eyes.

Carey kissed her with a hunger that bordered on roughness as he peeled back the thin gauzy fabric of her blouse, freeing her full bronze breasts. In delicate strokes, he caressed and lovingly fondled the firm warm flesh beneath his palms. Leela's eyes fluttered open. She slumped against the weathered, hard boards, her body trembling, her hands now stripping Carey's damp shirt from his shoulders.

Naked to the waist, silky golden skin moist with perfumed desire, Leela arched her back and gave herself over to Carey's embrace. Now his kisses came in deliberate slowness, moving sweetly, in agonizing titillation from her forehead, across the space beneath her chin, over her sloping shoulders, to her hardened nipples pressing up against his chest.

Leela laced her fingers through Carey's wavy hair to bring him closer to her bosom and sighed at the magical sensation of his touch in this frightful yet wondrous surrender.

"I want you, Leela." Carey moved one hand to the small of her back and pulled her forward until they were welded together. "I've wanted you since the first time I saw you." His words were tormented, his expression sincere. "You want me, too. Don't you?"

Leela had no answer.

"You must want me, Leela. I know you do."

"I feel . . ." She broke off, turning her head away, unable to put her feelings into words, not really sure what she wanted to say. Her mind whirled as she confronted what burned deep inside. Yes, her body ached to surrender to Carey's thrilling touch. Yes, her arms longed to wrap themselves forever around his warm, smooth shoulders. But the inner voice that had plagued her for days kept telling her she'd better be careful.

"Wanting you and having you . . . how can I . . . ?" Leela gripped Carey's shoulders with both hands and searched his face for an answer. "It's impossible to justify this, Carey. Impossible."

He put a finger to her lips, silencing her fears, and held Leela tightly with one arm. Their eyes remained locked on one another as Carey traced the outline of her mouth with steady fingers. Then he lifted her chin very gently and covered her face with tender kisses.

"Come away with me," he said suddenly, as if reaching for her answer. "Leave this backwoods patch of dirt and my sanctimonious brother. Come with me. We'll see the world together, get out of this godforsaken place. We can be free of people judging us, badgering us, telling us what to do."

Leela moved back slightly, trying to gather her thoughts. "I have a child. This is my home. It's not so easy . . ." Her words stopped at the sound of footsteps entering the barn. Her eyes widened in horror and she placed her fingertips to her mouth.

A puzzled scowl darkened Carey's boyish face. Quickly, he signaled Leela to stay put, stay silent. They remained frozen in their embrace, listening to heavy boots mount the ladder leading to the loft, the crunch of dry brittle straw under plodding deliberate steps, the sound of heavy, rasping breathing growing louder every second.

In a panic Leela pushed Carey away and bent down, groping for her blouse. When she straightened up, she found herself staring into the tormented eyes of T.J. Wilder, standing tall and straight, shoulders pulled back in taut indignation, holding his long-barreled rifle firmly in one hand. He looked from Leela to Carey, squinted his eyes nearly closed, then positioned the gun and took aim at his brother.

"I ain't taking this gun off your back 'til I see you disappear into the woods. And if you ever set foot on my land again, I'll kill you, Carey. I swear I will."

Leela stood at her parlor window and watched the sun go down, hours after Carey had disappeared down the road. Engulfed by shameful guilt, she dabbed at her swollen red eyes with a pink lace handkerchief and fought the wave of nausea sweeping through her stomach.

T.J. and Carey are finished, Leela thought, anguished that the ugly confrontation had shattered the tenuous relationship forged between the brothers. I've driven a deadly spike through the heart of my marriage, she lamented, but if T.J. doesn't turn me out, I'll dedicate my life to easing this pain I've caused. I love my husband. I love my son. I want nothing more than to stay here with my family and I will live on Rioluces forever.

Chapter Eleven

By noon, the sun could not rise any higher. It centered itself in a shapeless mass of white-hot rods, shooting out from the core of a shimmering pool of light. Leela tilted her face heavenward, letting scorching rays of sunshine burn deeply into her skin. Through narrow slits, she squinted in anger at the cloudless blue sky, cursing another day without rain.

Through the shade of her circular straw hat, Leela surveyed her land where acre after acre of knee-high vines curled in thick, sultry patches. Not a hint of moisture dampened the hard crust covering one hundred and sixty acres planted with Black Diamond melons.

Two weeks after the Fourth of July, six weeks without rain, the parched Texas landscape stretched its thick dark skin over the northern half of Limestone County in perverse acceptance of the harsh sunlight cutting to its core. So accustomed was this land to such abuse, it no longer threw up its lush, protective prairie grass, allowing determined farmers to clear narrow spaces, plow larger patches, and work the land until it bloomed white with cotton or shimmered green with corn, beans, squash or melons. Crops grew but withered in the sun, waiting for the rains to fall.

Today, shiny green magnolias, broad leaves upright and stiff, stood in bold defiance of the sun's constant glare. Oaks, elms, and even the hardy chinaberry trees, starving for water, dropped their leaves as if it were November, and the shriveled foliage lay exactly where it fell, undisturbed by the absence of wind and rain that had hung over the farm for nearly two months.

At four o'clock each afternoon, dark clouds filtered in from South Texas and piled up across the horizon in gray puffy masses heavy with water. When thunder shattered the silence and lightning streaked in jagged flashes to the ground, the cattle huddled in nervous clusters under twisted, knotty mesquite trees. Leela waited for the sky to crack open and drench the arid land. But rain never came. Not even a cooling wind. The dark clouds simply drifted on, floating away in stringy disappointment to gather in false anticipation in the next county.

Leaning on her hoe, Leela stared at the backside of her house. Once gleaming military blue, the frame dwelling now stood weathered and gray, clutching a bed of gravel infused with dandelions and Queen Anne's lace. The sprawling place begged for attention.

Leela's eyes traveled upward to a large open window centered in the back of the second story.

Today she couldn't see T.J., but she knew he was there: watching her, following her every move, waiting for her to come up to his room. The sickness that now ate away at his lungs kept him trapped like a rabbit in a too-small cage. Some days, while working in the fields, she saw her husband clearly, his face glowing yellow against the backdrop of his darkened room, his dark, piercing eyes focused on her. But today he hid his face in the shadows, and Leela was glad she could not see him.

He's been watching me for seven years, she thought, attacking the hard soil with her hoe. Just as I have been watching him, with no words to overcome the shame I brought.

Leela scratched around the melon vines and let her thoughts go back to the day Carey disappeared down the road. T.J.'s failure to curse her, accuse her, or even speak of her disgraceful behavior had been the condemnation she could hardly endure. But they had a child to raise, a farm to manage, and as the years passed, they settled into the routine of life on Rioluces, the shameful incident buried deeply in the fabric of their marriage.

Moving steadily among the tangle of vines, Leela worried that the crop might already be lost. Two more weeks of dry weather, she knew, would bring all her work to naught. T.J.'s illness had put the burden of bringing in the melons on her.

As the intense July heat filtered into her bones, Leela unexpectedly thought of Grandma Ekiti; her jet black face, glowing with a regal pride that bordered on arrogance, jolted into the center of Leela's troubled thoughts. She could almost hear her grandmother's voice telling African tales of sacrifice and ritual, delivered in reverent hushed tones under an incandescent moon, or chanted in breathless urgency while wind and rain pounded at their door. Such stories had filled Leela's childhood with vivid images of strong dark women who worked the melon fields of her grandmother's native village in the northernmost tip of Cameroon.

According to the ancient storyteller, those proud tillers of the soil with their shiny oiled torsos stripped naked to the waist and long slender necks draped with colorful beads and feathers had so pleased the sun god that he had gifted their fields with torrents of water and blessed their village with the sweetest fruit in the region. Those yearly offerings of beautiful images, which the sun god coveted and treasured, had slaked his thirst and given him reason to relent and let the rain god take over for a spell. When black clouds split open and water drenched the arid land, the huge green melons grew fatter and juicier, were coveted like treasure and ferreted from the fields by nomadic tribes passing down from Chad and Niger on their way to the coastline for trade.

While other villages withered and died without rainfall, Grandma Ekiti's prospered as no other in the region, and the men of Cameroon grew to worship these women, true saviors of their settlement on the high grassy plain.

He must be looking down on me, Leela thought of her grandmother's sun god. And for the first time in many, many years, Leela was filled with the need to connect with the mysterious woman who raised her. As a very young girl she had worshipped with Grandma Ekiti, mouthing the rhythmic chants to keep evil spirits away.

"I need your help, Grandma," she said boldly, her face turned to the sky. "Please help me save my crop!"

And at that moment, Leela decided to woo the rain god onto Rioluces with a token offering to end the sun god's ceaseless vigil, an earthly gift the god could take behind gray clouds to savor. The melon crop must survive.

Stepping more deeply into the profusion of pale fleshy vines and spiky green leaves that blanketed the land beneath her feet, she raised her eyes heavenward. And as a deep, throaty laugh rumbled up from her belly, Leela pushed her shoulders through the neck of her orange camisole, crushing the damp cotton blouse into a ball at her waist.

Sunshine washed over her high round breasts, stinging dark nipples with tiny pricks of fire, caressing the flesh to bring forth tiny beads of perspiration. Leaning back, Leela began to laugh.

"I have no pretty feathers to tempt you, or colorful beads to make you smile." She offered herself to the expansive blue sky, challenging the glare of the punishing sphere. "This is all I have to give you, Sun God. Take this glimpse of earthly pleasure and go away. Go sit behind the swollen rain clouds to gather strength for time of harvest, and let the rain god visit my land for at least three days. I do not want to see your shining face tomorrow."

Leela stood laughing into the distance, voice tumbling through still, hot air, feeling as if her grandmother's arms were clasped around her once more. But the sun god did not move. Did not even blink his one burning eye, only continued to stare at the lovely, bare-chested woman laughing in the field. And all around her, lying on the parched earth, shaded by their own leafy umbrellas, swelling in the torrid sunlight, the Black Diamonds continued to suck every drop of moisture from between the grains of dirt, to hide the precious water away, to grow darker, sweeter, and heavier as the rainless days slipped by. Leela hoped these hardy vines, warriors of African ancestry, could feed off themselves until the rains finally came.

Tucking away memories of Grandma Ekiti, Leela shrugged her sweat-drenched camisole back over her shoulders. Perspiration streamed from her temples, dripped down her flaming cheeks and soaked the front of her thin cotton shirt. The fabric clung to her full breasts like a second skin. She wiped a dusty hand across her neck, streaking mud into the sweat glistening on her torso, then slipped the hem of her long cotton skirt into the waistband and returned to work. Soon red blotches spread over the tender swell of Leela's thigh and the sun toasted her skin a darker hue.

Using short choppy movements, Leela shattered clumps of earth, showering dirt to all sides of the field. A fine brown mist glazed the vines and clattered off the swollen fruit. She tasted sand in the back of her throat and grimaced as she swallowed it. A black garden snake slithered toward shade. Smiling at this lucky sign, Leela moved quickly. With her long-handled hoe, she searched, poked, and prodded, lifting spiky green leaves to expose pale, bloated bellies until uncovering the slithering reptile. Rearing back, she brought her sharp tool down with a thud. With steady hands Leela scooped up the headless snake and quickly skewered its bleeding body on the limb of a nearby tallowwood. Lifting a solemn face toward the sky, Leela summoned the words of her grandmother's ritual and called out to the bold yellow globe. "With this offering, Sun God, the rains must come. Bring water to this land."

Leela stood trembling for a moment, letting the spiritual fusion ebb away. Turning slowly from the bloody snake, she looked past the sagging split-rail fences surrounding the farm to the single dirt road leading up to the house. A wild summer's growth of juniper vines and hawthorn bushes, undaunted by near drought, threatened to close off the road with a tangled, creeping mass of vegetation.

The run-down condition of Rioluces saddened Leela. Less than two years ago the split rails had stood firm and that white arched gate, topped with the letter R, had glistened so brightly in the sun, Leela had often shaded her eyes against its reflection. Now it was rusted brown like the earth. The gravel drive, once lined with spikes of red summer salvia, had disappeared completely beneath a blanket of weeds. The farm had deteriorated quickly after T.J. fell ill, and Leela worried that her husband might never leave his room upstairs, might never walk his land again.

The drone of a thousand cicadas wrapped their chirping melody around Leela. The afternoon sun peaked in its fury, pressing the land to absorb its wrath.

Down the road a thin stream of dust rose and drifted over trees surrounding the lane to the farm. Leela watched intently, leaning forward to gauge her visitor's distance.

As the whirring motor of an automobile cut the air, Leela laid her hoe aside, keeping one eye on the road.

During the past year and a half, visitors had rarely come to Rioluces. Leela knew the unpaved road leading from nearby Mexia to her isolated farm on the northern edge of the county snaked and coiled its way through sagebrush, thick mesquite and low-hanging Spanish moss. T.J. had just begun to clear and grade that last quarter-mile stretch from the main road up to the house when he collapsed at the highway, convulsed with fever. Kenny had found him on the ground, hardly breathing, staring vacantly into a stand of pines. Together, they had managed to get T.J. home and into bed before sending Pully Simpson, the sharecropping boy from across Cedar Creek, to fetch Dr. White.

Consumption, the doctor had diagnosed. The white plague. And with those words, T.J. Wilder's world was funneled into that tiny room upstairs and Leela's world split wide open, leaving her alone to manage three hundred forty acres of cotton, corn and melons.

Though panicked at the prospect of taking charge of the farm and terrified of watching her husband waste away before her eyes, Leela had plunged into the farmer's cycle to salvage the crops and keep the farm alive. During ten years of marriage, T.J. had been a devoted, hardworking provider. Now it fell to her to scratch their living from the stubborn land.

The sweet perfume of magnolia blossoms floated over the fields, and Leela inhaled deeply as a brand-new Model T Ford chugged through the gate.

"Wesley Sparks." Leela spat the words into the sandy field as a knot formed in her stomach. What the hell did he want? she wondered, quickly unhitching the hem of her skirt, letting the bright cotton fall in wide folds over her too-warm thighs. She entered the front yard as the square-topped Ford ground to a halt at the foot of her steep limestone steps.

The balding man who stepped gingerly from his car onto Rioluces did not look up, but kept his eyes downcast as he fiddled with the door handle. Leela glared at Wesley Sparks, smelling the newness of his car, the strong scent of leather and shiny chrome, new rubber melting in the raw Texas sun.

"That's some drive out here, ain't it, Mrs. Wilder? Never thought it'd take so long, even in this here new car. Somethin' ain't it? It'll go fifty miles an hour, on a good road that is." Sparks pulled a stained handkerchief from the pocket of his dark-vested suit and wiped the balding top of his pink head.

Leela said nothing, watching as the fat white man wiped dust from his sleeves and closed the car door.

"I'm glad to find you here," he went on, raising his watery blue eyes to hers as he shoved the handkerchief back into his pocket.

"What can I do for you, Mr. Sparks?" Leela forced herself to sound calm, cordial.

"Well, I just hated to have to come all the way out here, Mrs. Wilder, but there's been a few changes at the bank and . . ." he stammered and looked away. "Well, the arrangements we made with your husband last year . . . well, uh, they just won't do anymore."

"What do you mean, they won't do?" The knot in Leela's stomach seemed to grow. She could not speak. She stared directly at the man and waited tensely for his answer.

"As I said, there've been some changes at the bank." He glanced nervously past Leela. "Is Mr. Wilder home?"

"What kind of changes?" Leela asked, ignoring the question. "We've been paying you fine for years. What changes?"

Sparks reached back into his open car and took out a thick brown envelope. He fanned himself with the heavy packet as he moved toward the porch.

"Reckon I could sit down? Sure is a hot one, ain't it?"

Leela walked deeper into the yard as Sparks, wheezing for air, settled his huge body in the middle of the white stone slab. He opened the envelope with short, pudgy fingers.

"Is Mr. Wilder here?" he asked again.

Leela crossed her arms, looking down on the top of the man's shiny head. Her straw hat shaded her face, but the sun deeply burned the back of her neck.

"He's here, but he's not well."

"Sorry to hear that. But if he could just come look over these papers, quickly. He needs to know what this means."

"He's too ill," Leela said curtly. She was getting scared, but she wasn't about to upset T.J.

"Well, all right. I guess I can explain this to you." Sparks shrugged his shoulders and opened the square envelope.

"Five years ago, your husband borrowed fifteen thousand dollars against the two hundred acres he already owned and bought up another one hundred forty. I was willing to pledge the money against cotton, corn and melons, knowing your husband's reputation for the kind of crops he's been growing out here for years." The banker halted, glanced around, then stood to look out over the fields. "I see he didn't put in cotton this season."

"No. Only melons and corn since he's been sick."

"Well," the banker continued, "he's paid back twelve thousand . . . sometimes a little late, but still, it's been paid." He cleared his throat with a loud cough. "Now, this year's payment of three thousand dollars was due in January and, Mrs. Wilder, here we are in July with the payment still due." He peered up at her from under his wire-framed glasses.

"We arranged to pay in September. Don't you remember? After the melons are shipped out." Leela did not understand what the problem was. She distinctly remembered Wesley Sparks arranging for T.J. to pay in the fall. He had stood right here on this same porch last year and agreed to that. The Black Diamonds would get to market, Leela would make sure.

"I've been patient, Mrs. Wilder, but . . . I'm afraid we can't handle the note that way. The payment is due sooner."

"How much sooner?"

"I couldn't wait much more than thirty days."

Leela pulled off her straw hat, shaking out a mass of blazing curls that fanned out in a wedge from her face. An intense heat that did not radiate from the sun filled her up and burned her face. Gritting her teeth, Leela walked to stand within a foot of the fat man filling her porch steps.

"Just what are you saying, Mr. Sparks?"

The banker leaned back as Leela came closer and found himself looking up through the space between Leela's protruding breasts. Flustered, he pushed his buttocks up onto the next step in an effort to meet Leela eye to eye.

"If it were just up to me, now, there wouldn't be any problem," he started. "I've known and respected Mr. Wilder for a long time." Sweat suddenly beaded on the top of his sunburned head.

"But it's not up to you?" Leela asked. Here we go again, she thought, throwing blame all over somebody else. "Didn't you make the loan to my husband?" Leela's mouth turned down at the corners and her high cheekbones flamed with anger. "Didn't you agree on the way to repay the money?"

"Yes, I did, at the time. You're right. But the review committee . . ." He tried to stand, thought better of it and sat back down on the top step. "The review committee at the bank is demanding the note be paid off as soon as possible. I can only give you thirty days." When he finished speaking, his lips peeled away from tobacco-stained teeth. "And that's stretching it, Mrs. Wilder."

Leela stepped back. "You see those melons layin' out there in the field?" She swung her arm in a wide arc and glared at Sparks. "There's your three thousand dollars. Layin' in the sun . . . about to turn into dust. And we haven't had rain in over six weeks. The harvest can't start for at least two more."

"Better harvest sooner than that," the banker pressed.

"That's impossible," Leela threw back, no longer intimidated by this man's threat. "You don't treat Black Diamonds just any kind of way. They need more time to mature and a lot of rain. Then we'll cut 'em off the vine. They have to be shipped, money collected . . ."

"Say what you want," Sparks interrupted, his voice starting to rise. "Do whatever you want to, I don't care. But the payment is still past due, and if you don't meet the bank's deadline, you can just hand over the land." With great effort Sparks stood, peeping down into the front of Leela's camisole.

Leela propped her battered straw hat against her hip. "What's this really all about, Mr. Sparks? Seems kind of strange, all of a sudden the Mexia Community Bank needs our money. What's going on down there?"

A dirty gray tomcat crawled out from under the house and leapt onto the running board of the shiny new car.

"Shoo. Shoo. Get offa my car!" The banker jumped off the steps and fanned at the cat with the thick brown envelope, frowning as the small animal fled down the road into thorny tangled bushes.

Sparks opened his car door and held on to it as he spoke. "Guess you don't hear things so fast out here."

"What kind of things?"

"All the talk about oil. Got everybody in town land-happy." He removed his jacket, stained dark with sweat under the arms, and threw it over the front seat. "Now, I think that's the real truth, Mrs. Wilder. Land around here's being talked about. The bank wants a clear title to this place or a paid-up note. That's just the way it is at this time."

Leela sucked her full bottom lip between her teeth as she thought about his prediction. So those old tales were surfacing again. Rioluces: River of Lights, the Spanish settlers had once called this land. There wasn't really any river on the place, just Cedar Creek, which did run full after a heavy rain, and the earth no longer oozed that greenish black water the early settlers had skimmed to burn for light and warmth. Tall cattails, swamp cane, and gnarled scrub oak did flourish along the creek bed, their twisted limbs creating dark shady places and swampy pools of marsh land which Leela knew T.J. had never ventured into.

At the point where the creek tapered off into tall pines a ledge of white limestone jutted out above the water. Kenny played there, lying flat on his stomach atop the jagged flat rock, throwing pinecones and pecans into the swampy water, watching them sink slowly into the slimy black hole.

"A man from Oklahoma's puttin' down a test well three miles from here," Sparks continued. "The Rogers place, that's where the drilling is going on right now."

The Model T hissed as the radiator spewed water onto the ground where it settled in beads on the rocky, gravel drive. Leela stared at the fat white man, wondering if what he said was true.

"Folks been talking about oil in Limestone County for years," Leela finally said. "Nothing ever comes of it."

"I think this one's gonna be a strike," Sparks replied, his thin pinched nose twitching downward with each word as he eased himself into the car. His soft, protruding belly pressed against the steering wheel. "People have a lot of faith in this sink. Most figger something oughta show soon."

"So the Mexia Community Bank wants our land to look for oil."

"That's not what's going on here, Mrs. Wilder. The bank needs to be paid. Next month."

"I know what you're saying," Leela answered, walking to stand beside the open car window. "My husband's been on this land since he was a boy. He picked cotton here for fifty cents a day before he owned it. When he borrowed that money to expand this place, nobody wanted this jungle of a backwoods stretch." Leela threw her hat to the ground and anchored both fists on her hips. "So fast to make a loan, you were. So willing to tie up this land so you could snatch it back when you got ready." Leela measured her words as if her life depended on them. "Don't think for one minute, Mr. Sparks, that you're going to push us out of your way."

"That's not the case here, not at all. Your husband has a debt and he needs to pay it off. It's as simple as that. We need three thousand dollars or he'll forfeit the land. That's all."

"That's all!" Leela was furious. "You come all the way out here demanding that kind of money with the melons still layin' in the sun and you act like that's nothing? We need more time. There's no way to raise that kind of cash before the melons are shipped out."

"I understand your predicament, I do." The banker tried to sound sympathetic, but his flat, toneless voice chilled Leela in spite of the raging heat. Sparks slammed the car door and put his heavy arm out the window.

"Here's the call papers on this loan. You take 'em to your husband." He tossed the brown envelope into the dust at Leela's feet. "He's gotta pay up . . . or get off this land."

CHAPTER TWELVE

The screen door slammed shut behind Leela. Hurling the banker's papers across her parlor with an angry thrust, she hurried to the window, letting pages scatter over the dark brown carpet. She watched Wesley Sparks's shiny chrome bumpers reflect blinding patches of sunlight as he steamed and hissed his way toward the main road.

He's got a lot of nerve, Leela thought, grabbing the back of her sofa to steady herself. Coming out here with a demand like that. Treating me like I don't understand a thing. I don't need him pushing his greedy nose into my life right now. I've got a sick husband and a melon crop to worry about.

Sparks's devastating news sickened Leela, and suddenly she felt as if she'd been fooling herself, working the land and caring for her husband as if, sooner or later, everything would return to normal. The banker's visit had unsettled her, challenged her faith that the crop would survive. The tedious cycle of life on Rioluces had been fractured and broken, would never be the same.

It was awful enough to face each day not knowing if it might be T.J.'s last. And how dare the Mexia Community Bank threaten to strip them of their home, their future, the hard-earned legacy T.J. had created for their son. Leela followed the banker's car with narrowed eyes until dust rose thinly in the distance.

"Oil." Leela murmured the word aloud and her anger eased slightly as the reality of what might be at stake took hold. That's what this is really about, she thought. Oil. On Rioluces. With a test dig just a few miles down the road, Leela could feel the greedy edge to Sparks's threat and the heat of the land-grabbing fever of the Mexia Community Bank.

If there's oil on this farm, Leela thought grimly, it won't do a bit of good right now. I need three thousand dollars in less than thirty days. The Black Diamonds would be harvested, but there was packing and shipping time to consider, and with T.J. unable to get out on the road, the local buyers would have to come out to the farm to pick up their fruit. She needed at least ninety days to bring in the cash. Leela ran a shaking hand across her brow as the possibility of losing the farm sank in.

Trying not to panic, she wondered where she would go if T.J. died and the bank took the farm. Back to Aunt Effie, now widowed and alone? Into a small dark room where she'd have to raise her son by herself? Impossible, she thought bitterly. She'd never leave this farm. There must be a way to solve the issue with the bank.

Sighing, Leela rested her head against the windowpane and looked out across the sunlit acreage of Rioluces. Pressing her mouth into a gritty line of determination, Leela made up her mind not to let Wesley Sparks push her to cut the fruit too soon and peddle small, tasteless melons on the market. She'd make no profit at all, and T.J.'s reputation for the finest produce in the county would be destroyed.

A burst of trailing clematis shaded the wide front porch with purple shadows, mirroring the single square window. Leela placed her palm against the pane, the shiny glass surprisingly cool. She studied her muted reflection.

Pressing dry fingers to her red-brown cheeks, Leela stared. Her complexion now looked like mud. Texas mud. The same grainy brown dirt she had been scraping off the bottom of her shoes for all twenty-nine years of her life. The rich auburn underglow of her deep bronze skin was fading, eroded from hours of work in hot, parched fields and dulled with worry over what the future might bring. Leela ran a finger over her cracked, peeling lips. Not a very pretty sight, she thought.

She leaned closer to the mirrored window, trying to see the youthful bride who had settled on Rioluces nearly ten years ago, but without wanting to, she saw the misguided woman who had fallen for shallow compliments and nearly destroyed her marriage. Oh, yes, she admitted ruefully, I was much more beautiful then, but I was also very, very foolish to risk T.J.'s love.

The pain of her encounter with her husband's brother was never very far from the surface. But Leela had learned to live with it, keeping it submerged under a focused effort to regain T.J.'s respect. Now she gave him all the attention and care she could possibly manage, vowing to do everything possible to make his last days comfortable.

Leela stepped back from the window to clear away the memories and watched the harsh edges of her reflection melt away. Smoothing the folds of her cotton skirt across the slight swell of her stomach, she turned and glanced at the Rochester clock ticking softly over the fireplace.

It's been twenty-four hours with no change, Leela thought, making her way through the darkened room to the bottom of the stairs. She listened, gripping the banister fiercely as each grating, hollow gasp ripped through T.J. Wilder's infected lungs, filling the rooms below.

Pushing tired fingers through rumpled hair, Leela took a deep breath and headed toward the kitchen at the back of the house.

Splashes of sunlight streamed through high double-paned windows on two walls of the large warm room. Kenny sat at the heavy trestle table, pushing string beans and new potatoes around on a large china plate. When the child lifted his face to hers, Leela saw T.J.'s golden tan complexion and high flat cheekbones peering back. His perfect features tugged at her heart. His wide-spaced eyes, rimmed with dark feathered lashes, begged for answers. Suddenly, Leela wanted to pull her son onto her lap, cuddle him closely, kiss the top of his beautiful head and wrap him in the comfort she knew he needed now.

The questions were coming. Leela could feel them forming. They were coming now.

"Why'd you send for the preacher from town?" Kenny's forehead knotted in anxiety and his voice rose slightly with anger.

Leela went to stand behind Kenny and touched his brown curls.

"Who told you I sent for the preacher?" She was annoyed.

"Pully." Kenny glared at her. "I was in the barn this morning when he told me. Said Reverend Pearson is on his way." His voice cracked as the words rushed out. He threw down his fork and sat pouting.

Leela tried to hold Kenny's shoulders. "I thought it was time," she started.

"Time for what?" Kenny asked, voice shrill with fright. Swiftly, like a cat freeing itself from an unwanted caress, Kenny pushed back his chair and wrenched his shoulders from beneath Leela's hands. He faced her with eyes tormented by love, hardened by dreadful anticipation of what his mother might say.

"He's not any better, Kenny."

"But the doctor said the medicine . . ."

"Would help Pa's cough, let him rest easier, that's all," Leela finished.

"But he's better," Kenny insisted, as if he could make his mother believe. "Pa ate breakfast today. See?" He pointed to his father's half-eaten meal turning hard on a tray set atop the bleached pine sideboard. "See? He's eating again. I think he's getting better." Kenny's nervous chatter cut through Leela's heart.

She reached for Kenny, hoping she could hold him. He clutched her sleeve, his small fist gathering cloth into a hot, crumpled ball. Leela gazed down upon this golden miniature of her husband's face, shining back at her in sunlight, full of innocence and promise. Her hand covered his tight fist, and though he resisted, she pulled him into the folds of her skirt.

"Kenny, you must understand. The medicine helps Pa, but won't cure him. Dr. White said the consumption has done too much damage to Pa's lungs. It's too far advanced to cure. We can keep him comfortable, follow the doctor's instructions and sterilize everything . . ." Her calculated tone trailed off as she gave in to her own grief and fatigue. Tears gathered in her eyes and she blinked to push them aside. "I know this is hard, but we have to be strong."

Kenny quivered under her hands, sobs muffled in her thick cotton skirt. Leela put a hand under his chin and lifted his small face to hers. She slid her trembling fingers over his tan cheeks, wiping tears from beneath his large brown eyes.

"We have to be very strong. Both of us. It's going to be hard, but we must accept what Dr. White has said."

Kenny shoved his mother's hands from his face, knocking her arm against the table.

"That Pa is going to die?" The accusation was shrill. "Is that what you mean? That Pa is going to die? Today?" He pushed past Leela, headed for the back door.

"No, Kenny, I didn't mean . . ." But he stumbled angrily onto the porch. The screen rattled shut in Leela's face.

Kenny took all three steps in a leap and tore off across the dry yard, past the barn, and disappeared into the woods at the edge of the creek. Leela stood watching after him until dust settled over the barnyard.

It had taken her nine-year-old son to say the words: T.J. Wilder was dying from tuberculosis and, according to Dr. White, would be gone in a very short time.

Kenny's reaction did not surprise her. Leela had been dreading this moment, putting it out of her mind, out of their lives for as long as possible. On very bad days she prayed the earth would split open at her feet, create a deep, dark crevice and pull her away from the madness her life had become. On better days she focused on Kenny, and thanked God her marriage to T.J. Wilder had brought her such a blessing.

Kenny was hiding now, probably stretched out on the limestone ledge above the swampy creek. Throwing stones. Propelling his anger, fear, and disbelief to the bottom of the hole in a frenzy that would exhaust him.

Leela sighed aloud as she thought of her son's future. Kenny already knew as much about planting cotton and marketing melons as any farmer in the area. T.J. had taken his smart, curious son all over the state: loading and unloading railway cars filled with produce, buying and selling livestock, joking with the black farmers, doing very careful business with the white ones. At his young age, Leela knew from the questions he asked and the intense way Kenny watched his father, he understood the subtle differences of doing business with the whites, blacks, Mexicans, and Indians who populated the territory from Mexia to the Oklahoma border. Leela prayed Kenny would someday walk the land as its heir and owner with the same dedication and quiet determination as T.J. Wilder had done.

"He'll make it," Leela murmured to herself, relaxing taut muscles in her face as a smile involuntarily tugged at the corners of her mouth. She was proud of Kenny. He had an air of strength about him; carried himself like a freshly strung barbed-wire fence, all tight and shiny in the heat of summer but not so easy to touch. Leela nodded. It would take time, but Kenny would overcome the devastating loss of his father. Time would pass. He would mature and grow into the ownership of Rioluces, but could she hold on to the farm until Kenny could take over? Spiraling anxiety gripped her like a tightening coil.

Leela's eyes roamed the landscape. Beyond a slight rise in the land, uncultivated fields stretched to the horizon. Stragglers from the last cotton harvest dotted the fields, prompting memories of seasons when the land had bloomed fluffy white as far as she could see. Lines of empty drays, no longer needed to move the heavy loads, stood as skeletal reminders of the height of the picking season when the wagons had rolled off the farm in a continuous clatter, twenty-four hours a day.

Now it was all too quiet. The scorching sun had forced all living things into shady places; no cattle lingered in the pastures, chickens scattered themselves in the musty rafters of the barn, and Kenny's spotted hound slumbered in the shadows of a tallowwood tree, too drained to even lift his head when his young master sped past.

A feeling of desertion pervaded the farm. One by one, the help had left, moving on to steady work on other farms, in other towns. The slowdown had started when T.J. collapsed, and now Pully Simpson and his two brothers from across the creek were the only help remaining.

T.J.'s weak, brittle cough seeped through the floorboards and filtered into the kitchen. Leela turned slowly from the back door and walked toward the front of the house. She paused at the foot of the stairs, then stepped outside onto her shady porch.

From a distance, she easily recognized Reverend Pearson. The pastor of the Bethlehem Primitive Baptist Church in the nearby community of the Woodlands waved his heavy arms in half circles. His large bulky frame leaned precariously to one side.

Leela did not gesture back, but stepped down onto her white stone steps, twisting an embroidered handkerchief between two fingers, watching her visitor approach.

"Mornin', Sister Wilder," Reverend Pearson's words boomed up from the overgrown yard. He reined in his big dappled grays and brought his rubber-topped runabout to an abrupt halt. Yellow-brown dust blew up in Leela's face. The reverend mopped sweat from his ebony forehead and shook powdery dirt from his black frock coat.

"Good morning, Reverend Pearson," Leela replied in a voice she did not recognize. She had meant to sound in control. But her words rang thin and hollow, rising from a trembling place deep inside that threatened to start her whole body shaking.

Heaving his body over the wagon side, Reverend Pearson left the golden circle of July sunlight and mounted the steep white steps. Only then did he raise his eyes to hers. The solemn set to his face frightened her, unexpectedly drawing her closer to the ritual and ceremony which would mark the end of T.J.'s life.

As he approached, the preacher's shadow devoured Leela, pressed her back toward the screen with its smell of horseflesh and sunlight. He stopped before her and extended a hand. Leela took it, holding firmly. She longed to tap into his mysterious calm and ease the anxiety plaguing her today.

"Brother Wilder is passing through a most difficult hour." The black shadow rumbled and swayed from side to side. "You were right to send for me."

Leela stopped breathing and pressed her tongue thickly against the roof of her mouth to keep her face from quivering.

"Have courage, Sister Wilder," Reverend Pearson continued, squeezing her hand. "Have courage."

Together they entered the parlor.

Adjusting to the darkness, they stood awkwardly for a moment. The preacher removed his black felt hat, allowing tufts of tightly coiled white hair to spring from behind each ear.

Leela sat stiffly on a worn velvet piano bench and crossed her ankles, waiting as Reverend Pearson eased himself onto her horsehair sofa. He filled it completely.

"Thank you for coming all the way out here," Leela began, words sticking in her throat.

"I'm here to help you and Brother Wilder," he said, sliding his battered hat through thick fingers.

Leela noticed that the preacher's frayed shirt collar was stained yellow and soaking wet.

"We've stayed away from church so long," Leela blurted out.

"No need for talk like that, Sister Wilder," Reverend Pearson comforted, hunching his broad shoulders over his knees, looking down at his scuffed black boots. "The Lord has never left your side. He'll see you through this dark hour."

Leela crossed the room and knelt at the arm of the sofa, chest heaving with the effort not to cry. "Reverend Pearson, I'm so frightened."

Just as she hoped it would, his calm, strong voice began floating over her, soothing her, bringing her sobs to an end.

". . . and that's what you must believe, Sister Wilder," he finished. "Peace comes in time." The confident, rock-solid man of God clasped Leela on the shoulder in a fast grip, and together, they recited the Lord's Prayer.

In the silence which followed, Leela wiped her large brown eyes and Reverend Pearson pushed himself up from her sofa to make his way to the room at the top of the stairs. He entered without knocking.

T.J. Wilder used all the energy he could muster to pull himself upright in his bed. He would not meet the preacher lying on his back. Damn it, he thought, I'm not dead yet. It was true, consumption had leveled him. Humiliated him. Left him a useless stranger in his own home. His forty-year-old body throbbed with pain day and night. Shrunken and twisted, it had shifted into a hideous mutation of his former self. Unable to stop the rapid deterioration of his feverish flesh, T.J. had stopped raging in silence over his misfortune and now pressed his failing energy into composing the speech he intended to deliver to Reverend Pearson.

For the first time in his life he felt anxious to talk. And it might as well be the preacher who heard what he had to say.

Reverend Pearson quietly entered the stuffy room and sat in a chair at T.J. Wilder's bedside. The ailing man looked his visitor over closely, shook his hand weakly, then settled back on the pile of feather pillows propping him up.

"I ain't got much time, I know that, Reverend. And I ain't mad that my wife called you out here . . . kinda glad, really. I got a few words I need to say. Never was one to raise a fuss over things. Gotta just let some things work their way out. You know?"

Reverend Pearson nodded. "The Lord has you in the palm of his hand, Thomas Jacob. You have nothing to fear as you approach this dark valley."

"Don't mean no disrespect, Reverend, but I do have a few fears been worrying me lately."

"Tell me what's on your mind, Brother Wilder."

"You knew my half-brother, Carey Logan, didn't you?" T.J. asked bluntly.

"I knew of him," the minister replied.

"Thought you might, knowing how our momma's got so much kin 'round here." T.J. nodded slowly, as if assuring himself that talking to the preacher was, indeed, the right thing to do.

"I understand your half-brother left the county."

"That's right." T.J. steadied himself on one elbow. "You know why Carey left Texas?" His question was sharp and cutting, spit out on the edge of a searing slice of pain.

"His leaving could have been due to any number of reasons," the minister offered. "I heard rumors . . . I admit. But I'm sure you know better than anyone else the circumstances forcing your brother from Texas."

T.J. tilted his head back sharply, stared past the reverend, out the open window.

" 'Twas only one reason Carey took off and stayed away this long, Preacher. Wasn't about them charges Bird Dog Taylor brought against Carey over in Waco. They'd been dropped a long time ago. And Claude Varnet's spilled more corn liquor on the dirt floor of his barn than Carey ever coulda stole from him." T.J. coughed more blood into a soft cloth. "I gotta tell you this . . . It was over my wife . . . Leela . . . that's the reason he's been gone. And don't nobody but me know nothin' about it."

Reverend Pearson wiped perspiration from his upper lip and leaned closer to the dying man.

"More than two years after I'm married," T.J. started in, "here comes Carey, on the lam, his arm all cut up and bleeding. I told him he could stay a week, maybe two at the most. He stayed two months and charmed the good sense out of my woman. Had to pull a gun on him to get him off my place."

T.J. took several deep breaths and tugged the bleached sheets more closely around his thin frame. The sick man winced as a pain ripped through his chest. "See what I mean, Preacher? He's gonna show up. Soon as I'm gone. Mark my words, wait and see if he don't."

Reverend Pearson stood to clear his head and take in what T.J. had just told him. "I wouldn't stir up a lot of worry over that," he cautioned, trying to ease the agitated farmer. "I doubt Carey's interested in coming back here. It's been close to eight years, Brother Wilder. That's a long time to stay away."

T.J. shook his head. "Last I heard he was gamblin' in New Orleans at the Chalmette Hotel. I sent a letter out there six months ago. Never heard a word. I wrote him I was doing poorly, but warned him not to come back here, not even for my funeral. He's my blood, I know, but he's bad luck, too. He'd swindle my boy's future from under him in a second and lead his mother down some trail of promises that'll kill her."

Reverend Pearson paced back and forth in front of the open window. "Those are pretty strong words you're using against your brother," he said, anxious about the ugly frown now creasing T.J.'s face.

"You gotta promise me, Reverend. Don't let Carey Logan get

close to my wife and don't tell Miz Hattie what I said about him probably being down in New Orleans."

"That's no easy promise to make, Brother Wilder. Your wife's a grown woman. Not much I can say about how she lives her life once you've passed, and I don't like making promises that put me in a tight spot." Reverend Pearson did not want to become involved in this long-standing family feud.

"You'd do no good by telling my ma where Carey might be," T.J. countered. "She'd wind up building up her hopes that things would be different, but Carey ain't never gonna change. She's better off he's gone. She still don't believe he'd cut a man's throat to get what he wants and lie in court to keep it."

"You got legal papers on this place?" The clergyman changed the subject.

"Wesley Sparks is holding all my papers in the Mexia Community Bank safe. And I done writ it so Leela and my son's the ones to get this place. Old man Sparks is holdin' my papers 'til Leela settles with him . . . she knows what needs to be done. I hate to say it, Reverend, but I don't want Miz Hattie getting her meddlin' fingers on my land either . . . my momma's not much better a person than my brother, Carey."

T.J. frowned and squeezed his eyes shut for a minute, exhausted by the emotional confession with the minister. A single tear slipped down his cheek.

Reverend Pearson placed his large sweaty hand over T.J.'s. "Don't worry, Thomas Jacob," he said, anxious to end this conversation without making promises he knew he could not keep. "Miz Leela's a good woman. She's got enough sense to do what's right by the boy. I doubt she'd stand by and let a schemer like Carey bring the devil into her home."

T.J. nodded weakly and slumped down in his bed.

Feeling T.J. needed to be alone, the holy man stood up and clasped T.J. on the shoulder for a moment, murmuring the Twenty-third Psalm in a calming tone before he quietly left.

Leela raised expectant eyes toward the reverend as he lumbered down the frail staircase.

"Is Doc White coming back today?" he asked.

"He said he'd be back this evening, after a stop at Widow Harris's place." Leela was struck by the nervous timbre in the preacher's usually calm voice. The constant knot in Leela's stomach twisted and thickened.

"You better go sit with Brother Wilder until the doc gets here. I hate to say this, Sister Wilder, but I don't think there's much time left."

CHAPTER THIRTEEN

The sparsely furnished room smelled of disinfectant, of lye soap, and of a man who had lain too long in his sickbed. A single open window filled the better part of one wall and illuminated the stuffy cubicle, allowing T.J. a view of his farm. Warm air pressed down on his wasted figure lying with sheets stretched up to his chin. On the bedside table, close enough to touch, stood a silver framed wedding picture of T.J. and Leela. Fingerprints smeared the brown-tinted images and a thin film of tarnish darkened the filigreed frame. Leela picked it up, rubbed it briskly and held it for a moment, remembering the day as one of her happiest, but also as the day she first met Carey.

Raw guilt struck her once again. Almost eight years had passed, yet she felt as if she'd never be cleansed of his presence. Leela carefully set the picture next to a vase of wilting roses.

Stirring in the narrow bed, T.J. opened his eyes, now glassy brown with fever. Awful sunken places hollowed the flesh beneath his cheekbones and his once-handsome features had shifted into a skeletal mask. He looked nothing like the man Leela had married.

She reached over and touched T.J.'s hand, feeling heat rising from his bony fingers, fever throbbing in his burning palm.

"I hope you weren't upset that I asked Reverend Pearson to come out." Leela leaned over T.J. as she spoke.

"Naw," he said lowly, his voice a grating whisper. "If I ever needed prayin' over, guess now's the time." His gruff reply did not surprise her. Though her husband had chosen to hold on to his wife since that terrible afternoon in the barn, his tone and manner had grown more distant and surly over the years. It wasn't hatred Leela heard in his voice, but the kind of disappointment that changes a man forever.

"Reverend Pearson is sending for your mother." Leela's tone was tentative and probing. Maybe he doesn't want to see her, she thought, watching T.J. closely.

"Um hum," he nodded tiredly, accepting the preacher's decision. "And if Kenny ain't back by dusk," he suddenly started, "you send Pully after him. Don't need to be wanderin' off like that. I saw him runnin' toward the creek." T.J.'s voice was mean with pain. "There's a rattler's nest under those ledges. Told him to stay clear of that place."

The sick man reached for the rope pulley attached to his iron bed which allowed him to hoist himself upright and look out over the back of his farm. Leela knew he tried to keep up with all that happened on Rioluces and guessed he had seen her tempting Grandma Ekiti's sun god. He had probably enjoyed watching her, but would never say a word about it. When Leela moved to the far end of the bed, T.J.'s hand fell limply onto the sheet.

"Don't worry about Kenny," Leela started. "He's upset because Pully told him I sent for Reverend Pearson." She locked eyes with T.J. "He'll come around. This is hard on the boy."

She floundered. She had reluctantly accepted the doctor's prognosis but remained angry at the thought of being widowed. After all, she thought, what did Doc White really understand about her struggle? He had not suffered with T.J. as she had: massaging his chest night after night, his breathing so thick and slow she had to force air into lungs that rattled like dry bones clicking together. He hadn't stripped sheets off the bed four times in one night, so heavy with sweat they dripped on the carpet. And how much blood had he wiped up? Spots of blood everywhere. Tiny droplets of her husband's life scattered all over the room. I can't and I won't give up until the end comes, Leela thought.

T.J. shifted on his bed to better see Leela. "Things have gone down bad, haven't they, Lee?"

"Not so bad," Leela said as she placed a stack of clean towels on the dresser, surprised he felt like talking. "Things still move along. The Simpson boys, especially Pully, really help me out. They need the work and say they're waiting for you to get well."

T.J. frowned. "Don't look like that's gonna happen anytime soon." He broke away from her gaze, turning to stare out the window.

"We're managing, T.J." Leela insisted.

"Too much for just you and three overgrown boys. Don't know what you're doin'. I kin see the melons cookin' in the sun. The rains ain't comin', Lee. Might as well cut 'em loose. Ain't gonna get any better'n they are right now."

"The weather's bound to break. We're giving it a week," Leela said, surprised at her own determination to see the melon crop through.

"You ain't got a week," T.J. wheezed. Coughing up blood between the words, he spat into a crumpled cloth. "Them Simpson boys don't know a thing about growing melons. Gonna make you lose the crop."

The cutting remark hurt, but Leela shrugged it off. Nothing was going to stop her from bringing in the melons and paying off the bank.

"Heard a car out there," he went on. " 'Bout noon, wasn't it?"

Leela should have known he'd hear that car. What else did he have to do except lie in that narrow iron bed and listen to the land, and the house, and the melons growing in the fields as he slipped farther and farther away from his world?

"Who'd come all the way out here in this heat?"

"Wesley Sparks," Leela said quickly. "Just wanted to see how the crop was coming along. Surprised we didn't plant cotton this season. Said the last payment's still due about the end of October."

She hated to lie, but there was no need to worry T.J. about this business with the bank. Not a thing he could do about it.

"We gotta make that note on time, too," T.J. said in his usual stern voice that always sounded like an admonishment. "The melons are worth close to three thousand right now if you get 'em off the vine. Wait too long, you and Pully gonna be pickin' up dust balls outta that field."

Leela threw back her head, her thick, wavy hair standing out wildly about her face. His challenge provoked her.

"Three thousand dollars to the bank and what's left to live on?" she wanted to know.

"We'll manage," T.J. countered. "There's winter greens and squash could be planted."

"I'm going to get enough from those melons to live off for a while," Leela vowed. "All this work, through spring and summer. For what? To bring in half a crop? I've seen you play this waiting game with the rains . . . for years. And you always said to me, 'I'll wait another week.' Didn't you?"

T.J. looked at her as if she were a stranger. Never had Leela spoken to him with such conviction, and never had she dared challenge him. She'd been a good wife, he had to admit, and he'd long ago forgiven her misguided infatuation with his brother. She cared for the boy and the house like she ought to, but the crops—they remained his business, even if he could no longer leave his bed. For more than thirty years he'd worked this land and now Leela had replaced him.

"You ain't been at this business of tendin' melons long enough to take that chance," he told Leela gruffly.

"Well, you always waited, and it always rained," Leela went on. "And you always brought the melons in at the highest price. I'm going to need a lot more than three thousand dollars out of those fields. You think I can't do it?" Her eyes flashed a dare.

"I dunno," T.J. said, rubbing his chest to ease the pain. "Just don't play it too close, Lee. Wesley Sparks . . . coming out here today . . . you pay him soon as the melons are sold." He gave his wife a troubled look. "Can't figger why he's so darn fired up about that note. I been doing business with old man Sparks for years. Never pressed me for money before."

Leela said nothing, turning back to the dresser to pick up a fresh towel, and avoided his eyes as she handed it to him.

"I been in this room the better part of a year now, and it don't look like I'm gonna get down those stairs again." T.J.'s voice was husky, strained. He floated away, shrinking into his sickness, speaking to her from within his pain. "Don't be late with Wesley Sparks's payment. I gave him my word on that loan, and my word's always been good for any deal I ever made. You settle right with him," he ordered. Leaning forward, he peered at Leela oddly. "All my papers are in Sparks's bank. You get him to give 'em to you when you pay him."

Leela watched her husband closely. He sank back onto his pillows with an exhausted moan and shut his eyes tightly, his glassy stare shuttered against her worry. Leela knew he would not sleep, only pull into himself as he often did to gather a little more strength.

Uncurling his long legs, T.J. pressed one foot against the iron bed rail. "Rioluces will be paid up soon. Finished . . ." His husky voice tapered off, and his sallow skin glowed yellow against bleached cotton sheets.

At these words, Leela flinched. I cannot let him down, she thought.

She remembered the day five years ago when T.J. had decided to borrow that fifteen thousand dollars from the Mexia Community Bank. She had laughed at him, openly and brazenly, thinking it a crazy notion. Just because Wesley Sparks had loaned him a couple of hundred dollars years ago was no reason to believe he'd come across with the kind of money T.J. needed then. But the self-assured farmer put on his blue serge suit, walked into the banker's richly paneled office and came out with a sheaf of papers that tied his land to the bank for the next five years. And now, with only one more payment to go, the title would be clear again, Rioluces finally theirs.

Leela crossed the room and placed one foot on the low sill that rose a few inches from the floor. A banded purple butterfly, wings erect, clung to the rusty screen, and Leela tapped at it, watching as the exquisite creature soared off over the porch, past the bushy chinaberry trees to light on her deep pink rosebush.

T.J.'s labored breathing rattled through the room and startled

Leela. His time is short, she thought. Too short to be burdened by threats and demands from the likes of Wesley Sparks.

"You worked hard for this place," Leela said, the words out before tears could stop them. She had to tell him now. She had to let him know how much he meant to her, even if he didn't want to hear it. They had avoided speaking of feelings for too many years and Leela sensed it was time for her to state what crowded her heart today.

"You worked yourself into this sickness." She knew he could hear her. "You gave yourself away for this land . . . for me and Kenny." A tear slipped over her cheek. "There was a time when I didn't appreciate you. A time when I ignored your faithful devotion and love. I am sorry, T.J. Truly sorry." She watched him squirm uncomfortably in his bed. "We've let this lay like a stone between us too long. I have to tell you now how much you mean to me."

T.J. ran his fingertips across his feverish brow. "Ain't no need for talk like that. 'Twas more my fault than yours. I should never have let Carey stay here. Never should have put you in his way."

Leela crossed the room and sat on the edge of the bed. "But T.J., I should have seen through his charm and flattery. I was the one to let you down and I'm sorry. Very sorry."

Lifting his hand he touched Leela's cheek. "You never let me down. Don't ever think that. You been the kind of woman I needed but never thought I'd have. Taking good care of me and the boy. You been a good wife, Leela. I ain't judged you by my brother's disrespecting me. Oh, no. That day I long since put to rest." His trembling hand stroked her sunburned skin. "But I feel I'm slipping away now, and I don't like what's happening to you. You can't go on doing the work of a man."

"Don't you worry about me," Leela said, wiping her nose, taking a deep breath. She smiled and took T.J.'s hand in hers. "I learned my lesson years ago. Nothing will keep me from doing what I can to hold on to our land, our home."

She hadn't meant to bring up the old, hurtful past, but there it was—out in the open after too many years.

She went on. "I've worried about you so long. Planting in the rain, harvesting with hands nearly frozen solid. Traveling all over the state when the sun was so hot even cows took to shade. You refused to take care of yourself, to listen to my concerns. You shut me out of your life. I felt so alone, so isolated . . ." She shook her head, unable to go on.

"I know, I know." He nodded. "But it was the only way I knew how to make a living. A decent living, you understand? I had to work hard, Lee. I had to." Each word took effort to pronounce. "You know that. I'da been just another poor, landless colored man if I hadn't worked so hard, and I made up my mind when my momma turned me out of her house that I'd never ask a man to feed me and no woman would ever tell me what to do."

Leela had never heard him speak with such emotion. "Yes, I understand." Her voice fell to a low whisper. For ten years she had labored in isolation with him, lived the dull plodding days and long empty nights with an absence of friends and companionship that almost drove her mad. She turned a tearstained face to him.

"Look at what all that backbreaking work did to you. To us." A painful lump lodged in Leela's throat, and she put both hands over her face and let angry tears roll forth.

At last she cried openly, shamelessly, disregarding the doctor's advice as she cradled her husband's shrunken head in her arms. Angular shoulder blades poked up through his nightshirt as she stroked his thin, bony back. His tears stained the front of her orange camisole . . . the only tears she ever saw him shed.

The Rochester clock chimed five.

"I know I put in the work of four men, every day of my life," T.J. muttered. "I was strong. I could do it. This is my land, the best-looking spread in the county." He stopped and struggled for more air. "But . . . I never planned on this," he growled, slumping back onto his feather pillow.

Leela wiped tears from her husband's sunken cheeks, then gently placed one hand on his quivering chest. She saw tiny spots of blood on his undershirt.

"Neither did I, T.J. Neither did I."

Before Hattie Wilder could make the trip from Waco to Rioluces to see her dying son, the emaciated farmer was leveled by a coughing spell so severe, it only ended when blood flowed swiftly from his infected lungs and spilled down his chin to settle in a thick dark pool in his lap. T.J. looked up at Leela through a veil of terror and apology, sending them both back to their beginnings. And the violent crush of his hand upon hers, as he resisted the journey he knew lay ahead, left purple bruises from Leela's fingertips to her wrist.

CHAPTER FOURTEEN

Two days later, on July 22, 1920, Thomas Jacob Wilder's skeletal body lay in an open coffin in the farmhouse parlor. Black farmers from around the county, Negro merchants from Mexia and Groesbeck, and what appeared to be a large contingent from the Bethlehem Primitive Baptist Church thronged to Rioluces. Buggies, wagons, hacks, horses, and even two brand-new Packards and a red Ford touring car pulled into the tangled yard and lined both sides of the narrow road. Solemn-faced men and women gathered on this steamy afternoon, deep in the wooded farmland of Central Texas, to say good-bye to one of their own.

Leela sat on a straight-backed chair pulled up close to the open casket and bravely accepted polite expressions of sympathy from people she hardly knew. Many of these strangers had cut deals with T.J. over truckloads of melons, swapped livestock with him to upgrade their herds, or borrowed lamp oil from him in the dead of winter.

Leela peered into the casket again, thankful for the peaceful, rested appearance on T.J.'s face, relieved that his yearlong struggle against the ever-present pain and the slow rotting of his body had finally ended.

Perspiration gathered in small beads on the sides of Leela's face, and her damp hair clung to the back of her neck. After more than two hours of the vigil, Leela's heavy black mourning suit, soaking wet from her armpits to her waist, had fused her to the chair. She half-heartedly swatted at an iridescent horsefly circling the steamy room, then looked over at Kenny, sitting glumly on the sofa.

Kenny had stayed to himself for the past two days, not speaking more than three audible words to his mother. The pain in his face today nearly brought tears to Leela's eyes.

Hattie Logan Wilder inched down the stairs and entered the parlor. Her tall hulking figure, wrapped in folds of black linen, dominated the room.

She's determined to make me out a liar, Leela suspected, thinking Hattie had most likely emptied drawers, searched the closets, and poked around under the bed for any piece of paper that might resemble a will. If the greedy old woman only knew the truth, Leela thought as she stared at Hattie in disgust. The Mexia Community Bank might soon own it all, and if there was a will among T.J.'s papers, Wesley Sparks would not turn it loose until the debt was paid off. But that was none of Hattie's business.

Leela stiffened as Hattie placed yellow, work-worn hands on either side of Kenny's face, pulling his small round head into the soft flesh of her perfumed bosom. At least she looks sober, Leela observed.

A cluster of women in pleated black skirts with lace-collared blouses broke away from the crowd and eased themselves into the kitchen. Hattie's trio of friends had work to do: a grieving family needed food.

The ladies rattled pots and pans as they fussed over the trays of cornbread, mounds of potatoes, and steaming bowls of rice and chicken. They talked lowly among themselves. Their voices crept along the baseboards, tumbled across the faded carpet, and reached Leela in ragged bits and pieces.

"Done lost both her sons now."

"Carey ain't dead. I heared he's livin' down on . . ."

"Been about eight years, Elvina. Sounds lost to me."

"Somebody oughta find him, get him back here for Miz Hattie's sake."

"Leela'd have no part of that. She run him off in the first place. You know that, Inez. Carey Logan left town 'cause he couldn't charm Leela inta hookin' up with him."

"I heard his brother run him off."

"Half-brother, Martha. They had different daddys."

"Yeah, and ain't a soul in the county knows who Carey's daddy was. Well, same difference. They was both Hattie's boys."

"And remember how much they looked alike? Even with all them years between 'em, they was two of the handsomest men I ever saw. But the white plague shore did T.J. in, didn't it? You see how thin and wasted he looks in that box?"

"I never believed Leela run Carey off. More'n likely T.J. run his half-brother out the county to keep him away from Leela."

"Naw, I don't think so, Inez. T.J. Wilder never would of pushed his own flesh and blood from here, not even over his wife."

"Well, I think Martha got it right. Leela Wilder knows more than she ever told."

"Pray for Sister Hattie. She be the one needing us now. I can understand how she's feeling. Maybe T.J.'s passin' gonna make Hattie and Leela get straight."

"Don't bank on it, Inez," Elvina Hopper began. "I been knowin' Hattie Logan since she lived in the country. Goes after what she wants. Raised that boy Carey to be just like her. And she's ragin' mad 'cause T.J. ain't left her nuthin'. That old woman's a fright to reckon with when she don't get what she thinks she's due." There was a short silence. "I ain't never tol' this but you remember that fire what almost destroyed the Crenshaw place? Well . . . Hattie told me she got so mad when old lady Crenshaw refused to pay her extra for Saturday ironing, she just walked out the house and deliberately left the flat iron smokin' hot in the laundry room. Burned two rooms plum to the ground. Lucky Miz Crenshaw didn't die from the smoke. Now would you tangle with someone like that? If Leela's smart, she'll give up a little piece of this place and settle with Hattie."

Leela froze, stunned at the vicious words coming from her kitchen. Her insides boiled with such force that a numbness flashed from her legs through her shoulders. She felt hollow. Shaken.

How dare they? she thought. Coming into my house with all that old gossip. And with T.J. lying cold in his casket right in front of them. I should have known this would happen, Leela chided herself. Letting these distant cousins of Hattie come over to "do the food" was a mistake.

". . . held her looks. Ain't even hit thirty yet," the voice from the kitchen continued. "Won't be long before she takes another husband. How else she gonna hold on to all this land?"

"You right about that, Elvina. She gonna be cozying up to some man soon. Spreading them long legs to catch him. She ain't gonna be able to work this place and keep it widout no man out here. Worked T.J. to the grave for all this, she ain't gonna let no time pass 'fore she gits another one to keep this place producing."

"You gotta give it to her, Inez. She held her looks. She be a catch for some lonesome farmer. Really. She be looking 'bout the same as I remember."

"Every man who wants a wife 'tween here and Waco gonna be callin'."

"Even them what don't want a wife."

A burst of muffled laughter followed.

Leela jumped to her feet. In her hurry to rise, she knocked over her chair and did not stop to set it straight as she charged down the darkened hallway toward her kitchen. Throwing open the slatted door, she stood facing the three women.

All conversation stopped.

"Get out of my kitchen." She struggled to control her voice.

"Why, Miz Leela. We was just settin' out the food," Inez replied, taking a pan of rolls from the oven.

"I won't need your help after all," Leela remarked sharply. "I want you all to leave my house."

Martha wiped her hands on the bottom of her tiny apron, then propped them on her protruding hips. "Miz Hattie asked us to do the food, Leela. She wanted her kinfolk here today. Help out, you know."

"Yes," Leela threw back. "Help out. I know how you help out . . . by starting vicious rumors, bringing up old lies. I can get along without that kind of help."

"I don't know what you talking about," Martha started.

"Hattie's gonna be real upset over this, Leela," Inez added.

"This is not Hattie Wilder's home," Leela shot back. "It's mine and I want you to leave."

The three women shifted eyes from one to the other, shrugged in resignation, then picked up their straw baskets from the kitchen table and headed toward the back door.

"Ain't no reason for you to act like this, Leela Wilder. Ain't no reason at all." Martha threw a red-and-white dish towel on the sideboard and scooped up a tray of fried chicken. "I'll just be takin' my chicken on back home, then."

Elvina came around the other angry ladies and positioned herself in front of Leela.

"You ought not treat us this way. We come out here 'cause Hattie wanted us to help out with her son's wake. I'm kin, too, you know. Hattie's my second cousin, once removed. We just being sisterly at this sorrowful time." Elvina snatched off her apron and shoved it into her purse. "I hope you treat Miz Hattie better'n you's treatin' us. If you don't . . . you could be real sorry. Mark my words. I can just feel the troubles coming your way. They's coming, Leela Wilder, they's coming."

Narrow blue-green clouds, glistening like shards of turquoise glass, streaked boldly across the horizon and partially hid the descending sun. From the porch, Leela watched the horse-drawn hearse from the McBay Funeral Home carry T.J.'s body through the rusted gates of Rioluces. A double team of white carriage horses slowly pulled the ornately carved wooden coach into dense pines rising between the farm and the main road.

A fitting way to leave his land, Leela mused. He deserved to go off in style—like the dignified man he was.

"Oh, T.J., I will miss you," she whispered into the calm, fragrant air. The ache in her throat spread into her chest. Leela bowed her head slightly and murmured, "Farewell."

The ceremonial gathering had exhausted her. Curiosity, Leela knew, had brought many of the mourners out, enticing them, in the middle of July, to pull on dark woolen suits and heavy black dresses trimmed with big lace collars and hitch up their buggies to make the dusty trip to Rioluces. Now everyone had left except Hattie.

Sinking onto a wicker settee, Leela closed her eyes and let her head fall back onto the rough canvas cushions, legs stretched out, tingling with fatigue.

I hope their curiosity was satisfied, she thought, knowing what many of the wives had come to find out. She smiled and absently ran her hands from her waist to her hips. She had not gained an ounce of fat or one wrinkle in her face in ten years of marriage, though her wardrobe of plain cotton dresses did nothing to flatter her appearance. Soon that would change. She fingered the fabric of her black mourning suit. Aunt Effie still had bolts of fine linen and sheer cotton she had put away for Leela. One day, she determined with a twinge of guilt, when the proper time had passed, she'd have Aunt Effie make her the kind of dresses she'd always wanted.

The screen door rattled open and Leela sat up quickly, feeling Hattie Wilder's anger smoldering against her back.

"Damn you, Leela. You had no cause to treat them so."

Leela did not turn around.

"Out of the kindness of their souls, they come all the way out here to do your food and you treat 'em like they done stole somethin'."

"They might as well have," Leela fumed, thinking it ironic that Hattie would bring up the subject of theft. Turning in her chair, Leela faced her mother-in-law.

"What kinda nonsense is that?" Hattie raged on. "Elvina's my cousin, she's kin to T.J.! After you told me to ask her to come do the food, you gotta go raisin' a fuss . . . throwin' my people out, embarrassin' me! If you didn't want them out here, you coulda told me not to ask them."

"You think I'd let those women tell lies about me in my own kitchen and do nothing?" Leela growled through clenched teeth. "Those harpies love twisting their tongues around things they know nothing about. They're crude, jealous women who don't care how I feel. I had hoped things would be different, Hattie. I had hoped T.J.'s death might smooth things out for us. Guess I was wrong." Leela clamped her lips together and frowned.

"I'm not a stupid woman, Leela. You think you got this all sewed up like you want it, don't you?" Hattie rubbed her hands together in jerky, rapid strokes, a habit Leela knew signaled agitation. "Well, things ain't so simple. You got no cause to do this." She locked and unlocked the fingers of both hands.

Leela bristled at the hateful words. "I don't know what you're talking about."

"It's bad enough you done treated my kin like trash, but telling me T.J. didn't leave a will! That my son didn't leave no writin' about this farm! I don't believe it. T.J. and me had our differences, but we'd just about patched things up. You didn't like that, did you? He'd come around. He told me he wanted things to be better between us, and I know he woulda left something for me. If it wasn't for me sending him here in the first place, he'da never owned it."

"Why do you think you deserve this land? You never set foot on this place until Kenny was born. Then all you ever did was press T.J. for money. Money to bail Carey out of jail. Money to buy a horse because Carey took yours and sold it. How can you believe he'd leave this farm to you?"

Hattie snorted loudly. "You just shut your mouth about Carey. Whatever went on between me and my son ain't none of your business." The old woman shrugged her wide shoulders and wiped perspiration from her top lip. "I'm gonna claim what's mine, Leela. Part of this place is mine!"

"You're talking crazy," Leela hissed, knowing the greedy woman could keep this tirade going for hours if not stopped. "I'm not going to start in with you about this. Not tonight. Not ever. I was T.J.'s wife and this farm is mine."

"Well, I ain't crazy and I ain't gonna stop till I get what's due me. And Carey, too. I'm gonna find Carey and get him back here. We'll show you who's telling the truth."

"Hattie, just leave things be. If T.J. had wanted you to have any part of this place, don't you think he would have discussed it with me . . . with you . . . with somebody? Anyway, this is Kenny's inheritance, not yours or mine."

"I ain't trying to deny the boy anything. But fair is fair and I'm gonna put what time's left to me inta finding my Carey. And now that it's come up, why don't you tell me what you know about Carey leaving Limestone County in the first place? Why not? T.J.'s dead. You can finally talk about it, Leela. After all these years, you can tell me what happened the day Carey ran off. You can tell me why my boy's been lost to me all these years. Tell me, Leela, where did Carey go?"

As much as Leela did not want to, she raised her voice and lied to her mother-in-law. "There's nothing I can tell you, Hattie. I don't know where Carey went or why he left."

Hattie pushed out her chest, drew her large shoulders up around her ears and craned her neck forward, placing her lips near Leela's face. "You're lying!" She spat the accusation. "And you been livin' with that lie for all these years."

"I'm telling you the truth," Leela shot back as she pushed past Hattie toward the door. The smell of grape wine rose up in Leela's face. "Your lips are flapping 'cause you've had too much to drink."

Hattie moved quickly to block Leela's path.

"Well, I'm not lying and I'm not drunk. You're gonna stay on this porch and hear me out. I was smart enough to ask some questions . . . and I know Carey was still here at the farm when T.J. got back off the road. Pitting T.J. against his brother . . . that was a terrible thing you did, Leela."

"Whoever told you that was lying. I did no such thing. And trying to blame me for your troubles is wasting your time. You just can't stand the fact that T.J. wouldn't let you into his life, let you come here to live, that he made out just fine when you tossed him aside to make room for your precious Carey. Isn't that the truth, Hattie?"

"No, it's not!" Hattie slammed her palm down hard against the back of the wicker chair as her voice rose to a thin wail. "I wouldn't be living in that shack of a house in Waco if you hadda let Carey alone." In her anguish, Hattie reached back into her past, gathering up tarnished dreams to fling at Leela. "You made T.J. run Carey out of town. Carey had plans to build himself a little house, a five-room house off Woodland Road with a room just for me. I woulda had a decent place to live," she hissed.

"How can you believe that? Carey didn't have two bits in his pocket when he came through here. And there's lots more I could tell you about your precious Carey, but what good would it do? You've closed your eyes to his wicked way of life, living for the day he shows up at your door. Carey Logan had no use for anyone he couldn't profit from—in one way or another. Only reason T.J. let him stay as long as he did was because Carey was cut so bad. And for your information, Carey was the one who begged T.J. and me not to let you know he stayed on here after he got well."

"That's a lie!"

"It's the truth! I don't remember him being so happy to see you when you showed up here that summer."

Hattie stepped closer. "If he said that, it was just because Bird Dog Taylor was looking for him. They'd had a big falling out, and he knew Bird Dog would come 'round asking me if I knew where he was stayin'."

Leela laughed aloud at this. "I doubt Bird Dog Taylor would spend his time chasing after a two-bit gambler like Carey. That old man has hired thugs to take care of anyone who crosses him."

Hattie stiffened, opening her mouth to protest. "Say what you will, but I know you're the root cause for Carey being gone so long. The whole town knows it. Elvina and Inez only said what they know to be truth." Hattie pointed a long finger at Leela. "I always wondered just what went on out here to turn T.J. against his brother."

"Nothing," Leela stated flatly, her heart pounding.

"Oh, yes. Something happened all right," Hattie countered. "And one day it gonna come down on you like a hand squeezing the breath of life from your body. It'll spill out and cover you with troubles like you never seen before." Hattie moved toward the screen door. "I wish I hadda spoke to T.J. before he passed." Her deep voice broke and splintered with his name. "I'da promised him to find his brother." She lowered her square jaw until a layer of fat doubled beneath her chin and made her face loom large and pallid in the moonlight. "I'da asked him about his will, too," she said, piercing Leela with a determined stare. "You'll live a hell on earth for what you've done to my family. Wait and see." She stepped through the screen door and let it slam shut behind her.

The next morning, many of those who passed through the Wilder parlor offering condolences climbed a short flight of steps and crowded into the white frame building that was the home of the Bethlehem Primitive Baptist Church. Reverend William Pearson had been preaching to this rural congregation in the Woodlands community for over twenty years, and now he would minister the last rites to Thomas Jacob Wilder.

Leela and Kenny entered the sanctuary, making their way down the aisle as Hattie followed. The three family members sat in a pew very near the open casket, which stood banked with sprays of pink roses and white carnations. From her position it was difficult to see who entered, but unless things had changed, Leela could guess who would be in attendance. Little changed at the Bethlehem Primitive Baptist Church.

A small hand tapped lightly on Leela's shoulder and she peered through black netting to see Aunt Effie. Josephine's daughter, Penny, stood behind her grandmother.

It was a shame Aunt Effie had to raise that child, Leela thought as she raised her cheek for Effie's kiss.

She kissed Leela through the scratchy veil and whispered, "Have courage, dear. Have courage." She bent closer. "Please come out to see me. Soon?" Leela nodded and Effie took a seat under a large rendition of the Last Supper that showcased a brown-skinned Jesus and his obviously Negro disciples.

Leela marveled at how well Effie looked. The stylish seamstress wore a fashionable suit with matching cloche hat pulled down at just the right angle. It covered hair which had turned snow white two days after Uncle Bert died in his sleep five years ago. Her heart went out to her aunt and Leela decided to go visit her soon, as soon as she'd settled the problem with the bank.

Others from town arrived for the service and passed by Leela before taking their seats. Doc White nodded, deep sympathy clouding his face. She recognized Mr. Kirvin, the pharmacist, who had personally delivered T.J.'s medicine when the roads were too bad for Leela to travel. Her slow-witted neighbor, Red Walters, whom many ridiculed and shunned because of his crooked back and stuttering speech, slipped in and quietly sat near the door. He had been T.J.'s only neighbor for twenty years and had helped clear the tangled acreage when T.J. first inherited it. From the corner of her eye, Leela saw Pully come in alone, shuffle up from the back of the church, hat in hand, to say good-bye to his employer and friend. The young man did not look at Leela, but paid his respects at the casket and left by the side door, blowing his nose quietly into his red-and-white handkerchief.

The organist began to play "There Is a Place of Refuge," and Reverend Pearson adjusted the billowing sleeves of his black robe, threw back his heavy shoulders and strode to the pulpit. Holding on to the sides of the dark pine podium, he surveyed the small gathering before him. Candles flickered on either side of the altar and the smell of roses wafted thickly through the room. The hot air was stirred only by cardboard fans bearing messages from the McBay Funeral Home.

When the reverend began his words of comfort, Leela's hand flew up to her mouth. A veil of tears clouded her vision. Kenny grabbed his mother's arm, squeezing hard while Leela wiped tears from his face and cheeks. The two sat ramrod straight, holding on to each other until the final hymn was sung.

The simple, short eulogy lasted exactly twenty minutes. Then Leela turned her back on Hattie Wilder and followed the pallbearers out of the church, across the dusty grounds, to the gaping hole where T.J.'s shiny new tombstone stood in sharp contrast to the old carved headstones and crumbling brick markers that dotted the aging cemetery.

As the reverend administered the closing rites, Leela did not hear a word he said. She stared into the open grave, speaking silently to her husband. Thank you for the years of forgiveness you gave me, though I lived with my guilt every day. You've left me now, but I promise you I'll do everything possible to raise our son to be as generous and caring as his father.

Chapter Fifteen

When Johnny Ray Mosley's horse disappeared into the thicket at the end of the road, Josephine ran back inside her house and shook Oliver awake. The sleeping boy turned over, groaned and pulled his thin blanket more tightly to his chest.

"Oliver," Josephine urged, "get on up. Your pa's gone. Get on up now, we've got a lot to do."

The thirteen-year-old sat up and wiped his hand across his mouth, blinking his eyes more fully open. "Pa's gone?" he muttered, looking through the doorway as if he did not believe his mother.

Josephine went back into the cooking area and stood with her back to Oliver. "Yes, and he's going over to McLennan County, so he won't be back for a day or two. Get on up, boy. We're leaving." The words fell like heavy raindrops on the roof. "We're moving back to town." Swiftly, she gathered up the small amount of sugar, salt and flour remaining in the house and jammed the tins into a wooden box.

Oliver slowly drew back his threadbare blanket and swung his feet to the floor, contemplating his mother's words. "Pa's not gonna like it if he comes back and we're gone." He pulled on his pants, watching Josephine shove a stack of tattered linens into a box. "You sure we're leaving, Momma?"

"I'm as sure about leaving this place as I am about you being my son," she said, feeling relieved that for the first time in months, Johnny Ray had not taken the wagon. To Josephine this was a sign that it was time to make her move. Another opportunity might never come again.

She removed the thin gray blanket from her son's bed, folded it and put it in the box. "I told your pa we'd be going to visit Grandma for a day or two. Didn't seem to matter to him . . . but that's not the truth, son."

Oliver frowned when he saw her face. The egg-sized bump above Josephine's right eye flared angry and red on her translucent skin. "You lied?"

"Yes, I did," she said quickly and boldly, " 'cause we're never coming back here to live."

"Did Pa do that?" Oliver asked, remembering the frightening sounds of his parents' voices, raised in anger last night.

"Yes." Josephine touched the ugly bruise and winced. She reached over and put her arm around Oliver, then sat on his bed and pulled him close. "I've tried to make it work, son, and I don't expect you to understand these grown-up affairs. But you've been living in the middle of all your pa's hatefulness right along with me and you're old enough to see we gotta go."

He looked at her with confusion in his eyes. "So Pa's gonna be here all alone?"

"I reckon so, I can't stay with him any longer."

"Where we gonna go, Momma? To Grandma's?"

"No, I've found a little house not far from Grandma's. We'll have a place of our own."

"Is Penny gonna come back and stay with us?"

Josephine hesitated. "If she wants to . . . it's up to her." She felt her voice crack. "But if she'd rather stay with Grandma, that's all right. We won't be that far away."

She turned him loose and went into the next room, listening to the sound of his bare feet as he scurried around to collect his meager belongings.

Thank God I got Penny out of here, Josephine reflected, a painful sense of failure closing in around her heart, eased only by the sense of relief she felt that her daughter had not seen or heard what happened the night before. Josephine could still feel the weight of Johnny Ray's drunken body over hers and the sting of his palm across her face. Over and over. Until the room spun in terrifying circles, then went totally black. After thirteen years she'd had enough of his torment, and as difficult as it was to admit that her mother had been right, Josephine was ready to do so.

This ought to make Momma happy, she concluded, hurriedly stuffing her frying pan between the sheets and blankets filling one crate. I am leaving Johnny Ray, the father of my children, but I'll never move back home. Never. No matter what I have to do to make a living for myself, I won't run home to her. I'm a grown woman and I'm not so dumb that I can't make it on my own. I'll show her and that smug Leela, too. Now that she's a widow, what's she got? A farm she'll probably lose within the year. Josephine smiled to herself. We'll see who's the clever one. If I put my mind to it, I know I can find a way to get by. And I won't do days' work for some white family, either. I'll never clean up after someone else.

Josephine and her son moved through the house in silence, loading a few chairs, a washbasin, some oil lamps and a scarred pine table into the wagon. The pink china dishes Effie had brought over were carefully wrapped in brown paper. Josephine bundled all of her clothing in a heavy quilt and even took the feather pillows off the bed. She knew she could never come back.

After stripping the house of everything that was useful, Josephine started off toward the shed at the back of the house. "Oliver, bring the wagon 'round back. There's a few things in the shed I'm taking."

Josephine entered the dark musty outbuilding and stood for a moment as her eyes adjusted to the dim light. Waist-high barrels of

Mister Harry's corn liquor lined the walls. The room was filled with containers. She quickly rolled one over on its side and pushed it out the door.

"Come help me get this in the wagon," she called to Oliver, struggling to angle the big barrel into place.

"What you takin' this stuff for, Momma?" Oliver asked as he laid out a plank from the ground to the wagon.

" 'Cause it's about the most valuable thing on this place. The only thing worth any money at all."

Together, they loaded four kegs of the white lightning, tied them down securely, then set off toward town.

Josephine didn't say another word to her son during the one-hour ride into Mexia, until they pulled onto Denton Street and headed to the end of an unpaved road. "Here we are," she remarked, indicating a small frame house sitting in an overgrown yard.

The low four-room dwelling sat far back from the street, fronted by a cracked brick walkway that had nearly disappeared under a tangle of weeds. The porch sagged in the middle and several screens were missing, but it had a good roof and a chimney at each end. Thorny hedges and rambling rosebushes crowded the entrance, creating such a fearsome barrier Josephine and Oliver had to circle the house and go in through the back door.

Inside, the dark empty rooms smelled of mildew. Paper shades hung at angles over three of the four windows, and piles of trash lay in clumps in the corners. The impoverished life of the former renters still clung to the scarred walls and warped pine floors, but the kitchen had a real sink and a big gas stove, and there was even a cracked tub to bathe in.

After unloading the wagon, Josephine started to sweep. Oliver walked through the house and found a broken three-legged stool he thought he could fix. He propped it up against the wall and sat down. The place was scary to him, all dark and strange. He wanted his mother to say something, but she just kept sweeping trash out the door as if she no longer knew he was there.

Maybe his mother wouldn't cry so much now and look sad all the time, he decided, as he got up and slipped out the back door to explore the tangled yard. At least, for now, he wouldn't have to go hide in the woods like he used to when Johnny Ray came home roaring drunk.

Guiding her small buggy down the dusty road, Leela savored the sunlight warming her back. No wind stirred the cotton fields on either side of the highway, though wispy gray clouds floated in ragged puffs to the south. Shafts of sunshine, gleaming like molten gold, burst from the sky and spread a shimmer of sparkles over the ground.

Heading east on the Mexia-Comanche Crossing Road, Leela rehearsed aloud what she planned to tell Wesley Sparks.

"The melons will be harvested tomorrow morning. My help has already turned back the vines, the Black Diamonds are looking as good as any prime crop, and the wagons stand ready in the fields. If you could just extend the payment deadline, I will be able to settle my husband's debt." It sounded very reasonable and fair to her. If only he would listen and grant her a few extra weeks.

Near the edge of town, Leela turned off and took the rutted Mexia-Groesbeck Highway to Palestine Street, pointing Taffy, her chestnut mare, toward Aunt Effie's house. Before pleading her case at the bank she wanted some advice. This meeting could not be left to chance.

"I'm so glad you came," Effie said, when Leela entered her cluttered kitchen. The tiny birdlike woman lifted a box of books from the kitchen table, shoved aside a stack of folded linen and motioned for Leela to sit down.

"Excuse all this mess," she said, laughing. "I got it in my head this morning to clean out all this stuff Bert held on to and never would let me throw away. He was funny that way. Kept everything."

Leela smiled and nodded as she noticed the crates of scrap iron, hardened pieces of leather, rusted-out tools and boxes of frayed rope scattered around the room. Uncle Bert had been dead five years and Aunt Effie was just now getting around to doing what she herself hadn't done: sort out T.J.'s things. She watched her aunt with sympathetic eyes.

"Look at these old gloves," Effie sighed, turning the worn leather pieces over in her hand. "He wore these to work for fifteen years. See how thin and smooth they are."

Leela did not reply. She could still see Uncle Bert laughing as he entered the house, pulling off those stiff leather gloves as he lifted lids from the pots to see what Effie had cooked. During all the years they lived together, Leela had never heard Uncle Bert raise his voice in anger or utter an ugly word about anyone. His jovial personality had filled the house with love. A comforting silence settled over the two women.

Effie laid the gloves aside and shoved a small leather trunk from beneath the table.

"Now that this is empty, I ought to get it out of my way." She closed the lid gently and snapped the lock shut. "This trunk belonged to Bert's father. He had two of them . . . just alike. Parker took one when he left for Chicago. I tried to give this one to Josephine when she moved out, but she flat refused. Said she didn't have any use for such an old thing. Kinda hurt her poppa, I think."

"How is Josephine doing, now that she's living in town? Do you see her more often?" Leela asked.

"Oh, not really. Penny's still here with me. Josephine comes around now and then, but she's gotten so independent and free, she hardly has time for her daughter."

"How in the world is she managing?"

"Don't ask me! I wish I knew. She won't let me help her and she keeps talking about this 'little business' she's started, but won't tell me a thing about it. She knows how to sew a pretty good seam. Maybe she's taking in sewing."

Leela could hardly imagine Josephine sitting down before a sewing machine even to sew for herself, but said nothing in reply.

Effie set a pot of coffee on the table, and Leela poured herself a cup.

"Have a little something to eat, honey. Don't look like you been eating too good. Want me to fix you some eggs? I got some fresh hog sausage Willie Green brought over yesterday. I can fry up a couple of—"

"No, thanks," Leela interrupted. "I'm not hungry. Just a little tired, I guess."

Effie reached over and patted Leela's hand. "Only been about a month and I know you miss him. T.J. was a good man, a bit quiet, a tad stubborn, but a fine husband and father, that much I know." She squeezed her niece's fingers. "We all miss him and it's going to take some time for you to get your strength back. Nursing him like you did for over a year! That'll bring any woman down low. Now, take care of yourself. I don't see how you managed, with so little help."

"It was hard, toward the end, it was very hard," Leela acknowledged. "But I've managed to hold on to the crop."

"That's a big place. You gonna need more help than you got to keep it going. Kenny's not yet the man I know he's going to turn out to be."

"Effie, you're right, he's such a strong boy. T.J.'s death hit him hard, but he's doing better than I ever imagined he would. After the funeral he dried his eyes and put his crying aside. He's trying to act so grown-up. I worry he's covered up his sorrow too fast."

"He'll mourn in his own way. Everybody has to. Even you."

"I miss T.J. terribly. I do," Leela admitted, remembering her farewell promise to him. "Everything is so different with him gone, but for Kenny's sake I'm trying hard to keep things as normal as possible. The work on the place goes on."

"I understand. Bert's been dead for five years and there're days, let me tell you, I don't want to do a thing except feel sorry for myself. Maybe today was one of them," she mused, running her hand over the humpbacked lid of the leather trunk. "You know, I'd like Kenny to have this." Her words were softly spoken. "I think Bert would want that, too. Josephine already said she doesn't want it, and I'd like to keep it in the family."

"That's a nice thought, Aunt Effie. A gift like this would be a very special reminder of his uncle." Leela leaned over and kissed her aunt on the cheek. She saw sadness creeping into the fragile skin around her eyes. "Why don't you help me put it in the buggy right now," she said, breaking the somber mood. "If not, I'll probably forget it."

The two women easily carried the trunk outside, stowed it securely in the back of Leela's small buggy, then returned to the table to continue their visit.

"I got the most wonderful letter from Parker," Effie told Leela as she opened the drawer under her small sideboard. "Here, let me read it to you. He asks about you, and this news is so good, I'm certain he'd expect me to share it. Just listen."

Effie settled comfortably in her seat, took out the letter and began to read:

August 19, 1920
Washington, D.C.

Dear Momma,

I just had to write immediately and thank you for the shirts you made for me. They arrived yesterday and I am wearing one of them now as I sit down to compose this letter. You know I can buy my own shirts here in Washington, Momma, but having these made by you is so special. Wearing them makes me feel closer to you.

I was so sorry to hear of T.J. Wilder's death, though I guess it was not unexpected. That's a terrible blow to Leela, I'm sure. How is she getting along now? She's not living out there on that isolated farm all alone, is she? Times are changing everywhere and she ought to be careful out there so far from town. Please give her my love and ask her to let me know if there is anything I can do to help her in this difficult time. I will be writing to her very soon.

The news that the *Banner* has closed down is also most distressing. At seventy-nine, Mr. Foreman needs to take it easy, I guess, but it's a shame no one is willing to step in and continue his work. You know, Momma, I've been seriously thinking of coming back to Mexia to take over the *Banner* myself. It's just a thought right now, so don't go getting excited, but Margaret and I have discussed it and the possibility sounds more appealing each day.

It is good to know that Josephine has moved into town and is closer to the family. Please give her and Leela my love and tell them all is well with me. Margaret has recovered very nicely from the terrible cold I wrote you about last month and has resumed teaching her small group of students. She enjoys her work very much and I've told her if we come back to Mexia that she would be very welcome at Halsey School, I'm sure.

It's stifling hot here in the capital. It's been as warm as

ninety-two for the last week. I'll bet it's not much better there, is it? Well, I'm a Texan and used to it, and I'll write you as soon as I've made up my mind whether or not now is the time for me to return.

All my love,
Parker

Effie's hands fell limply into her lap as she finished reading the letter. "Wouldn't it be grand to have him back home?" she remarked, leaning her head to one side. "You know, Leela, I really believe if Parker came home he might be able to get through to Josephine, get her back to the family." She slipped the folded pages back into the envelope. "He'd be a big help to everyone if he returned."

"I agree," Leela murmured. "And right now I could really use his advice." She got up and walked to the window, running a nervous hand over her brow as she stood looking out.

"What's wrong?" Effie probed. "I knew when I saw your face at the door this morning that there was something important on your mind. You can't hide it from me, honey. There's something powerful weighing on your shoulders."

"You're right, Aunt Effie, and that's why I came. I'm on my way to see Wesley Sparks at the Mexia Community Bank."

"Whatever for?"

"There's a problem about the farm. Sparks is pressing me for payment on a loan he made to T.J. five years ago."

"Pressing you? What do you mean?"

"Well," Leela started, squeezing her hands together in anxiety, "he's threatening to take the farm unless I can pay off the note. Soon."

"How much is it?" Effie asked.

"Three thousand dollars."

Effie stared at Leela in disbelief. "Three thousand dollars? T.J. owed that kind of money?"

Leela nodded. "And I can pay it. Just not right now. I've got to bring in the melons first, then I can settle with the bank."

"Won't he wait until the crop's sold?"

"He says the review committee wants the debt cleared up sooner.

The harvest starts tomorrow. But even then, I won't see the kind of cash he wants in time to make his deadline. I'm going over to ask for more time."

"What's with old man Sparks? I never knew him to be demanding like that. Bert had some dealings with him a long time back. Seemed kind of sympathetic to us. Once helped Bert get a good job making steel vaults for the new bank building. I thought he carried some weight over there."

"Not when there's talk of oil," Leela began, going on to tell Effie of her conversation with Wesley Sparks and of the test well being drilled on the Rogers place. Effie grinned and nodded her head at the news.

"I was born seventy-two years ago, exactly two miles from your farm. That sticky black stuff showed up all through that area back then—you know that's why they named that area Rioluces. My momma and others who knew how to do it used to scrape that black slimy stuff up off the river bank and burn it. I can still remember the smell. Strong and smoky. Stayed in your clothes for weeks. Most folks thought it a nuisance. Horses and cows wouldn't drink from the creek, and superstitious folks thought the water was cursed. I always figured somebody would sink enough money into that land to bring up oil in my lifetime. Bet Wesley Sparks and those men at the bank know more than they're telling you."

"I think so, too," Leela replied.

A curious frown wrinkled Effie's brown face. She sat silently for a moment before she spoke.

"There's a man in town you might want to talk to," she said. Her voice fell into a whisper as if telling a secret. "A colored man named Victor Beaufort. He came here a few weeks ago with a jacket that needed repairing. Said he was new to Mexia, from Oklahoma, and was looking for land to lease. Seems he's in the oil business. Can you imagine? I never thought too much about it until hearing what you just said. They been talking oil in these parts so long, I kinda let his words slip right through without notice. But I must admit, Leela, I never heard tell of a colored man talking oil before."

"Where is he now?"

"Told me he has offices in a building near Mildred's Cafe, over on Belknap Street." Effie turned in her chair to face Leela more fully.

"Why don't you talk to him? He might know more about this drilling that's going on. Honey, don't you let Wesley Sparks run you off your land. Speak your piece when you meet him and let him know you're no fool. You're a right smart woman. You can talk real good. T.J. worked hard for that land and you deserve to keep it. I can smell some dirty business brewing. When you go to the bank, you be careful. Don't sign any papers 'less somebody legal looks them over. Why don't you go on over to Belknap Street and talk to this man, Victor Beaufort?"

Feeling encouraged by her aunt's words, Leela soon said goodbye and climbed into her buggy, picking up the reins to hold them tightly. Effie's right, Leela thought. I ought to talk to someone about this business of oil on my land. I sure wish Parker were here. The men at the bank would listen to him. He'd make them see how much I need more time. He'd know exactly how to handle Wesley Sparks. Leela sighed, suddenly saddened anew by Parker's absence.

As Leela tied her sunbonnet over her hair, she was surprised to see Josephine coming toward her on the street. She waited until her cousin drew nearer.

"Good morning, Josephine." She lifted her hand in a wave.

Josephine muttered hello and nodded, coming to a stop in front of Leela.

"I heard you're living in town. Everything going all right?" She didn't wait for Josephine's reply. "If there is anything I can do to help you, let me know, Josephine. I mean it. I hope this move will make things better."

"I am doing just fine and I don't need any help. Oliver and I are managing very well, thank you." She sounded bored and weary.

"That's good! Really! I worried so much about you out there with Johnny Ray. I mean . . ."

"Don't bother yourself, Leela. I know just what you mean." Josephine lifted her chin and took a deep breath, peering around Leela to see what was in the back of the buggy.

"What's that you're carrying around?"

Leela turned slightly. "Oh . . . Aunt Effie is giving this to Kenny."

"Isn't that Poppa's trunk?"

"Yes, it was Uncle Bert's and your mother wanted Kenny to have it."

"That's my trunk and she had no right to give it to you." Her words were flatly possessive.

"She said you didn't want it, that you wouldn't care if—"

"How dare you come into my parents' home and take things that don't belong to you? You've no right to that, neither does Kenny. It's mine." Tears gathered in her eyes. "Poppa always said I could have it."

Oh, God, Leela thought. Why did I accept this? I should have known Josephine would make an issue of the gift. She started to climb down.

"Well, if I had known how you felt, I never would have let Aunt Effie give it away." She reached into the back of her buggy and tugged at the heavy trunk. "Give me a hand. We can get it out."

"Don't bother! I want nothing to do with it now that you've had your greedy hands all over it. How disgusting you are! Greedy and disgusting. Didn't that land-rich husband leave you enough money to buy your son his own trunk?"

"That's not the point and you know it, Josephine."

"You take and take and take, don't you, Cousin Leela? You just have to have your own way!" Her voice shrilled through the street, bringing Effie to the front porch.

"Josephine. Stop that awful talk. And all out in the street, too. I gave the trunk to Leela. You said you wanted no part of it. Now apologize. Don't be so ugly about this. It's just a misunderstanding."

"This is no misunderstanding, Momma. Leela always gets what she wants—you make sure of that, don't you? Well, I will not apologize. Not ever! Leela is evil and greedy and I'm the only one in this family who has ever seen right through her deceitful ways." She took a deep breath to stem the tremble in her voice. Tears ran down her puffy cheeks. Her colorless skin flamed red with anger. "Keep the trunk, Cousin Leela. And every time you look at it, I hope you think of me and how you took advantage of me to get it."

She turned on her heel and walked quickly down the street.

Leela got back in the buggy and sat staring after her cousin, feeling unfairly assaulted by such vindictive words. She gave her aunt a bewildered look, shook her head sadly, then clucked loudly to Taffy and snapped the reins. As the horse started off down Palestine Street, Leela watched Josephine's bulky frame move slowly around the corner and wondered if even Cousin Parker's return would make a difference.

Chapter Sixteen

After Leela departed, Effie had trouble getting back to her work. She tried to finish a dress she had set aside, absently running two seams which she had to pull out, her mind crowded with thoughts of Leela's predicament.

So much money was needed to save the farm. Soon. And with so much at stake. She wished she could help, but had nothing to offer. Bert had been a hard worker and a good provider, but his death had left her with fifty dollars in cash. Her sewing was more than a way to make ends meet; it kept her mind off her own nagging worries—like Josephine and her new situation. Thank goodness she had the good sense to leave that brute, Effie consoled herself, recalling the last time she saw Josephine with a badly bruised cheek and a swollen left eye. So far he hadn't come around looking for her.

With a yank Effie pulled the last thread from her ruined seam and pushed the delicate fabric once again under the sharp needle. As the whirring machine ran its line of stitches, a thought came to Effie that made her stop in midseam. She quickly stood, went straight into her darkened bedroom, got down on her knees and pulled a long, flat pasteboard box from beneath the bed. The musty-sweet odor of faded white roses and dried clumps of lilac wafted up as she pulled the dusty container open. With light fingers she hurriedly riffled through the papers and photos and letters which represented a faded collage of Effie's past. At the bottom of the box, yellowed and nearly crumbling, lay a letter she had received close to thirty years ago. With trembling hands Effie opened the envelope, pulled out the single page and read:

Dear Sister,
My writings not too good, but I wanted to tell you my news and let you know I's fine. Got a job cooking on the railroad, the MK&T from Ft. Worth to Galveston. Mabel's glad bout the steady work but don't like me been gone so much. Grandma's still with us so she kinda keeps Mabel compny. Soon as the baby's a little older, we all gonna come for a visit. Named the baby Leela, a name Mabel picked out by herself. I been paying up on something the boss man calls a railroad bond. Started the day I got hired and I add on every month. Boss man says long as I keep doing this, my baby always gonna have some way to get money. This is all new to me, but it more than I ever thought I'd have. Things is going real good for us. Glad to hear your baby Parker got over his sickness.

Your brother, Ed

Effie wondered what happened to that bond as she put the letter into her pocket. Unless Grandma Ekiti cashed it, which she seriously doubted—the old woman couldn't read or write a word of English—the bond could still be valid. But where was it? And after almost thirty years, considering how big the MK&T was now, Effie wondered how much it might be worth.

The main thoroughfare rumbled with activity. Road wagons, buggies, and heavy drays pulled by as many as three teams of mules vied with top-heavy Model T's for space along the dusty avenue. A slight wind lifted Leela's skirt from around her knees as she snapped the reins impatiently and headed down Commerce Street. She looked up at the sky and noticed more clouds gathering on the horizon.

Neatly painted signs, flapping gently in the rare breeze, hung suspended before recently constructed frame buildings, still oozing sap from freshly cut boards. Leela's mare brayed loudly and reared back on hind legs when a wagon piled dangerously high with lumber swerved past. The driver yelled at a pack of wild dogs blocking his path, then roared away in a huge cloud of dust. On the other side of the street, a white foreman barked orders at his black bricklayers, cursing the men for wasting mortar.

Leela inched her way through the tangled crowd to halt in front of an old brick building set with tall limestone-block windows. Stepping down, she shook out her skirt, removed her sunbonnet and let her copper curls settle in a blaze on her shoulders. She ran a flowered handkerchief over her cheeks and wiped gritty road dirt off her damp face before entering the Mexia Community Bank.

Inhaling deeply to still the nervous flutter in the pit of her stomach, Leela could taste the oiled mahogany, polished brass and pungent pipe tobacco smells settled so thickly over the lobby. The petal-shaped blades of a gray ceiling fan, droning like a metal dragonfly, did not cool the room, but lazily circulated streams of hot air throughout the stuffy space. The staccato pecking of the receptionist's typewriter echoed sharply in Leela's ears.

Throwing back her shoulders, Leela grasped her heavy purse more firmly, crossed the lobby, and took her place in line behind an elderly white couple and an attractive young Indian woman whose long dark hair fell in heavy braids past her waist. Leela waited as the frail young man in the paneled counting cage completed his transactions; then she stepped up to the window. The pock-faced teller finished counting a stack of bills, stowed them in his cash drawer and looked up.

"Yes?"

"I'd like to see Mr. Wesley Sparks, please."

"Mr. Sparks is not here," the teller said with little expression.

"When do you expect him?" Leela asked, already making up her mind to wait for him, no matter how long it took.

"Well, I'm not sure." The young man's words were uttered

slowly, as if calculating his odds of saying the right thing. He shifted on his stool. "What do you want with Mr. Sparks?"

Leela stepped back slightly as the teller pushed his thin face closer to the glass partition separating him from his customer. His eyes narrowed and moved from her face to her waist and back up again.

"I'd really rather speak to Mr. Sparks," Leela stated firmly, watching the young man's jaws tighten as she refused his question. "Perhaps I should come back later? Or wait?"

"I don't think so," the teller replied, an indignant tone creeping into his voice. He placed another stack of bills into his cash drawer, locked it with a flourish, then stood. "If you just tell me what your business is, perhaps our manager, Mr. Bernard, can help you."

"It's about a loan," Leela began.

"A loan from this bank?" He ran the tip of his tongue over bluish lips.

Leela nodded.

"Oh, well, I'm sorry. You've made a mistake." A hint of a smile eased onto his face. "We don't make loans to colored at this bank. You'll have to try someplace else." By now his small white teeth were completely bared, and he faced Leela in undisguised contempt.

A sinking feeling washed through Leela. She took a slow, deep breath and pressed on.

"I already have a loan from this bank and I would like to talk to Mr. Sparks about it." Her face remained immobile, as if carved from polished wood, but her hands shook so badly she hid them inside the folds of her skirt.

The irritated man pulled down a white shade in Leela's face. Big black letters said CLOSED. He strode away from his teller's cage and entered a door at the back of the bank.

The peck-peck of the receptionist's typewriter stopped, and Leela stood very still, staring straight ahead at the shaded window, waiting. Curious eyes bored holes into her back. She felt the burning mockery and smug scrutiny of those milling around the busy lobby. Standing tall, spine stiff, chin lifted, throat closed, Leela remained at the head of the line, determined not to leave.

Damn Wesley Sparks, she fumed. Where was he? Why must I

go through this humiliation? I probably own more land than he does, she thought.

Minutes ticked by, and those standing behind her moved to another window, served by another teller. Leela refused to budge. She thought of Wesley Sparks driving all the way to Rioluces to threaten her with his call on the loan. And now he refused to leave the sanctity of his cubicle and meet her face to face.

As Leela's resolve began to weaken, and it appeared she'd been completely dismissed, a bespectacled man stepped forward and motioned her toward an open door at the rear of the building. Leela nodded to him, strode briskly across the lobby and followed him into an office.

"Please sit down, Mrs. . . . ?" The man waved a freckled hand toward a dark green chair.

"I'm Mrs. Thomas Jacob Wilder," she told him, settling into the wide chair, carefully placing her handbag on her lap.

The strong smell of cigar smoke penetrated every corner of the room.

"I'm the bank manager, Mr. Bernard," he said, moving to sit behind a desk cluttered with folders, books, letters and maps. Crossing his arms on his chest, Mr. Bernard leaned back in his swivel chair and fixed his eyes on Leela. The light from the open window behind him illuminated his silver hair and reflected brightly off the round brass ashtray piled high with half-smoked cigar butts and ashes.

"I understand you have a loan with this bank?" Bushy white eyebrows moved higher onto his forehead.

"My husband, Mr. Wilder, did," Leela replied. "He passed away several weeks ago." Reaching into her handbag, she pulled out the original loan papers and placed them on the desk. Mr. Bernard made no move to pick them up.

"Was your husband a colored man?" the banker asked bluntly.

"Yes, sir, he was," Leela answered, equally blunt. "And Mr. Sparks made him a loan five years ago."

"What was used for collateral?"

"Rioluces." Leela said.

"Rioluces?"

"Our farm, six miles out of town. Out off the Mexia-Comanche Crossing Road."

"How many acres you got out there?"

"Three hundred forty."

"What'd your husband grow? Cotton?"

"For some time, but when he fell ill, I could only manage melons and corn. The melon crop's fine and should bring in enough to meet the note."

"Um-hum," Mr. Bernard muttered, gingerly fingering the folded document Leela had placed on his desk. "How much money did your husband owe the bank when he died?"

"Three thousand dollars. But he had everything arranged with Mr. Sparks. That's who I really came to see today," Leela said, wondering why this man was asking her all these questions. Why didn't he just pull out the records? Everything was there.

The banker finally picked up the document before him and flipped through all three pages.

"Where is Mr. Sparks?" Leela broke the silence. "He knows all about this. With my husband passing away, well, I need more time to settle this. A few months," she rushed on, wanting to get the bold request behind her now that she'd gone this far.

Mr. Bernard acted as if she had not spoken, reading through the papers. "Your last payment was due in January," he noted, peering at Leela over the tops of his small round glasses. "It's August, Mrs. Wilder. You're going to have to settle this immediately. If not, the Mexia Community Bank has no choice but to move forward to foreclose on your farm."

"But," Leela dared to protest, "Wesley Sparks agreed to let my husband settle the debt in the fall, after the melons were shipped. Check his records. We always paid Mr. Sparks on time, in hard cash, and always in the fall."

"Do you have proof of those payments? I see the original loan was for fifteen thousand dollars." He hesitated as if considering what to say next. "That's quite a sum to be borrowing, and honestly, Mrs. Wilder, I knew nothing of this arrangement. We've never made loans to Negroes. This is all very irregular and disturbing."

"I have receipts signed by Wesley Sparks for every dollar my husband paid him." She now pulled four slips of blue paper from her bag. "Here," she said, passing them to the banker. "They're all signed and dated by Mr. Sparks himself." She waited tensely as Mr. Bernard examined each one carefully.

In the silence that followed, Leela decided she had nothing to lose and began her plea for an extension.

". . . and the harvest will start tomorrow morning," she finished. "I know the crop will bring in enough to make this payment by the end of November. If you could just . . ."

Her earnest words were quickly interrupted. "Well, Mrs. Wilder," he began, pushing himself up from the desk as he spoke, "there are two things you need to know." He went to the open window and stared out into the busy street. "First, Wesley Sparks no longer works at this bank. In fact, Mr. Sparks has disappeared. Vanished almost two weeks ago with a great deal of the bank's cash and all the files from his desk." Mr. Bernard pulled out his watch fob and checked the time. He went on. "We have no idea where he went, and none of the directors at this bank had knowledge of this loan to your husband. As I said, we don't loan money to Negroes. Mr. Sparks, unfortunately, did not follow our policies."

By crossing her ankles tightly and pressing herself farther back into her seat, Leela tried to still the nervous tremble she felt rising inside. What did this mean? she wondered, clenching her hand into a tight, painful fist.

"You said Mr. Sparks took all of his files with him?" Leela asked, a fearful tremor in her words. She bit her lip, anticipating his answer.

"That's right. And it's caused the bank quite a few problems. Apparently Wesley Sparks was in the habit of holding deeds and other legal documents for customers. Highly irregular, let me assure you."

Leela sat tensely, waiting to hear what else the banker had to say.

"How many acres you say you got planted in melons?"

"One hundred sixty," Leela replied.

Mr. Bernard went back to his desk, sat, and carefully folded the four blue receipts around the three-page loan and dropped the bundle into his top drawer. Leela leaned forward to protest, thought better of it and sat back, staring uneasily as the banker locked his drawer and put the key into his vest pocket.

"We'll have to draw up new papers," he explained, tugging the drawer to make sure it was locked. "First, we need to inspect your melon crop. See what it's worth. A representative of the bank will be out to your place tomorrow morning." He folded his hands in his lap as if dismissing Leela. When she made no move to leave, he went on. "If the crop is as large as you say and the melons look as if they will bring in the cash, I'll consider an extension. That's all I can offer you at this time, Mrs. Wilder." He stood, giving Leela a definite look of dismissal.

"I appreciate your understanding," Leela forced herself to say, swallowing the anger in her voice. She wondered how many other black families Wesley Sparks had used to steal money from the bank. "An extension will truly help me out." She paused, hand on the brass doorknob, and glanced back at Mr. Bernard. The banker had his head down in a pile of papers and did not even bother to make a reply.

Leela stepped into her waiting buggy, settled down on the warm leather seats and started off toward Rioluces. She felt hopeful; her worry over losing the farm began to slip away. The constant knot that had lain like a stone in the center of her soul eased for the first time in months, and an unfamiliar though welcome rush of energy broke through her doubt and despair. She would not lose Rioluces.

Crossing Belknap Street, Leela remembered Effie's warning and her mention of the black oilman who was scouting land to lease.

I don't need him now, she thought, pulling onto the main road. If there's oil on Rioluces, it will be there after the melons are sold. Maybe then she'd talk to this Victor Beaufort.

An overcast and threatening sky stretched slate gray overhead. Leela slapped the reins sharply and urged Taffy forward to get off the road before the storm broke. As she rolled into the yard, Pully Simpson ran up, grabbed hold of her horse and led the buggy into the drafty old barn.

"Looks like the rains is comin', Miz Leela," Pully said, helping her step down.

"Yes, it does," Leela agreed, brushing dust from her skirt, holding tightly to the young man's rough hand. "It will probably rain most all afternoon. When it clears," she said, stepping briskly toward the high door, "I want you to get Indy and James and see if Red

Walters's hands can help and finish turning back the vines. We're harvesting the melons in the morning."

"We's ready, ma'am. Yes, we'll get everything done before nightfall. Just soon as this spell of weather pass."

"An inspector from town will be here early. When he's through, we can start the harvest, not before."

"Yes, ma'am. Hope he come out real early, ma'am. Won't be no good ta start pickin' in the heat of the day."

"No," Leela agreed as she started toward the house, "it wouldn't, but we can't do a thing until he's come."

"Looks like this one gonna drop water," Pully shouted above the rising wind.

"Let's hope so, Pully," Leela called back. "Every farm in the county needs rain." She rushed toward the house as a sudden gust of wind scattered gravel and dust in her face.

Kenny bolted out the back door, jumped over three steep steps and met his mother halfway across the yard. He grabbed her arm and ran alongside her.

"Ma, this is gonna be some storm. Look how dark it is and it's only 'bout noon."

"Just a long overdue summer rain," Leela reassured him. "It will pass. Look how fast the clouds are moving. And we've got to have this rain."

Inside the dim kitchen, she had to light a kerosene lamp before starting her chores. She pulled out a basket of turnips, picked out the biggest ones, then washed them at the faucet. Kenny sat at the table eating a raw tomato.

"Did you get what you wanted in town?" he asked.

Leela kept peeling the rough skin off a large turnip. "No. I didn't see any fabric I liked. Guess I'll have to go over to Groesbeck and try McKelvy's or Clay's." What could he possibly understand about the complicated situation she was in? she worried as she kept on peeling. "The Black Diamonds come off the vine tomorrow," she said, changing the subject. "If you want, you can ride in the lead wagon with Pully."

Kenny smiled at this news, got up and tossed part of his tomato out the back door.

"Ma," he called, "the wind's blown that big poplar tree nearly double. Come look, Ma." He stepped onto the porch as Leela came out behind him.

Dark clouds dipped close to the fields, hanging in deadly silence like the grayish black aftermath of an explosion. The wind strengthened as Leela watched, shaking her bloom-filled rosebushes in a jittery frenzy, throwing a flurry of pink petals into the air.

She waved to Indy, James and Pully, who had just finished herding all the livestock into the barn. They secured the door, then headed out toward Cedar Creek, where they would wait out the storm in their two-room cabin a quarter mile from Rioluces. There was nothing to do now but wait.

By four o'clock, darkness fell so heavily and quickly, Leela lit more oil lamps and candles to illuminate the kitchen. Still, no rain fell. Sinister clouds continued to gather on the horizon, while sporadic winds gusted angrily and threatened to splinter the wood-frame house.

The Rochester clock chimed six when Leela and Kenny sat down to eat dinner. While they ate, the storm swirled into a crescendo of lightning and thunder, shattering the silence between them. Heavy and plump, like clumps of dirt hurled against the walls, the first raindrops plummeted from above. They clattered onto the roof, struck the dark windows sharply and thudded into puddles on all four porches.

Kenny left his supper cooling on the table and ran to the front parlor window.

"Come back and eat," Leela said. "You can't see a thing out there."

"Please, Ma. Just a few minutes. I want to watch."

Leela held her peace. Kenny shoved his nose against the cool dark pane and caught a glimpse of the raging storm when a shocking bolt of lightning lit up the pitch-black yard. Leela shuddered as the house rattled and creaked on its foundation, the vicious storm vibrating the floor.

"Can't see much," Kenny complained. "It's like a black hole out there, but water's standing in the yard, Ma. A lot of it."

"Come finish your dinner," Leela urged. "This squall will be passing on through. The land really needed a drenching."

Rain continued to pummel the earth far into the night. The storm screamed through the eaves, charged the night with electrical flashes and emptied torrents of water over the county.

As Kenny slept, Leela lay in her bed, listening to the echo of water splashing into the washtub she'd set under the leaky spot in the parlor roof. The minutes ticked by and she dozed off, slipping away from the storm into a dream-filled slumber.

She was taking the train to Dallas. Dressed in a red silk suit with matching hat, she approached the ticket window, money in hand. The helpful stationmaster explained that her train was boarding now, and she had better hurry if she planned to take the 9:22 that day. Leela bought her ticket, rushed onto the platform, and was about to step onto the train when it suddenly began to move. It simply pulled away from the station as if she were not there. Leela looked up to see the conductor and all the passengers waving good-bye. The train slipped down the tracks in a cloud of steam, hissing off to the north under a soulless black sky.

Stop the train, Leela yelled. Wait for me!

When it blasted its whistle and roared away, Leela jolted awake with a start.

Huge spoked wheels grinding over metal track, the groan of heavy cars straining to follow, the haunting whistle. The sounds assaulted Leela in the middle of her darkened bedroom. She pushed herself to a sitting position, pulled a sheet up to her chest and looked around in confusion. She distinctly heard the huge iron horse thundering directly toward Rioluces. The wailing whistle hurt her ears so badly, she pressed her hands to her head. Within seconds, an explosion ripped through the house. A thunderous crash propelled her to her feet, just as water burst through the ceiling in an alarming fury and flooded down into the room. Leela fled, screaming at the top of her lungs as black water rose under her feet and the wind tore the bedclothes from her body.

Pieces of lumber fell down around her. She groped her way toward Kenny's room. The water rose rapidly around her ankles and sharp splinters of wood pierced her bare feet.

"It's a tornado!" Leela shrieked as she threw Kenny's door open. "Get up. Kenny, get up. Come with me. We've got to get into the cellar." She shook the sleepy boy awake, threw a blanket over his head and dragged him along behind her as she bolted out the front door, wading through knee-high water to get to the side of the house.

Soaked to the skin and fighting against the powerful wind, Leela struggled with the heavy slanted door protruding from the ground. Together, she and Kenny finally forced it open and squeezed inside. They stumbled down the steps and collapsed on the cold dirt floor. The heavy door slammed shut with a thud overhead, trapping them in the dark moldy space.

Leela managed to untangle her soaked nightgown from around her legs and huddled protectively on the floor beside her son. Shivering in wet clothes, she put an arm around Kenny, and together they sat in darkness until the storm above them eased its fury and the first rays of sunlight filtered through the cracks in the cellar hatch.

When all was quiet, Leela shook Kenny from a fitful half-sleep and they cautiously emerged into the steamy morning, stepping out into thick muddy water swirling nearly waist-high as far as they could see. The house seemed to sit in the center of a shimmering lake, water rippling in the last breezy remnants of the devastating tornado. Leela immediately saw that most of the roof had been blown away. Luckily, the barn remained intact, but she could hear frightened animals clamoring to be freed.

As her eyes flitted across the misty landscape, Leela began to shake. A chill inched over her damp skin, her legs grew unsteady, and she held her breath as she took in the sight before her. Acre after acre of bloody red pulp, twisted and smashed, floated in murky brown water with chunks of vivid green rind. Her precious Black Diamonds, her African warriors, which she had groomed and nurtured to withstand the drought, now lay vanquished and defeated, broken into pieces, their entrails hurled in angry mutilation across the vast acreage of Rioluces.

Chapter Seventeen

"Who you say you lookin' for?" the old woman asked, stopping in midstroke to lean against her well-worn broom.

"A Mr. Beaufort," Leela replied. "Victor Beaufort. I was told he has an office in this building." Leela pointed toward the open doorway behind the woman, who shook her head slowly, then resumed her sweeping.

"This here's Mildred's Cafe," she said, stirring up a cloud of dust at Leela's feet. "My cafe. I'm Mildred. Don't nobody office in here."

"Do you know where I might find Mr. Beaufort?" Leela asked, stepping out of the woman's path.

"What's he look like?"

"I've never met him," Leela hesitated, "but I understand he's new to Mexia . . . an oilman from Oklahoma."

"Oh." The woman's dark lips curved at the corners. "The colored oilman." She stopped to wipe her hands on her frayed apron. "I never could recollect his name. Such a fancy-sounding name. He comes and goes. Real businesslike, he is. Always in a hurry. Don't stop and chat much with folks 'round here. I think the man you lookin' for is over there." She pointed to a redbrick building with three arched windows facing them across the street. "Try that building, up on the second floor."

"Thank you," Leela said, turning quickly, heading toward the two-story structure. She pushed open a weathered door and climbed a short flight of stairs.

Victor Beaufort did not immediately stand when Leela entered the room, but leisurely tapped his still-smoking pipe against the rim of a gray metal ashtray.

Standing in the doorway, poised to speak, Leela hesitated for a moment, scrutinizing the man before her. He lifted his head from the pile of papers spread across his desk and pushed his ink pen into its holder, allowing his light brown eyes to lock briefly with hers.

His short dark hair, trimmed neatly and precisely with a razor-sharp part on one side, tapered stylishly into sideburns on either side of his face. As the oilman's darkly chiseled features softened, his carefully trimmed mustache spread thinly across a firm yet sensitive mouth. Like melting chocolate, a slight smile eased over his handsome face until the skin at the corners of his eyes crinkled in welcome. The look he gave Leela sent shivers up her arms. He appeared smartly dressed in a crisply tailored pale beige jacket with an arrow-straight tie down the center of his chest. Leela relaxed suddenly, allowing herself to be immediately drawn into the soft brown curves of his face.

"Are you Victor Beaufort?" she asked, knowing her sudden intrusion had caught him off-guard.

"Yes, I am," he replied, drawling his response, obviously trying to compose himself.

Leela moved toward his desk, breaking his curious stare.

"What can I do for you?" he asked.

"I understand you're an oilman," she blurted out.

"I guess you can call me an oilman. And you are . . . ?"

"Mrs. Thomas Jacob Wilder," Leela said matter-of-factly, then added, "recently widowed."

Victor Beaufort stood, waving his hand toward a cane-bottomed chair that looked worn to the point of breaking apart.

"Please sit down, Mrs. Wilder."

Leela slipped into the chair, clutching its scarred arms as she crossed her ankles. Her stiffly pleated skirt hit her leg at midcalf, then rose a few inches higher as she slightly raised one knee.

Victor Beaufort's eyes traveled over Leela's legs. She was surprised to find she did not resent his candid interest.

"I've heard about you," Leela plunged ahead in a businesslike tone. "I understand you worked in the Osage fields in Oklahoma, and now you're looking for oil in Texas."

"That's pretty close," he admitted, leaning back in his chair, stretching his long legs beneath the ornately carved table that served as his desk. His jacket fell away from his chest, and Leela saw the initials VB monogrammed on the pocket of his starched white shirt.

"Do you think there's oil in Mexia?" she asked, her eyes flitting nervously from his broad shoulders to the charts and graphs covering his desk.

"I most certainly do," Victor answered with conviction. "Me and a whole lot of folks. Oilmen from all over the country are swarming in here like flies to an open jar of molasses. Everybody's waiting to see what Colonel Humphreys brings in."

"Colonel Humphreys?" Leela frowned. She had never heard the name before.

"A. E. Humphreys. The wildcatter who spudded in the Rogers test well. The way I heard it, when the locals went bust, old man Humphreys jumped in with enough cash to skid the derrick from the lost hole and keep on drilling. He's made and lost three fortunes, and most folks believe he'll make another one right here in Mexia. If the test proves out, this town's gonna boom." Victor now leaned forward and placed both elbows on the table. "Might be bigger than Spindletop. That's what old-timers are saying." He rested his chin between his hands and stared directly at Leela. "What's your interest in all this, Mrs. Wilder? Why'd you come here looking for me?"

Before Leela answered that question, she decided to ask one herself.

"What are oil leases going for?"

"You mean per acre?" He quizzically raised one eyebrow and studied Leela's face.

"Yes. How much money would be paid to a landowner to let someone like you look for oil?" Leela's unflinching stare matched his.

"Not much," Victor said seriously. "Sometimes as little as ten cents an acre, sometimes as much as a dollar." Victor saw the crush of disappointment begin to creep over Leela's face.

"A dollar? That's not very much," she said.

"It's enough to slap a permanent smile on the face of a farmer who's never seen fifty dollars in hard cash. Especially if a gusher comes in." His light brown eyes glinted in eagerness as he spoke of the promise of a strike. "And it can happen. I've seen black gold shoot out of the ground like . . ." He abruptly stopped talking, put his hands flat on the desk, embarrassed by his own enthusiasm. He picked up his pipe to light it again. "Mind if I smoke?"

Leela waved her hand distractedly, thinking about what he had just said.

"And how long does that take?" she wanted to know.

"What?" He seemed puzzled by her question.

"For a gusher to come in," she replied.

Without answering, Victor threw back his head and laughed aloud, propping one booted foot on his knee.

"That depends on a lot of things, little lady." He rubbed a slim, ringless finger along the intricate tooling on his calfskin boot. "Could be weeks, could be months, years even. And as I have seen more times than I like to admit, maybe never."

The creeping disappointment began to strengthen, making Leela very uncomfortable. She felt herself wilting.

"Why all the questions, ma'am? Seems like I'm upsetting you." His words verged on an apology.

"I had hoped you might be able to help me. But if one dollar an acre is all I could get for a lease . . ." She paused and let her voice trail off, discouraged that the small amount a lease would bring was a far cry from what she needed.

"Hold on, now, Mrs. Wilder. Why don't you just tell me what's going on? I can see that something's worrying you. If I can help, I'll try." He settled back to listen.

Feeling relieved that Victor was willing to hear her out, Leela absently twisted the lace on the wrists of her gloves as she related her tale.

She told Victor the history of Rioluces, reliving the painful memory of T.J.'s death, the horror of the destructive tornado and the total loss of her melon crop.

Unexpected tears welled up in her eyes as she explained to this stranger how desperate she was to hold on to her farm.

"And what's the bank's position now that the Black Diamonds are lost?" Victor asked.

"The bank examiner never came," Leela said. "Water stayed high for days. No one dared travel the Mexia-Comanche Crossing Road for nearly a week—the entire highway washed out in the storm. Today's my first trip to town, and with the crop gone . . . well . . . I couldn't face Mr. Bernard again, though I'm sure I'll be hearing from him soon enough. I decided to come here and talk with you."

They both fell silent for several long seconds, the atmosphere stuffy in the cramped, hot room. From the street they could hear the voices of two men arguing over the value of a load of lumber while a dog whined loudly as if it were hurt.

Without saying a word, Victor put down his pipe. He quickly stood and began pacing back and forth in the space behind his desk. There were frown lines in the smooth brown skin of his forehead. He ran a hand over his neatly cut hair several times before he spoke.

"So, you need three thousand dollars very soon, don't you?"

"Yes." Leela's barely audible voice cracked.

"I can tell you right now, Mrs. Wilder, no land man is going to pay you three thousand dollars for a lease on your farm. Not just yet. Maybe in another four, six weeks and that's only if the Rogers test proves good. The most I suspect you could get right now is about five hundred dollars."

As much as she dreaded hearing this, she steeled herself for the truth. He was right. Only a very foolish man, or a very wealthy one, would dole out three thousand dollars on untested land, especially before a show of oil somewhere in the area. And she could see that Victor Beaufort was neither foolish nor wealthy.

The room suddenly seemed unbearably hot, and Leela peeled off her short cotton gloves, wringing them between sweaty fingers as she waited for Victor to continue.

"Let me explain how this business of looking for oil comes about. As a leasebroker, or land man, I purchase as cheaply as possible the right to look for oil on someone's land. That gives me, or an oil company if I sell my lease to them, access to the land for a specific period of time, usually five to ten years. In your case, for example, you would get three hundred forty dollars a year from me until oil is brought in."

"Have you leased any land in Mexia yet?" Leela asked, curious about this self-assured man who seemed to have all the answers. She watched his eyes narrow at her inquiry.

Victor stopped pacing and put both hands on the back of his chair. He leaned slightly forward as he answered. "I don't usually talk about the deals I make. That can be tricky, you know?"

But Leela wanted to know more and pressed Victor until he told her.

"I've got a seven-year lease on the Varnet place, just east of the Rogers farm. You know the area?"

"Claude and Mary Bell Varnet's farm? Of course, my cousin lived very near them. They've got about fifty acres, don't they?"

"And before you ask me any more questions, I'll tell you I leased it for ten cents an acre, and the only reason they took my offer is because they're near starving to death on their own land."

Leela didn't say a word but reckoned that the reason Claude Varnet took that little bit of money was to buy more fifty-gallon drums to brew his corn whiskey in. The lazy man was content running hooch through the county and was well known as the local source for anything from Johnny-mash to White Mule.

"What happens if you don't find any oil?" Leela wanted to know.

"At the end of my lease I have to abandon the property and the owner can sell the lease to someone else or back to me to try again."

"And if oil is found?"

"The landowner gets one-eighth of the oil. This is called a royalty, your share of the profit I'd get for the sale of the oil."

"And how much does a barrel of oil bring?"

"About a dollar right now. And that's before the expenses of getting it to the refinery, where it's processed for sale. If the man who brings it in can't get it to the refinery cheaply, he'll wind up making about fifteen cents a barrel. Pretty risky business, you see."

Leela's disappointment grew with each word Victor spoke, though she nodded in understanding, fearfully asking one more question.

"If there is oil on my land, how long would it take after it's discovered for me to receive any money?"

The creases in Victor's forehead softened and disappeared. He wove his fingers together and pursed his lips, knowing the importance of his response. "Ma'am, if a gusher blew in on your land today, it might be six months before you'd see a penny."

Leela crumpled her gloves into a sweaty mass of cotton and jammed them into her purse. She rose to leave.

No use pursuing this, she determined, hating the awful surge of despair that threatened to make her cry. I need money *now* to keep my farm. That inspector from the bank will show up any day. And when he learns I have no crop, Rioluces will be taken immediately. Pushing back her chair, she stepped toward the door.

Victor crossed the room and unexpectedly stood behind her, very close to her, so close she could smell the mixture of pipe tobacco and cologne that clung pleasantly to his clothes. She turned to find herself staring into Victor's intense brown eyes.

"Don't go. Not yet, Mrs. Wilder. Please believe me, if there is any way I can help you, I'll try. But you must understand how things work."

"Very slowly, I can see," Leela said bitterly. She backed away slightly, feeling a little dizzy, unsettled by Victor Beaufort's steady gaze.

"I'd like very much to see your land," he said lowly. "Might be we could work something out. How would it be if I came out tomorrow morning?"

The smell of him, the nearness of him, the small offering of hope he extended made Leela tremble. She tilted her face up to his and smiled for the first time since entering the office. Holding herself stiffly under his penetrating eyes, she finally managed to say, "I'd be proud to show you Rioluces. Please come out as early as you can."

Victor Beaufort startled Leela as he reined in his stallion and stopped just outside the barn door. From inside Taffy's stall, Leela listened to him speak soothingly to his overheated horse.

"Hold on now, boy. Let's see if anybody's here."

Taffy snorted and pawed the ground, smelling a new horse on the place. Leela stroked her chestnut mare, remaining silent behind the cracked partition.

She could see Victor clearly, sitting tall, wearing a light brown Stetson that gave him an air of importance. It suited him well, in shape, size and color, reminding her of an advertisement for hats she'd seen in the *Saturday Evening Post.* Two shiny pieces of silver, the size of dimes, dangled from the ends of leather ties hanging loosely under his clean-shaven chin, and his chocolate-colored vest, made of velvet-smooth suede, closely fit his broad shoulders tapering to a lean waist. It was splashed with colorful glass beads sewn in an elaborate tribal design Leela recognized as Osage. She noticed that Victor had replaced the fancy tooled boots of yesterday with a pair of sturdy, knee-high riding boots fit with spurs and a small pocket for his Bowie knife.

Leela watched the easy, confident way he dismounted and casually tossed his reins over the hitching rail.

"Mrs. Wilder?" Victor called out, striding closer. He hesitated before entering the dim, open space.

Leela stepped from the shadows with one hand shading the early morning sun from her eyes.

"Why, Mr. Beaufort, you startled me," she replied, moving quickly into view.

"The young man at the gate said I'd find you here."

"Oh, Pully? Yes, I told him to be on the lookout for you."

"Just call me Victor," he told her, nodding his head in greeting.

"When you say 'early' you mean it, don't you?" Leela joked, though she had lain awake most of the night anticipating Victor's arrival and had risen at the first show of daylight.

"Any serious riding to be done today had better be done before noon. Looks like we've got another scorcher on us." Victor moved aside as Leela passed him, stepping into the light. Leela circled Taffy once around the yard, mounted the anxious mare and looked down at the oilman.

"Are you ready to see Rioluces?" Before her guest had time to respond, Leela galloped off toward the west, headed toward fallow cotton fields stretching for miles in the distance.

Victor quickly caught up with her, guiding his painted stallion over the soft soil that had so eagerly absorbed the torrential rains of a few days ago. Prairie grass that had chafed and cracked under the sapping glare of the sun now rustled green and supple in a refreshing wind that blew in from the south and tempered the late-August morning.

The luxurious breeze would not last, Leela knew, for it was only seven o'clock. The sun had not yet heated the crust of the land, had not sucked the remaining moisture from damp, shady places to create the stifling, swamplike atmosphere that severely tested anyone caught riding late in the day.

Together, Leela and Victor passed clumps of feathery cypress, their long fronds swaying ever so slightly toward the ground. Stands of red and white oaks, sturdy trunks topped with finger-shaped leaves, captured sunshine in their leafy crowns and glistened along the trail. The long-awaited downpour had even forced wisteria vines to burst forth mistakenly with small purple buds long past their short blooming season.

As they galloped toward the west, they scattered jackrabbits, armadillos, skunks and raccoons from hidden nests, disturbing one coiled rattlesnake that raised its clattering tail in angry defense.

With Victor at her side, Leela surveyed her land and felt proud. The expanse of Rioluces was as impressive as the richness of its resources. Thick banks of soaring pines, their spiky branches tufted in vivid green, crowded together in a swell of timber marching uniformly to the west. Broad-leafed vines coiled to the tops of sturdy trees and layered their purple grapes so thickly and hungrily around the bores of the posts, not a glimpse of craggy bark remained.

To the east, gigantic live oaks stood in groves, their thick, cablelike branches stretching out across the land, their gracefully balanced limbs bringing salvation to the sun-beaten livestock gathered in their shade.

To the south, beyond Cedar Creek, waves of impenetrable forest rose in a slight incline and set the remotest boundary of Rioluces.

Victor brought his stallion to a halt and sat staring when he and Leela reached the destroyed melon field. The sickening stench of rotting watermelons assaulted them. The fermenting fruit, exposed to the scorching sun, lay in a tangled mass. Flies buzzed in thick, dark hordes, and hungry birds pecked furiously through the wasteland, scavenging for seeds. Huge pieces of rind, chunks of red flesh, twisted vines and even whole melons lay abandoned like fallen soldiers after a bloody battle.

Leela put her riding glove to her nose as she spoke. "You can see what a mess the storm left behind. It will take a long time to set this straight. I've allowed Pully and his brothers to sell any salvageable melons. I can't pay them wages and there's no profit left in this field."

In the distance, wild dogs rooted through the spoilage, and a determined raccoon tugged at a piece of melon with its tiny human-like hands.

"This is incredible," Victor said, urging his anxious mount to stand still. "I've seen the aftermath of tornadoes in Oklahoma, but never anything like this."

A gutted corridor of felled trees, pulverized crops, uprooted undergrowth, and twisted barbed-wire fencing ran nearly a mile in the distance, leaving a well-defined imprint of the storm's vicious wrath. Oddly, a good portion of uncultivated land had been spared, as if the storm clouds had deliberately targeted Leela's precious Black Diamonds.

"Makes a man humble, doesn't it? Seeing how everything he's got can be taken away in just a few minutes." With a sudden jerk, Victor turned his piebald stallion southward toward the creek and rode away from the devastation.

Leela urged Taffy forward to catch up with him, guiding the mare closer to take advantage of her position and look quietly over at the oilman.

The sun-creased bronze of his profile captivated her. Head held high, jaw thrust forward in thought, his rugged beauty drew her in. His long muscular legs pressed into his mount as he rode effortlessly across Rioluces. Like a hunter with his prey just ahead, Victor's graceful sprint toward the south told Leela he was an experienced rider with a genuine love for the land.

In some indefinable way, Victor Beaufort reminded Leela of her cousin Parker. Maybe it was his purposeful manner of speaking, as if every syllable uttered brought him closer to the truth. Or perhaps because he had found a way to manipulate the white man's world to establish a place for himself. Victor radiated that same confidence bordering on arrogance, a self-assurance seemingly bred from the knowledge that he controlled his future and knew exactly where he was headed.

Leela's heart pumped rapidly when he turned toward her and gave her a smile. Feelings of her youth surged forth, and she remembered her yearning for someone to embrace with the passion she had not found with T.J.

Is it possible, Leela thought as she urged Taffy forward, that someday I will find such a love? She swallowed and took a deep breath to clear her head. I'm here with Mr. Beaufort to look for signs of oil, nothing more, she reminded herself.

A short time later, the two arrived at Cedar Creek. Wide and fast-moving, it cut a path toward the Navasota River, where it divided Leela's land from Red Walters's farm. When they dismounted to water the horses and take a short rest, Leela pulled a canteen of water and two red apples from her saddlebag. She tossed an apple to Victor, then went to sit on a huge log rolled up to the bank of the creek. In the delicious cool of the shade, she stripped the gray bandana from around her neck and patted perspiration from her temples, removing her straw hat to let her mass of copper curls fall free.

But Leela could not relax. She sat tensely, twisting the bandana in her fingers. Did the lay of the land mean anything to him? Did he see any potential for oil? Would he take a chance on Rioluces?

Stealing a glance in Victor's direction, Leela realized how much she hoped he saw promise in her land. So much depended on his opinion. As she looked out over the rippling water, dotted with hovering dragonflies, she knew it would be impossible to ever leave Rioluces.

Victor finished watering his stallion and walked toward her. She raised expectant eyes to his and held them for a moment before she was able to speak.

"Tell me about yourself, Mr. Beaufort. What does being an oilman really mean?" She adjusted her split riding skirt and shifted on the log to make room for him to sit beside her. Victor sank down next to Leela, facing slightly away from her, and stared at the forest of pines in the distance.

"Well, I lived all my life in Oklahoma. And after thirty-four years I've decided to try life as a Texan." He pushed back the brim of his Stetson and pulled his bandana from his neck. He absently polished the apple as he spoke. "I came here as a land man, but I've decided to stay on as a wildcatter." He seemed to find this amusing and smiled broadly as he bit into the crisp red apple.

"Are people in Oklahoma talking about Mexia?" Leela wanted to know.

"Oh, yes. When I came to Mexia, my intention was to only buy and sell leases . . . buy up a lease on a large tract of land very cheaply, divide it up into smaller parcels and resell them for much higher profits."

"Is that what you did in Oklahoma?"

Victor chuckled lightly, and Leela watched his handsome, dark features melt into sunshine. "No, not at all," he replied through his laughter. "My two brothers and I started out in the oil fields digging ditches and laying pipe. You were right, I worked the Osage fields, some of the most productive in the state. But I got no profits from that oil, only two dollars a day as long as my hands and my back held out, and only if the gang pusher was willing to tolerate a colored man on his team. Some were more agreeable than others."

Leela said nothing, knowing what he meant. Victor finished his apple and tossed the core far into the middle of the creek.

"It was dirty work but there was a lot of it, so my brothers, Cap and Frank, and I just went from gang to gang over the area. Wherever we could hire on is where we stayed. But we had bigger ideas and eventually pooled our wages to buy up a load of rusted pipe. We cut and retooled the pipe and sold it to an oil company for four times what we paid for it. That got us hooked, and there was no way we would ever go back to digging ditches after that. Our little pipe company has done so well we've got enough money to buy up a few leases, and I want to try my luck at wildcatting."

"That means you drill the well, doesn't it?" Leela asked.

"Exactly. A wildcatter takes a risk when he spuds in the well and does all the work to bring in the oil. My brothers and I know everything a man needs to know about sinking a well, though the white oilmen would never admit it. Sometimes it's just a matter of getting our hands on the right tools. If the suppliers won't sell them to us, we can do a pretty good job of making our own. We've become very inventive over the years, and now we've got all the rigging we need." He paused and let out a deep breath. Leela could feel him shifting beside her. "What the devil. Sometimes a man's gotta take a risk or two if he wants to get more out of life than a handout."

"Does your company have a name?"

"The Beaufort Drilling Company," he said proudly. "We may be the only drilling company of colored men looking for oil in Texas."

"Why don't you sink your well in Oklahoma?"

"No way to do it there." Victor's tone was matter-of-fact.

He turned squarely toward Leela and leveled his eyes with hers. "You must understand one thing. The oil business has no place for black men. Even in the fields, digging ditches, pushing pipe, my brothers and I rarely saw another black face. We grew up in the shadows of the derricks of Tulsa when the Sue Bland well came in at Red Fork. We played hide-and-seek between red-hot boilers and built ant farms at the foot of wooden storage tanks."

"Did your parents work in the fields?" Leela asked.

"Oh, no. My brothers and I were oil field orphans, never did know who our parents were. A Cherokee woman named Annie Bowlegs kind of raised us. She was a field cook at the drilling site. So the white men in the oil fields knew us. First job I ever had was carrying water from derrick to derrick at Red Fork. Twenty-five cents a day from sunup to sundown. And I loved it."

As Victor talked Leela watched him closely, impressed by the way he spoke of his childhood with both pride and sadness, yet never sounding bitter. He's so much like Parker, she reflected again. He made his own road map for his future.

"We got to be pretty well known on the drilling circuits," Victor continued. "A good word from a former boss man helped us get jobs. But we were the exceptions and it's still that way. Looking for oil requires money, trust and a common bond between men willing to rely on a handshake deal . . . and I don't know any white man who feels comfortable doing that kind of business with a colored man. I think my chances are better in a place like this."

"Why do you say that?" Leela wanted to know. "What's so different about Mexia?"

"Negroes in this county own the land and I can get the cash together to buy the leases. After I find the best possible location, my brothers and I will be ready to take the chance."

"What about your lease on the Varnet place? Will you drill there?"

"I'm holding that lease to turn a deal. Just praying the Rogers test proves out. If it does, I can sell my lease on the Varnet place for just about any price I call. That will give me the cash to support my wildcatting, if I can find the right place to sink my well."

Leela got up and walked to stand under the low-hanging boughs of a willow tree at the very edge of the water. She stripped off a branch and tore tiny leaves from it as she thought about what to say.

"And do you think Rioluces is that place?" she asked, almost afraid to raise her eyes to Victor's.

The land buzzed with horseflies, bees and hornets. A multitude of birds chirped and cackled from all parts of the meadow. These familiar sounds of the Texas landscape seemed magnified and unusually shrill to Leela. She waited for Victor to answer.

"I don't know," he said firmly, leaning forward with clasped hands dangling between his knees. "You're three miles from the Rogers place. This land is just like any other land I've looked over, and there's no reason to believe there's oil here and not on the neighboring farm. No surveys have been done. No one has tested the soil. Although this business of searching for oil is very chancy, my brothers and I can't afford to sink our first well on hunches."

Leela crushed the willow branch into a ball, twisting the tender green twig with both hands, and glared into the water. She dared not look at him.

So he wants no part of Rioluces, she surmised. Why did he lead me to believe he could help, when he really has nothing to offer? Leela fumed. He only came to Rioluces to get closer to me, impress me with his oilman talk and his fancy Indian clothes. She hoped he could feel the anger in her thoughts.

"As I said yesterday, Mrs. Wilder," Victor went on, his clasped hands tensing as he looked away from her, "this oil search here in Mexia is still in the early stages. Until a test well proves good, no one will be taking chances on leases around here. Your farm certainly is in a location that would favor an underground reserve, but I couldn't offer you more than five hundred dollars for the lease, if I decide to take it."

Leela's anger at Victor Beaufort boiled to the surface and stung her bitterly. Hadn't he listened to her story of the settlers who scraped and burned pitch from this creek bank for years? The rumors of oil on Rioluces had been handed down for generations. What more did he want?

When at last she turned to face him, her heart fluttered lightly and her mouth went dry. My God, she asked herself, what is it that draws me to him? Suddenly, she felt angry for being so attracted to him. What in the world was she doing? Wasting time with a man who could not help her save the farm. Allowing herself to be conned by a handsome stranger.

Leela stomped off toward her horse, throwing the willow branches in Victor's face as she passed him.

"What an awful man you are!" she cried. "Using your ploy to look over the land to get close to me. How dare you lead me to believe you can help, when all you ever wanted was to prance along on your fancy horse and spread your smooth charm around? Well, I'm not at all impressed and really wish you'd never come. I don't need to hear your talk about hunches and chance and untested soil. I need an honest man who can help me save my farm."

As much as she hated for him to see her cry, tears burst forth, rushing down her cheeks, interrupting the tirade of words she wanted to throw at him. Her effort to present a strong front fell apart. Too embarrassed to say more, Leela shoved past Victor and swung herself up onto Taffy.

The sudden mounting frightened her mare and the skittish animal reared up on hind legs, whinnying loudly. Confused, Taffy took off toward the creek. Leela screamed and clutched the reins.

"Whoa! Taffy, whoa!" She pulled the leather straps as hard as she could.

Taffy stopped abruptly and Leela felt herself falling backward as the hind end of her horse sank beneath her.

Victor rushed forward to block her fall.

"Watch out! Oh, my God!" he cried as he slipped beneath the horse just as Leela tumbled into his arms. He pulled her close and quickly flipped her onto her stomach, shielding her from the horse's flailing hooves. Victor groaned loudly as he took a blow on his back. Leela tried to push free of him, but he only clutched her more tightly.

"Hold on to me," she heard him say as they rolled from beneath the horse to safety.

Once clear, Leela sat up and began to wipe sticky black mud from her face. "What in the world?" she muttered, angry that her cowhide skirt was ruined, mad at Victor for holding her so tightly.

"Look!" Victor grabbed her by the arm. "Look!" He started to rise. "Can you believe that?" He stared at Leela's horse, mouth open in surprise.

Leela pushed a tangle of curls from her eyes and followed Victor's gaze. Taffy whinnied and snorted as she struggled to stand, but it was impossible. Her hind legs were trapped, completely mired down in a slimy black pool of oil.

Chapter Eighteen

The Alzonia Quartet, usually loud, brassy and syncopated, turned the volume down with a muted version of "The Fade Away Blues" and eased its soulful tune out over the crowd. Brilliant points of light burst like sparklers from an elaborate chandelier in the center of the hall, bouncing off the chipped gilded trim on the red velvet chairs pulled up to tables set for blackjack, poker, craps and roulette.

Tonight the patrons in the Versailles Room of the Randolph Hotel, sipping bourbon from Baccarat goblets and nibbling smoked oysters from thin china plates, made an exotically festive portrait. The men and women who perched themselves on reproduction Louis XV chairs looked nothing like the Anglo-Saxon lords and ladies in the faded tapestry hanging over the massive oak bar. No powdered wigs curled around thin white faces. And the men who propped their feet on the brass rail beneath the smooth marble counter wore dark patent leathers draped with sparkling white spats instead of high-heeled slippers set with big golden buckles. The women among the swaggering group of seemingly powerful men sat like artists' models in their beaded flapper shifts, patting finger-waved hair slicked back like rows of satin ribbon.

Under the huge crystal light suspended above their heads, the elite of Baton Rouge's black society laughed and drank, gossiped and flirted, tossed money on the gaming tables with heavily bejeweled hands and settled smugly into themselves, knowing how special they were.

The weight of the delicately etched brandy snifter in the palm of his hand made Carey Logan think of Dallas—the Valeta Hotel—the steamy foul kitchen where he had washed glasses just like the one he now held and where he had learned to swallow the bitter taste of hunger and mask the shame of empty pockets and threadbare clothes.

Never again, Carey thought, detesting those bitter memories now edging too close to his current situation. I've gotta shake this place real soon and I ain't leavin' town without my money. Pieces of paper don't spend where I'm going. Doyle Brisko's gonna be sorry he cried broke tonight. I'm sick and tired of these geechie gamblers.

Abruptly, Carey pushed his empty glass across the slick bar and began forming his plan to raise cash. Tonight.

"Hit me again, Toby," he said to the white-jacketed barman polishing champagne glasses with a soft towel.

"Yes, sir, Mr. Logan," the bartender replied, reaching for the dark brown bottle of brandy stashed behind a cluster of decanters filled with whiskey, gin, rum and vodka.

Carey watched the amber liquid settle into his brandy snifter, picked it up and held the glass under his nose for a moment. He was tempted to down the drink in one gulp, let it slide down his throat in one blissful numbing stream. But he knew Ada Lache was watching from her table in the shadows; she'd had her eyes on him all night. He swirled and sniffed and handled the brandy in a manner he knew would impress her.

Carey stared into his drink. Yeah, he'd known lots of women like Ada: classy, tempting, bored. Hungry for a little excitement. They were everywhere. Decorating the speakeasies and private clubs of Baton Rouge, spicing up the action as the men rolled dice, dealt cards and sipped bootleg bourbon from fine crystal glasses.

I think it's time to make my move, Carey decided, and I'll need Ada Lache to pull it off.

"Been a lucky night for you, Mr. Logan?" Toby asked as he handed a frothy mint julep to a tall Creole man.

"Pretty good, Toby," Carey lied, trying to bury his anger at the chickenshit way he'd just been treated by Doyle Brisko. "I've seen better action, but can't complain." Carey glanced into the mirror behind the bar and connected with Ada Lache. "I got a feelin' my luck's gonna change. Think I'll share a little of my take with Miss Lache. Seems she's all alone this evening."

"That's right. Mr. Struthers ain't been 'round just yet."

"Send over a bottle of champagne," Carey said, placing his last twenty on the bar. He straightened his jacquard cravat, picked up his brandy and walked toward Ada's table. She did not look up when he sat down, but lowered her eyes to the candle flickering beneath a rose-colored shade in the center of the table.

"Use a little company, Ada?"

She raised gray-blue eyes at Carey. "Yeah," she breathed in a husky voice. "Damon's out of town."

"Hope that's not the only reason for letting me sit with you."

"I didn't mean it like that, Carey. You know I like your company anytime."

"Anytime Damon's away, you mean." Carey inhaled her Midnight Orchid perfume as he slipped into a chair. She smiled widely, deep dimples making perfect impressions on either side of her oval face.

"Where's your shadow, anyway?" Carey asked, hoping her tough-guy boyfriend might have left Baton Rouge for good.

"He'll be back in a few days, probably by the end of the week," Ada said, leaning closer to Carey, allowing her silky black hair to brush the linen tablecloth.

"A coupla days?" Carey tugged at the wide French cuffs protruding from the sleeves of his white dinner jacket and watched as Ada examined his sapphire-studded cuff links. He raised one finely arched eyebrow when he spoke.

"A lady can get pretty lonely in a space of time like that." He sat back and ran a manicured finger over his neatly trimmed mustache.

Ada was the kind of woman most men wanted hanging on their arms: flawless brown skin, "good" hair cascading over her shoulders, teeth so white and even they hardly looked real. And the black satin dress that defined her shapely figure was so elegantly stylish it must have come from Chicago, or maybe even New York.

She was also the type of companion Carey easily tolerated when the chips were falling his way, but when his luck turned sour or he'd lost heavily at the tables, he shied away from females—too much trouble and too damn hard to please. Tonight, Ada appeared sexier and more exquisite than the last time he'd seen her, or maybe she just seemed so irresistible because, for the first time in months, she'd come into the Versailles Room alone.

"Damon must have a pretty good deal working to leave you alone like this."

"I think he's moving some merchandise up around St. Louis."

"Bourbon? Gin? West Indian rum?"

"Don't ask, Carey." Ada leaned back in her chair and frowned. "I told you I don't get that involved in Damon's affairs. It's better that way. You know? He's a businessman and his business is private. Understand?"

"Sure, I understand." Carey backed off. "Just curious. Sounds like Prohibition's been better for Damon Struthers than any other man in this town. Black or white. Guess when it comes to getting a decent drink, folks don't care who supplies the whiskey, long as it's strong and there's lots of it around. Keeps this place shaking along, I see. Have to admit, Damon made a smart move opening up this room."

"Seems so," Ada murmured, looking around, obviously uneasy. Carey began to wonder if Damon had more claim to her than he thought, or maybe she had other reasons for her restlessness. He decided to give her the space to let him know.

The bartender set an iced-down bottle of champagne on the table, uncorked it with a flourish and poured a small amount into Ada's glass.

"Sure would be nice to get to know you better, spend a little time alone with you," Carey began, watching Ada's full red lips curl over the side of the frosty glass.

"Think so?" Ada replied, lowering slanted eyes, as if truly considering his proposal.

"Yeah," Carey said with confidence, taking his cigarette case from his breast pocket. "I think we'd get along real fine."

Ada said nothing, but swished the champagne around on her tongue, swallowed, then spoke to Toby.

"Perfect," she said, holding her glass out for him to fill. "Be sure to tell Mr. Struthers I'd like you to keep this brand around."

"I'll pass it on to the boss," Toby said, filling Carey's glass before stepping away from the table.

Ada raised her drink in mock salute as she threw back her head and shook her hair from her face. Then she edged closer to Carey's side of the table.

"Congratulations. I heard you laid out a hand at the poker table that whipsawed Doyle Brisko out of that fancy Packard he's always bragging about."

Carey fished a scrap of paper from his watch pocket.

"That's what it says here." He pressed his thin lips together as he laid the IOU on the table. "Bad part is, I can't lay claim for twenty-four hours. Musta been crazy, falling for that hard-luck story of his. Sorry bastard. Gave him 'til tomorrow night to raise the cash to clear this. If he doesn't, the car is mine."

"He'll pay it," Ada said seriously. "That car's worth a whole lot more than the couple a hundred he probably owes you."

"I haven't seen it," Carey said, "but if it's really a Packard Twin-Six, it's gotta be worth at least three thousand."

"Try six," Ada replied, lifting her softly pointed chin as she spoke. "Custom-made in Detroit. Heard it's set up about like a luxury compartment on the Southern Pacific. The finest motorcar ever built. A man could drive it from New York to California, so I've heard."

"What else have you heard about Doyle Brisko?" Carey asked. This conversation, he realized, might turn out to be real valuable.

"For starters, he has a lot more money than he'd ever let you know. Just won't carry any of it with him." Ada tugged at the straps of her skimpy satin dress and secured them over her elegant brown shoulders. "He comes through here a couple a times a year, on his way to New Orleans, I hear. Surprised you haven't tangled with him before now. You know how many times he's used that car to settle a wager, then reclaimed it the next day? Most any regular at the Versailles Room has held claim to that car, at one time or another. He always gets it back," she said stretching her words out for emphasis. "Always."

Carey folded the IOU into a small square and offered Ada a lighted cigarette. She took it and inhaled deeply as she went on. "You know, he's got more money than all the so-called high rollers of Baton Rouge put together. He could have paid you off in cash tonight if he'd wanted. But wagering that car is like . . . well . . . his little game of power. He goes around bragging about how many times he's put up that car and not lost it."

"Someday he just might not get it back." Carey didn't like what he heard. He needed cash. Tonight. If he didn't pay off his hotel bill, his clothes would be in the lobby in the morning. And Slim Moran expected him at the Keystone Hotel by midnight tonight to clear up a little business from last night's game. Doyle Brisko was going to be sorry for involving him in his worthless power play. He'd won that hand fair and square, in front of witnesses, and Brisko owed him four hundred dollars.

"Where'd he get his money?" Carey asked, scowling over at the bull of a man whose protruding belly forced him to turn sideways to place his chips on the roulette table.

"Oil. Texas oil. Ever heard of Spindletop? Biggest gusher to ever come in. Just across the state line in Beaumont. I got family living over there. My Aunt Mary told me all about Doyle Brisko. His daddy was one of a handful of black men to own a little piece of land right in the middle of it all. Had half an acre and got rich overnight when Spindletop blew in. Doyle's momma and daddy died soon as the cash started flowing, and being the only son, he got it all."

Carey blew smoke rings above their heads and stared at the ceiling. He reached over and stroked Ada's hand. She sat quietly and let him trail his fingers up to the soft crook in her arm.

"How would you like to go for a ride in that car?" he asked slyly, leveling his face with hers.

The Alzonia Quartet swung out with a jazzy rendition of "Ragtime on the Bayou," and Ada hummed along for a moment, considering his offer, then lazily pushed her long fingernails into the heavy tablecloth before taking Carey's hand in hers. She squeezed it softly.

"And just how do you think you could manage something like that?" she asked in a whisper.

"Do me a favor," Carey prompted. "Go over and sit with Brisko at the roulette table. Just talk to him real sweet for about twenty minutes. I'm sure you could do a real good job at that." Carey searched her face for assurance. "That's all you need to do. Then tell him you gotta go powder your nose, or something like that. Be sure he thinks you're coming back. Come down the back stairs behind the kitchen and meet me at the door facing Meyer Alley." Carey reached up and boldly threaded his slim fingers through tendrils of Ada's dark hair, then tossed down the rest of his drink before rising. "And bring along another bottle of that champagne you like so much." He winked at her as he turned away. "Tell Toby to charge it to my room."

It took less than ten minutes for Carey to bolt up three flights of stairs to his sparsely furnished room on the top floor of the Randolph Hotel, pack everything he owned into a floral carpetbag and finalize his plan for leaving Baton Rouge. After rechecking the single closet and all the drawers in the tall highboy, Carey sat at the desk with a sheet of white paper, his Falcon pen filled with black ink. He opened the IOU from Doyle Brisko, studied the man's handwriting for a few seconds, then started composing his note.

Finally satisfied with his handiwork, Carey blew the ink dry and folded the note in half. A familiar rush of pleasure, brought on by the well-executed forgery, filled Carey and eased the tension in his face.

A light rain began to tap against the windows as he picked up his bag to leave. While locking the door to the room that had been home for nearly two years, he thought of the one hundred and eighty-seven dollars he owed the manager, shrugged and glanced around the hallway, opting to leave by the empty back stairs.

After quietly stashing his bag inside the door at the Meyer Alley entrance, Carey doubled back into the brightly lit lobby and handed his note to Frankie, the doorman, who stared at the paper in silence. Carey calculated the odds that Frankie could even read.

About a thousand to one, he'd wager, watching the old man struggle to decipher the note.

"Frankie," he began, "Mr. Brisko wants me to run an important errand for him. Get me his car keys, will you?"

The uniformed doorman snapped to attention at the authoritative tone in Carey Logan's voice. He shoved the note into his pants pocket.

"Yes, sir, Mr. Logan. Right away."

"Thanks," Carey said, tipping Frankie a quarter as he accepted the gold chain holding a single key. He twirled it around on his index finger as he stepped from the hotel into light misty rain.

Without looking back, Carey walked quickly down Gracie Street, the stiletto tap of his patent leather shoes echoing on the wet pavement. He turned the corner toward the lot where he knew the Packard would be parked, calmly opened the door, slid into the driver's seat and smiled when the smoky-sweet smell of padded leather and new chrome caressed him. Sitting inside the big touring car, gripping the expansive steering wheel, Carey felt as powerful and important as a captain at the helm of his ship.

Instinctively, he leaned down and ran his hand under the front seat. I figgered as much, Carey thought, folding his fingers around a fat leather pouch which he held up to the gas lamp shining just outside the window. Inside, he found the official registration for the Packard Twin-Six, stuck between a thick stack of bills: tens, twenties, fifties and even a wad of hundreds. Grinning, he pushed the money bag into his breast pocket and stuck the key into the ignition. The big motor purred to a soft start.

Carey enjoyed driving the long car as much as he relished the sense of control it gave him. Slowly, he made his way over to Meyer Alley. Before reaching the Randolph, he pulled into the shadows at the end of the block and waited until he saw Ada emerge, a gauzy red scarf thrown over her hair.

As smoothly as possible, Carey swung up to the curb, but miscalculated his distance and thudded loudly onto the sidewalk. Ada screamed and jumped back. Carey bolted from the car.

"I'm sorry," he called out. "Don't worry, I'll get the hang of it. It's a beauty, isn't it? Just like you said." He walked past her, retrieved his bag and opened the door on the passenger side for his charming companion.

Ada set the bottle of champagne on the floor, then pulled the damp scarf from her hair. She sank onto the soft leather cushions.

Carey stowed his valise into the trunk and eased himself down beside her. He turned to ask, "How far you wanna go?"

Ada snuggled seductively against his shoulder, lifting her face to his. Carey knew what she wanted and gently pulled her chin toward his. He leaned down and placed his lips over hers. She kissed him back, fiercely, reaching up to wrap her perfumed arms around his neck.

"Seein' as how you're drivin'," she murmured when their lips finally parted, "I'll go as far as you want to, sugar."

Massive chestnut trees dripping with Spanish moss caught the yellow beams of the Packard's big headlamps and rose up eerily in front of Carey. Speeding along, with the windows rolled down despite a continuous drizzle, he felt light-headed with freedom, exhilarated to be putting Baton Rouge into his past.

He'd knocked around Louisiana for almost eight years, gambling his way from Shreveport to Alexandria, over to New Orleans, finally settling in at the Randolph Hotel in Baton Rouge. The years had twisted through golden yellow highs, filled with deliriously good luck, then plunged into deep purple periods when nothing fell his way. All in all, Carey guessed he'd evened things out, especially on this last hand with Doyle Brisko.

Eight years was a long time to be gone, he thought, hoping things had cooled enough in Texas for him to reenter the play. He was anxious to get back to pure honest gambling, where a debt was settled, good or bad, on the spot. Those Louisiana folks had kept him off-balance with their clannish way of gambling—rules made to suit themselves. They let all kinds of quirky deals go down. Just like this business with Doyle Brisko. A regular at Bird Dog's never could have dodged a debt like that and lived to either tell it or collect.

He and Ada rolled along in silence through the dark countryside, the smell of stagnant lowlands drifting mustily through the windows. With her stocking feet tucked beneath her legs and her head against his shoulder, Carey knew Ada had made up her mind to stick with him, go wherever he was headed; she sure as hell couldn't go back to Damon Struthers's bed. Carey stole a glance at her lovely face and inhaled the perfume rising from her hair. He reluctantly admitted that the last thing he needed was involvement with this woman and her tough-guy bootlegger of a boyfriend who, most likely, would chase Ada across state lines. Though he hated to, Carey knew he'd have to cut Ada loose. Soon.

A thick veil of fog drifted in from shallow swamps along the highway, and Carey strained to hold his course as he maneuvered the heavy car over ruts and fallen branches with a concentration that taxed his impatient nature. Navigating the pitch-black road was frustrating when he bristled with excitement to plunge into his future, looking forward to the shock and envy he knew he would cause with his unannounced return to Mexia.

The car whizzed along, powerfully eating up the miles through Lafayette Parish, into Lake Charles, and edged its way toward Orange. Carey's mind raced with plans to turn this spontaneous escapade into a profitable adventure.

First thing I gotta do, he thought, is ditch Ada at her aunt's house in Beaumont. She can't come along where I'm headed, and I sure don't need Damon Struthers on my tail. With a little fancy doctoring of the Packard's registration, I can easily convert the car into cash, though I may have to detour farther south to do it. Better not head straight back to Mexia. Then I'll buy a first-class ticket on the Santa Fe and fast-track it back to Limestone County in style. The envelope of cash warmed his chest.

Carey thought of his mother's letter, which had miraculously followed him to Baton Rouge from the Chalmette Hotel in New Orleans.

So T.J. was dead. For the first time since getting the news, he let the reality of his brother's death sink in. He wasn't sure how he felt about it. Too many years of anger got in the way.

Ma needed him now, Carey told himself. But not because she missed him. Carey tried to suppress the disappointment rising up. She wanted him to help her deal with Leela over T.J.'s affairs, claim what was due her. Might be lots of land and money at stake.

Though thoughts of his mother agitated him, thoughts of Leela brought a tightness to his chest, igniting vivid memories that had smoldered too long. Memories of a summer eight years ago. Memories of the musty-smelling barn where Leela's heavy, warm breasts, bare and luscious, had been pressed against his chest. The vivid scene inflamed him and brought a surge of desire to the surface.

Carey swallowed, feeling his mouth go dry. He had never wanted anything or anyone as much as he wanted that woman. And she wanted him. Oh yes, she did. Why else would she have let him see her half-naked? Why else would she have crushed his head to her breast, driving him mad with the smell of her? And if T.J. hadn't spoiled things, bursting in, waving that old wartime rifle in his face, he'd have taken her completely and convinced her to leave his dull brother and come to Louisiana with him.

But things were different now, he reflected. T.J. was gone and he was coming back with money in his pockets. She'd be impressed. She'd be glad to see him. Nothing was going to stop him from having Leela now.

Chapter Nineteen

The Indian summer of 1920 baked the countryside with waves of blistering days folding one into the other. Throughout Limestone County, maples, oaks, and bushy locusts faded yellow, then orange, then red, and shook their fiery branches toward the vast Texas sky. Sporadic rains broke the relentless heat for an hour or so in the afternoons, then fizzled thinly into parched fields to rise in steamy vapor throughout the night. Withering creeks shrank away from dry banks and threaded listlessly toward the Gulf of Mexico. Kenny complained to his mother that his favorite swimming hole now rose only to his waist and was hardly worth jumping into anymore.

Victor Beaufort had a chat with Mr. Bernard, convincing the banker that the Wilder place showed no signs of oil, stating his assessment with such arrogant assurance that the banker agreed to give Leela until the end of the year to pay off T.J.'s note.

On November 19, 1920, when the first frost of the season

painted the land with a sprinkling of ice, the Rogers test proved good. The well came in small, with little fanfare, verifying the existence of oil in Mexia by belching forth a paltry fifty barrels a day. Undeterred, the visionary wildcatter, Colonel Humphreys, swiftly bought up leases on all adjoining land and Victor Beaufort was paid ten thousand dollars for the ten-cents-an-acre lease he held on Claude Varnet's farm.

Two days after the deal was struck, Victor traveled to Rioluces to celebrate with Leela.

From her seat at the dining room table, Leela could see Kenny chasing fireflies over the lawn. He jumped and snatched at the air, then carefully placed each flickering point of light into his jelly jar. Leela noticed it was nearly full.

She smiled to herself. Kenny seemed to be recovering better than she'd hoped from the blow of his father's death.

A sigh of contentment escaped Leela's lips as she leaned closer to Victor Beaufort.

"I'll remember this day for a long, long time," she said, feeling happiness swell in her chest. "The future finally seems to hold promise."

"All you have to do is take that check to Mexia Community Bank and get a clear title to this place. I've already wired my brothers in Oklahoma to get on down here. It's time to spud in Rioluces Number 1."

Victor's light brown eyes turned up at the corners as he began to pour more champagne into Leela's glass. When she lifted a hand to protest, he took it gently in his and said, "Just one more toast, Mrs. Wilder. I don't think that's too much to ask."

"Call me Leela, please," she laughed, allowing him to hold her fingers. They burned against his palm. She struggled to compose herself. "This is my first taste of champagne and I like it very much. But I fear I'm a little overwhelmed by all this excitement. You've been so generous, advancing me the money to pay off the bank. Not only can I finally clear the title to my farm, I'm going to have an oil well, too."

"Yep," Victor said quickly, releasing her hand. "Things are going to change real fast for you. And when the cash starts rolling in, I bet you'll be taking the train to Dallas once a week to shop in the finest stores in Texas."

"It's unbelievable," Leela said, noticing again how utterly captivating Victor Beaufort's eyes really were. Such an unusual shade of brown. Light, intensely glowing behind long black lashes. And he acted as if he had no idea of their unsettling effect on her.

Leela relented, allowing him to fill her glass, and lifted it to him across the table.

"What shall we toast this time, Mr. Beaufort?"

"Didn't I ask you to call me Victor?" His tone was gentle. It stirred her, bringing a rush of warmth.

She nodded, smiling.

"Well," he started, becoming solemn, "the success of the well is one thing, but I'm hopeful this venture will bring more than barrels of oil and bundles of cash."

"And what might that be?" Leela asked, her fingers beginning to tremble slightly as she clasped the cool glass.

"The opportunity to get to know you better." He ran the words together as if he feared slowing down might keep him from getting them out.

The breath he took was audible, and Leela could not help noticing the nervous way he pushed his broad shoulders back. His velvet-trimmed jacket fit him perfectly. The striped silk tie on his starched white shirt seemed the most elegant she'd ever seen. She just looked at him, unable to respond, then tapped her glass against his and took a small sip of the sweet, cool wine.

They talked for the next two hours. When darkness descended, Leela lit the tall candles on the sideboard, called Kenny inside to get ready for bed, then sat once again across from Victor and listened, enthralled by his stories of oil wells, wildcatting and Oklahoma Indians.

She learned that he had literally created the opportunity to apprentice in the oil field when he beat up the sickly white boy who held the watering job and showed up in his place the next day.

"How did you know you'd be hired?" Leela asked, not at all surprised at his brazen behavior.

"I didn't," Victor said, shaking his head as he remembered. "The gang pusher said he didn't hire niggers as a rule, because they were lazy and he couldn't trust them."

"What did you say?" Leela sensed the incident still pained him.

"Say?" Victor threw back, his eyes wide. "A ten-year-old oil field orphan doesn't say anything. I wanted the work real bad, so I remember standing straight up in his face, not giving him any sign that I was leaving. The man just stared at me, shook his head and finally handed me a bucket. He told me I'd get twenty-five cents a day to climb the derricks and get water to the men, and I could have all the kitchen scraps the camp cook threw out." Victor ran a hand over his face and looked at the ceiling. "And I was the happiest little colored boy in Oklahoma that day. I had a job. A real job. The first time I climbed a derrick to pass a ladle of water to a roustabout, I knew I was going to be an oilman. No matter how long it took or what I had to do, I wanted to have my own outfit and take my chances drilling holes in the ground."

"And your brothers?"

"After a time, I did my work so well, the boss accepted Cap and Frank into the crew. Some white men didn't take too kindly to it. Remember, in the oil field, the heaviest, dirtiest, most dangerous work has always been done by white labor: men who are glad to get two dollars a day and are quick to defend, sometimes at gunpoint, their right to keep blacks out of the fields."

Victor settled back in his chair as if melting into his memories.

"Now you've got your chance, Victor." She liked calling him by his first name. The intimacy of their conversation warmed her and she stared at Victor, knowing she could easily surrender her heart to him. "And I'm glad," she added, "that Rioluces is where you'll sink your first well."

He made no reply, though his expression told her he understood her happiness. Then Leela stood and began to clear away the dishes, slightly exhausted from the excitement of the evening, the intensity of Victor's stories and the heady champagne.

As she gathered plates and glasses, Victor left his seat and came toward her, blocking her path, piercing her with his cool, light gaze. She turned her face from the clutter of platters and wine goblets scattered over the table. He gently placed one hand on her shoulder. She stepped toward him and raised her eyes to his, allowing him to guide her into the circle of his arms.

His kiss was soft, not urgent or probing. So soft it felt more like a caress. But beneath the gentle touch of his lips upon hers, Leela felt the strong vibrations of his heart.

No sooner had Leela stepped out of the Mexia Community Bank than she felt a sharp tug at her elbow and turned around to see Hattie Wilder standing there, hat askew, eyes watery and glazed, clutching a battered purse to her chest.

"What's this about oil out on the farm?" Hattie's tone was so surly, so biting, so accusing that Leela recoiled sharply from her mother-in-law and stepped back toward the protection of the bank door. Hattie slid closer to Leela and craned her wrinkled neck forward.

"What are you doing in Mexia, Hattie?" Leela asked, surprised to see the old woman.

"I live here now," she answered. "Elvina Hopper asked me to come live with her, so I quit my job at the clinic."

"You quit your job? When did that happen?" Leela watched Hattie carefully, wondering if she were lying. As far as Leela knew, the only thing Hattie had ever done well was show up for work every day.

"Yes. I quit. I'm tired of living all alone, so when Elvina asked me to come stay with her, I said I would. It's more than my other kin has done," she said bitterly, shrugging her big shoulders in a heaving sigh, twisting her face into a frown.

"I'm sorry," Leela began, not knowing what else to say.

"Don't be pityin' me," Hattie lashed out. "You ain't never cared what happened to me. If you hada owned up to T.J.'s will, I wouldn't be in this situation."

"No will was ever found," Leela said slowly and deliberately, resignation in her voice. She hoped to avoid another draining confrontation.

"That's just you talking." Hattie's tone was gruff and accusing.

"No, it's not," Leela countered. "And even if T.J. had a will among his papers, it's gone now. Wesley Sparks disappeared. The bank manager said he ran off with a lot of the bank's money and every scrap of paper T.J. gave him for safekeeping." Leela stood silently for a moment, trying to summon the patience to remain civil.

She would never really know what her husband had given Wesley Sparks, but Leela truly believed T.J. had not left as much as a square foot of Rioluces to either Hattie or Carey. He would have told her so.

Hattie spoke up. "And now I hear you foolin' around out on the farm with some oilman. You oughta be ashamed, Leela Wilder. My son ain't in the ground six months and already you got some man in his house."

"Don't start, Hattie," Leela said through clenched teeth. "You take that crazy talk someplace else. I'm not fooling around with anyone, and if I were, it would be none of your business."

But apparently fueled by homemade wine, Hattie proceeded to deliver an agitated tirade, her voice booming down the center of Commerce Avenue.

"None of my business! You plain stole my share of the farm from me, making out like T.J. never left me a thing when you know part of that place shoulda come to me. You ain't never gonna get away with this, Leela. And ain't no good gonna come to that stranger who done sweet-talked you inta signing up with him. The whole town's talking 'bout him. Goin' around actin' like he's white. He ain't got no sense at all. He better be careful. Folks around here ain't gonna let him dig for oil and throw his weight around town. There'll be trouble for everyone. We don't need his kind stirring things up. Uppity nigger edgin' in on white folks' business, that's what they sayin' about him. Gonna slip that farm right out from under your flighty nose and make you lose everything. Mark my words, and it'll serve you right. Wasn't for Kenny, I'd have nothing more to do with you. But he's my grandson, only real family I got left. And you ain't gonna keep me from interfering if I want to. Wish I never had to cross your path again."

Leela wanted to slap Hattie's face, but the gawking passersby stilled her hand and made her control her tongue.

"Hattie, I refuse to stand here and argue with you over something that's been long settled. If you'd let me, I could help you."

Hattie's sad appearance and desperate accusations suddenly drained Leela of anger, leaving her unexpectedly flooded with feelings of pity. She feared Hattie would be a thorn in her side until the day she died, but it was a sorry state of affairs to have one son gone and the other missing.

"You just go on, Leela," Hattie ordered. "Git away from here with your pitiful excuses, 'cause I got help coming." Hattie's voice rose shrilly as she followed Leela toward her buggy. "Carey's coming home, I can feel it in my bones. Bet you didn't know T.J. sent his brother a letter. Weeks before he died. That's news to you, ain't it? And according to Reverend Pearson, T.J. told Carey he was sick. Bet he begged Carey to come back and take over the farm." Hattie threw back her head and laughed.

"I don't think so," Leela said, the hurt in her voice clearly showing. Why would Reverend Pearson do such a thing and not tell her about it?

"And the preacher told me where to find Carey," Hattie continued. "So I sent him a letter, too. How does that sit with you, huh? My Carey's gonna come help me set things straight. So you just go on over to Belknap Street, Leela. Go visit the black oilman and tell him this: I ain't gonna let him bluff his way through here, and when my Carey gets home, we'll see who's gonna profit from all that oil your lover man thinks he's gonna find."

Leela rushed to the street and climbed into her buggy. When she looked down, she saw Hattie smash her straw hat more fully onto her graying head and make her way down Commerce Avenue, turning into Mr. Kirvin's pharmacy at the end of the block.

Three miles out of town, Leela's hands finally stopped shaking. Hattie's bruising words settled over her like wet sand. She was sick of hearing about Carey Logan but Hattie's confidence in his return was beginning to unnerve Leela. She cringed at the prospect of seeing T.J.'s half-brother again.

The incident with Carey now had no meaning at all, she reasoned; in fact, nothing had really happened. And no one had seen her with Carey except T.J., and he was dead. The chill in the air made her tremble.

To restore her courage, Leela reached into her purse and pulled out a heavy packet of folded papers. She gingerly tugged at the red ribbon holding the document together, allowing the loose pages to fall apart in her lap. She examined the last one, stamped PAID IN FULL in dark blue ink, and let her eyes caress the seal of the bank, the flourishing signature of Mr. Bernard, and the scratchy handwriting of the receptionist who had witnessed the transfer. Rioluces was safe at last.

With Victor Beaufort's loan of three thousand dollars against future oil royalties, he had freed Rioluces from the threat of foreclosure.

Riding along the desolate road, thoughts of Victor Beaufort began to filter in, easing her turmoil, smoothing out the wrinkles in her brow. Leela bit into her bottom lip as she tried to think sensibly about the powerful feelings Victor had stirred in her.

Hattie's tirade may have served a purpose, Leela reluctantly admitted. After all, how much did she really know about this man she now trusted with her future? And what might be the consequences of having signed the lease with him?

Leela was no fool. She had enough education to read the oil lease contract, though the complicated document did contain some fancy phrases and technical words she didn't understand. She had been reluctant to admit this to Victor. If only Parker were here, she thought, he'd explain it all to her.

For the first time Leela worried about her decision to support the colored drilling company, the colored oilman. Who had ever heard of such a thing? Had she been naive in her decision? Had she let her heart rule her head? Could the greedy white men in dark vested suits who now filled the streets of Mexia stop Victor from realizing his dream? Could Hattie Wilder be right?

Leela's heart sank as she turned Hattie's words around in her mind. The bitter woman may have sent Leela a belated message of caution: Negroes had their place in Limestone County, and to think otherwise brought only disappointment and trouble.

She knew Victor Beaufort flaunted his independent attitude in an arrogant, dangerous manner. She didn't know about Oklahoma, but in these parts no black man ever tested the system so openly. She found Victor's confidence and fearless ambition exhilarating, yet his relaxed attitude about issues of color and segregation frightened her, made her feel he had deliberately blinded himself to the rough road that surely lay ahead.

Leela sighed and pushed her fears away, reaching for more pleasant thoughts of Victor. She had seen him every day for the past four weeks, sometimes from afar as he surveyed her land, at other times more closely, while sitting to sign papers. Every time the opportunity presented itself, she let her eyes roam the length of his body, studying the graceful strength in the curve of his neck when his head was bent from her.

Sometimes Leela would deliberately stand too close to him, accidentally touching his hand while handing him a pen, or brushing her bare arm against his. She watched him feign control, his eyes steady, often not leaving her face for long seconds, his breathing suddenly becoming rapid or, at times, so shallow Leela swore he was holding his breath.

Leela had never met a man like Victor and, gingerly, in the tiniest ways she could allow, she let herself be drawn to him, sensing a deeper relationship lay ahead.

Victor's charming manner both pleased and annoyed Leela. She found herself filled with conflicting emotions when he quickly captured Kenny's admiration. The boy followed the oilman all across the property, holding his instruments, asking all kinds of questions. She was grateful for Victor's patience and genuine interest in Kenny, but it also intensified her lingering guilt over T.J. Their marriage had lacked passion, but Leela couldn't deny that T.J. had truly loved her and their son in the only way he could.

But whatever she felt for Victor, wildcatting Rioluces was the first priority. She must not allow herself to be distracted. Besides, he probably had a string of beautiful women pining over him from northern Oklahoma right into Central Texas.

As Leela pulled her buggy onto Rioluces, a NO TRESPASSING sign greeted her. On her instruction, Pully had made the sign, hanging it over the rusty gate with a heavy iron chain. She looked around for Victor's familiar Model T, then remembered he had driven to Dallas to pick up his brothers, Cap and Frank. They would arrive from Oklahoma on the Silver Eagle Limited at six o'clock that evening, and tomorrow the Beaufort Drilling Company would break ground to spud in Rioluces No. 1. Though Victor had only been gone for less than a day, she hated to admit that she already missed him.

A lone farmer, whom Leela recognized as Red Walters from across the ridge, ambled up from the creek path toward her.

"Mornin', Miz Wilder." Red stopped at the side of her buggy.

"That's some hole in the ground back there. Things be lookin' up 'round here, I reckon."

"Looks that way, Red. Folks been coming through here for days. You can't imagine how happy I am over this. Like a gift from heaven, it is. Just when I needed a miracle."

"Oh, I reckon you's happy, all right. Only wisht T.J. coulda lived to see it. My, my, what you think he woulda made of all this?" Red Walters spit a stream of tobacco juice into the grass and chuckled. "My, my, who woulda thought it? Right here on T.J.'s land."

"He'd be as happy as I am, I'm sure," Leela replied, noticing for the first time that a shiny Pierce Arrow sat parked near the side of the house. Red saw Leela's puzzled look and offered what he knew.

"Pully told me that's a white man from some big oil company wants to talk to you. Seems like he's been waitin' since right after you left for town. Don't look like he's got nuthin' else to do 'cept sit and wait, does it?"

"I'd better see what he wants," Leela said, waving good-bye to her neighbor as she guided the buggy up to the front door.

Approaching from the rear, she could see the back of a man's head, his dark felt hat pushed back, one arm hanging out the window. Leela got down from her buggy and walked up to the sleek red automobile as the man put his newspaper aside and got out of the car.

"What do you want?" she asked, looking over the youngish man standing before her in a deeply wrinkled seersucker suit.

"You the owner of this farm?"

"Yes, I am."

"I'm Thornton Welch, president of Starr Oil Company. I understand there's been a show of oil on this place."

"That's right," Leela answered, not taking her eyes from his face.

"One of your help here let me go see the site, and Starr Oil wants to offer you ten dollars an acre for the lease."

Leela's heart raced, throbbing so strongly in her chest it threatened to close off her breathing.

Victor had paid her one dollar an acre. She tried to calculate the difference as she stared at Mr. Welch. But, she reminded herself, Victor also advanced her three thousand dollars because he believed there was a pool of oil under Rioluces that would put the Red Fork discovery to shame.

"It's already leased," she said in a firm, nonnegotiable tone.

"Who leased it?" The man was visibly shaken. Surprised. His easy confidence faded. "Starr has been buying up leases in this area for the past two months. Who got here before us?"

"I've signed with the Beaufort Drilling Company." Leela took a deep breath, clamped her hands together and drew herself up as tall as she could manage. "Victor Beaufort is the owner."

"Who? I never heard of him, and I been leasing through Texas a long time. How much he pay you?"

"I'd rather not say," Leela hedged.

"Don't matter. Whatever he paid, we can double. Just tell me where to find this man Beaufort and we can work it out."

"I doubt he's willing to sell his lease," Leela said on Victor's behalf.

The white man threw out a curt laugh and slapped one hand on the side of his expensive new car. "Offer enough money, any man will sell. Just tell me where to find him."

Confused, off-balance, not sure what this meant, Leela decided to let Victor work it out when he returned.

"His office is near town, on Belknap Street," she told Thornton Welch.

"Belknap Street? Over in Niggertown? You must have it wrong, lady. Ain't no oil company over there."

"Yes, that's where he has his office," Leela said.

Thornton Welch reached into a folder of papers and pulled out a rectangular white card. "Here, take my card and when you see Mr. Beaufort, tell him to get in touch with me. I can make him a real good deal for that lease."

Leela took the card and slipped it into her skirt pocket as Mr. Welch got into his car. He turned and looked up at her as he started the engine.

"I can ask around town and probably find him, but I know you got the street wrong, lady. Ain't no oil company across the tracks in Mexia."

Chapter Twenty

The early months of 1921 saw a frenzy of activity on the western edge of Mexia. Colonel Humphreys's second well, Blake Smith No. 1, came in at two hundred barrels a day, followed very quickly by the Occidental Oil Company's Liles No. 1, which spewed twenty barrels of crude every hour. These astonishing strikes verified citizens' belief that black gold was settled beneath their sleepy town, and news of the rich potential of the Mexia field spread rapidly throughout the nation.

Random drilling and fortunate hunches, often referred to as "yardstick geology," spurred a frantic rush of exploration by many who only weeks ago had been grocers, carpenters, trappers and even professional men in northern cities. Landowners, willing to accept as little as twenty-five cents an acre for leases, provided the cheap vast tracts that attracted a deluge of independent oil companies, operators, traders and wildcatters. Speculators rushed to tie up every acre within the gently curving fault that defined the Mexia field, and construction began on a refinery two miles south of town. A muddy web of new roads inched through cotton fields and fallow farmland, growing more intricate every day as farmers stood on the edges of their acreage, collecting as much as a dollar for each wagon, motor car or buggy wanting to cut across their property.

Risk takers with access to capital promoted their ventures with much success, attracting investors who were willing to sell their wives' wedding bands and the family milk cow for the cash to purchase a drilling outfit. With very little money a man could sink his shallow well and run the operation with a skeleton crew. Such entrepreneurial ventures usually sported names relative to their risky nature—"Lucky Ten" or "Texas Chance"—and often found their investors in the ranks of wealthy widows with large tracts of land.

On the southwestern edge of Rioluces, the Beaufort Drilling Company labored in patient isolation, forcing their cable tool rigging to cut deeper and deeper through layers of shale, sand, mud and limestone, probing the earth for oil. More than fourteen oil companies approached Leela for the rights to Rioluces. As she firmly refused each offer, sticking with her commitment to the Beaufort Drilling Company, she was cursed, threatened, harassed and generally made to feel that she'd made a very big mistake putting her faith into the likes of Victor Beaufort.

When a midnight fire destroyed all the lumber that had been cut and honed for the derrick, Victor refused to get the sheriff involved, knowing it would do no good, and enlisted the help of neighboring farmers to quickly replenish his supplies.

The Negro community of Limestone County turned out in droves to help Victor and his brothers sink their well. Not only did they cut new timber for the derrick, they helped string the new wire cable and even stood guard during the night to chase away thieves who routinely crept onto the drilling site; a red hot boiler or a tally of pipe could be spirited away and sold before morning.

Six weeks into the drilling, Thornton Welch visited the site, warning Victor that it was highly unlikely he would be able to secure the equipment or cash to continue drilling if his first well should come in a duster.

Victor had made no reply, continuing his work as Mr. Welch probed further. Just where did Victor plan to store this oil he was hoping to bring to the surface? Sheet metal for storage tanks was scarcer than a boardinghouse room in town. And how did Victor plan to pipe the stuff to the railroad cars to get it to the refinery? Didn't he know that pipe was now so hard to find that even Starr Oil, one of the biggest and most powerful oil companies in the field, was shipping its pipe in from Oklahoma?

Victor shrugged off Thornton Welch's doomsday talk, firmly declining his offer to buy the lease at any price he might offer.

Leela supported Victor's refusal to sell, remaining confident that Victor knew what he was doing and would not let her down. But a shiver of fear did slide over her heart when Thornton Welch predicted that she would need Starr Oil sooner or later. "We can wait . . . for a little while, Mrs. Wilder," he'd threatened. "But mark my words, Beaufort can't do this alone." Then he roared off in his big Pierce Arrow, his words stinging Leela's ears.

Townsfolk were very vocal about their disdain for the Beaufort brothers' company. Pully told Leela what he had overheard while standing outside Ed's Barber Shop: one oilman referred to Victor's outfit as "those coons punching holes in the ground" and lamented that such valuable land remained tied up with such a folly. Another, standing with his map spread out on the wooden sidewalk, had spoken brashly about scaring the daylights out of "the stubborn widow who was blocking progress." He said he could force her to reconsider her refusal of legitimate offers. Fires, explosions, and underground cave-ins could happen anywhere, anytime.

The cold drizzle that seeped into the neck of Victor's jacket and filled his heavy field boots was discomforting but tolerable. He tugged his soggy Stetson forward, bent his head toward the ground and blocked his mind to the chilling wet fabric that clung to his torso from his shirt collar to his waist. Cold air bit into his cheeks and prompted a rash of chilblains over his arms and hands. He shoved his frozen fingers into the deep pockets of his coat.

He had sloshed his way through many treacherous Oklahoma oil fields, enduring violent blizzards, swirling dust storms, torrid heat waves, and rainstorms that literally washed the roads from beneath his feet. This Texas winter of freezing rain was a nuisance, but nothing compared to what he had known.

As Victor dodged between two slow-moving railway cars, he left his brothers, Cap and Frank, behind to secure the remainder of their cargo and headed toward the refuge of his car. He slid behind the wheel, stripped off his sodden hat, and quickly started the engine, pulling away from the Mexia depot with sudden, jerky turns. As the headlamps of his Model T illuminated the slimy road, he cut sharply, skirting huge holes in the ground, and thought about what had just happened.

Staring ahead in grim silence, he could feel his anger rising. His feet were so numb with cold he could hardly feel them on the pedals. He pressed his lips into a thin hard line, then cursed lowly under his breath.

"Damn those greedy peckerwoods," he muttered. "If they think this will stop me, they've got another thing coming."

He took a sudden curve too fast and the heavy car swerved across the road. He was seething with hatred and disbelief that pipe-hungry thieves had robbed him of a good portion of his cargo. He had been waiting for this shipment for nearly a month. And now, somewhere between Houston and Mexia, at some desolate outback of a railway crossing, desperate hijackers had assaulted the freight cars and spirited away not only his pipe but also a set of bull wheels and the precious sheet metal he needed to construct his storage tank.

The loss stunned him, but he was not entirely surprised that it had happened. Mountainous loads of valuable oil field supplies rumbled and thundered across Oklahoma and Texas twenty-four hours a day. Armed guards rode shotgun on the tops of trains, pointing their big Gatling guns out across the fields.

He pressed the gas pedal to the floor, pushing his motorcar to shake and sputter as it sped toward Rioluces. But why was his shipment, according to the freight clerk, the only one that did not survive intact? This was bad news, but he had to break it to Leela. The robbery would mean another delay.

Victor turned off the Mexia-Comanche Crossing Road and entered the dark passageway to Rioluces, leaving the lights of the boomtown behind.

Cap and Frank would salvage what they could, he consoled himself, and arrange to get it out to the site in the morning. Victor would have to decide how to replace the equipment. Where in the world would he find sheet metal and pipe before the well came in?

There was no question in Victor's mind that he would find what he needed, even if he had to leave Mexia and search all over Texas. Nothing was going to stop him from bringing in Rioluces No. 1. The setback only intensified Victor's drive to plunge more deeply into the challenge of striking oil on Leela's farm.

His tension eased as soft yellow lights in the farmhouse windows emerged in the distance, glowing warmly against a pitch-black curtain of isolated acreage, inviting him to let images of Leela displace his troubled thoughts.

He could picture her now, moving from room to room, full skirts falling softly over gently curving hips. A brightly colored shawl dripping fringed lace onto the swell of her breasts. Sitting in her parlor, her long, graceful legs stretched out toward the warmth of the fire. His chest tightened and he gripped the steering wheel as he thought of Leela.

So quick. So intelligent. So full of curiosity. Those were the qualities he cherished in her, the strengths he admired. She raced through his blood, seeped into his bones and tingled the remotest corners of his consciousness.

He thought of her copper-colored hair catching winter sunlight, brown eyes wide with interest, a reflection of gold on her satin, bronze skin. The lively gestures of her small hands and the delicate way she held a pen should have remained insignificant observations. But such details sprang so vividly from some hidden source they made him catch his breath.

He felt at ease in her presence, as if he had known her for a very long time, as if he were meant to be with her forever. Her determined support of his drilling company and her fierce belief in this wildcatting venture in the face of such ugly opposition drew Victor closer to Leela and inspired him to prove himself worthy of her faith. For the thousandth time, he silently vowed he would not let her down.

He knew she fit with him, hungered like him, wanted everything life had to offer and was willing to go after it. She settled comfortably within his plans for the future, and it was no longer difficult for Victor to admit to himself that he loved her with all his heart. But his desire to see Leela this evening was tempered by the bad news he had to break. He shifted the car into low gear and rolled up to the high rusty gate.

The sound of Victor's car rumbling onto the property brought Leela to the window. The sight of his Model T, glistening black and shiny in the freezing rain, sent a ripple of joy up her spine. She had hoped he would come back to talk with her tonight. When the sample core taken this morning had come up oily and black, Victor had been more genuinely optimistic than he had been in weeks. She had actually heard him humming to himself as he left for the train station to claim his cargo.

Kenny had been so excited at the prospect of oil actually gushing over the derrick, he lingered at the site until very late and had come home exhausted, going to bed directly after dinner.

Leela let the sheer curtain fall back into place over the ice-covered window and pulled the door open before Victor could knock.

"I was hoping you would come back out tonight," she said, smiling as she stepped back to let him into the hallway. He stood dripping water from his hat, his jacket, his sodden leather boots.

"I thought I'd better let you know what's happened." He did not return her smile, but remained stern as Leela took his hat and jacket and spread them by the fire.

"Sit down," she said, suddenly nervous. She'd never seen Victor quite so serious. He eased himself into a big chair near the fire and placed his damp feet close to the hearth.

"Did the shipment arrive?" Leela asked, knowing how vital the pipe and rigging were. They had already discussed the imminence of the strike and she understood the scarcity of supplies.

"We got about a third of what I paid for," Victor said slowly, staring into the fire as he spoke. "Seems like somebody turned a blind eye on my cargo somewhere between Houston and Mexia. Lost a tally of eight-inch pipe, a set of bull wheels and the better part of a crown block. Not to mention all the sheet metal I'd contracted for delivery. Don't know exactly what happened, 'cause nobody else seemed to lose a thing."

Leela did not know what to say. She watched Victor fold his hands between his knees and lean closer to the fire.

"This will set us back a spell." He glanced over his shoulder at her.

Leela shivered as she ran her eyes over his handsome profile, illuminated by the golden fire. The disappointment in his face cut straight to her heart, and she resisted an urge to place her hand on his cheek.

"How far back?" Leela asked, grateful once more that Victor discussed the progress of the well with her. She was curious about the venture and had learned a lot about wildcatting. He made her feel as much a part of the company as if she had put her own cash on the line.

"This might mean a delay of two or three months. We can bring it in, but Lord knows how we'll store and pipe it." Victor's words had a desperate edge.

"And financially? What does this mean?" Leela asked.

"It means that everything hinges on Rioluces Number 1 coming in soon and big and without complications. I can't stop drilling," Victor answered, "but if we make a strike with no pipe or storage, I'll just have to run the crude into a sump."

"A sump?" Leela repeated, raising her brows.

"Something like a dam or an above-ground cave. A shallow area on land to collect the oil in a surface lake. Not the best way to handle the crude, but it's sure been done lots of times. In Oklahoma, some fields looked like slick lakes of oil, like black water as far as you could see."

"Victor," Leela started, "maybe you ought to contract with Starr. You know Mr. Welch wants your lease."

"I know," Victor admitted with a sigh. "But what he's offering won't even make up for what I've already spent. He wants everything. Entire control of the field. Why should I move over and let him take what we've got? I had everything worked out to handle this find . . . on my own."

"Things happen for a reason," Leela prompted. "The pipe and sheet metal are gone, so maybe we should reconsider."

"It's serious, but it's not going to stop me." Victor's tone was sharp. "There's enough timber on this place to make wooden storage tanks. Might take a while, but it could be done. I'll bet I could put together a crew of men just from the neighboring farms. We could do it," he finished, turning back toward the fire.

"And the pipeline? How would you manage that?"

"If I can get it stored, I'll find a better deal than what Thornton Welch is offering. Occidental is interested."

"You're too stubborn! Stop holding out just to prove that the Beaufort Drilling Company can do it. Why don't you go see Thornton Welch? He wants in." She moved closer to Victor and put her hand on his knee. The damp fabric of his heavy woolen trousers felt cool beneath her palm. "The delay would take all the money you need to pay the men on your crew. You're going to need every dollar to spud in the next well." She watched him cautiously as he lifted his chin and cocked his head to one side.

"Why are you so fired up about a deal with Starr?"

"Because I'm afraid for you, Victor," Leela blurted out. "I hope you don't think I'm putting my nose into your affairs, but—" She hesitated, then stood and walked to stand by the fire. She watched shadows play over his worried face. "I know every dime you have is riding on that well, and each day of delay means a day when something could happen."

"Like what?" he said curtly, slumping back in his seat. "Are you worried I'll be murdered in some dark alley or that there'll be an explosion at the site?" He tried to make light of her concerns.

"There's a lot of angry talk going on in town." Leela turned her back to him and faced the warming fire.

"I'm well aware of what's being said about me and my company," Victor shot back.

Leela spun around, letting him see her pain. "Then you must understand why I'm worried." Her husky words caught in her throat and fell into a whisper.

Victor nodded, rising to take both of Leela's hands in his. "I understand your concern. Really, I do. No one's ever brought me up short before. At least no one I cared to listen to." Small drops of perspiration gathered on his brow and he stood silently for a moment, as if resigning himself to the truth; then he slowly moved his hands along her arms to wrap them around her shoulders. Leela stepped closer and laid her head on his chest. "You may be right," he murmured. "There's a lot of tension around here. Maybe I better sign on with Starr and put us on an even keel. I can't risk losing this oil once I've brought it in. And that could happen with things as uneasy as they are right now."

The heat from the fire seemed to scorch the side of Leela's face, yet she refused to move, remaining in Victor's arms.

"Don't think of this decision as selling out," Leela cautioned. "Bringing in the oil will be proof of your success. Then just think of all you can do with your millions!" She laughed lowly, leaning back to watch the taut lines in Victor's face disappear. "Just think of this as a business decision that will make you rich."

"Make *us* rich," Victor corrected, his voice so level and determined Leela thrilled to hear it.

Without another word Victor pulled her closer and kissed her deeply, stroking Leela's hair as she melted into the warm cocoon of his arms. She savored the feel of him, the smell of him, the strength of his muscular body against hers.

"We're in this together, you know?" His words pierced her and his question left no doubt in Leela's mind that she would follow Victor Beaufort wherever he wanted to go.

As the fire crackled and spewed colored points of light into the chimney, Leela allowed herself to be kissed over and over. On her lips, her neck, in the soft hollow between her breasts. She clung to Victor and silently cried for joy, knowing this was the passion that had been denied her in marriage. The urgent emotion that now bloomed between them filled Leela with a soaring happiness. And as Victor's hands roamed through her thick soft hair, down her back toward the warm spot at the base of her spine, she knew that Victor Beaufort was all she wanted, all that really mattered, and all the oil in the world could never change that.

On February 7, 1921, a crush of curious onlookers gathered at Rioluces. A stream of heavy, square-topped motorcars churned the soggy rutted fields, though mule-drawn wagons fared much better in the sticky mud, inching slowly toward the whirring thump of the cable tool rig as it plunged and rocked its way toward a strike. The Beaufort Drilling Company had persevered in spite of harassment, theft and the loss of several strings of tools and had now reached a depth where pay dirt was expected. The soil samples had grown more oily and thick as each day passed, convincing Victor that he was very close to breaking through.

Pully leaked the news to Red Walters, who quickly told Claude Varnet, who leapt from his bed to tell Johnny Ray and Harry Mosley that Rioluces, the land called "river of lights," would soon live up to its name. Within hours, the news had spread like wildfire throughout the county.

Farmers, local businessmen, gamblers, roustabouts, lease-brokers, hobos, drifters, housewives and cowboys—all crowded excitedly beneath the wooden derrick to witness what each one hoped might be the biggest gusher of the field so far.

Many stood gawking at the crude gangly pump while others turned eager faces skyward to view the monstrously narrow pyramid soaring eighty feet into the clouds. Inside the slatted derrick, suspended by thick cables, hung the heavy string of tools used to service the well.

Leela stood up in her wagon to see Victor. He was standing on the platform alongside the huge bull wheels that dwarfed all the men in his crew. She wondered what he was thinking. Shadows from his wide Stetson prevented her from seeing his face, but she knew how anxious he was.

Leela surveyed the site. Where in the world had all these people come from? The place looked like a carnival campground. Ladies appeared in flat straw hats, brims loaded with paper roses and lily of the valley. They fought the strong February wind to keep their bonnets on their heads. Others looked as if they had just laid aside their dish towels, stripped off their kitchen aprons, and headed straightaway to Rioluces.

Excited children squealed and tumbled about in the mud, and she noticed Kenny was right in there with them. Most parents were paying little attention to the youngsters, intent on watching the sway of the pump or the hissing steam engine that sputtered and strained to keep the rhythmic pump in motion.

Leela searched the derrick for Victor. He was now halfway up the wooden structure, standing on the double board, checking the ropes to the draw works. The sight of him stirred her again, and there was a flutter in that soft space between her throat and her chest. Remembering the feel of his hands on her body, his lips on her neck, she was suddenly embarrassed. She shook her head and smiled, then took a deep breath.

Daylight hours ticked by. Oil talk slid off excited, jovial tongues. Stories of the boom passed from wagon to wagon, stranger to neighbor, each person telling a taller tale. The prattling went on far into the day until the sun broke through the misty veil of winter clouds.

Leela sensed electricity in the air. The atmosphere crackled with expectation, quivered with hope, setting the stage for this wildcatter and his crew to come through with the expected performance—a real Texas gusher.

Cap and Frank handled the heavy string of tools with bare, callused hands. Other men with dirt-streaked faces and grizzly beards labored under the derrick, checking gauges, measuring depth, handling the thick wire cables with firm, strong hands. The mud-covered roustabouts paid little attention to the crowd, focusing on the ceaseless pounding of the pointed bit as it ground its way deeper and deeper into the soil. Leela could hear rock shattering beneath the earth as the bit clawed toward the ancient reserves lying within the compacted soil of Rioluces.

Victor searched the crowd and saw her. She waved at him, pleasantly surprised when he jumped down from the platform and headed her way. Leela's mouth went dry as she watched him approach, and her eyes ran shamelessly from the top of his Stetson to his mud-covered boots and back up again. He was beautiful.

Leela raised one hand to shade her face from the white-hot glare of the sun as it slid, again, from beneath one of the few clouds remaining in the sky. Her wagon jolted suddenly and she instinctively reached for the reins to steady her horse, which did not take kindly to this crush of people and the clamor rising from the crowd. At the same moment Kenny yelled, "Ma!" and jumped up into the wagon. He clasped Leela fiercely around the waist, pulling them both down to the floor.

The ground beneath them trembled. A gurgling, swishing noise rushed forth and silenced the excited gathering. A low, menacing rumble echoed beneath their feet. All eyes remained focused on the hole in the ground, all breathing seemed suspended and necks stretched forward, mouths hanging open as the hopeful witnesses followed the strange noise with their hearts.

All at once a big chunk of mud flew up out of the six-inch hole, its forceful expulsion booming like a cannon shot over the heads of the onlookers. They screamed in surprise and scattered back a few feet as a stream of mud showered them and splashed up into the derrick. Then all became silent. Anxiously, the crowd waited.

In rolling thunderous waves, the earth screamed for release until the clap of an explosion and the blast of an eruption forced a thin column of gaseous oil vapor up through the narrow pit in the ground. It exploded in a shower of black mist. The geyser ripped away more than six hundred feet of wire cable, threw the hardworking bit into the air, and tore through the derrick, taking a good portion of the rigging with it. The force of the explosion pushed the crew from the derrick floor, just as a fountain of black liquid followed.

"Strike!" the men yelled, dropping wrenches, heavy metal bars, stout pieces of lumber and hammers as they fled, dodging flying bull ropes and shards of metal as they scattered frantically toward safety.

A thunderous "Ya-hoo" rose up from the crowd in a uniform voice claiming victory. Hats sailed through the air, looking small and insignificant as they floated strangely away on a shower of oil drifting southward. Men and women hugged each other and clutched slimy children while the enormous black fountain raged uncontrolled.

Victor leapt into Leela's wagon, scooped Kenny up on his broad shoulders and grabbed Leela into the circle of his oil-soaked arms.

"We did it!" he yelled above the joyous uproar, tossing his favorite hat into the fray. "We did it! Rioluces Number 1 is on the map!" As the slick black rain began to settle in shallow pools at his feet, he put one hand beneath Leela's streaked face and told her, "I want you to marry me, Leela. There will be no happiness in this without you." He gave her no time to even think about an answer before he kissed her fiercely and hungrily, ignoring the waves of black gold that fell in sheets upon the oil-drenched land.

Chapter Twenty-One

At first they brought their own jugs and bottles, crowding the back porch with dollar bills in their hands, arriving as soon as the sun went down. Josephine had welcomed them, smiling as she ladled out the whiskey, happy to take the money so eagerly pressed into her hands. She was never quite sure who promoted her business, but secretly thought Oliver spread the word that she had white lightning to sell.

Business was steady and profitable. Josephine now sold the corn liquor in clear glass jars she bought for a nickel at Mr. Green's store and charged her customers an extra quarter for the container. They paid a dollar for a pint. No one complained. The farmers, shopkeepers, carpenters, singers and gamblers looking for a source swore that the black-white lady on Denton Street had the best-tasting hooch in town.

As Josephine sat at her table counting the day's take, she smiled to herself, feeling satisfied that she'd cleared enough to pay the ten-dollar-a-month rent she owed on the house, buy the malt, corn and potatoes she would need to make the next mixture of whiskey and get Oliver a pair of shoes; he was going to start school this term, whether he wanted to or not. Though he was close to fourteen and big for his age, Josephine knew he would feel out of place and felt guilty that the boy could neither read nor write.

She had dropped out of Halsey when she was fourteen, but at least she could add and subtract and read the newspaper. He ought to be able to do that much.

It had worked out fine, she told herself, sipping a glass of tart Johnny-mash. She had not been much of a drinker before moving out on her own, but now she looked forward to a little taste occasionally to make the lonely hours pass more quickly. Oliver was gone most of the time, running around with a gang of boys who lived in the neighborhood. She had no friends and shunned male companionship, still relieved that Johnny Ray had left her alone.

"Johnny-mash is the only friend I need," she said under her breath. It don't talk back or cause trouble, she thought, though lately it had started giving her those terrible headaches. She'd just have to be careful not to drink so much.

Momma may say this is the devil's work, Josephine mused, remembering Effie's bitter words. But what else could she do? Those kegs of whiskey kept her from starving, and she could see there was a lot of money to be made. So what if liquor was illegal? The steadiest customer she had was the deputy sheriff from across the county line.

Nothing looked the same to him. Mexia's sleepy, small-town atmosphere, which he had chafed against as a young man, but now longed for as an adult, was completely shattered. The striking turquoise skies Parker had bragged about to Margaret were gone, tainted by surging clouds of black mist and oily vapor rising up from the ground as far as he could see. The once-grassy pastures spreading out behind the house now lay oil-soaked and churned into rutted fields of useless muck. Even the porch steps, stained black with droplets of the ever-present crude, had not escaped the touch of Mexia's new treasure, though the nearest derrick was at least a quarter mile in the distance.

The impatient blare of horns rising from traffic snarled in the center of town could barely be heard above the constant train whistles that shrieked around the clock. Though early spring roses trailed onto the porch, Parker could not smell them at all, and he wiped his nose with his linen handkerchief to fend off the acrid smell of sulfur gas settled so thickly over the town.

Parker didn't like what he saw and didn't like what he had been hearing about Mexia. But his decision to come home had been carefully thought out. He hoped to set things straight with his sister, get to the bottom of the pain he knew she was causing their mother, and as the new owner of the *Banner*, he planned to publish a paper that would tell the truth about what was happening to the Negroes in his hometown. Not all he had seen was cause for celebration.

Effie Alexander came out onto her back porch and slipped her arm around Parker's waist.

"It's just so good to have you back home." She had to raise up on tiptoes to kiss her son on the cheek. "You and Margaret. But I'm a little upset you'd make such a trip with Margaret in that condition."

"The doctor said if we planned on leaving Washington we'd better make the trip before the end of April." Parker returned his mother's kiss and patted her arm. "If we waited too long, we'd have had to come after the baby was born."

"When I got your letter last month, I could hardly believe you were really coming back for good."

"Well, Momma," Parker started, spreading an old copy of the *Banner* on the top step, "it wasn't an easy decision." He sat down, then shifted to make room for his mother to sit beside him. "With Mr. Foreman passing away so suddenly, I knew the office of the *Banner* would be stripped bare, the presses destroyed, if I didn't move quickly to save them. This town should not be left without a colored paper, not at a time when Mexia, especially the colored folks here, are in the center of all the news across the country." He paused and inhaled deeply. "Margaret and I talked it over and decided, if I was going to come back and run my own paper, this looked like the time to do it."

Parker spoke with the passion of a newspaperman who knew he was living through history. The oil boom that had exploded in his hometown would be written about for years to come.

"Do you realize, Momma, that important men with the big oil companies believe the Mexia fault will bring in more oil than all the crude discovered so far? The huge reserves have hardly been tapped. Can you imagine what's to come? The stories that I'll write about Mexia will be carried from Texas to New York, maybe as far as Europe."

"Make some sense of it, son," Effie said pointedly. "There's so much confusion and so much greed. Somebody needs to write the truth of it all."

Parker nodded slowly, giving his mother the reassurance she sought. He felt excited to accept her challenge.

"I'm proud of you, Parker," she said, patting his knee. "You left here under the worst kind of circumstances. Your father and I worried and fretted every day you were gone. And now look what's happened. Well, it makes me teary to think how blessed our family's been. All you ever wanted to be was a newspaperman, and now here you are, back home, the owner and publisher of the *Banner*." She lifted her chin toward fast-moving clouds, dark and ominous on the horizon. "This town won't ever be the same." A pained expression came over Effie's face and her words, though not bitter, were fiercely said. "Lives are changing quickly, Parker, some for the better, many for the worse. Take your cousin Leela, for example. The oil's been an absolute blessing . . . a miracle when she needed one. But for others. Well, it's brought out the devil at his worst, breaking up a whole lot of families, black and white."

Parker nodded and clenched his teeth. In the twenty-four hours since his arrival, he had heard news of two hijackings out on the Mexia-Groesbeck Highway, a murder on Belknap Street and a violent fight in a gambling parlor in the center of town that ended only when the place was burned to the ground.

"The *Banner* will cover more than the violence of the boom," he assured his mother. "There must be some good coming from all this money people are making."

"Maybe to some," Effie replied, tired resignation in her voice. "But as far as I can tell, it's ruined your sister."

Parker felt his mouth go dry. It was time for him to face the problem. Placing his arm around Effie's shoulder, he asked, "Momma, what is really going on with Josephine and why hasn't she come around to welcome me home?"

* * *

Margaret Alexander sat up in the bed, pushed her long dark tresses back from her face and wiped sleep from her eyes.

"But it's so late, Parker. Can't you wait until morning? Then I can go with you."

Parker went over and sat beside his wife, gathering her slender body into his arms. He was glad they'd come back to Mexia, that his first child would be born in his hometown. And Margaret needed his mother, too. She was frail and delicate, in need of constant attention, and nothing would make his mother happier than having Margaret to fuss over as she waited for her grandchild.

Parker's love for Margaret surged through him as he placed his hands on her shoulders and gently urged her back onto the starched white pillowcase.

"It's only nine o'clock. You've been asleep less than an hour, and I want you to stay here, in bed. I won't be gone long." He kissed Margaret gently on her lips and caressed her soft brown cheek. "Momma said Josephine is living over on Denton Street since she left Johnny Ray."

"What about her children?" Margaret asked.

"Penny stays here with Momma most of the time, but Oliver runs the streets just like his father did, and Josephine has taken up selling whiskey to earn a living. Did you ever hear of such nonsense? My sister, a bootlegger? Sounds like she's lost her mind." Parker rose from the bed, went to the tall wardrobe and took out his hat.

"Maybe it's not as bad as you think," Margaret said, trying to comfort her husband. "Bootlegging is illegal. Surely Josephine wouldn't risk being put in jail!"

"Apparently she doesn't care." He put on his hat and leaned down to squeeze Margaret's hand. "She's just a few blocks from here and I know you want me to stay, but I've got to see Josephine tonight. Whatever's going on with her has got to stop."

It didn't take Parker long to make his way to Denton Street where he immediately recognized the house. It was set back from the street on a lot that at one time had been lovingly landscaped. Though now overgrown and trailing wildly, the rows of bushy hedges lining the sidewalk remained as stalwart proof of some gardener's skill. Two stately bur oaks rose on either side of the porch, and the bearded iris at the foot of the steps struggled to put forth deep purple blooms.

Parker stepped onto the sagging porch and knocked impatiently on the door. Immediately, Josephine answered.

"Hello, Josephine," Parker said, looking at her, then peering into the dim rooms spreading out in the shadows behind his sister.

"Parker!" The startled young woman tugged at her soiled blouse, which hung loosely on her bulky frame, and laid her hands on her stomach. "Parker!" she said again, squinting her pale eyes in disbelief. "You're home." Her words were flat, without emotion, as if she had no life to give them.

"Yes," he replied uneasily, horrified to see how desperately overweight and puffy his sister appeared. Red creases ran the length of her face. He must have awakened her. His heart filled with sadness and a lump rose in his throat, but he smiled broadly and reached out to hug her. She stiffened in his arms.

"Home for a visit or for good?" she asked, as if the length of his stay would determine whether she asked him in.

"For good," Parker answered, moving closer to the door, edging past her into the narrow hallway.

Josephine shrugged in resignation, stepped back slightly and allowed her brother into her house. She shut the door quickly, walked in front of him and led Parker down the hall, past rooms filled with broken furniture and piles of rags, through a jumble of discarded bottles and jars along the baseboards. Tangled dingy curtains separated one room from another.

They entered what appeared to be the kitchen. Parker was not certain, for it did not look as if the stove had ever been used for cooking anything other than sour mash or distilling fermented fruit.

The kitchen table was set up for bottling and sealing jars of white lightning and bottles of wine. The table, the countertops, and all the space along the floor were crowded with earthen crocks, bottles and jars, some full, some empty and dirty, waiting to be filled. He'd never seen such an operation in his life.

"How can you do this?" Parker started right in, though he had planned to ease slowly around to the bootlegging issue. No wonder his mother's heart was broken.

"Do what?" Josephine threw back innocently, flinging herself into a chair. Parker remained standing, glowering down at his sister.

"Do what?" she asked again. "Try to make a living for myself? If Momma sent you to preach to me, you can leave right now."

Parker noticed that his sister's pale, smooth skin was blotched with eruptions.

"Momma didn't send me. I came to see you," Parker told her. Josephine stared at him with distrust and resentment.

"Well, here I am," she said in a sarcastic tone. "And don't get any ideas that I'm broke and desperate. Just because the house is a little dirty. I haven't been feeling well for the past few days. Upset stomach, that's all."

"You do look like you've been under the weather," Parker agreed, wondering how much of this stuff his sister was drinking.

"I'm doing real well now. The boom's brought me a way to make my own money. I don't need Momma or Johnny Ray or anyone else. I like my life just as it is. And I'm fine, Parker. Just fine."

"You don't look fine to me." His tone was stern, yet brotherly. He made up his mind not to bite his tongue. "And this place is more than just dirty . . . it's revolting! You were raised to do better than this. How can you disappoint Momma so?"

"Disappoint Momma! Is that all you care about? Can't you give me a little credit for taking charge of my life? I'm doing the best I can!" she yelled at Parker. "And I'm not living my life for Momma."

"What happened, Josephine? I know things with Johnny Ray didn't work out, but you could have gone home. You have two children. There's no reason to be living like this."

"I'm happy," she cut him off, slumping in her chair. "I make enough money to live by myself and—"

"You let Oliver run the streets day and night, so I'm told, and you gave Penny to Momma to raise," Parker interrupted, unable to understand how his sister could content herself with such a life. "When was the last time you visited your daughter? Momma says she does not see you for weeks at a time. How can you do this to her?"

"She wanted Penny to come live with her. She badgered me for months until I decided, why not? If that's what makes Momma happy, why not?"

"Because that's not what makes Momma happy," Parker said in

a most serious tone. He paced back and forth, his eyes still on his sister. "And you know it. She's devastated, Josephine. Really hurt. She feels she's lost her only daughter."

Saddened by the tears welling up in Josephine's opaque eyes, he knew he had hurt his sister.

She bit into her bottom lip and glared at Parker.

"Her only daughter! What a joke! You know she turned her back on me the day Leela entered our house. Don't say you didn't see it, Parker. You saw how Momma fawned and fussed over Leela. She still does. And now that this oil has come in on her place, you'd think she was royalty the way Momma carries on. Leela bought this and Leela bought that. That's all she ever talks about when I go to the house. Still comparing me to Leela. Well, I don't want to hear it . . . so I stay away."

"I'm certain Momma does not compare you to Leela. Don't take it that way, Josephine. She loves both of you, that's for sure, but you should never think Momma considers Leela better than you. It's all in your mind, Josephine, and you really ought to try to be a part of the family. Staying away for months and you live only four blocks from home! That doesn't make sense to me."

Josephine shuddered and wiped her nose on the sleeve of her blouse.

"First Leela, then Penny," she went on, voice quavering with pain. "Why wasn't I enough, Parker? Why was Momma so fast to replace me? Always looking for a better daughter in somebody else?"

"That's not true," Parker said, confused by his sister's words. How long had she been tormented by such thoughts? And why in the world didn't she talk to anyone?

Josephine bent her head and continued to speak through muffled sobs. "Leela is a witch, you know. She even turned you against me. Convinced you to leave me and go up north." Josephine stopped, giving her brother a scathing look.

Parker quickly circled the table, pulling Josephine to her feet. He held her tightly as she shook with grief on his shoulder.

"You've got it all twisted, Josephine. Cousin Leela had nothing to do with my leaving. I had to go. I couldn't stay here. I don't know what Poppa told you, but he and Momma wanted me out of Mexia. There was no future for me in this town."

"You didn't have to leave me alone with Leela," Josephine protested. "She was always hateful and mean to me, and it got worse after you left. So I moved out to the country with Johnny Ray. To have a life of my own."

"You shouldn't have done that."

"Well," Josephine screamed, pushing Parker away, "I did! And I'm not sorry. Not sorry at all!"

"I wrote to you and tried to explain. You never answered a single letter. How do you think that made me feel? I don't know where you get these strange ideas that Momma turned away from you." In frustration Parker slammed his fist onto the table. He felt he had lost all control. And this stream of odd, vindictive talk from his sister . . . where in the world was it coming from? He took a deep breath and went on. "You were always the special one, the one Momma loved most."

Josephine pulled back to spit the words at her brother.

"Special! Oh, yes, she called me 'special.' Only because I had white skin! I was her special black child who didn't look like anyone in the family. That's the only reason Momma ever called me special . . . and I know underneath all her talk, she hated me and thought me a freak!" Josephine picked up a jar of corn liquor and smashed it against the wall. The strong odor of whiskey immediately filled the room.

Parker grabbed her arms, afraid of what she might do next, but she flailed wildly and wrenched free, forcing him back.

"Stop it, Josephine," Parker pleaded, tears now standing in his eyes. He hated the torment his sister was in; his heart bled for her anguish and unfounded pain. "Let me help you," he began.

"What could you possibly do to help me?" Josephine widened her strangely colorless eyes. "There's nothing you can do. Do you hear me, Parker? Nothing! You can't help someone who's nobody. And I'm nothing! Nothing! Nothing!"

CHAPTER TWENTY-TWO

Leela Wilder had everything she could possibly want. The extent of her happiness was frightening at times, swelling up on sunny days to smother her with joy, creeping into ordinary moments to surprise and excite her without warning.

Rioluces No. 1 was producing nearly five thousand barrels a day. No. 2 had come in last month with a shocking burst of three hundred barrels an hour. And though there was evidence of a slowdown on No. 1, Victor had already spudded in Rioluces No. 3.

When Victor hired six armed guards and posted them around the site, the Beaufort Drilling Company was finally taken seriously and all harassing threats immediately stopped.

Kenny had returned to his childish, carefree self, having tucked away the loss of his father in a secret place that no longer plagued him, and Victor Beaufort had just confirmed his love for Leela with a ruby-and-diamond ring.

Leela reached over to touch Victor's cheek. Her hand trembled, and she felt a surge of happiness claim her heart as she told herself, again, I am the luckiest woman on earth.

The house was quiet. Kenny had gone to spend the evening with a schoolmate in town, and dinner alone with Victor had been pleasantly romantic. Leela smiled to herself as she thought about the evening.

Their conversation had been lively and crowded with talk about oil wells, railroad lines and Prohibition. When they discussed the recent wave of Negro artists fleeing to Paris to live and work, Victor decided that he would take his bride to France for their honeymoon. The thought of traveling by ocean liner thrilled Leela, and the idea of walking with Victor through the streets of the most romantic city in the world was slightly overwhelming.

By the time the final sip of brandy passed her lips, Leela knew this evening would come to a very special end.

She walked to the oil lamp on the mantel and held the rich red gemstone up to the light. It caught the dull yellow glow from the lamp and its brilliance radiated back. Now it is official, she thought. I will soon be Victor Beaufort's wife. And the man I've chosen to be my husband understands me and loves me as no one has before.

Carefully setting her brandy glass on the mantel next to the Rochester clock, she reached down and took Victor's hand. He stood, towering over her, the expectant look on his face warming her and making her feel secure. He lightly touched her hair, then wove his fingers into the tendrils at the nape of her neck and lowered his lips to hers.

His kiss was magical, cutting them off from the rest of the world, setting the course she was ready to follow.

When Leela gently pulled free, Victor held her tightly for a moment, then softly followed her into her candlelit bedroom.

There was no need to say anything. They'd been talking for hours. Days. Weeks. Not a day had gone by when they were not together. And Leela relished the hunger that smoldered constantly between them, anticipating its glorious fulfillment tonight.

The soft cotton sheets on her fluffy featherbed felt soothing and cool against her neck. Leela searched Victor's face above hers. It was strong, handsome, flushed with desire. She ached to possess him totally, brazenly, without taking her eyes from his. She began to undo the tiny buttons on his shirt.

In a blur of gentle movements, they disrobed. The feel of his warm, muscular arm beneath her shoulders nearly brought tears to her eyes. She could hardly bear the tenderness he brought to their embrace.

Leela surrendered to a flurry of kisses sweeping over her forehead, her eyes, her cheeks. Victor nuzzled the soft skin at the back of her neck. The sweet mellow scent of him enveloped her and she moaned slightly, arching her back to caress him with every inch of her thirsty bronze skin.

The intimate joining of their naked bodies sent a ripple of shudders through Leela. Her eyes fluttered closed as she savored his touch, her lips parted slightly as desire surged to the surface and engulfed her.

Victor smiled down at the woman beneath him, rejoicing in the way the soft candlelight illuminated her flawless golden skin. He pulled her closer to his smooth, hairless chest.

Leela's eyes opened slowly and the look she saw on Victor's face was reassuring. He had a trusting, solid confidence about him that made her feel warm and safe. With Victor in her life she felt whole, as if her years with T.J. had been years of marking time, waiting for this union to bring the jagged pieces of her soul together.

Victor trailed his fingers lightly through the blaze of soft curls spread out on the pillow, then buried his face tenderly among them.

"I love you," he whispered into her ear, inhaling the perfume of her presence, the scent of the flickering candles, the comforting odor of pine logs in the hearth. He stretched his lean body alongside hers and reveled in the long-awaited touch of his skin against hers . . . the joy of finally possessing her. He didn't know why she had chosen tonight after so many months of gentle refusal, but he never pushed her—knowing that was the surest way to lose a woman like Leela. Tenderly, he moved his hand over her shoulder, along her side to the swell of her hip, across the supple skin of her thigh. He felt her stir beneath him. The half-lit room swirled with passion and he crushed his lips to hers.

Leela kissed Victor as if she feared he might vanish from an incredible dream. She felt herself floating, shimmering within his caress, transported by a love she had almost convinced herself did not exist. When their lips parted, she leaned over his shoulder and murmured into his ear.

"I've been waiting for you a very long time. I'll always love you, Victor. Always."

He did not reply, but pressed his face between her breasts and groaned, his warm breath charging her with passion. She slid her palms down his spine and urged him to take her.

The intensity of Victor's lovemaking did not shock her, but flushed her body with raw hunger, propelling her to satisfy the very essence of her desire. She gave herself over completely to him, trusting in the strength of their love. No dark thoughts of regret shadowed her surrender. In fact, the smile Victor could not see that played lightly over her lips was wickedly delicious, frightfully risqué. Leela sighed and was glad he could not see it. This night would be treasured like a gift, to be tucked away in the most secret part of her soul.

Hattie Wilder stopped at the corner of Titus and Denton, squinting up and down the darkening street. She felt lost, confused. The sun was rapidly disappearing and she'd have to hurry if she hoped to find the place before dark. Her breathing turned ragged and shallow. Her chest began to ache, but she leaned more heavily onto her gnarled stick and turned north, creeping painfully up Denton Street, looking carefully at each house as she passed.

A big house with two bur oaks in the front. That's what the ragman had told her. That's where she could get a small jar of whiskey. Just a little taste to help ease the pain in her chest.

When Hattie saw the house, she crossed the street, followed a broken brick path to the back, and tapped lightly on the sagging frame that held a screenless door without a knob.

A brown-skinned boy with nappy, dirty hair appeared and looked down at Hattie. He didn't say a word, just surveyed the old woman with blank, disinterested eyes.

"Yo' momma home?" Hattie asked, straightening up as much as she could.

"Uh-huh," the boy uttered, stepping aside to let Hattie in.

"Momma!" the boy yelled through the house. "Momma! A lady

here to see you." Then he pushed past Hattie and ran off into the shadows.

Hattie stepped into the kitchen. The horde of flies circling the room and the acrid stench of fermentation almost drove her back outside. But she waved her handkerchief in front of her face and gratefully sank onto a chair at the cluttered table.

"You wanted to see me?" Josephine asked in a distracted tone as she pushed her way through the dirty curtain at the door. Her hair was combed today, neatly braided and pinned across the top of her head. Her translucent skin appeared painfully flushed.

"Mister Jonas tol' me I might be able to get a little taste here . . . you know? I got a touch of rheumatism and arthritis, too. Sometimes a taste o' corn helps ease the pain."

Josephine had nothing to say. She walked to a cabinet, took out a pint jar of clear liquid and placed it on the table in front of Hattie.

"Eighty-five cents," she said, fixing her pale eyes on the old woman.

Hattie pulled out her tiny black change purse and counted out the coins onto the table. She started to put the jar into her big purse, then stopped and looked up at Josephine.

"You reckon I could taste a little before I go? I got a long walk over to Preston Street."

"It's your whiskey," Josephine said curtly as she reached into the cupboard and pulled out a teacup. She handed it to Hattie. "Help yourself."

Hattie quickly screwed off the lid, poured a small amount into the cup and swallowed it with one gulp. She slumped back and let the warm liquid work its way through her tired, crippled body.

Josephine eased down into the chair across from her visitor and gave the woman a sullen stare.

This girl looks familiar, Hattie thought. I've seen her someplace in town.

"Have a drink with me, baby," Hattie offered. "Ain't no good for an old woman drinking alone."

Josephine hesitated for a moment, then reached up and got another cup, holding it loosely as Hattie filled it halfway.

Josephine took a sip and set the cup back down.

"What's your name?" Hattie asked, trying to break the awkward silence.

"Josephine," came her answer.

"Seems like I seen you before," Hattie said. "You always lived over here?"

"Grew up over on Palestine, near Preston. My momma's Effie Alexander. Maybe you know her. She sews for a lot of the ladies around here." Warmed by the whiskey, Josephine relaxed, glad to have some company.

"Alexander," Hattie repeated flatly, taking another sip of liquor. "You possibly kin to someone named Leela Alexander? She married my son T.J."

Josephine threw back her head and laughed in a crude, mocking tone. "Leela Alexander? You got it all wrong, lady. Leela was never an Alexander. She's some long-lost cousin of mine who took my family name. She was Leela Brannon when she came to Mexia. And that was a long time ago."

Hattie's hand stopped in midair. She quickly set the teacup on the table and leaned across the stained oilcloth to see Josephine better. "Brannon, you say? Her name was Leela Brannon? A kinda redheaded woman? Lives out in the country? On that place where they done found all that oil?"

"Yeah, that's her," Josephine said, boldly pouring herself another shot from Hattie's jar. "We're not close. Once I got married and moved from my momma's house, we stopped speaking. I just moved back into the city a short while ago."

Hattie's eyes widened with each word Josephine spoke. A pain gripped her chest and forced all air from her lungs. She struggled to swallow another sip of whiskey.

"You know my cousin?" Josephine asked dully. How strange, she thought, that this old woman would know Leela.

Hattie was speechless. She continued to stare at Josephine over the rim of her cup.

"Well, she's a greedy, selfish woman who never thinks of anyone but herself," Josephine volunteered, glad for an opportunity to vent her feelings about Leela. "I never believed she was really my cousin, even if my momma said so."

"What you know 'bout her?" Hattie forced each word on a rush of ragged breath. She felt her insides shrink against her ribs. The pain was excruciating. "How you know her name was Brannon?"

" 'Cause my momma was a Brannon. Had a brother named Ed. He died in some fire on a train and left his baby girl for my momma to raise. But she never came to Mexia 'til she was close to grown. That's why I never believed that story. If she was my cousin, why'd Momma wait till the gal was grown to bring her here? Coulda just left her where she was."

Hattie let out a sigh that bordered on a moan and slumped back heavily in her chair. The dirty room rocked before her eyes. Ed's child. The baby girl he had talked about. And to think—T.J. had married her! Though no blood relation existed, the coincidence of Benny Wilder's child marrying the daughter of the only man Hattie had loved was chilling. She began to sicken with the stunning revelation. Her stomach cramped with the jolt of memories that suddenly assaulted her: Carey's painful birth, that train ride to Fort Worth. The bond.

She gripped the edge of the sticky table and pulled herself more upright. Her bleary eyes did not want to focus and Josephine seemed very far away. "Yo' momma ever talk about her brother? Your Uncle Ed?"

"Not when I was growing up. Not that I can recollect." Josephine burped loudly, giggled and took another drink. "But you know something strange? Really strange?" She slurred her words together despite straining to speak distinctly. "Not six months ago, when I was at my momma's house, a letter came to her from the MK and T railroad. She said she had been waiting a long time for that letter. Well, she finally got it—some business about some bonds Uncle Ed was supposed to have. I asked my momma, 'Why you fooling around now with a dead man's affairs?' She said she was trying to find out what happened to a bond that belonged to Cousin Leela." Josephine's face twisted into a scowl that nearly closed her eyes. "Always doing something to help Leela out. She never lifted a finger for me. Always trying to help Cousin Leela."

Hattie blinked rapidly, rubbed her bleary eyes and put the cap tightly on her jar. She'd heard enough. Pushing herself back from the table, she stood looking down at Josephine.

"Thank you kindly, Miss Josephine, for the whiskey and your company." She shoved the jar into her bag and snapped it shut. "I best be getting on home."

Hurriedly, she left through the back door, clumsily maneuvered the porch steps, and stabbed the soft ground with her gnarled walking stick as she headed south.

"Can't hardly believe what I just heard," Hattie mumbled, ignoring a gray cat that ran across her path. "If what that gal said is true, there's trouble brewing. I can feel it. Leela and Carey. Brother and sister? How in the world did things get so twisted? And if that gal's momma is trying to find Ed's bond, no telling what trouble might be stirred up."

She walked the rest of the way home in a daze, thankful to make it back without passing out. She was light-headed and dizzy, and the pain in her chest seemed to spread all through her shoulders, down her left arm.

Hattie struggled to climb the steps onto Elvina Hopper's porch.

Well, she decided as she entered the house and pulled off her hat, if the law comes 'round asking questions, I don't know nuthin' about any of it. Nuthin'. And nobody can prove I do.

Chapter Twenty-Three

Street noise from busy Commerce Avenue seeped into the office through a half-open window and shattered the strained silence between the two men. Victor Beaufort uncrossed his legs, placed both feet flat on the floor and eased himself back into his chair. He stared in disbelief at Thornton Welch.

"That's a pretty tough bargain you're trying to strike," he said bluntly, not at all happy with the deal he'd just been offered.

"I think it's a fair approach, Mr. Beaufort. We need each other and this way we both profit. Without Starr Oil piping your crude out of the ground and shipping it to the refinery in Corsicana, what do you really have, Mr. Beaufort? Nothing but a sump full of crude that will deteriorate daily. Subject to fires and contamination, too. Not a very good way to store oil."

"That's not news," Victor replied glumly. "Why else do you think I agreed to our original deal? Rioluces Number 1 came in so big and so fast I was glad to sign up with you. And Number 2 is holding its own, though I know production might be slipping a little. But eighty-five percent? I'm sorry, Mr. Welch, that's a big chunk of my lease on Rioluces."

"I don't think so. Not when you stand to lose the entire lease unless production increases substantially. With all due respect, Mr. Beaufort, you know the terms of our contract. Based on your projections you guaranteed production of 750,000 barrels of oil by the end of the year. Rioluces Number 1 has fallen from 5,000 to 2,500 barrels a day. Number 2 is declining steadily and you've got a ways to go on Number 3. The way it looks, unless Number 3 comes in big and we can get production out of it very quickly, you're not going to make the terms of your contract."

"Don't write me off just yet," Victor protested, feeling the hairs rise on the back of his neck. "That gas explosion last week set me back. I'm sure somebody deliberately triggered it." He remained rigidly erect as he said the words, but was inwardly shaken as he wondered, again, if one of his new guards had had a hand in the tragedy.

"I know nothing about that. In fact, I only heard about the explosion today."

Victor raised one eyebrow, a smirk of disbelief on his lips. "At any rate, it tore everything up. Injured two on my gang. One man's burned so bad he'll probably never recover."

"Those things happen in the oil field," Welch said with no emotion. "Gotta be able to press on, Mr. Beaufort. If you don't have the money to replace your equipment and bring Number 3 in according to schedule, I'll be forced to sue for the lease."

"Or give up eighty-five percent right now? That's what you're offering?" Victor snorted and pushed himself to the edge of his chair.

"That's more than fair, Mr. Beaufort." Welch remained calm, as if nothing Victor could say would ever bother him. He began cleaning his fingernails with his small pocketknife. "Most oil companies wouldn't even offer you that. There's no reason why we can't continue our relationship. But Starr needs assurance that future production is coming. We need some proof of your ability to bring in Number 3—not that I have any reason to believe your outfit might fail." Mr. Welch smiled blandly at Victor. "Laying pipe and transporting crude costs money, you know? And before we start laying out the pipeline for Number 3, I think it's best we conclude this deal."

Victor took a deep breath to still the nervous quaking in his chest and locked eyes with Thornton Welch. "I just can't turn over eighty-five percent of my lease to you right now. I've got to think this over, talk to Mrs. Wilder."

"I don't see what there is to talk about. It's your lease. The landowner's got no say about what you do with it."

"Well," Victor drew out his response, "I'd feel better letting her know what the situation is."

"I'll give you a little time." Exasperated now, Welch stretched both arms out on his desk. "If you put up a flat ten thousand dollars as security, we'll continue our relationship as originally agreed. For two more months. Then we'll check production figures again."

"When would you want the money?" Victor asked.

"Oh, let's say . . . I guess I could give you a week." The oilman did not blink an eye.

"That's impossible!" Victor rose halfway from his seat as he protested. "You know all my cash is tied up with Number 3." His words were sternly spoken. "And I've only received one payment from you for all the oil you've already piped out." Victor slumped back down and continued his negotiation. "Maybe in thirty days . . ."

"That won't do, Mr. Beaufort. This is really a very simple and generous proposition. Eighty-five percent of Rioluces right now, or pay Starr ten thousand dollars within a week."

"Or?" Victor prompted.

"Or Starr will be forced to sue for the entire lease."

"That's the rawest deal I ever heard," Victor snapped as he stood to leave.

"Better read the fine print in our contract. You'll find it all in there." Welch took out a cigarette and lit it. "And, by the way, Mr. Beaufort, don't try to shop this deal to any other oil company. I had a chat with some fellas last night at the Cozy Cafe. I've got the support of any company you might try to approach. Seems like we're all in agreement on this issue." He averted his eyes, seeming to dismiss Victor's palpable fury. "Might want to start thinking about pulling out."

Victor slammed his Stetson on his head and strode to the door.

"You're not forcing me off Rioluces," he told the smug man. "I plan to go over that contract again. I don't remember any such terms.

This is going to be settled, Mr. Welch. You can count on me settling this matter. Whatever it takes."

"Well, you've got till this time next Friday, Mr. Beaufort. I'll be right here waiting for your answer."

Parker tilted his face toward the sky and inhaled deeply, feeling very pleased that he had decided to buy the Buick convertible and not the coupe. "It sure feels good to be out of the city," he told Leela, savoring the rare breeze that floated over them. "Must be something about the direction of the wind. I can hardly breathe the air in town, and I rarely drive with the top down. Oil everywhere."

Leela laughed under her breath. "Just wait," she cautioned her cousin. "After you've been home for a while, you'll see there is no place that escapes the oil for very long. There are days right here on Rioluces when it seems to be raining black mist."

"Yeah," Kenny piped up from the backseat. He leaned forward and placed his folded arms on the soft gray leather upholstery. "When the well blew in on Red Walters's place, it took three days to cap it. Boy, you couldn't go outside at all. The ground was all black and sticky for weeks."

Parker turned slightly in his seat to look back at his young cousin. "From what your mother tells me, you don't let it stop you from going fishing."

"Oh, no," Kenny agreed, picking up his cane pole, balancing it in his hands. "The oil don't bother the fish. Pully and I come out to the creek almost every day. They been biting real good, too. I hope we get some today."

"It's been a long time since I dropped a hook into Cedar Creek," Parker admitted. "Let's hope the catfish are hungry."

Leela adjusted her new tan Stetson to better shade her eyes and gave Parker a smile. "You look so prosperous and important, driving this wonderful car."

Parker could not keep from smiling, feeling rather pleased with the way things had turned out for him.

"Victor and I have talked about getting an automobile. Maybe you can help us pick one out."

"Sure," Parker said, a hint of humor in his voice. "It's time you gave up the horse and buggy."

She laughed and playfully swatted Parker on the arm. "All right, you've made your point." Then her tone turned more serious. "I read your article in the *Banner* urging the city to enforce a curfew. You're right. I'm so glad you're back, Parker. This town needs you. The family needs you." She suddenly reached over and gave Parker a hug. "So much has changed since you left . . . you don't know how many times I wished you were here. I've needed your levelheaded advice more than once."

"You've got a lot to deal with, Leela," Parker said as he rotated the big steering wheel and turned off the main road. The shiny touring car came to a stop at the edge of Cedar Creek. "Two producing oil wells. Another on the way. A son to raise. A wedding to plan. You're going to be mighty busy for quite a while."

"You know, Parker," Leela began as she opened her door, "after all I went through to finally secure the title to this land, nothing seems impossible to me."

Parker nodded in agreement as he unloaded the fishing tackle and helped Kenny bait his hook. The boy was soon happily settled in a shady spot under a big post oak. Leela spread a quilt nearby.

"Well," she prompted, "what do you think of Victor?"

Parker chuckled. "He's a fine man. When he came into the *Banner* this morning to introduce himself, I was covered with ink and could hardly stop to really chat with him. He certainly is determined to stay on top of his lease."

"It's a struggle," Leela admitted. "The whites haven't taken too kindly to his presence, but he ignores all the talk. I used to worry, but now I see he'll do what he wants to do no matter what I say." Leela gazed across the fast-moving water. "You know, I wouldn't want it any other way. He's been tested again and again, and he still gets past the obstacles the big oil companies throw up. He'll never give up his lease."

"So far, you've both done well," Parker said. "But Leela, be careful. There is so much money at stake, and too many cruel and greedy people have moved into Mexia. Schemers are literally stealing land and leases with all kinds of tricky deals."

"I know," Leela admitted. "A new derrick shoots up every day."

"And the celebrating never stops. You wouldn't know Belknap Street anymore. It's the wildest, most dangerous area of town . . .

they call it Little Juarez now. A curfew is needed. I wouldn't want to be caught there after dark."

"That's where Victor has his office," Leela said quickly, remembering how quietly pleasant the street used to be.

"Really?" A flicker of concern passed over Parker's face. "Well, he should watch his step over there. Everyone's toting a gun."

"There was a terrible hijacking off Woodland Road last week," Leela said, as Parker secured his line and joined her on the blanket. "Makes me nervous just to think about something that awful happening right up the road."

"That's why you and Victor need to be very careful," Parker warned. "Do you realize the population of Mexia is over twenty thousand now and growing every hour? The boom has changed our town completely. Used to be I knew everybody I passed on the streets. Now I see the most awful looking roughnecks and speculators hanging around town. You and Victor are prime targets for those who would like to have this land."

Leela took a peach from the small wicker basket and rubbed it as she went on. "We have armed guards now, but in the beginning, we did have some trouble on the place. After Victor contracted with Starr Oil to pipe and ship the crude, things began to settle down. Thornton Welch is a man we can trust. I didn't like him at all at first, but now I truly believe he's looking out for Victor's best interest."

Parker glanced sidelong at Leela, wondering if she understood the shrewd tactics of the company that aimed to control the Mexia field. "Don't be too fast to accept everything Welch has to offer," he cautioned Leela. "He plans to keep Starr Oil in the dominant position in this boom. Don't ever forget that. Victor Beaufort seems like a pretty smart man, but the leasebrokers and developers working for that company have loads of experience and resources, and they know tricks we've never even dreamed of."

Back at his office, Victor pored over his contract with Starr Oil to find the clause that allowed Thornton Welch to push him around like this. Unfortunately, the convoluted wording did indeed give Starr the right to ask for up to eighty-five percent of the lease if production began to decline.

The Beaufort Drilling Company hasn't failed yet, Victor thought angrily. But even if he could scrape up the ten thousand for Starr, it wouldn't be long until the perilous balance between creditors and production caught up with him.

With ten percent pledged to his brothers and another five percent to the farmers who had been working for him, meeting the terms of Thornton Welch's offer would leave Victor with nothing at all.

How did I miscalculate production by so much? he lamented. Wildcatters were cutting deals with oil companies on little more than a dirty handshake and a slap on the back. And he thought he had all the bases covered with this fancy complicated contract.

They were going to do their best to run the colored wildcatter off the block, Victor reluctantly admitted. Rioluces was just too valuable, and it galled them to see it making a black man rich. Well, it would never happen, he vowed, shoving the papers back into his file cabinet. If it wasn't for Leela, he'd torch the field before he'd hand Starr a single percent of his lease. But right now he had to pull every string he could to get ten thousand dollars together.

Victor lowered his face into his hands, trying to clear his thoughts. If Leela got wind of this, she'd be real upset. He couldn't let her down. But he couldn't tell her he had overlooked the fine print on the Starr contract either. He had put his own company in jeopardy! What kind of respect would she have for him? He had really bungled this venture. Rioluces was rich . . . they'd just tapped the surface. He couldn't let Starr Oil take it. And he couldn't allow Leela to lose confidence in him . . . the man she was engaged to marry! How could he have let this happen?

Victor remembered how quickly he had made his projections. How eagerly he had signed the contract. Now it was all coming back to haunt him.

He had to find the money, and Leela must never know a thing about it.

CHAPTER TWENTY-FOUR

Carey Logan smoothed out a crumpled copy of the *Houston Informer* and held it up to read. The paper was nearly a month old but he didn't care; he was anxious for news about the black folks in Texas, he'd been out of touch too long. Now he was finally headed toward Limestone County, where he should have gone six months ago.

As the train swept into a deep curve, then roared across the Brazos River, Carey strained to read the headline, which immediately caught his eye.

March 17, 1921 . . . Mexia Negroes Rich From Oil Discovery!

Carey pulled the paper closer and began to read:

A tract of land owned by Mrs. T. J. Wilder, leased for drilling purposes by the Beaufort Drilling Company (the only Negro drilling company operating in the field) was the discovery site for Rioluces No. 1, a 5,000 barrel a day gusher which came in on

February 7th. It was followed by Rioluces No. 2 which just blew in yesterday at 300 barrels an hour. Mrs. Wilder is only the first of many Negro families who can look forward to becoming overnight millionaires as exploration progresses at a fast pace along the dense fault line that borders the western edge of the city. Mrs. Wilder will receive one-eighth of all oil produced, or 1,525 barrels a day. Inasmuch as the Beaufort Drilling Company, of which Mr. Victor Beaufort is the president, has recently contracted with Starr Oil Company to sell its oil at $1.10 a barrel, Mrs. Wilder will be paid $1,677 a day as long as such production continues. Oilmen predict this is just the beginning of an unprecedented boom in the once quiet town of Mexia.

The bold black letters chilled Carey, yet left him perspiring so profusely his starched white shirt stuck against his chest. Oil on T.J.'s farm! Leela was a rich woman! The story mesmerized Carey and he had to reread the article to believe it.

Carey's hands shook as he tried to refold the newspaper. He impatiently balled it up and shoved it into his valise.

I should have gone on back to Mexia like Ma wanted, he grudgingly admitted. I never should have listened to Ada and got tangled up in that deal in Galveston. If I'da followed my instincts, I'da dumped her in Beaumont right off.

Carey cursed himself for letting Ada Lache get him offtrack, though the excursion to Galveston had proven very profitable. He had willingly drifted down to the island, where high rollers stepped off steamers every day and the casinos along the seawall teemed with gamblers around the clock. The experience had been glorious: sitting on his bougainvillea-draped veranda, sipping rum punch all afternoon, rising in the evening to dress in elegantly tailored clothes to saunter in and out of blackjack parlors, roulette rooms and glitzy hotels where poker games went on for days without end.

He had done well, too. Turning the luxurious Packard into six thousand dollars had been easy. Doubling that amount at the roulette table was even easier. And during the entire time spent on the island, he had experienced an exhilarating streak of good luck. The cards, the dice and even the tiny ball spinning around the roulette wheel had fallen his way. Now he was carrying nearly all his winnings home, with a bundle of cash lining both sides of his new leather valise.

Coming upon a copy of the *Houston Informer* had also been a lucky sign. He had picked it up off a bench in the train station, unaware that his sister-in-law's good fortune was the headline story.

Good thing I ditched Ada in Houston, he thought, his mind racing at the prospects of what he'd find in Mexia. He had no regrets about leaving her behind. She'd gotten too possessive and demanding. Besides, he doubted she'd be alone very long. Ada needed a man around all the time, but Carey had to move on and travel light. His jaw tensed as he gritted his teeth. He had a lot of catching up to do.

Carey reached into his valise and searched through the jumble of papers and clothing filling the heavy bag. He pulled out the letter from T.J. that had been forwarded to him from New Orleans. Carey studied the evenly spaced letters of T.J.'s handwriting. This would be real easy, he decided as he took out a sheet of white paper and his trusty Falcon pen.

In 1921, approximately sixteen thousand miles of railroad track crisscrossed the state of Texas. The Missouri, Kansas and Texas (MK&T), the Atchison, Topeka and Santa Fe (Santa Fe) and the Houston, Texas and Central Railroad (HT&C) carried the majority of passengers and freight into Central Texas. As news of the Mexia boom circulated throughout the nation, all three lines became virtually paralyzed with traffic.

Railroad cars groaned under the weight of pipe, sheet metal, lumber, casing and valuable oil field supplies as they pushed their way up and down the tracks between Houston and Dallas, all freight destined for Mexia. It became virtually impossible to feed the hunger for raw materials the new boomtown demanded.

Like scenes of an exodus, an endless parade of wagons, hacks, and buggies struggled into Texas. The popular automobiles, which fared no better than horse-drawn hacks on unpaved dirt highways, quickly sank into muddy gumbo soil when the inevitable rains began to fall.

Strangers from all parts of the country flocked to Mexia and became its newest residents. Many were legitimate Texas oilmen, glad to have a new discovery in the wake of depleted pools like Spindletop, Desdemona and Burkburnett.

Less honorable men and women swarmed into the area, anxious to make their fortunes from the weakness, greed and ignorance of many who benefited from the oil. Gamblers, prostitutes, bootleggers, and fast-talking hustlers with a plethora of schemes quickly set up house, at times in tents or even outside, as shelter became very scarce. Many housewives rented their spare rooms, their front porches, and the shady spots under their broad leafy oaks for as much as eight dollars a day.

Space was even rented in shifts. Men who worked during the day left beds to be occupied by equally determined oil field workers who would come into the fields at night. No one complained. There was too much money and too little time to make it for a man to worry about a thing like sleep.

When Carey Logan stepped off the train at the crowded depot in Mexia, the first thing he noticed was the smell of sulfur gas that filled the air; it had a sickening, sweet odor and burned his eyes. Crated freight, stacked high all around the depot, waited for pickup under the watchful eye of armed guards. Families of oil field workers roamed the platform, searching through the crowd for fathers, brothers, or uncles who had come ahead of them, carrying all their possessions in cloth sacks and pasteboard boxes.

On the street, leaky trucks waited in line to transfer oil into railroad tank cars, leaving a slick river of crude to settle in pools around the tracks. Young colored boys, no older than seven or eight, hawked fresh water outside the station for twenty-five cents a dipper.

As Carey pushed through the throng of people gathered outside the station, he automatically circled the depot and headed away from town. If there was a room to be had for a colored man in Mexia, he would find it on the west side of the tracks.

He was lucky to find suitable lodging not too far away from the depot. The sunny room above Mildred's Cafe suited Carey just fine. The long narrow space, running the width of the cement block building, had windows at each end which allowed him to watch the bustling activity on Belknap Street and gave him a clear view across the railroad tracks into the center of town. The meager iron bed, cracked washbasin, and rickety table and chair were not nearly as luxurious as what he'd had at the Randolph Hotel in Baton Rouge. But he was lucky just to find a room. Mexia had certainly changed.

As soon as he settled the rent with Mildred, he opened his big valise and began to unpack. The musty armoire accommodated his array of fine suits: dark gabardine with wide notched lapels, a classy pinstripe with red silk lining, a double-breasted woolen with a belted jacket. His custom-made shirts with monogrammed pockets and stiff French cuffs were carefully coordinated with more than a dozen silk ties of a variety of colors. Alligator boots, soft leather tie-ups, patent slippers and sturdy cowhide boots rounded out Carey's selection of footwear. He had six different hats to choose from.

One good thing about spending time in Galveston, Carey thought as he hung up his clothing to air, was that he'd found an excellent tailor. Now he had the look he needed.

Carey pulled off his travel-worn clothes and splashed water over his face. He shaved carefully, slicked back his dark hair with a big glob of Royal Crest pomade and eased into his favorite brown suit, the one with brass buttons and slant-cut pockets.

Looking out the window facing west, Carey strained to see Rioluces. Tall derricks punctured the skyline, smoke curled up from gas fires along the fault, and the crowded Mexia-Comanche Crossing Road was jammed with a solid line of slow-moving traffic.

The beginnings of a shantytown, the inevitable gathering of oil field workers into their campsite community, snuggled against the business district and bordered the Negro neighborhood. He watched three men fight the gusty April winds to finish construction on their hastily erected shotgun shacks, made of two-by-fours, canvas, tarpaper, and tin.

Carey surveyed the chaotic site, thinking of all the riches that lay beneath the land. Soon, he told himself, part of it was going to be his.

Carey reached into the secret compartment of his valise and took out a bundle of cash. He riffled the bills, loving the feel of the money, peeled off two thousand dollars and put it into his pocket. That should be enough to turn Leela's head, he mused, locking his door, starting off toward town. My brother was such a niggardly bastard, he never understood Leela's nature. A woman like her wanted a man with cash to throw around. And now Carey had it. He grinned and adjusted his handsome fedora as he entered Harrison's to rent the most impressive automobile available.

The trip to Rioluces was a nightmare. Though eight years had passed since Carey's last visit, he knew the trip should have taken less than twenty minutes by car. He'd been lucky in town, leasing a big Studebaker touring car for fifty dollars for the week. He relished arriving at Rioluces behind the wheel of the shiny black convertible; he wouldn't dream of sitting behind the rear end of a horse. But the roads were terrible. He'd been detoured and sidetracked a number of times, stuck for an hour behind a huge wagon hauling timber that hogged and obstructed the road. Thank the devil he'd had enough foresight to wear his long duster over his good clothes.

When the traffic eased, Carey turned off the main road and sped toward the farm. The sight of two tall derricks rising up like wooden towers behind the farmhouse shocked him. He could hardly keep his eyes on the road as he maneuvered the heavy car down the narrow lane, through the arched gate of Rioluces. He had been unprepared for the actual presence of the wooden spikes that signaled riches.

The house itself had not changed—in fact, he thought it could use a new coat of paint. Looks like Leela could use a little help around here, he mused. I think I've come just in time. His heart raced at the thought of seeing her again.

Evidence of oil field traffic was everywhere. Ruts were filled with slimy black mud, and standing pools of oily water dotted the entire landscape. Nothing pretty about this, Carey thought as he stopped the car at the front porch. He got out and looked around.

Out of curiosity, he decided to go around to the back of the house to get a better look at the derricks. He carefully stepped over the oily grass and walked as far as the barn. From his position, he could see a small crowd of people lingering at the base of one of the derricks. A lettered sign read RIOLUCES NO. 2. Two black men stood on another platform less than a hundred feet away, pulling thick ropes and lifting heavy tools, urging the drill bit deeper into the earth. A third well was under way. There was no question in his mind that the lone woman sitting on a chestnut mare, blazing tresses catching the golden rays of sunshine, was Leela.

Carey went numb. She was more beautiful than he remembered. Even from a distance he could see that the years had treated her well, perhaps, if possible, had even enhanced the wholesome loveliness that had nearly driven him mad. He nervously licked his lips, remembering that hot, lazy summer he had spent on this land. That summer when Leela had carefully bandaged and nursed the awful gash in his arm. That summer he had floated through, entirely captivated by Leela. He trembled at the memory of his brazen kiss and the feel of her lips as she had dared to kiss him back. Desire surged through him anew as he recalled how obligingly she had let him slip her gauzy blouse to her waist. The remembrance of her silken breasts beneath his palms warmed him now, and he took a deep breath, certain he could still smell the perfume of her hair.

If T.J. hadn't interrupted them, waving that rusty Marlin repeater in Carey's face, he would have claimed her. She would have surrendered. His life would have taken an entirely different direction.

But it didn't matter now. Carey shrugged and pulled his hat down lower; he didn't want Leela to see him. Not just yet. He was back. Ready to claim the woman who still set him afire.

Several minutes passed before Leela noticed the stranger standing in the shadows of the barn. She groaned aloud and called out to Cap.

"Looks like another one of those damn leasebrokers chasing a deal. I wish they'd let me alone. Seems everybody in the county ought to know by now that this land is not up for grabs."

"They just not gonna accept the truth, Miz Leela. We're here to stay," Cap said as he stopped for a moment, straightened up and peered across the acreage toward the stranger. "Well, this one here's 'bout the best-dressed one to come on the place, anyway." He chuckled and shook his head, resuming his work as Leela clicked the reins and urged Taffy up the hill.

The closer she got, the more familiar the man appeared. His wide-brimmed hat, pulled down at a stylish angle, prevented her from seeing his face. But there was something familiar about him. He stood with a slight slant to his body, almost like T.J. did, Leela thought shaking her head as she remembered. T.J. had that way of holding one shoulder higher than the other. She'd only known one other man with a stance like that. Her heart fluttered and she gripped the reins more firmly. He stepped from the shadows and the sun bathed his face.

Carey Logan. Leela didn't dismount as she greeted Carey, but evenly welcomed him back and invited him in. She entered the back door and watched him sit at her table. Whatever he was up to, she wanted no part of it.

Handing Carey a cup of coffee, Leela settled in at the far end of the trestle table. He had not shown up to console her over T.J.'s death. That much she knew for certain.

"Don't feel like you gotta keep your distance from me, Leela. I won't bite, you know?" Carey smiled and brushed the lapels of his spotless gabardine suit. He picked up his brown felt hat, ran his fingers around the brim, then set it back down. "Been quite a spell, hasn't it?"

"Yes, Carey. It has. I'm very surprised to see you."

"I don't know why. You know I care about you."

Leela stiffened at these words. Care? she thought. But she kept silent as Carey went on.

"As soon as I got Ma's letter and learned T.J. had passed on, I took the first train out of Baton Rouge and headed here. You can't imagine how it hurt me, learning my only brother was already dead and buried before I even heard about it."

"Well, you never did let anyone know where you were. You're lucky Hattie's letter caught up with you at all." Leela watched Carey closely. She did not know him well, but had spent enough time in his company to sense he was uneasy: hedging the truth, trying too hard to impress her. She poured a little more coffee into her cup and let Carey explain his absence.

". . . and when I got the bad news," he continued his story, "I told Damon Struthers he'd have to find another partner for his club because I had to head back to Texas. Of course, Damon was real upset. He had to buy me out. We were fifty-fifty on the deal and I'd been manager of the Versailles Room at the Randolph Hotel so long, he had to pay me quite a sum. Also, I think he was scared of losing business. No one else could book ragtime bands and singers into the place and keep the crowds shouting for more." Carey paused and fingered his trim mustache, obviously waiting for Leela's reaction. Her lack of response spurred him on. His voice rose slightly and his words came faster.

"During the five years I was there, the Versailles Room became the hottest night spot in Louisiana. I even got Eubie Blake and Mamie Smith to come through for a gig." Carey lifted his chin and shifted his eyes. "But you know, Leela, I was really getting tired of the club business. Long hours, all kinds of crazy folk to deal with. Musicians can be temperamental pains in the . . . uh, neck," he finished, getting up from the table to go stand by the kitchen window.

Leela stared at his back. His stance was so much like T.J.'s. But the resemblance to his half-brother stopped there. Carey's flippant braggadocio grated against the memory of T.J.'s sober, modest existence.

"Sounds like you've done well for yourself," Leela prompted, certain most of what Carey told her was a lie. He still oozed magnetic charm, but she knew his attractive posture camouflaged a shallow, self-centered hustler.

"Extremely well," Carey agreed, turning to face Leela. "But enough about me. Looks like you're not faring too poorly either." His engaging smile startled Leela. It brought an uncomfortable sweep of memories. He broke into soft laughter. "All this business with oil in Mexia!" he exclaimed, moving quickly back to the table, where he bent forward and placed both hands flat down next to Leela's arm. He gazed into her eyes. Leela hated the flutter in the center of her chest and tried to avoid his intense stare, but gave up and looked directly back at him.

"Word never got to Louisiana about all this!" Carey said, leaning closer. "First I knew what was going on was when I got off the train in Mexia. Such excitement. And to think . . . right here on T.J.'s land." Carey eased one hand onto Leela's warm wrist. He stroked her arm softly as he went on. "A shame, isn't it, that T.J. never lived to see the fruits of his labor? Such good fortune for such a good man." Leela saw how easily Carey was able to say those words. His hypocrisy was disgusting.

"Yes," Leela conceded, removing her arm from beneath his cool fingers. "Your brother deserved good fortune. He had a very difficult time toward the end. It was hard on all of us . . . especially Kenny."

Carey sat down again, now in the chair closest to Leela. His expensive cologne wafted to her. The smell triggered memories of a dark hayloft, sun pouring in, heating her bare skin. She had not been up there since.

"Where is Kenny?" Carey asked. "Guess I wouldn't know the boy. How old is he now?"

"He'll soon be ten," Leela replied, distracted, confused, wishing Carey would go away. "He should be along any minute. Pully, one of my hands around here, went into town to pick him up from school. It's a long day for the boy, but Halsey is the best place to send him, so I manage to get him in and out of town every day."

"That's a good idea. The boy needs the best education he can get. But I wouldn't expect any less from you, Leela. You always struck me as a pretty smart woman."

She wanted to get up and run. Looking at him, remembering, hearing his voice. It was too much to tolerate now. Leela wiped her face with a damp kitchen towel and stared uneasily down at the table.

Carey paid no attention to her mood, preoccupied with his own mission.

"Now that I've returned, there's a few things I want to talk to you about," he began, his tone suddenly turning serious.

Here it comes, Leela thought. The real reason he's come back.

"What do you mean, Carey?" she asked innocently.

"Well . . . I don't know if you ever knew about it . . . but T.J. wrote me a letter." Carey reached into the inside pocket of his expensive suit.

"No," Leela lied, letting him go on, "he never said anything to me about writing you."

"I got this letter some time ago. Not too long after he got sick. I never dreamed he'd pass so quickly and I had kinda put this letter away. You know? I didn't want to think about him passing on. But it seems like I ought to share this with you."

"May I see the letter?" Leela asked, extending her hand.

"Of course," he said as he gave her the single page.

Leela gingerly accepted the white paper and looked it over.

T.J.'s evenly spaced, printed letters jumped up at her from the page. Her hands began to shake as she read:

Dear Carey,

I hope this letter catches up with you before things turn too bad for me. I got the white plague and it don't look like I'm gonna git over it. I know we done had our differences, but

I'm hoping you will come on back to the farm and help Leela out once I'm gone. This ain't easy to ask, but I want you to watch over affairs on the place and help Leela keep things going. Help her with the boy, too. She's about worked herself to death since I been laid up. Do what you can to hold on to the farm. This farm is all I got to leave her and I want you to help her with any plans she got for the place. In my thinking, Rioluces is as much yours as mine.

Your brother,
T.J.

Leela let the paper slip from her fingers and settle on the table. She lifted angry, confused eyes at Carey.

"I don't believe T.J. wrote this letter."

"Now, now, don't get upset. That's T.J.'s writing, isn't it? Nobody ever made letters like his." Carey picked up the letter and folded it in half. "I'm sure he didn't want to get you more worried about his sickness than you already were. It's gotta be hard for a man to admit he's facing up to death. Musta been a difficult time for you . . . and Ma. I'm gonna go see her tomorrow. But don't you worry, Leela. I'm here now. I've got plenty of money." He paused and pulled the stack of bills from his pocket, fanning them onto the table. "I'm gonna help out with everything from now on. T.J. wanted me on the place, that's clear, and that kinda makes us partners, doesn't it?"

Incensed, Leela jumped up and crushed the stiff new bills in both fists, then shook the money in Carey's face. "How dare you come back here with a fake letter from my dead husband and act as if nothing ever happened? You have no respect for anyone's feelings, do you? There is nothing here for you!" Her flare of temper startled Carey, who drew back sharply as if she had slapped him. "You think you can saunter in here after eight years, throw cash all over my kitchen table and buy your way back into my life?" She hurled the bills to the floor. "Get out of here!" Disgust flooded her face. "Things have changed, Carey. Your smooth charm won't work anymore, you've played that hand one time too many."

"Calm down, Leela," Carey started, regaining his composure. "I'm just trying to be helpful—like T.J. wanted."

"Ha!" Leela gave him a short, curt laugh. "All T.J. wanted was for you to stay off his land. Remember, Carey? The last thing your brother said to you was 'Stay off my land or I'll kill you.' I heard him—I was there!" Leela went to the door, yanked it open and anchored both hands on her hips. "Now pick up your dirty money and *go*!"

Chapter Twenty-Five

The gentle swish-swish of the oil pumps floated like jazz riffs over the farm. Echoing eerily up from the drilling site, the soft yet grating refrain filled the room like the rustle of angels' wings quivering nervously above Leela's head. The rhythmic beat of the balance bars tipping one way, then another, usually brought comfort and solace to Leela, made her good fortune seem concrete, solid, beyond the reach of greedy men who threatened to take her oil-rich land. But tonight, instead of lulling her to sleep, the steady rocking created an anxiety that wound tighter and tighter as the hours slipped by. When the Rochester clock chimed three, Leela groaned and turned onto her side, staring glumly out the window.

Lace curtains fluttered lazily as a cool breeze entered the room. Leela took a deep breath, then raised her eyes to the intricate pattern of shadows playing darkly on the ceiling. Reluctantly, she opened her mind to the dreaded reality that Victor's contract with Starr might be in jeopardy.

Production was declining daily. The crew, though doggedly continuing with the drilling, had not been paid this week. When Leela had offered to meet the payroll from her personal account, Victor had curtly refused, cutting her off before she could finish making her offer. Later, he apologized for snapping at her, but Leela still worried that he was under too much strain. If only he would set aside his pride and let her help. Though the equipment needed to complete No. 3 had been replaced, according to Victor's calculations they remained three weeks behind schedule.

Leela placed the back of her hand over her brow and added one more worry to her list: Carey Logan. Her head began to throb at the thought of the complications he might bring to a situation which already verged on exploding. She lay quietly, but her mind refused to rest.

At last Leela turned back the coverlet and slipped out of her bed. After lighting the lamp, she went to her desk and pulled out her copy of the lease. Pushing a tangle of curls from her face, she moved nearer the light and reread the contract.

Rioluces No. 3 had to come in before the end of next week, she calculated. Moving to the window, she looked out over her land, feeling both proud and saddened at the sight of the monstrous derricks soaring into the starry sky and the slick pools of oil reflecting moonlight like mirrors. Leaning her head against the window frame, Leela thought of Victor's plight and her heart went out to him.

"Don't worry, my love," she whispered into the night. "We've come too far and worked too hard to let people like Thornton Welch or Carey Logan crush our dreams. Have faith, Victor, hold on to our future. Our love is stronger than anything we might face."

"Finish those eggs, Kenny," Leela called over her shoulder as she fried sausage at the stove.

"You know I don't like them like this," the unhappy boy protested, stabbing the lumpy yellow mass with his fork.

"What's wrong? They're scrambled, aren't they?" Leela snapped, too tired from tossing and turning all night to argue with her son about his breakfast. She had more important things on her mind, like hearing from Victor. Why hadn't he come by to tell her about his meeting with Thornton Welch?

"They're hard." Kenny folded his hands in his lap. "You never make them hard like this, Ma. Never."

Leela glanced down at the overcooked eggs in the center of Kenny's plate. "Well, don't eat them, then." She cut the conversation off, knowing Kenny had reason to complain. "Just eat your biscuits and get along," she said, softening her tone. "Pully's waiting in the buggy for you now."

She went over and laid her hand on the top of Kenny's head. "Here's your lunch," she said apologetically. "Fried chicken and another biscuit, with honey inside. I'm sorry about the eggs."

Kenny got up and smiled at his mother, brushing his lips lightly on her cheek before running down the hallway to the front door. Leela followed him onto the porch.

Crowding up to the front of the house, an early April showing of purple iris swayed gently in the breeze, nodding their heavily budded stems nearly to the ground. The clear blue sky, with its hint of warmth to follow, helped Leela forget her long sleepless night.

As she stood waving good-bye to Kenny, Victor's Model T pulled through the gate. She watched him come to a stop at the foot of the steep limestone steps and felt a slight catch in her throat at the sight of him.

"Good morning," Victor called, coming toward her.

Leela lifted her face to his kiss and allowed herself to be swept away for a moment. She hungrily pressed her lips against Victor's and wrapped her arms around his neck.

"Good *morning*," she replied when their lips finally parted; then she led him into the house. "Had breakfast?" she asked, picking up Kenny's untouched plate, frowning at the mess she'd made of his eggs.

"Nope. The line outside Mildred's Cafe was close to the end of the block. You know, it's darn near impossible to get a meal in town. Folks are swarming all over the place." Victor stretched his long legs under the table.

"Ham, sausage, eggs?" Leela asked as she pulled her black iron skillet onto the flame.

"Whatever you cook, I'll eat," Victor said, laughing. "Haven't you learned yet how easy I am to please?"

Leela said nothing as she put a thick slice of ham into the skillet.

"Victor," she prompted, turning serious, "how did the meeting with Starr Oil go?" She kept her back to him as she spoke, unable to face him in case the news was bad.

"Very well." His exuberant words filled Leela with relief. "Welch is so sure Number 3 is going to come in big, he's not concerned at all about the decline in production."

Now Leela swung around, amazed. "Really?" She broke into a wide smile. "There's no problem with the contract? With the delay?"

"None whatsoever," Victor told her. "We just need to keep moving forward. He said declines are to be expected as underground pressure fluctuates. No reason at all to be concerned." He took off his fringed jacket and hung it over the back of the chair and moved to stand in front of Leela. He circled her waist with his hands. "So you stop all that worrying, you hear?" He ran a finger softly over the faint frown line on Leela's brow. "Leave the details to me. Everything is going to be just fine."

Pulling from his embrace, Leela turned back to the stove. Victor gave her a puzzled look and stepped back. "What's the matter?" he asked warily.

"We might not have problems with Starr," she began, "but I'm afraid there may be trouble brewing elsewhere."

"What are you talking about, Leela?" He turned her toward him and searched her face. "What trouble?"

"Do you remember me telling you about T.J.'s half-brother? The one no one's seen for so long?"

Victor took the plate of fried ham and eggs from Leela and set it on the table. He pulled out his chair and sat down to eat. "Sure. Carey Logan. He's been gone for years you said."

"Well, he's returned to Mexia," Leela said sharply, coming to the table to sit near Victor.

"You saw him?"

"Yesterday. Showed up out of the blue not too long after you left to go meet with Starr." She took a linen napkin from the table and nervously twisted it as she spoke. "I think Carey's trying to start some trouble."

As Victor ate his breakfast, Leela recounted her brother-in-law's visit.

"Do you think that letter means anything?" Leela asked, frowning.

"I guess a judge would have to rule on that. But why do you think it's a fake?"

"Because T.J. and Carey were never close. My husband never planned to leave any part of this farm to Carey. He worked hard for this land, lived out here all alone for years. During the ten years of our marriage, T.J. saw his brother twice—on our wedding day and two years later. And the last time Carey set foot on Rioluces, he came to hide from cutthroats out of McLennan County who were hunting him down over some sour deal involving bootleg whiskey. When he left a few months later, headed toward the Louisiana border, T.J. was holding a gun to his back. Carey Logan is a lowlife con artist, and he forged that letter to steal our profits."

"Why did T.J. pull a gun on him?" Victor asked.

Leela's nostrils flared as she inhaled deeply, averting her eyes from Victor's. "I . . . I'm not certain," she stuttered. "They'd had a violent argument that morning. I remember T.J. threatened to call the sheriff if Carey didn't clear out. That was eight years ago. No one's heard one word from Carey since."

"What'd they argue about?" Victor pressed, laying down his fork, giving Leela his full attention. There's something she's not telling, he thought, as he asked her again, "What happened?"

"I never knew." Her clipped response was defensive. "Probably some family mess from way back before I married T.J. They had lots of problems . . . I think Hattie was the root of it. T.J. felt his mother kind of threw him away when Carey was born, and she never owned up to who Carey's daddy was. That kind of mess, you know?"

"Well, there's no reason for you to get all upset," Victor offered, feeling rather put off by her obvious discomfort. "Sounds like he's looking for a business proposition. You said he had a lot of cash?"

"He laid at least two thousand dollars on this table."

"Well, since he's family and all, we might want to consider letting him buy into a little piece of the lease." Victor saw the look of horror on Leela's face and quickly added, "Might be a whole lot easier than fighting him in court if he tries to press that letter from

T.J. as a valid will. The judge might rule that the lease you signed with me is not valid."

"Not valid? Why?" Leela did not like the sound of this.

"It could mean that you did not have the right to lease the land without Carey's agreement. A court action like that could tie up everything. Maybe for years. If that letter holds, he'd have equal share of Rioluces with you." Victor finished his ham and wiped his hands on his napkin. He tossed it onto the table. "And I don't think you want that. Might be a sight easier just to let him in."

"Never!" Leela snapped. The thought of Carey squeezing into her life, her future, was nauseating. "The letter's a fake! T.J. never would have written such things. Don't you dare sell him an interest in your lease! Promise me, Victor." She gripped the edge of the table and leaned forward. "Carey is a gambler, a hustler, a cheat. He's conned his way through life, using people like chips in his poker games to get whatever he wants. He'll do anything to turn a deal to his favor. Lie, forge, probably even steal. I want nothing to do with him. I won't have him involved in our affairs."

In a panic, Leela grabbed Victor's arm, forcing him to his feet. "You've got to promise me, Victor. You cannot bring Carey into our lives. You cannot encourage him in any way. You've got to make him stay away from here." Leela was so upset, she hardly felt Victor's hand on her arm as he attempted to loosen her grip.

"Leela! Calm down!" Victor tried to step back, but she refused to release him.

"Things could turn very ugly, Victor. If he tries to make an issue of the letter, let him. I'll be the one to take *him* to court. That will make Carey back down. There are warrants for his arrest in at least two counties; he can't afford to get tangled up with the law." She slumped against Victor and trembled. "Please, go find him. Tell him to stay away from me and my land. Please, Victor, do this for me."

"Where is he staying?" Victor gently brushed his hand over Leela's hair and held her close.

"I didn't ask," Leela replied. She ran her hands up to Victor's shoulders, reassured by their solid width. "But he's driving a big black Studebaker around town. It won't be hard to find him."

* * *

It hurt Carey to see how much she had aged. The deep furrows lining her cheeks spread down her chin, ran the length of her neck, and created folds of withered flesh at the base of her throat. Her dull brown eyes flickered shut for a moment; then she smiled and opened her arms to her son.

Carey Logan averted his stare and let Hattie pull him to her bosom. He could hardly embrace his mother. The sour stench of day-old whiskey clung to the tattered shawl thrown around her hulking shoulders.

"I knew you'd come home, son. Nobody coulda told me different." She squeezed Carey with a frail hug and stepped back to look him over. "Mighty fine, you look. Mighty fine."

She held on to his arm as she moved toward the cluttered sofa.

"Elvina done gone visit her sister in Corsicana, so things ain't so proper 'round here," she apologized as she cleared a space for him to sit beside her. Carey sank down next to his mother.

"Don't worry, Ma. I came to see you." Embarrassed, he glanced away as he saw the crystal shine of tears in Hattie's eyes. "Just got back yesterday. Took me a while to find where you were staying."

"Had to leave Waco. Wasn't so easy trying to make it alone." Hattie wiped her eyes with the hem of her apron.

Carey accepted his mother's subtle reprimand without comment and edged himself to the far end of the sofa to see her better. Bloated by alcohol, yet withered by age, she appeared at the same time oddly swollen and skinny.

"I'm better off living here," she tempered her remark. "Me and Elvina kinda help each other out. Things is a sight better than they was in Waco."

"Well, I'm back now, Ma. And things are gonna change."

Hattie's dim eyes raked her son. "You gonna stay in Mexia? For good?" As her lips parted, her crooked yellow teeth emerged. "You not leavin' me again?"

"That's right, Ma. I'm here to stay. And I didn't come back broke either. Here." He reached into his pocket and took out a fifty-dollar bill. "You take this and get whatever you need."

Hattie let him push the bill into her palm.

The minutes ticked by. They talked haltingly and uneasily about the past eight years, though Hattie skirted the details of T.J.'s death. Carey watched his mother's face become darkly troubled when the discussion turned to the discovery of oil on the farm.

"I went out to Rioluces and saw Leela yesterday," he told her. "Looks like T.J. didn't know what he was sitting on, did he, Ma?" They shared a little bit of strained laughter. Carey crossed his legs and smoothed a wrinkle in his dark navy suit. "There's a fortune in oil on that place." His voice was calm but intense.

"And," Hattie began, her tone low, conspiring, "you know we shoulda got a part of that land. Thank God Reverend Pearson took pity on me and told me where to write you. Now you can see for yourself what's going on. I been prayin' you got my letter. Leela's got no right to all that land, and she's been lyin' about T.J.'s will since the day he died."

"Don't worry, Ma." He gave her his boyish grin that always brought a smile to his mother's face. "Let me handle Leela."

Hattie's taut jowls relaxed as she listened to her son.

"I'm working things out. Might be a little tricky, but we're not gonna be left out. Not on your life. With that much money at stake, on your son's land? My brother's farm? She'll never be able to keep it from T.J.'s kin. Just leave it all to me. Only wish I'da got here sooner," Carey half apologized. "But I was caught up in business, you know?" He sat up straighter and assumed an air of authority. "I've got plans to get our share of Rioluces. And you know what, Ma? I've got my sights set on Leela, too. I think it's time for me to marry, settle down."

Hattie stared at her son in abject horror. "You don't mean that!" She scooted to the edge of the cushion. "You can't get involved with that woman!"

"Don't be so prudish, Ma. She's good-looking. About to be the richest woman in the county. Sitting out there all alone on that big farm. So what if she was T.J.'s wife? I understand her better than he ever did. I know her kind." He grinned, almost sheepishly, and looked down at his shoes. "She needs a man to take care of her. Who better than me?"

"Guess you ain't been back long enough to hear what's going on." There was a tremor in Hattie's voice. For the first time she thanked God for Victor Beaufort. "She's all tied up with that colored oilman what done brought in the wells. From what I hear, they carrying on out there something awful." She reached over and clutched Carey's wrist. "Stay away from her, son. She ain't nothing but trouble. Just set your mind to getting us a piece of that land."

Carey waved one hand back and forth at his mother, dismissing her concern. "You think I'm going to let some greasy wildcatter scare me off? I read about Beaufort in the newspaper . . . already had some problems at the site, I understand. White folks don't have any use for him, and the colored can't do a thing to help him now. Well, his problems are about to get a whole lot worse. When I finish with him, he'll wish he'd never come to Mexia." Carey stood up and tugged his hat over one eye, adjusted his tie and flashed his charming smile at his mother. "Don't worry so much, Ma. You'll see, I'm gonna have Leela and the farm and all the oil that's on it. You can count the colored oilman out."

After Carey drove off, Hattie stood on the porch for nearly half an hour. Her legs throbbed with pain and her ankles began to swell, yet she could not make the effort to go back inside. Gulping air in short, shallow gasps, she struggled to still the nervous cramping that churned her stomach. She thought she'd be sick right there on the porch.

He's gotta know the truth, she told herself, dreading the aftermath of such a revelation. As much as she didn't want to stir things up, she couldn't let him go off courting his half-sister.

Oh, God. Hattie steadied herself against the splintered railing. How'd things get so twisted? All this mess coming back to haunt me, after so many years . . . and just when Carey seems to be acting like he oughta.

At least he had tried to be civil. More civil than Hattie ever remembered. It was the first time they had had a real talk together. No arguing. No accusations. Maybe Carey had finally grown up.

Hattie shuddered and remembered Josephine's revelation. Effie Alexander was investigating, and the MK&T railroad had records.

What could they do to her? Bring charges at this late date? Almost thirty years after she cashed that bond? Hattie's mouth felt as dry as parched corn.

With painful, jerky steps she left the porch and walked through the tiny house, going straight to the kitchen, where she opened the cupboard door. The whiskey she attempted to pour into her glass splashed across the table and down the front of her dress, but she managed to get the glass to her lips.

As the fiery liquid dribbled down her chin, she wiped her face and mumbled, "I'm not saying a word 'less I have to, 'cause it will all probably come to nothing. Carey just better set his mind on gettin' that land and leave that woman alone."

Carey tapped his foot as music from the honky-tonk joint blared into the early evening, wove itself into the din of motorcars, street vendors, barking dogs and lumbering drays, nearly overshadowing the clamor of people drifting through Belknap Street.

An exotic-looking girl in a tight red dress stood arguing with a man outside the smoky club. A few feet away, sprawled in the gutter, a drunk lay trembling and shaking with jake foot, nearly paralyzed by his consumption of denatured alcohol. Excited pedestrians stepped over the palsied man, rushing along, going about their business on the teeming, lawless avenue.

Gunfire erupted two doors down. A bleeding man stumbled from Jimmy's Dice Parlor, turned to curse his assailant, then staggered into an alley. The cluster of ladies congregated outside their "dance hall" paid little attention to the injured man as they preened and postured on the corner, trying to snag a few customers for the evening.

Carey Logan took a long drag on his cigarette and continued to survey the activity from his upstairs window. He was killing time, waiting for Victor Beaufort to show up. Mildred had told him the oilman officed and lived in a suite of rooms across the street, but usually left before dawn and returned long after midnight. It didn't matter to Carey how long he had to wait; he had nothing else to do except keep his vigil. Besides, the sights on Belknap Street were very entertaining.

Belknap Street—Little Juarez—the most dangerous area of town. A variety of tough-looking, fast-talking men and women ruled the muddy thoroughfare with their swaggering presence. Oil field workers, bootleggers, prostitutes and sharpies, all with too much cash in their pockets, treated every evening like Saturday night.

The sheriff and his deputies casually dismissed the senseless killings and blatant robberies as inevitable consequences of the boom and turned away from their duties, throwing up their hands in resignation, no longer even patrolling the area.

Riotous laughter shrilled up from the cafe below, and Carey heard someone shout that another gusher had just blown in on a five-acre plot leased for five dollars. The celebrating would go on all night.

The noisy cafe did not bother Carey. In fact, he thrived on the pulsing energy that crackled in the wide open pub. The people who frequented Mildred's Cafe were people like him: charged up, excited about being in Mexia and more determined than ever to snag their share of the boom.

But tonight, all Carey wanted was thirty minutes alone with Victor Beaufort. That's all he'd need to bring him to his knees, Carey determined, lighting another cigarette, and Victor wouldn't even know he'd been leveled.

By three-fifteen, Carey had a cramp in his neck and his shoulders throbbed. He had dozed off sitting in the window. He woke with a start at the sound of a motorcar and looked down. Victor Beaufort had just come home.

Tall, brown-skinned, hair parted on the side, probably wearing a fringed suede jacket. That's the way Mildred had described him. And there he was, parking his big Model T in front of the building.

Carey waited until he saw lights appear in the second-floor windows. Then he emptied his valise of all its cash, stuffed the money into a heavy paper envelope and wedged it under his shirt. After checking his appearance in the cracked Cheval mirror, Carey went downstairs and crossed the street.

Chapter Twenty-Six

With an angry flip of his wrist, Victor turned the pages over, placed them flat on his desk and stared at the blank white sheets before him. He could no longer stand to look at the words on the damnable contract. He had read it over so many times, he had memorized the stranglehold conditions threatening to strip him of his valuable lease.

He lowered his head between his sweaty palms and squeezed his eyes shut.

How will I ever explain this to Leela? he worried, feeling the strain of the long evening begin to seep into his bones. He had talked to every possible source for cash in Mexia. No one was willing to advance him the ten thousand he needed to get Starr off his back. It was a conspiracy, he decided, a shutout by all the majors who secretly wanted Starr to triumph so other, more profitable deals could be cut. There were so many leases to be had for a dollar, who needed entanglement with him and his bitter dispute with Starr?

Victor stood and walked to the window. Looking down into the street, still alive with raucous commotion, he felt his anger ebb into an aching sensation of hopelessness. He gripped the windowsill to steady himself, frightened at this weakening, this slipping away of his confidence.

If he could not save his lease, he'd leave Texas and return to Oklahoma, Victor vowed. He could never face Leela. What would he say? That his miscalculation and naive trust made him easy prey for a man like Thornton Welch? If Starr took over Rioluces, he would not stay in Texas a ruined man.

He thought of his brothers, Cap and Frank, who after months of solid support and backbreaking labor, would each lose their ten percent stake in the lease. Even Pully and his brothers, who had been promised a moderate cut, would be left with nothing to show for their work, cheated out of their dreams, as he surely would be.

Only Leela will continue to benefit, Victor realized. Nothing could stop her royalties from pouring in. He knew she had more than enough cash to pay off Thornton Welch, but he'd rather lose it all than go begging to her.

Victor watched a cluster of drunken, loud-talking men toss dice in the middle of the block. They carelessly threw down handfuls of crumpled bills with no thoughts of tomorrow.

Victor recognized the same small gathering of men who met nightly at the end of the block. They carried on, running through the streets, all hours of the night, not a worry, not a care, he observed. Pockets full of dollar bills to be wagered or used on drink and women. They thought the oil had brought them happiness. Victor choked back the awful pain that washed over him. Maybe they were the lucky ones; they had no plans for the future, so they could not be hurt as he had been.

A soft tap on the door roused Victor from his thoughts. He pulled out his pocket watch to check the hour. Three-thirty. He took a deep breath, went to his desk and swept his contract under a pile of papers, then cracked the door just enough to see a well-dressed man standing in the shadowy hallway.

"Yes?" he asked cautiously. He had never seen this man before.

"I'm looking for Victor Beaufort," Carey said in his most proper, dignified tone.

"And your business?" Victor was leery of this late-hour visitor who knew his name and appeared too smooth.

"I understand the Beaufort Drilling Company is in need of an investor."

Victor opened the door a little wider and stepped back.

"Your name?"

"Carey Logan. Perhaps your fiancée, Mrs. Wilder, has spoken to you about me." Carey walked boldly into the room, passed Victor and positioned himself with his back to the window. "I would like about thirty minutes of your time, Mr. Beaufort. I have a proposition I think you'll be interested in hearing."

It took Victor less than twenty minutes to make his decision. As he drew a clean sheet of paper from the center drawer of his desk, he wondered why Leela had been so upset about Carey Logan's return. He seemed like a very impressive young man to Victor. And after all, he did have a letter that could be pressed in court. Why bother with all that? Victor knew just how to settle this affair.

"Mr. Logan," Victor started, "there is one rather complicated condition to accepting your money." He pulled the Starr Oil contract from beneath the pile of papers. "The current contract with Starr prohibits me from selling off any more than five percent of the lease to anyone other than Starr." He cleared his throat and watched Carey closely. "Rather prohibitive, of course, but this condition will lapse after Number 3 is brought in."

"Five percent's not a whole lot," Carey said, loving his chance to pressure Victor. "My cash should buy a better percent than that. Maybe I ought to take my investment elsewhere. Might be a better return."

Victor reached over as if to caution Carey.

"No need to do that. It would just delay everything. We can work around it, Mr. Logan. Hold on, now. We can work this out together." Victor hesitated, then plunged forward. "However, I will need your assurance that our agreement remain confidential until Rioluces Number 3 is producing. No one can know of your investment, especially not Mrs. Wilder."

Carey nodded in agreement.

"After that," Victor went on, "Starr has no say in what I do with my lease." He did not add that by then he would have proven to Leela that he could make good on his promise and bring in his wells as he'd predicted.

"What's your offer, Mr. Beaufort? What can my ten thousand buy me tonight?" Carey was getting tired of Victor's rules and conditions. He wanted to get on with the paperwork.

"Your ten-thousand-dollar investment will give you five percent of my lease on Rioluces right now and twenty-five percent of Number 3, which ought to blow in any day. Also, your ten thousand will be treated as a loan, to be paid back at ten percent interest as soon as Number 3 is producing."

"Any restrictions on my share?"

"None. It'll be yours to do with as you please."

"And twenty-five percent of your take on Number 3? As long as it's producing? No time limitation?"

"That's right, Mr. Logan. And believe me, we're just scratching the surface of this field. The potential is enormous." Victor hoped his anxiety over this agreement did not show in his face. He'd have to square this deal with Leela eventually, but right now he had to save his lease. If it meant doing business with Carey Logan, so be it.

"Well, Mr. Beaufort. I think you've got a deal. Can you draw up the papers right now?"

"Well, I can draft them, but in the morning I'd have to get the typist at the bank to type the contract up proper, in the right form, you know?"

"Don't bother with a typist, Beaufort. Either we cut the paperwork right here and now, or there won't be a deal with me." Carey set his finely turned mouth into a grim line and waited.

Victor nodded and pulled out his fountain pen.

As dawn broke over Mexia, the sky changed very little, remaining dark and overcast, filled with the dismal black vapor that poured from the earth. Back in his room, Carey held his document closer to the smoky oil lamp and read it again. He studied the way Victor Beaufort crossed his T's with a flourish and ended each sentence with a bold dash.

The small percentage of the lease did not bother Carey. He had all he needed: a handwritten contract executed by Victor Beaufort and legal ownership of a part of his oil lease on Rioluces. Carey was on his way to having everything he wanted . . . Leela, the cash and the farm.

Carefully, Carey folded the contract and slipped it into the secret compartment of his big valise, then opened his armoire and took out a gray pinstripe suit with matching vest.

He would get to the claims office later, he decided, after he had settled everything with Leela. He could afford to move slowly, let Victor Beaufort get on with his work. He had a well to bring to completion before the really big payoff rolled in.

Carey poured cold water into his washbasin and absently began to create lather in his shaving mug. A ride out to the farm was in order, he decided. He ought to go look over his newest investment.

The line at the county lease office wound twice around the block. Victor had arrived at nine, and by noon he was still standing outside. The crush of hopefuls with leases to file pushed and jostled one another, knowing that filing their papers as quickly as possible might be the only guarantee they would be paid.

With so much activity going on around the clock, leases changed hands with the throw of the dice or the fold of a poker hand. A combination of faulty mathematics and just plain ignorance caused dangerous, volatile situations; payoffs were made to leaseholders on a first-come, first-served basis, and it was not unusual to come up empty-handed as a result of an oversold lease.

Victor examined the handwritten document again and nodded to himself, glad he had insisted Carey wait at his office until two copies of the contract had been executed and signed. By filing his copy at the claims office, he was making the deal public record, though taking a chance: for the news could get to Leela before he got to her to explain.

But there was no way to get around it. If he did not register the contract, the deal was null and void. The last thing he wanted was a lawsuit from Carey on top of everything else.

Victor felt a ripple of satisfaction as he recalled the look on Thornton Welch's face when he had put the ten thousand on his desk this morning. Absolute shock. The man had believed Rioluces was his.

A smile lit Victor's face. It's over, he thought, and the lease was still in his control. As long as Carey Logan kept his word and said nothing to Leela, no harm would come. She might be a little upset when he finally told her, but she'd come around, even be thankful, when Number 3 blew in at thousands of barrels a day.

When it did, he mused, Leela would laugh at herself for being such a pessimist. She'd see he was right to bring Logan in on the deal to keep Rioluces in the family.

"Hold on, Kenny! I don't think we're going to make it!" Leela yelled above the growling roar of her brand-new roadster. With the top down and the wind whistling so loudly, she doubted Kenny could hear a word she said. The enormous thunder of wheels grinding over gravel filled the air.

In a protective gesture she reached over and braced one arm across her son's chest. "Close your eyes and put your head down! We're going off the road!"

From the corner of her eye she saw Kenny duck his head into his lap. She yanked the steering wheel to the left, trying to veer the big car around a log blocking her path. The low-slung roadster bounced into the air and landed with a thud on the side of the road in a soft grassy bank.

Leela held on, guiding the car as best she could. She pushed down on the brake pedal, but nothing happened.

The car continued on, gaining momentum, the shiny red machine plunging forward at a frightful speed. It did not stop until they crashed head-on into the base of an old bent willow.

"Oh, dear!" Leela screamed. "This is awful! Kenny! Kenny!" She reached over and shook him by the shoulder. "Look at me! Are you hurt?"

Kenny lifted his head, looked through the cracked windshield at the steam rising from the hood and admonished his mother in a stern grown-up voice.

"You should have waited for Victor, Ma. He told you not to try it alone."

Leela rose up from her seat and peered over the top of the hood. The entire front end was smashed. She looked over at Kenny. The two locked eyes, then broke out in laughter.

"I can't believe I did this," Leela said, gasping to catch her breath. "And don't you say another word, young man," she challenged Kenny. "It was an unavoidable accident. Could have happened to anyone trying this ridiculous road for the first time." She pulled off her white straw hat and tossed it onto the backseat. "Thank God . . . we're not hurt," she started, pushing against the door. It creaked and groaned, then finally popped open. Leela slipped from behind the wheel to go inspect the damage.

Her new Lenox roadster was crumpled and folded like discarded newspaper. A headlamp dangled from its socket, the bumper lay twisted on the ground.

Kenny stopped laughing long enough to join her at the front of the car.

"Victor's gonna be mad, Ma. He told you it was gonna be hard to control the motorcar. Now look at it. It's all ruined." The disappointment in his voice touched Leela. She put her arms around him and murmured in consolation, "No one's hurt. That's all that matters. And don't you worry about the car . . . or Victor. He just picked the car out. I bought it. And it looks like I'll just have to buy another one."

Rubbing Kenny's back she went on. "That's the good part, son. We have enough money to buy another one."

"But I liked this one. The red one."

"Then that's what I'll get. As soon as Victor can take me to Houston."

Leela reached back into the car to retrieve her hat, tied it firmly on her head, then turned to face the road.

"Guess we'll have to walk back home. I'll get Pully to take you to school." Badly shaken but not hurt, Leela stepped carefully out of the muddy grass and waited for Kenny to catch up.

"Get your books, Kenny. You'll still have to do your lessons."

"Oh, Ma," Kenny groaned. "Can't I just skip it today?"

"Stop complaining," Leela said, "the spring term's just about over. You'll be finished with your lessons soon enough."

"You should have let Pully take me in the wagon," Kenny said as they made their way up the road. "As usual, Ma."

"I thought I'd get in a little practice. I've had the car for two weeks now. What good were all Victor's driving lessons if I was never going to drive?" Leela replied, annoyed with herself for bungling her first attempt, but not in the least bit worried about the car.

As they walked back toward the house, Leela thought about her words, slightly surprised at how nonchalantly she considered buying another car. She could hardly believe her own changed attitude about things that at one time were as out of reach as the moon. Having more money than she could possibly spend did take the edge off the uncertainty of the future.

Now Leela loved her shopping sprees to Waco, Dallas, Fort Worth, even Groesbeck and looked forward to remodeling the farmhouse from cellar to rooftop. A telephone line had been strung last week, and tomorrow the instrument itself would be installed. A telephone! She could use it to call anyplace in the country.

It was frighteningly delicious to be able to spend hundreds and hundreds of dollars with no thought of running out. Once Rioluces Number 2 blew in, Leela's weekly royalties totaled nearly three thousand dollars. Her Lenox roadster had scarcely made a dent in her funds.

The sound of an approaching car brought Kenny and Leela to a halt. When Leela turned to look back, she didn't like what she saw. Carey Logan's black Studebaker was bearing down on her.

"See you've had a little accident," he called from his open window as he slowed alongside them. "Get in. I'll give you a lift to the house."

The ride back to the farm was made in awkward silence, with Leela holding her breath when Carey introduced himself to Kenny. Luckily, the boy was pleased to see his uncle again and very impressed with his shiny black car. Carey was brash and expansive, bragging about his travels and, against Leela's protests, he pressed a half-dollar into Kenny's hand.

By the time Leela got her son settled into Pully's wagon, Carey had already promised to come around on Saturday to take his nephew fishing. What could she do? Refuse him and make an ugly scene? Kenny was so taken with his new uncle, he would never listen to a thing she might say.

If only Carey did not resemble T.J. so much, Leela thought as she watched Kenny's animated face as he told his uncle about his favorite fishing hole.

Pully slapped the reins and started off toward town. Kenny turned around in the wagon three times to wave good-bye. Not to his mother but to Carey, for Leela could see her son's adoring looks directed past her to his fascinating new relative.

"Why are you here?" Leela asked Carey as soon as Kenny and Pully disappeared out of sight. She turned to go back into the house, not inviting Carey in. "What do you want?" Her tone was filled with exasperation and disbelief that he'd shown up again so soon after their row.

"Why, I'm surprised at you, Leela. You act as if I don't belong here. After all, the boy's my nephew and . . . ," he hesitated, then moved his eyes from Leela's face, across her chest, stopping at her trim waist. "We've always been friendly. Haven't we?" He arrogantly mounted the steps and followed her into the parlor. "Seems natural to me that I'd come around to see my kin. With T.J. gone, the boy needs companionship. I just thought . . ."

"You thought wrong, Carey," Leela interrupted, making her way to the far side of the room. "We're doing fine. And let's get something straight. Right now. You and I are not friendly. Not in the way you're trying to make out. I'm happily engaged to Victor Beaufort, and I don't want you coming around, trying to complicate my life. Don't try to dredge up a youthful mistake and make it anything other than what it was. A mistake."

Carey walked toward Leela. She backed away until her skirt brushed the edge of the hearth. The Rochester clock startled her as it rang out in chimes, nine o'clock.

"How can you call what we did a mistake?" Carey ran his tongue over his lips and moved closer. The hypnotic ring of his smooth voice chilled her. "Don't you remember, Leela? How beautiful it was with us? How much you wanted to be in my arms? How sweet my lips tasted on yours? That could never have been a mistake. Our timing was not good, I admit. But now . . . T.J.'s gone. There's no reason to worry. We can start over, get to know each other again." He reached up to touch her hair.

Leela stiffened. She could not bring herself to slap his hand away, nor could she stop the trembling in her legs.

"And you might as well forget about Beaufort. He'll never bring you any real happiness. All show—a front man, that's all he is. There's no man on this earth for you but me."

Leela edged to the left, trying to get around Carey. He blocked her path and put a hand on her waist. She could feel his unyielding grip through her dress. She tried to pull away. He slid his hand behind her, spreading his fingers to caress the small of her back.

"Don't you ever wonder just how it might have been?" he whispered into her ear.

Leela froze in his arms. "No," she answered, feeling more afraid than angry. "I never thought about you at all."

"That's hard to believe," Carey murmured, leaning closer. The scent of hair oil and cologne rose up.

Leela shied back, his breath on her neck, memories of that sultry afternoon eight years ago sweeping over her in agonizing clarity. Her flesh still tingled with a life of its own in the same, exact spots he had touched her before.

"Let me go!" She tried to pull away, but he held her fast.

"I didn't come back to fight you," Carey continued in an even, seductive tone. He paid little attention to her struggle. "You know, you really belong to me. Always have. We're alike, you and I. We go after what we want. And don't tell me that I'm lying," he said, crushing the fabric of her dress in his fist. "I'm back now. Things have changed. There's no reason at all why we can't just pick up where we left off, and settle in together to run this farm like we were meant to."

"You're crazy." Leela hissed the words at him and broke away. Carey grabbed her arm and pulled her to his chest. He forced his lips over hers and kissed her with the fiery depth of a man with no limit to his passion. His tongue parted her lips and filled her mouth with an urgency that nearly caused Leela to faint. He sucked at her, drained her, swept her resistance away.

Despite her struggle he moved his hands up and down her back, across her shoulders, over her breasts. He gripped the tangle of her hair within his fists, painfully pulling her head back with both hands, trapping her against the mantel. He pinned her cruelly beneath his tall, lanky frame. When Leela felt the weight of his body over hers, his stiff erection probing her thigh, she quickly dug her fingernails into the side of his neck and pulled down with all her strength.

"Damn you!" he cursed, grabbing his neck.

Leela managed to slip beneath his arm, tearing a sleeve from her dress as she fell onto the sofa.

"Get out!" she screamed, clutching the torn fabric. "You get off this farm and never come back."

Carey stood above her, laughing. "You're mine, Leela Wilder. Only mine. You can tell yourself you're in love with Beaufort if you want to, but I felt you kissing me back." He took out a handkerchief and wiped his neck. Tiny drops of blood stained the white cotton square. "It felt good, didn't it? My lips over yours. The passion's still there, whether you want to admit it or not. Nothing's changed about you." Carey put his handkerchief into his pocket and sauntered to the door. Before leaving, he looked back at Leela. "It's only a matter of time, sweetheart. When your oilman lover finally betrays you, where will you be? Set adrift out here on this godforsaken farm, that's where. Think about that kiss, Leela. You'll see. One day, maybe sooner than you think, you'll be glad to have me to turn to."

Chapter Twenty-Seven

Parker slammed a stack of newspapers on his mother's kitchen table and stood frowning, shaking his head in disbelief.

"What's wrong, Parker?" Effie asked, taking a handful of straight pins from her sewing basket and placing them on the floor where she sat. Leela turned to face Parker as her aunt began folding up the hem of her suit, fastening the delicate fabric with an expert tuck.

"I paid two boys a dollar apiece to carry these papers along Denton and Thomas." Disgust seeped out with each word. "And what did they do? Nothing! I found these bundles left by the side of the road, covered with mud. Ruined!"

"Not surprised," Effie commented, "everybody's running a scam these days. Can't trust anybody anymore."

Parker took off his jacket and loosened his tie. "Where's Margaret?"

"She's resting," Effie said. "I convinced her to lie down for a while."

Parker nodded, then slammed his fist on the stack of papers. "It's a damn shame, what's going on. I thought I was helping those boys out—they came to me and asked for work. Said they needed the money to eat. So I foolishly paid them in advance." He poured himself a glass of water as he circled the table. "Last time I'll get duped like that."

"Forget it, Parker," Leela advised. "It's just another example of the kind of people crowding this town."

Parker leaned against the stove as he finished his drink, then abruptly stated, "I guess I'll have to go back to the *Banner* and get more papers, then distribute them myself." He grimaced and pensively bit his lower lip. "Then I've got to get over to Josephine's. I don't know if it helps, but I still keep checking on her." He set the empty glass in the sink.

"How is she getting along?" Leela prompted, knowing how much Effie hoped her son's concern might turn her daughter around.

"Sometimes I think I'm wasting my time." His bitter reply surprised Leela. "I hate to say this but Josephine does not want to be helped. She's happier than you know, Leela. She has convinced herself that her bootleg joint is a successful business venture. The sheriff hasn't done a thing to shut her down. From what I hear, he's a big supporter. Hard to understand. I'm just worried she's going to get hurt one day, dealing with all that trash."

Effie looked up, soft blue silk still clasped between two fingers. "I know, son, and I wish I could say you're wrong. But as much as you've tried to help her out, seems like nothing ever changes." Effie stopped her pinning and spoke to Leela. "Parker offered to let Josephine work at the *Banner*. She's pretty good with figures and she could help him with the accounts. But she refused. Prefers to keep things just as they are."

Leela looked down and her eyes met Effie's. Painful memories of Josephine's youthful jealousy and continued estrangement passed unspoken between the two women.

"It's probably a good thing Penny's here with you," Leela began. "The child doesn't need to watch her mother deteriorate before her eyes."

Effie got up and sat at the table. "It's hard . . . real hard for me to see my girl like that." She wiped her eyes and sighed.

"What's this about a lawsuit?" Leela asked, stepping down from the footstool, smoothing out her skirt. "Victor told me he saw her filing papers in the courthouse against Johnny Ray. Is that true?"

"It's true, all right," Parker replied, crossing the room to sit in his father's old armchair. "You know Mister Harry died last year. That half-acre now belongs to Johnny Ray and he's leased drilling rights to Starr Oil. Predictions are good that a gusher will be coming in real soon. They're drilling around the clock out there. Josephine's filed suit to get her share. Johnny Ray's hopping mad about the whole affair and is telling everybody she doesn't have a chance of getting her hands on his oil."

"Well," Leela said, with a snip in her voice, "he never did marry her. She should have known no good would come from that relationship. Trying to act like they were husband and wife. That was a stupid thing to do."

"Maybe," Effie said cautiously, "but the children are his . . . they've got some rights. You know? Even though Johnny Ray never married Josephine, those are still his blood kids. When the well comes in, Oliver and Penny ought to get something."

"Don't count on it, Aunt Effie," Leela cautioned. "He's let you clothe and feed his kids all these years. Why should he change now?"

"Well," Parker cut in, "I advised Josephine to file a civil suit in the court, force Johnny Ray to acknowledge his children. Once the judge rules, it's out of his hands. The court will see after the rights of the children. There's a lawyer in Dallas I know who can help her. He's won a lot of cases like hers."

Walking to the mirror over the sofa, Leela appraised her new suit as she spoke. "Well, with all these oil wells coming in every day, I'd wager a whole lot of strangers are showing up from nowhere, claiming to be blood relatives as soon as the issue of money comes up."

Parker nodded. "I write about it all the time."

Effie stood and stretched. "Step back up on the stool, Leela. That hem seems a little uneven."

"That's a real fine suit, Leela. Some special occasion?" Parker absently picked up a copy of the *Banner* and opened it.

"I've got to meet Victor in Dallas," she muttered vaguely.

"Got to?" Parker lowered the paper and peered over it at his cousin. "You don't sound like you much want to go."

"Oh, I do," Leela said, standing still as Effie fussed with the hem. "It's just that there is so much going on at the farm. I don't think it's a good time to be away."

"You need to get out of Mexia if you ask me. It will be good for you and Victor."

"I guess so," Leela admitted. "It's just that . . ."

"What?" Parker asked, watching Leela carefully. "What's going on, Leela? You're upset. I can tell."

"It's just that there have been so many delays on the drilling, and this well must come in before Sunday. A lot is riding on it, Parker. More than you can imagine."

"Is Victor worried?"

The remark stung Leela for some reason and she shot her cousin a puzzled glance. "Of course he's worried."

"Well, why'd he go off to Dallas and leave you here to fret over his affairs?"

"That's not fair, Parker. Victor has business in Dallas. Money to raise."

"Money? He's got money problems?"

"That explosion last month destroyed a lot of equipment. Took a lot of cash to replace it. Then, there's the payroll for the crew. You know? Victor's got a lot to take care of . . ." Her words trailed off as she thought to herself: and then there's the matter of Carey Logan's return. A lump quickly rose at the back of her throat.

"Well," Parker began, settling back in his chair, "those are ordinary expenses for a wildcatter to incur. What's the big deal? It happens every day. Your farm has great potential, Leela. Quit doing Victor's worrying for him."

Inwardly, Leela stiffened at these words, insulted by her cousin's inference that Victor had dumped his troubles on her.

"Parker's right," Effie agreed, running an expert eye over the slim skirt. "Leave the worrying to Victor. He knows what he's doing. You just go on up to Dallas and have a grand time."

* * *

Victor met Leela at Central Track, the area in Deep Ellum where all the trains rolled in. He rushed to embrace her, kissed her hungrily and held her firmly by the arm, until they reached the front porch of Rosa Jones's home. He had rented two rooms from the lovely woman who routinely opened her house to Negro travelers who could not get a room in a downtown hotel.

As Leela unpacked her suits, dresses, shoes and hats, she recalled Parker's words of advice. He has no right to think Victor doesn't care, she told herself in her lover's defense. Yet *she* had been the one to put the crew off until Monday, assuring them they'd be paid just as soon as Victor returned. Though tempted to pay them herself, she hadn't, knowing how enraged Victor would have been. The disappointment on their faces had nagged at her all the way from Mexia to Dallas.

Sinking to the fluffy comforter on the high, four-poster bed, Leela sighed. She should be ecstatic about the party tonight. This trip was like some fairy tale. She shook out her pink organdy ball gown with bands of sequins across the shoulders which Effie had so lovingly sewn. Tonight she would put all thoughts of Rioluces out of her mind and be the carefree princess at the ball.

Taking her hairbrush from her traveling case, she began absently stroking her hair. She trusted Victor's judgment and would not give him reason to suspect her unease. Yet the face staring back at Leela in the mirror was strained and taut with anxiety. This would not do, she admonished herself, burying her trepidation under a brilliant smile as she fluffed out her hair and began to dress.

The ballroom at the Pythian Temple was the center of social events for the blacks of Dallas. Designed by the son-in-law of Booker T. Washington, it was the hub of black society in 1921, the gathering place for the new black professionals who returned to Dallas with their hard-won degrees from institutions like Fisk, Prairie View, Atlanta University and Howard.

When Leela stepped off the elevator onto the fourth floor, she was shocked by the grandeur of the ballroom. Gleaming mahogany floors, polished for dancing, reflected images of the magnificent velvet-draped windows dominating the room. Two stories high, arched at the top, the elegant portals lined each wall, creating a magical world. Darkly handsome men in stiff black tuxedos and sparkling ladies gowned in the very latest fashions, sat at small round tables along the dance floor. Pale pink roses and streams of satin ribbon were lavishly intertwined across the front of the stage. And the incandescent light from a huge sequined ball sent glittering patterns out over the crowd.

The sweet smell of perfumes, pomades, colognes and scented candles filled the air and made Leela slightly light-headed. As the orchestra struck up and the dancing began, she leaned more firmly against Victor's arm, clutching her handsome escort in excitement.

They danced for an hour without stopping; then Victor seated her at their table and crossed the room. As he stood talking to a heavily bearded gentleman, Leela sat and watched him, shamelessly observing her gallant fiancé, and let the wonderful sensation of loving him engulf her. In his cutaway jacket and satin bow tie, he looked so important and businesslike. Her heart swelled with pride and deep genuine love, and she chastised herself for ever doubting him.

He had taken his chances by putting everything into his company, calculating production, and signing up with Starr. And look at him now. The deal had turned out just fine. He had proven to everyone that he could hold his own against those who coveted his lease. And now, with Rioluces No. 3 on the verge of coming in, Victor had become so well-known throughout the state, he was sought after and listened to by the most important black businessmen in Texas.

Leela watched him approaching. There was no man in the room more confident, more assured of his future, or suited to build an empire from oil than her own handsome fiancé who now stood at her side.

The evening slipped past. Leela lost all sense of time and let her mind abandon the problems back home. She and Victor laughed and savored Ethel Waters's silky voice singing "They'll Be Some Changes Made," while discussing honeymoon plans to sail to Paris on a sleek ocean liner, enjoying the jazz artists making music across the Atlantic.

At two in the morning they entered Mrs. Jones's parlor and sat whispering in the dark like teenagers. Leela felt dizzy with happiness and chided herself for her unfounded worry. She had mentally recorded every detail of the evening, savoring this beginning of her new enchanted life.

"Come to my room," she whispered brazenly, guiding Victor silently toward the darkened staircase, thrilling to the feel of his lips on her cheek as he impatiently nuzzled her skin. With her arm around his waist, she led him into her suite.

Moonlight flooding through the windows gave a sleek silver polish to the ornately carved bed at the far end of the room. They sank down on the coverlet without speaking, and Leela threw her arms around Victor as he easily unfastened the silver buttons on her gown. The sequined dress fell to the floor with a gentle rustle. Leela tugged Victor's tuxedo from his shoulders.

Victor gazed down into her eyes for a moment, then slid his fingers into her hair and pulled her lips to his. A flush of desire surged through Leela, forcing a low, urgent moan from her lips.

"I've been waiting for this all evening," he said softly, hoping the feel of her in his arms again would dispel the guilt that plagued him. She'd never find out about the deal, he reassured himself, as he ran his hands over her smooth bronze shoulders.

As Victor eased her down onto the bed, Leela's fingers trailed lightly over his back, moving in ripples to the swell of his hips. "I've missed you something awful," she breathed, fighting the unwanted image of Frank Beaufort's angry face when he learned he would not be paid. "As soon as you left Mexia," she went on, "a part of me went with you."

Swiftly, Victor buried his face against her neck, inhaling her perfume as he thought: Oh, God, I've betrayed her and she must never know. I'd die if I lost Leela now.

Pulling up to see her, he murmured, "I never want to be parted from you again. Not even for a moment, not ever."

Leela reached up and brought his lips closer. "You're stuck with me," she whispered, trying to smile. "Nothing could force me from you." Yet when Victor's hand closed over her breast, she flinched, hating the sudden memory of Carey's hands on her.

"What's wrong?" Victor stopped and examined her face in the shadows. He could feel the tension in her body.

"Not a thing," Leela lied, pressing closer to him, hoping to banish her uneasiness. "Maybe I'm too anxious. A little eager, I suppose."

"Just relax," Victor urged, stroking her hair. "We have no reason to hurry. I'm not going to run away."

Leela softened in his arms and gently accepted him, struggling to maintain the magic of the evening.

As moonlight streamed through the window and bathed the troubled couple, Victor made love to Leela with tender restraint, his behavior thoughtful and soothing, but his lack of passion made Leela wonder if her own preoccupation had dampened the encounter.

When Victor Beaufort kissed Leela good-night and crept silently back to his room, he cursed himself under his breath for his deceitful agreement with Carey Logan. As he tugged the cold sheet over his shoulders, he vowed to clear the whole mess up and tell Leela the truth just as soon as they were back in Mexia.

CHAPTER TWENTY-EIGHT

Hattie took the three-page contract from Carey and squinted at the bold black letters, lips curling back as she mouthed the words, trying to read the handwritten document. A quiver of eagerness rippled through her at the sight of the strange new words. Many were complicated and difficult to understand, but the paper looked legal and important enough to convince her of its authenticity.

"How you manage to get fifty percent of that oil lease? Seems like a awful lot for that black oilman to be giving up. This is all legal, ain't it?"

"As legal as it needs to be for me to sell off a few percentage points myself," Carey replied, taking comfort in the letter from T.J. that he had safely filed away.

That was his trump card if this thing went bad. He could tie up the whole lease in court.

"That's where the money is right now, Ma," he went on, "in

selling off shares of my lease. It will take a little longer to see money from the oil, but Number 3 is due in any day. Then I get twenty-five percent. Just think how rich I'll be."

Hattie's silence prompted Carey to add, "How rich we both will be, Ma. 'Cause you know I'll be sharing whatever I get with you."

For the first time since his return, Carey saw a glint of interest in his mother's eyes, and the grin on her face was reassuring.

"Sounds good to me, son." She nodded as she spoke.

"Beaufort's so arrogant," Carey continued, "he doesn't even realize his time is running out. I just got it from a very good source that Starr Oil is planning to take over the whole field if Number 3 is not brought in by this Sunday. I'll bet Leela doesn't know it, either. And I've heard Victor Beaufort is not even in the city. What kind of businessman is that? Leaving everything in the hands of those ignorant roughneck brothers of his? He deserves to lose everything."

Carey tugged at his wide French cuffs and adjusted his pearl-studded cuff links. "I've got to hedge my bets, now . . . need a plan to keep me from being the loser. If Starr is really planning to move in on Rioluces, I've gotta use my lease to raise cash before Sunday evening passes. Ma, I can get a fortune for shares of my lease. I've already got some rich white men from East Texas standing in line to get their hands on my shares. New in town. Anxious to get in on the action. They've got connections with a Philadelphia company that's bankrolling them. All they want is an opportunity. And that's me, Ma. Me. The only in they've got right now. Think of it, Ma. These white fat cats coming to Carey Logan's door to make a deal."

Hattie handed the contract back to Carey.

"Guess you got it all figured out," she concluded, rubbing her hands together, locking and unlocking her thick fingers. Suddenly, she asked, "You talk to Leela about any of this?"

"She's got no say about what happens. She signed the lease with Beaufort. After that, it's fair game." Carey stopped talking and licked his lips, dropping his voice to a confidential whisper as he added, "But I have been out to see her. Twice. And you know what, Ma? Things are looking promising."

Hattie tensed at the serious sound of Carey's words. Agitated to the point of nearly blurting out a warning, Hattie rubbed her hands together more quickly.

"She's coming around to my way of thinking about me being the one she needs out there on the farm." He smiled so broadly, Hattie thought she could see all of his even white teeth back to the last molars. "Things couldn't be better, Ma. Everything's working out just as I planned."

Hattie slumped back on the sofa and narrowed her eyes at her son, fearing his desire for Leela had gone too far.

"What are you talking about?"

"I already told you my plans. I'm ready to get married. And Leela's the one I want."

"I told you to forget about that woman! You stay away from her!" Hattie looked warily at her son as he excitedly went on.

"Don't be so old-fashioned, Ma." Carey shrugged his shoulders, dismissing Hattie's warning, anxious to share his good news with his mother. "It doesn't matter to me that she was married to T.J." He leaned forward as if he had a secret to tell. "And if I weren't such a gentleman, I'd tell you a thing or two about her. I learned enough while I was staying out there to know Leela won't have a hard time getting used to me."

"It's got nothing to do with T.J.," Hattie shot back. "There's things about Leela you don't know."

"What things?" Carey quizzically tilted his head. "She's a good-looking woman, the kind I like to be around. That's all that matters to me."

"Don't move too fast, Carey. Just 'cause she's got a pretty face ain't no reason to get hitched up," Hattie threw out.

"Good enough reason for me," Carey snapped, starting to get riled by his mother's opposition. "A pretty wife, oil wells bringing in cash—sounds like the makings of a good life to me." He pulled back his shoulders and looked defiantly at his mother.

"There's things, I'm telling you, you don't know about that woman." Hattie refused to be quiet. Now was the time to tell Carey the truth, no matter how much it might hurt.

"What things?" he asked again, his face clouding over. He turned squarely toward his mother. "What could you possibly know about Leela? You never liked her. Never even talked to her if you could help it. And I know you did your best to stay clear of her all these years."

"That's true. I'da picked another type of wife for my son, if I'da had any say in it. But be that as it may, I just recently heard something about her that kinda shocked me . . ."—Hattie faltered—". . . something that got me to thinking."

"What?" Carey wanted to know. His boyish smile crumpled.

"Well, for one thing, she never went by her real name. All that time T.J. thought he'd married one woman and she was really somebody else."

"What are you talking about?" Carey wondered if the years of drinking corn liquor had taken their toll on his mother. Hattie squirmed and shifted around on the sofa, trying to push herself up from the torn soiled cushions.

"I don't care about her past, Ma. Don't start digging up old dirt to try to change my mind. I'm gonna have Leela as my wife. Soon. Just a little more time, you'll see. She'll be begging me to move out there with her. She needs a better man than Beaufort. Anyway, he's on the verge of ruin. Then what would she want with him?"

Hattie groaned as she struggled to get her bulky frame up off the deep sofa. Finally, she stood weaving back and forth, looking down at Carey, then shuffled painfully to the other side of the room, as if putting some distance between herself and her younger son would make it easier to tell him her story.

"There's some things you gotta know," Hattie started. "This ain't easy, son, but I guess it's time. You gotta be told."

The room fell silent. Hattie wheezed as she stood staring into space, stringing words together in her mind. How to say it? Where to begin? What damage was she about to inflict on her fragile relationship with Carey?

"Leela's real name wasn't Leela Alexander, like T.J. told me when he married her."

"So? What difference does that make, Ma? T.J.'s dead and I don't care what her real name was."

"You gonna have to listen to what I say, Carey. And you gotta promise this stays between me and you."

"What's wrong?" Carey watched his mother clasp both hands

firmly together, almost as if in prayer. He'd never seen such agony on her face.

"I been told that Leela's last name was Brannon. And she came to Mexia from Fort Worth."

"And?" Carey asked, sitting tensely on the sofa, waiting for Hattie to make her point.

"And I once knew her daddy. Ed Brannon was his name. A railroad man who passed through the county one night almost thirty years ago." A faraway look came over Hattie. She turned from Carey and looked out into the street. "I put him up one night when he was feeling kinda poorly. He left the next morning, snuck out before daybreak, and soon after, I heard he was dead." Hattie turned her face back on Carey and locked eyes with her son.

"What's the point, Ma? Who cares about Leela's daddy? You gonna tell me he was crazy or something? You know craziness don't always pass down. Sounds like that voodoo talk out of Louisiana. Heard enough of that while I was over there." He threw his hands down in a gesture of disgust.

"No. No. This ain't no made-up story. You gotta know 'bout Leela's daddy, 'cause Ed Brannon was your daddy, too." The words flew out in a rush, leaving Hattie staring numbly at her son. She let her face go slack and all life drain from her body as those long-repressed words hung in the air.

Carey stared at his mother, at first unable to put it all together. Stunned. Straining not to believe what his mother had just said.

"My daddy, too? What the devil does that mean? What kind of crazy talk is that?" He jumped up and crossed the room in two angry strides, stopping directly in front of Hattie. "You been dodging the truth about my father too long for you to all of a sudden come up with this. I don't believe you. How could you have kept this quiet all these years? You're lying to keep me from marrying T.J.'s widow. That's all there is to it. You're lying."

"I wish it wasn't true," Hattie whispered. "I wish I could tell you something different, but . . . it looks like what I heard about Leela being Ed Brannon's daughter is a fact. And I know he was your daddy. Ain't got no doubts 'bout that."

"Ha!" Carey roared. "No doubts, you say! When did all this become so clear? Huh? When did you finally start to remember who my daddy was?" He formed two tight balls with his fists and raised them in his mother's face.

Hattie shied back, turning away from her son. "I always knew," she whispered. "I never stopped thinking about Ed Brannon. He's the one man I never forgot."

Carey stood towering over his mother, fists clenched, breath coming in loud ragged gasps. Hattie felt the heat of his breath on her face and steeled herself for his angry assault.

"Go on, Ma. Tell me everything." Carey's voice grew angrier with each word. "There's more to this, isn't there? What is it? Huh, Ma? What's so dreadful that you had to keep it a secret all these years?" A frightened veil of anticipation descended over his face. "What is it?" he shouted, his rage engulfing Hattie. She covered her ears, eyes squeezed shut in shame.

Abruptly, Carey dropped his arms to his sides. He shook his head as he spoke. "Why did you brag all over the county that you didn't know who my father was? That you'd slept with so many railroad drifters you forgot which one might have been my daddy? I've spent every day of my life hating you for that. Trying to figure it out. What was so awful about this Ed Brannon that you never could even utter his name?"

"There was nothing awful about him." Hattie's eyes flew open as she slipped from beneath Carey's piercing gaze to grope her way to a straight-backed chair. Grabbing one arm, she lowered herself down. "It had nothing to do with him. Nothing. Ed was the kindest man I ever met, and his death really hurt me bad."

"Then why did you never speak of him? I begged you, Ma. I needed to know who my daddy was. What right did you have to lie like you did?"

"What right?" Hattie snorted in disgust. "The right to protect myself from jail. That's what! There was a legal matter about some railroad bonds, and once I got myself involved, I knew I could never mention Ed Brannon's name. I didn't want anybody ever connecting me with him."

"So you lied to me and kept your mouth shut?" He stared at her in disbelief. "Over some railroad bonds?"

"I forged his wife's name, took some money meant for Leela.

I'da been in deep trouble if anyone found out. But once it was done, I wasn't sorry. Not for a minute. If I hadn't done it we might have starved. Ed Brannon owed you something, too."

"So you thought you got what you were due?"

Hattie nodded, tears running down her wrinkled pale cheeks. "I thought so . . . but the pain it's caused me all these years ain't been worth it. I never wanted to hurt you, Carey. I guess I hoped you'd stop asking about your daddy."

"A man never stops wondering where he comes from, Ma. I hated growing up like a nobody. A real nobody. Even you said you didn't know where I came from. That's a painful notion for a child to sleep with every night, and the years passing by don't make it any better."

Carey smashed his fist against the wall. A flurry of stained wallpaper and rotting plaster scattered in clumps all over the rug.

"Thanks, Ma," he said at last, agony roughening his voice. He examined his bleeding knuckles, then wrapped them with his handkerchief. Not looking up, he repeated, "Thanks, Ma, for ruining my life once again." He raised wounded eyes to his mother. "Guess you finally set the record straight, huh?" He walked to the door and opened it. Turning, he looked back at Hattie. She saw perspiration dripping down the sides of his face, the front of his shirt stained with blood and tears.

"You know, it's too hot in here, Ma," he said strangely, yanking his dark red tie from around his throat. "I don't see how you can stand it."

Hattie had nothing to say.

Suddenly his misery slipped behind a mask of indifference. "I gotta go," he said. "I've got some important business to take care of, and it's gotta be done tonight."

The gas lamp in front of the cafe drew him toward it, guiding him like a beacon. Carey had no sense of direction, no sense of even walking, his mind was whirling crazily.

Leela. His half-sister! He'd undressed her as he had undressed women from Texas to Louisiana and back again. And she had loved every minute of it. Loved it! He had run his hands all over her body, kissed her so deeply and hungrily she had nearly lost herself to him. Why, he had even suckled her sweet breasts, feeling her thrill to his touch as much as he had to hers.

My sister! How in God's name did Ma let this happen? I'll never forgive her for this. Never. And I'll make sure Leela knows about it, too. Why should she be happy with her oil wells and riches, when I'm left, once again, with nothing?

Carey ran a finger over the scar on his neck where her fingernails had cut into his skin. It was still raw and painful, but it seemed it had happened a lifetime ago.

Raging inwardly, Carey strode up to the cafe, his blood boiling with disappointment and bitterness. As he pushed against the swinging doors, he buried his hostility and raised his chin, surveying the room with an impatient eye.

The four men sitting at the small square table in the center of the cafe set down their glasses when Carey walked in. They watched him expectantly and did not protest when he pulled up a chair.

Under different circumstances they would never have let this colored man come through the door, let alone sit at their table. But each one of them knew Carey was different: he had a valuable lease for sale, on that land west of town that Starr Oil was threatening to grab.

The well-dressed strangers were gamblers, not in the traditional sense, but they were willing to wager thousands of dollars that Rioluces No. 3 would come in before Sunday. If it did, they'd be rich. If it didn't they'd be broke, but a fifty-fifty chance seemed pretty good odds.

Carey buttoned his jacket over the bloodstains on his shirt, pushed back his hat and tilted his chair up on two legs. He looked at each man slowly, as if making sure he would remember their faces.

"Y'all gentlemen ready to do a little business?" he asked as he took out his faithful Falcon pen.

CHAPTER TWENTY-NINE

Sunday morning at eight o'clock, Victor drove Leela to the train station in Dallas. The ride through Deep Ellum was gloomy and silent, and Victor made no attempt to ease the strain.

What's wrong with him? Leela asked herself, as he rushed to stow her bags on the train. He actually seemed anxious for her to be leaving, though she knew he had no appointments that day.

When the train whistle blasted and the engine started up, he kissed her absently, then held her at arm's length. "I'm sorry I had to cut your visit short, Leela." He placed one hand on her shoulder. "But I've got a slew of people I need to meet with. It's better that you go on back today."

"I understand." Leela breathed the words, not at all sure she liked Victor's demeanor. He seemed preoccupied, unable to focus on her, and she was just as happy to be going home. With Rioluces No. 3 on the verge of coming in and Thornton Welch waiting in the wings, hoping to snatch Victor's lease, one of them needed to be on the property.

Victor had given her precise instructions: as soon as there was any show of oil, Leela was to wire him in Dallas, then contact Starr Oil.

Victor needed her help. He was a very busy man. And as Leela reluctantly kissed him good-bye and settled in for the train ride home, she was secretly frightened that her own behavior may have been the reason he wanted her gone.

As much as she understood Victor's need to raise money, she did not appreciate his sending her back to face the crew—or Starr Oil, for that matter.

Exhausted from the hectic round of social gatherings and a whirlwind shopping spree, Leela nodded off in her seat and drifted away from her troubles as the train rolled along.

She awoke with a start when the conductor barked out that they were pulling into the Mexia depot.

Stepping from the train, Leela pulled her satin-collared jacket more fully closed at the neck and looked around the platform for Pully. He had promised to be there at nine o'clock sharp. Not seeing him, she frowned and pursed her lips. Pully would never just leave her stranded. If he couldn't make it, he'd have sent Indy or James in his place.

The frightful steam engine hissed and cloudy vapor rose up at her feet. Leela waved her hand in front of her face, trying to see beyond the foggy drifts that had settled over the crowded depot.

I'll hire a car to take me home, she decided, starting across the platform. Suddenly she heard Aunt Effie calling her name.

"Leela! Over here! Hurry!" Effie waved frantically over the heads of passengers in her way.

How odd, Leela thought, for Aunt Effie to be here. As she elbowed her way through the crowd, Parker appeared at Effie's side. He had a troubled look on his usually relaxed face.

Leela stopped where she was, waiting tensely as the pair approached.

"What's happened?" she asked, certain that something had happened to Kenny. Why else would both Effie and Parker be meeting her at the station?

Parker pushed in front of his mother.

"Is something wrong with Kenny?" Leela blurted out, grabbing him by the arm.

"No," Parker assured her, removing his straw hat as he led her out of the tangle of passengers into a quieter spot. "Kenny's fine. But there's been a hell of a ruckus out on the farm."

"A ruckus? What do you mean?" Leela glanced at Effie, who averted her eyes and shook her head in resignation.

"Tell me what's going on," Leela said firmly, her heart sinking as she stared at her cousin.

Parker centered himself directly in front of Leela, placed both hands on her shoulders and spoke.

"Number 3 came in. Saturday night."

"And . . . did it come in big? Did Cap and Frank manage to get it under control?" When Parker didn't answer, Leela began to panic. "There's been a fire, hasn't there? That's what's wrong. Is there a lot of damage, Parker? Tell me everything." Leela feared what he would say. Parker's expression became more grim.

"The well came in huge," he said. "It spouted oil straight through the night before Frank and his crew could get it under control." He paused and took a deep breath. "But there's a problem, Leela. There was no fire, but four white men came onto Rioluces early this morning, ran the entire crew off the place and have chained up the gates. They say they've got the rights to the oil and no one's coming onto the property. They say they're in charge now."

"That's impossible! White men, you say? They're probably from Starr."

"No. They won't even let Thornton Welch onto the place. Got Gatling guns trained on the road, said they'll shoot anyone who tries to enter the gates."

"Oh, Parker. What on earth can be going on? Where did these men come from? Have you seen them? Tried to talk to them? What else do you know?"

"I just returned from there. They've got papers that look real legal, giving them fifty percent of the lease."

"*Fifty percent?* That's not possible. All but five percent of that lease was optioned by Starr Oil . . . until today. Only after this Sunday could anything more be sold. Anyway, Victor would never sell any part of his lease. When production slowed on Number 2 and he was worried about Starr taking over, we talked about that, but he didn't have to do anything drastic. Victor said he and Thornton Welch settled everything. Victor would never sell a percentage of his lease without discussing it with me. Especially not fifty percent."

Leela's words echoed in the back of her mind, reviving her doubts about Victor. Would he do such a thing? Was that why he'd been so distant and edgy? The possibility brought forth a nauseating wave of fear.

"Well, the men at the farm let me read the purchase agreement. The papers they're holding say a man named Carey Logan was the one who sold them their shares." Parker cocked his head to one side. "Isn't that T.J.'s half-brother? The one you said disappeared a long time ago?"

Leela wrenched her shoulders from beneath Parker's hands, her eyes wide with horror at the mention of Carey's name. She stepped back and looked from Effie to Parker, unable to speak for a moment.

"You saw this?" she asked.

"Yes," Parker replied, "and the documents they have look legal enough. I told them I'd be at the lease office in the morning to verify all their claims. If Carey Logan's purchase of fifty percent of the lease is registered at the county office, then there's not a thing you can do but wait for Victor to get back and explain this. He's got to know something about this deal."

"There'll be nothing registered at the county leasing office," Leela said with panic in her voice. "Victor . . ."—the coil of doubt about her lover's dealings wound tighter and tighter as she forced herself to speak—"would have told me of such an agreement. They're lying. These are schemers Carey Logan has hooked up with to try to take over Victor's lease. I'm not surprised Carey's the one behind this mess . . . Effie, didn't I tell you how crooked and vicious he could be?" Leela turned on her heel and headed to the exit. "Carey's going to pay for meddling in my affairs. He's going to pay for causing all this confusion." She stopped and turned to Parker. He held her by the arm. "Oh, Parker. What can we do?"

"Not much. I'll send a wire to Victor. He'd better hurry and get back here. In the morning I'll go to the county office and check on everything. Then you'll know where you stand."

"We can't wait until tomorrow. Something must be done tonight."

"Don't you try to solve this alone, Leela," Effie cautioned. "Leave it to Parker—he'll get to the bottom of it. You just come on home with me tonight and we'll set this straight tomorrow."

"No, I can't do that," Leela snapped. "Parker, get my trunk. I want you to take me home."

"To Rioluces?"

"Yes. That's my oil these men are claiming to have rights to. You think I'm going to stand by and let them get away with this? Please take me to Rioluces. Now!"

"I need a place to lay low, Ma," Carey said as he laid a stack of bills on the kitchen table in front of his mother. His hands trembled as he continued to count the money and arrange it in neat piles between himself and Hattie.

"Dirty lying bastards," he growled as he fingered the bills. "The rest of my money better show up soon."

He had had less than two hours of sleep and had even lain down in his suit. For the first time in more than three years, he was wearing the same clothes as he had worn the day before. He felt disoriented, dirty, pressed for time. His disheveled appearance annoyed him, but the turn of events at the farm today, coupled with the promise to get the rest of his money before daybreak, had forced him to leave his room on Belknap on short notice. Those men from East Texas hadn't come around yet, but he'd convinced Claude Varnet to get the rest of his money and hold it until Carey contacted him.

"What's wrong, Carey? You in trouble again? You promised you'd steer clear of the law. That deal went bad, didn't it? And you said all this money you was gonna get from the oil lease was legal." The accusation in her voice incensed Carey.

"It is legal," he said curtly, annoyed by her whining. "I just need to be scarce for a while. I'm not leaving Mexia without the rest of my money. They can't cheat me and get away with it! Not me! If

Claude doesn't get my money for me, I'll go hunting those bastards. I will!"

"Don't sound like a good idea to me, Carey. You'd best think about protecting yourself." Hattie watched her son closely as he handled the money.

"The men I'm dealing with have tons of money. They're gonna come through. They will. Just a matter of picking it up at the bank in the morning. That's all. And I'm gonna stay right here in Mexia until I get what's coming to me."

Hattie went to the cabinet, took out a pint of whiskey and poured herself two fingers, then put it back on the shelf. She quickly swallowed the welcome liquor.

"Anyway," Carey rambled on, "they're using some company's funds. Insured and all that. It really won't matter if they come up short." He tried to make light of his situation. "Just as long as I get my share. Here, Ma, this here's for you."

He felt oddly disgusted as his mother stared in disbelief at the stack of bills on her table.

"This is kinda scary, son. All this cash. You shore you ain't in no trouble?"

With a sudden sweep of his arm, Carey shoved all the bills from the table. They fluttered to the floor in a flurry of green, settling about his feet. He grabbed the small wooden table with both hands and sent it flying across the room. It splintered and fell with a crash.

"Don't you ever stop worrying, Ma? That's all I ever heard from you when I was growing up. Ever since I got kicked out of school. 'You in trouble, son?' 'You lying to me, Carey?' 'What'd you do, steal that pen?' Remember? Can't you ever believe in me? Why can't you just take the money and shut up!" He picked up the leather satchel containing the rest of the money and heaved it across the room. It knocked the whiskey bottle off the shelf. It splattered all over the cash.

"I'm not in any trouble, damnit!"

"Ah, Carey," Hattie moaned, seeming to shrink away from her son's pain. "Don't talk like that. Please, don't."

Exasperated, Carey wiped both hands across his cheeks and sat very still, trying to compose his thoughts. His contempt for his mother rose like bile in his mouth. "You never stopped letting me know how much I let you down when I dropped out of school," he said quietly. "You never even told me good-bye when I left. How'd you think that made me feel?" Carey slid his fingers through his dark wavy hair and let out a deep, heavy sigh. "And weren't you really glad when I was finally gone? Wasn't it easier without me around?"

"No," Hattie sobbed. "I been worried sick for eight years. You staying away is what ruined my life! I never stopped praying you'd come back. I thought about you every day. Didn't I write you letters and beg you to return?"

"Only after T.J. died." Carey stood, chest heaving, eyes running tears. He wiped his face with the back of one hand. "Well, here I am," he managed to say. "So, stop with the third degree. All I asked you was if you knew a place where I could lay low." He spoke through clenched teeth, towering over Hattie. When she didn't respond, he began restlessly pacing the length of the kitchen. The smell of his mother and the spilled whiskey was making him sick. "Is that too much to ask? Can't you do this one thing for me?"

Hattie dug her fingernails into her palms and shrank back into her chair.

"There's a girl who runs a bootleg joint over on Denton Street," she whispered in a frightened voice. "I think she might let you stay there."

Against his better judgment, Parker drove Leela out to Rioluces Sunday night. As they approached the farm, the headlights of his Buick illuminated the heavy chains wrapped over the gates and the two big guns positioned behind them.

Cautiously, Parker pulled to the side of the road and rolled down his window. He leaned out and yelled.

"I've brought Mrs. Wilder, the owner of this property! She wants to talk to you!"

"Let her step out of the car into the light," a man's voice cut the black night air.

"Be careful," Parker cautioned as Leela opened the car door.

"Don't worry. I'll be all right. I just want to see these papers they've got."

Leela slipped out, went to the front of the car and stood with the light behind her. She faced the thick, round barrels of two Gatling guns jutting out above the slats in the fencing.

"You have no right to keep me off my property," Leela shouted into the darkness, aiming her words at the faceless men behind the guns.

"We're just protecting our rights from Starr Oil. They say they got the rights, and we're not leaving until we get to the truth."

"That cannot happen until morning," Leela yelled.

"We ain't waitin' 'til morning. We got somebody checking this whole thing out right now. 'Til it's settled, nobody's getting past this gate. We got a legal purchase agreement here that says Starr has no control over this oil."

"May I see it?" Leela called out.

When no response came, she walked a little closer, extending her hand. One of the men tossed a paper to her feet. She stooped down, picked it up and went back to the front of the car to read it over. Parker got out and stood at her side.

"See, Leela? Doesn't it look legal? I think Victor better get back and straighten this out."

As Leela read the contract, her heart sank.

"Carey Logan will never get away with this," she told Parker. "I'll kill him before I'll let him ruin Victor."

After some discussion and Leela's assurance that she'd do nothing to force the men off the property, they relented and opened the gates. Leela and Parker entered the house, and she went straight to the telephone.

"I've never used this thing for a long-distance call. Parker, help me. We've got to get through to Victor."

They managed to get Estelle Simmons, head telephone operator of Mexia, on the line. She said she'd have to place the call, then ring them back. Might take a while, she cautioned, but as soon as the connection was made she would let Leela know.

By midnight they had heard nothing. Leela fell into her bed, exhausted and distraught, while Parker sat in a rocking chair at her bedside, T.J.'s old shotgun across his lap.

Anything could happen here tonight, he thought, wishing he had been able to convince Leela to leave. When she had insisted on staying, he knew he could not leave her alone.

At two in the morning the ringing telephone woke them both. Parker let Leela take the call. He stayed in the bedroom while she talked to Victor, but could not help overhearing what was said.

". . . that's right, Victor. They have papers stating that Carey Logan has signed over to them, giving them fifty percent of your lease. How can that be?"

There was a long silence.

"What do you mean, five percent? Five percent! You promised to stay away from Carey Logan altogether. You said nothing about this to me."

Parker's heart began to race for Leela.

"I trusted you to keep your promise," he heard her go on. "Now, see what you've done? I warned you. It doesn't matter that it's forged, it's still got everything torn apart. You're going to have to get back here and settle this with Starr. I'm sure Thornton Welch is raging mad. He thinks you've violated your contract. You know there was only five percent available to sell, plus Starr retained the rights to pipe any oil to come in before Sunday and the well came in Saturday night."

Parker could hear Leela crying, struggling to maintain control of her voice.

"How could you lie to me like that?"

Parker wished he could hear Victor's answer.

"Oh, yes, you did. By saying nothing, you lied. I knew something was wrong when you acted so coldly toward me in Dallas. I never would have dreamed you'd do something like this!"

Parker clutched the rifle and held his breath.

"I'll never trust you again, Victor. How could you deceive me and then make love to me as if nothing had happened?" Sobs muffled her words in a torrent of pain. "None of this would have happened if you had come to me for that money. Why did you go to Carey Logan? *Why?*"

More silence.

"Well, I have even less respect for you now!" Leela shouted. "I want nothing more to do with you."

Parker stepped into the parlor and stood next to Leela. She looked at him, her eyes bright with tears.

"No, Victor. Don't come back to see me. Come back and set your affairs straight. I really don't care if I ever see you again."

The sound of shattering glass jolted Leela and Parker awake. He dropped the shotgun in his hurry to get up, tripped over it and fell. She screamed in terror, leaning down to help him, grabbing the long heavy gun with both hands. A wide slice of pale moonlight streaming through the bedroom window gave them light enough to run through the house. The sound had come from the parlor. They eased down the hallway to see what had happened.

A stout piece of wood with a note tied around it lay in the center of the room. Parker motioned for Leela to stay back, then dropped to his knees and crawled to retrieve the message.

He and Leela went back into the bedroom, where she lit a single candle to read the bold black letters.

MR. BEAUFORT. CHEATER. LIAR. SWINDLER. YOU WILL PAY.

"Parker, this is serious," Leela gasped, feeling the danger of their situation intensify. She crushed the paper into a ball. The palms of her hands were clammy and cold. "Victor will be murdered if he returns now."

"But he must return and clear his name," Parker said. He frowned and rubbed his forehead. Leela could tell he was dead tired, but thanked God he had come out with her. His rational approach had kept her from spiraling panic and hysteria.

"You said Victor only sold Carey Logan five percent. If Logan's the one who misrepresented his share, then he's the one they should be looking for."

"This is awful." Leela paced back and forth in the low, dim light, the scrawled note clutched in her hand. "And I'd wager you everything I own that Carey Logan's not even in the county. He's left Victor to take the fall in his rotten dirty scheme." Leela blew out the candle and stood in the moonlight. "Parker, maybe they think you're Victor Beaufort. That's why they threw in this note."

"Stay clear of the window," Parker advised, taking Leela by the elbow, guiding her into the shadows. "We've got to stay put until morning. Nothing can be done before then."

Leela slumped onto the bed and buried her face in the crook of her arm. Parker moved toward the rocker, shotgun in hand. Before he could lower himself down into the chair, the roar of an explosion ripped across the farm. Like the deafening blast of a thousand locomotives, a tremendous boom paralyzed them, sent them cowering onto the floor.

"What in the world is happening?" Leela screamed, shocked when Parker shoved her head roughly against the carpet. "Parker! What has happened?"

"Stay down! Stay down!" was all he could manage to say, one hand firmly covering the side of Leela's head.

The shattering eruption of another detonation brought a shower of debris through the window. Parker swiftly threw his body over Leela's as glass rained down on his back. Instinctively, Leela struggled to free herself, straining to push her cousin away.

"Hold still, Leela. Stay here." He pushed her down again, wincing as he heard the thump of her skull against the floor. "I'm sorry, Leela. But you must stay down!"

"What is it? Parker! Let me up! Let me up!"

"Stay down!" Parker said in a firm, angry voice.

The smell of burning oil filled the room.

The air became thick with black smoke.

The farmhouse suddenly shuddered and creaked as another violent discharge erupted. Every window exploded into a shower of glass that shot through the rooms like hail. A sudden draft of hot air swept through the house, carrying papers and clothing, a vase of roses, anything not fastened down.

From the floor, Leela could feel the ground vibrating and hear the ripping groan of her house coming apart: walls caving in, the chimney crashing down, the roof opening up to the heavens.

The hot, acrid wind gathered strength, whooshing through the ruined house, threatening to suffocate the pair huddled on the floor.

"Show yourself, Beaufort! We know you and Logan are in this together." A chorus of hate-filled voices cried for Victor to come out and dare to explain himself to the crowd. Over and over, like the chant of a lynch mob, the angry men called for Victor Beaufort.

"You scheming liar," a male voice called. "It's all gone now, Beaufort. You'll never see a penny from this field. Come out and face the men you've robbed."

"Don't move," Leela told Parker, holding on to his sleeve with a firm grip. "They must have found out the papers signed with Carey are false. I told you they think you're Victor. You'll never get out of here alive."

"Don't worry," Parker said. "I have no intention of sacrificing myself for Beaufort. Just stay down and be quiet. They've done what they came to do. They'll probably clear out before long."

The hours dragged by while Leela and Parker remained on the floor, seated just below the broken window, where they suffered in silence, listening to the violent taunts of the frenzied mob and the crackling hiss of fire raging outside.

A bright orange light bathed the room in shades of hell. Leela watched Parker's handsome features shimmer in the eerie golden glow.

What would she have done without him? A sinking feeling in the pit of her stomach started to rise up again. Parker was the only one who had cared enough to be truthful and honest with her. He knew Victor had betrayed her, lied to her, let her fall into this deadly affair. She squeezed her eyes shut in shame. What a fool he must think her.

The crackle of burning wood echoed eerily over the farm.

She could trust Parker, Leela concluded, her bond with her cousin giving her strength. But where was Victor? she wondered in disgust. His reputation, his company—all ruined. And he had not even seen what was coming.

How could he put her land in such jeopardy? Leela's anger flared as she thought of the burning wells. And how could he have taken such a chance with her love? With their future?

Leela's throat ached as she struggled to swallow her tears. Crying would do no good, she reprimanded herself. Tears would do nothing but weaken her resolve to come out of this affair and go on, alone. Without Victor. This land belonged to her, oil or no oil. And no matter what these men did here tonight, Rioluces would always be hers.

She touched her cheek and felt the warm sting of the raging

inferno outside. Beads of perspiration gathered at her temples. The air was getting too thick and heavy to breathe.

Though she dared not rise up to look, Leela knew all three wells had been set afire, torched in angry revenge, and would burn out of control for days, maybe weeks, until the oil was depleted.

"Coward. Liar. Cheat. You deserve to die." Another hateful voice filtered into the house. It seemed to come from far away.

Parker and Leela stayed put, staring into darkness, until the first soft signs of daylight edged into the room. The farm grew quiet. The men began to drift away, for Leela could hear their motorcars starting up.

When she thought they had cleared out, she lifted her head and peeked over the windowsill, just in time to see a lone man dressed completely in black, hurl a lighted torch onto the side porch. He ran to his car and took off.

She stifled a scream and dropped to her knees.

"Parker! They've set the house on fire! We've got to get out of here, now!"

Parker yanked her by the arm and tugged her onto her stomach.

"Stay low. Follow me." He began crawling toward the front of the house. "Where did he throw the torch?"

"On the east porch," Leela said, feeling the first wisps of smoke fill her lungs. She coughed loudly and scrambled on her knees behind Parker.

At the center hall, Parker stood, pulled Leela to her feet and dashed through the door to the west veranda.

As they burst into the early morning air, flames licked hungrily at their backs. They managed to jump from the porch and run for Parker's car. As they stopped to look back they were shocked into silence by what they saw.

The east side of the house was engulfed in flames. More than half the roof was missing. The men were all gone, but out on the horizon, at the slope of Rioluces's only hill, flamed three tall red-orange towers of fire.

Like giant beacons of the dawn, they rumbled and burned convulsively. The wooden derricks, eighty feet high, splintered and crumbled, their huge timbers falling like scorched arms to the ground. In skeletal dignity they struggled to stand, but piece by piece the crossbars and rigging succumbed to the raging blaze that strengthened and flared as it fed off its unlimited supply of underground fuel.

All around the flaming towers, spreading out like a glittering blanket of gold, the fire raced swiftly across the oil-soaked grass. Right up to the barn. Down to the creek. Into the now fallow fields.

Leela's jaw tightened at the sight of her land, so savagely assaulted and bleeding before her eyes. *Victor Beaufort has destroyed my home, my dreams, the legacy my son should inherit. I'll never forgive him for this!*

CHAPTER THIRTY

A dull yellow glow filtered through the heavy curtains and painted the small room ochre. Leela flinched in pain as she opened her swollen eyes to stare vacantly into the warm golden space. Her eyes felt as if grains of sand had been embedded behind her lids. A wave of nausea swept up from the pit of her stomach and she took a deep breath, trying to shake the light-headed sensation that came with it. Lying very still, knowing she was at Aunt Effie's, Leela struggled to remember how she had gotten there. Slowly she ran her tongue over parched lips, feeling the cracks in her flesh.

A part of her did not want to remember, but haltingly the painful events of the previous night began to take shape. Glass shattering, thunderous explosions, the smell of burning oil: it still clung to her hair, her flesh, even penetrating the bed covers spread over her now.

Leela thought of Parker. He must have brought her here. Where was he? Was he hurt? Had he talked to Victor yet? And Kenny! Thank God she hadn't taken him to Rioluces last night. She wanted to see her son.

Leela tried to sit up, but the pain in her head forced her back onto her pillow. She lay exhausted while images of the flaming derricks swirled through her mind. Staring miserably into the glow of the afternoon sun smoldering behind the curtains, she let herself go slack, feeling all her courage ebb away.

Rioluces was in ruins. Not only the oil fields but the farmhouse as well. A terrible despair settled heavily over Leela, and she put her hands over her eyes to keep from sobbing.

All she had struggled to hold on to was gone. T.J.'s legacy destroyed! The wells would burn unchecked for weeks, and the land would be useless for years. Even cotton and melons could never be planted again! The hollow sense of loss that swept over Leela was almost too much to bear.

And Victor? Her heart convulsed with pain. She had given herself completely to him. She had surrendered with every fiber of her being. And what did she have now? Nothing! She wondered if he had returned to witness the results of his betrayal. Had he been to Rioluces to survey the charred remains of the future he had so carelessly wagered and lost?

At this thought Leela broke down. Her resolve crumbled, and tears of disappointment and broken dreams filled her eyes, spilled over and slid silently down her cheeks.

Everything she possessed was in her trunk, she realized, surprised the vandals had not taken it from Parker's car. And Kenny had no more than what he was wearing. They'd been stripped of everything they owned.

In the security of her girlhood bedroom, Leela let her tears come forth. She turned her face into the pillow and cried openly, her entire body shaking with the finality of her loss.

I should be blaming Carey Logan, Leela thought. But Victor knew! He had a choice, and he made the wrong one. She had told him Carey was nothing but a braggart and a hustler. Her hatred for Carey equaled her disappointment in Victor. If only he had listened to me, she lamented, all of this destruction could have been avoided.

There was a soft knock at the door.

"Aunt Leela? Grandma wants to know if you'd like to have some tea."

Leela raised swollen eyes to Penny's flat round face. The girl looked just like Johnny Ray. Her deep-set eyes were dark and intense, and her thick black hair was twisted into heavy braids. Though her paternal resemblance was strong and deliberate, Penny had escaped her father's nasty disposition, and thanks to her grandmother's guidance, she displayed none of her mother's selfish behavior. At eleven, she stood almost as tall as Leela.

Penny remained awkwardly in the doorway. "Are you all right, Aunt Leela?" She looked as if she feared her aunt was dying.

"I'll be fine. My eyes are burning like the devil and I've got a pain in my chest, but I'll recover. Tell Aunt Effie I'll be out in a few minutes. Let me get up and bathe and dress." As Penny backed out the door, Leela stopped her.

"Where's Kenny?"

"In the backyard with Margaret."

"Would you ask him to come in and see me?"

Penny nodded and disappeared, closing the door with a gentle thud.

Within seconds, Kenny appeared at Leela's bedside. She hugged him tightly and stroked his small back, sensing the fright that consumed him.

"Is the house burned down?" His eyes were wide with apprehension.

She was silent for a moment. "Yes, Kenny. I'm afraid so."

"Who did it, Ma? Why was our house burned down?"

"It's all a big mistake and very complicated. There was a misunderstanding, Kenny. That's what it was. A misunderstanding."

"Does Victor know what's happened to his oil wells?"

Kenny's innocence touched Leela and she hesitated, unsure of just how much to tell him.

"I'm not certain if he knows or if he's even back in Mexia, but he'll be the one to straighten it out. Don't you worry. He knows what to do." She couldn't bring herself to tell him more. And what good would it do? The boy had lost his father, now his home, and though he didn't know it yet, Victor Beaufort would no longer be a part of their lives.

Kenny squeezed his mother's hand fiercely. "And the barn and the horses? What's happened to Taffy?"

Tears surged to the surface as Leela thought about her horse. T.J. had given her the chestnut mare only months before he fell ill.

"Everything has been destroyed, sweetheart. I'm sorry, but that's the truth. When I last looked at Rioluces, everything was burning . . . even the grass and the trees and the fields." She held on to his hand as she spoke. "But the land is still ours. That's what's important. We can build a new house. I'll get more horses. We'll get through this and return to the farm."

"But when, Ma? How long will that take?"

"A while, Kenny. A while. But until then, we can stay here in town with Aunt Effie. We'll most likely be here when Margaret's baby is born. Now that's something to look forward to, isn't it?"

Leela brushed tears off Kenny's face and placed her cheek to his.

"I'm glad you weren't hurt, Ma," she heard him whisper into her ear. "I'm glad Cousin Parker was there to save you."

The house was so quiet Leela could hear the sounds of rosebushes rustling in the breeze outside. Parker and Margaret had taken Penny and Kenny into town to buy ice cream. Aunt Effie's idea. Might take the youngsters' minds off the ordeal of the night before, lift the cloud of doom hovering over everyone. Leela was glad for the time alone with her aunt. In great detail, she told her everything.

"I'm not sure you should blame Victor like that," Effie said. "He's a victim of Carey's scheme just like you are."

"He should have listened to me," Leela said with exasperation. "He promised he'd not do business with that man."

"Well, seems like his pride got in the way and made him ignore your warning. Not the first time such has happened to a man. Think about forgiving him, Leela. The two of you can bring Rioluces back."

"I'll bring it back alone. It's my land. There are plenty of oil companies who will still want a lease." She stopped and absently looked out the window. "That's if they get those wells capped and salvage anything. No telling how much oil has been lost."

"Parker went to see Frank. He's already got his crew together and they're on Rioluces right now, trying to get things under control. It's out of your hands, Leela. They know what to do. Just be glad you and Parker weren't hurt. Coulda been real bad, you know. Real bad."

"I know," Leela agreed. "And I'm going to get to the bottom of this. I'm going to find Carey Logan and make him pay. He's ruined my life and destroyed my son's future. He won't get away with this!"

"Be careful," Effie warned. "He's a threatening, unstable man. Don't you try to settle this alone. It's a complicated affair, Leela. Carey's got oil companies and white men all riled up. This mess could turn ugly and dangerous. You leave it to Victor to settle."

Leela took a sip of her tea, then set the cup back down in its saucer.

"I have nothing, Effie. Nothing." She twirled her ruby-and-diamond engagement ring around her finger. "I'd like to throw this ring in Victor Beaufort's face." Her words came out in a rush. "But I won't. I'm going to sell it and use the money to start rebuilding my house."

"Now, now," Effie cautioned. "Don't do something in haste that you'll regret. At least talk to Victor first. The two of you ought to try to work things out. You really need to try, Leela. I'd just hate to see you all alone again. And Victor's a good man. Really. So he made a mistake. These things happen. Try to get past it. Talk to him, please."

"Why should I? He didn't talk to me. When he needed money to give to Starr, why didn't he just come to me?"

The deep lines in Effie's forehead drew closer together as she considered Leela's question. "You already know the answer to that." Her tone was slightly impatient. "And it won't do any good asking it over and over again. Men just think different than women. Always have and always will."

Leela dropped her shoulders into a slump, sagging against the table as she told Effie, "Most of my royalties were in cash . . . in the house. Don't say a thing," she protested as Effie's mouth flew open. "I know I should have kept more of my money in the bank. But after that incident with Wesley Sparks, I figured my money was safer with me."

"That was a dangerous thing to do," Effie admonished, getting up from the table as she spoke. "With all the hijacking and robbery going on in this town, you never should have kept cash at the farm.

And look at what's happened. Gone, all gone." She stood staring down at Leela as if contemplating her next words.

"Well, there's nothing to be done about it now." Effie remained where she stood, hands clasped together, looking at Leela, perplexed.

"What's wrong?" Leela asked, uneasy under Effie's scrutiny.

"Leela, do you remember when the melon crop was destroyed by that tornado?"

"How could I forget? I felt just as I do now. As if God had forsaken me, abandoned me. And you know what really hurts? After all I went through to claim the title to my land, now I'm right back where I started. Why is this happening to me, Effie? Why?" She shook her head slowly, then raised tear-filled eyes to her aunt. "But why do you ask?"

"You came to me then, worried sick about paying off the bank to keep your farm. Your visit that day got me to thinking about a letter . . . a letter I got from your father, many, many years ago."

"You never mentioned this before." Leela tilted her head to one side. "What about his letter? Do you still have it? May I see it?"

"There's a little more to it than that."

Effie left the room and brought back the letter, waiting in silence as Leela read it twice.

"Don't you wonder what happened to that bond?" Effie asked.

"It's been almost thirty years. I'm sure it'd be worthless by now."

Effie's face lighted up. "Just the opposite, Leela. If that bond my brother took out for you is sitting in a drawer someplace, it could be worth close to one hundred thousand dollars. Think of how the MK and T has grown. It was just a few miles of track when your daddy got his job. Now that railroad line is part of a system that crisscrosses the entire country."

"But the bond may have been burned up or lost when he died," Leela said. "Grandma Ekiti may have even thrown it out. She couldn't read, you know, and had no sense of cash money, let alone paper bonds. Maybe the railroad gave it to her and she lost it or threw it away."

Effie took out another letter. "Read this," she said. "I took it upon myself to write the railroad and told them my brother's story. It took months, but I was surprised I even got an answer. Here." She handed the official looking paper to Leela. "What do you think of this?" She sat back, arms folded over her chest as Leela read.

Dear Mrs. Alexander,

In response to your inquiry about the Missouri Kansas & Texas Railroad bond issued to your brother, Edward Carey Brannon, our records show that his wife, Mrs. Hattie Brannon, cashed the bond shortly after his death. We have no additional securities registered in Edward Brannon's name. If we can be of further assistance please let us know.

John Hood
MK&T Securities Mgr.

Leela looked at Effie. "That's odd. My mother died before my father did. And her name wasn't Hattie, it was Mabel."

"I know." Effie leaned forward and put both elbows on the table. "Leela, you may think I'm crazy, but I only know one woman named Hattie."

"Hattie Wilder?" Leela watched Effie's face.

"And isn't it strange that Hattie Wilder's got a son with Ed's middle name?"

"What are you saying? Are you trying to . . ."

"I don't know," Effie cut Leela off. "But someone named Hattie charaded as your mother and cashed your father's bond. Now, that's a fact. And whoever she was, she knew what she was doing. She stole your inheritance. Think about it, Leela. I've heard the rumors about Hattie Wilder, how she carried on with railroad men when she was living near the Waco depot. Your daddy's route went right through McLennan County."

"You think Hattie knew my father?"

"Coulda been possible." Effie raised her eyebrows as she prompted, "Why don't you go ask that woman a few questions?"

There was absolutely no air coming into her lungs. Leela halted in front of Newton's General Store and leaned against a telegraph pole to catch her breath. The roar of her own pounding heart thudded rhythmically in her head and her stomach was knotted in pain. Leela's copper hair, flowing loosely about her face, tumbled in tangled ringlets to her shoulders. It caught the late afternoon sun, sparkling like spun gold, threaded with glints of burnished bronze. As she pushed the heavy tresses from her neck to cool her shoulders, she realized perspiration had soaked the entire bodice of her dress and her hem was splashed with mud. She'd torn her sleeve on the door when she'd rushed past Aunt Effie, yet she continued on, unconcerned. Frankly, her appearance was the last thing on her mind. She had to find Hattie Wilder. Now.

After checking her direction, Leela marched on, pushing through the crowds filling Belknap Street. She nervously chewed her bottom lip, shoving past the roughnecks and oil field workers idling on the sidewalk, swilling whiskey from canning jars and bottles.

Hattie Wilder had better have some answers, Leela thought, clenching and unclenching her fists as she stepped from the wooden sidewalk to circle a fierce German shepherd standing in her path. It was obvious the dog was not going to move.

That woman had acted strangely since the first day she had met her, Leela remembered, the image of Hattie pocketing Effie's silver clearly coming to mind. She would not hesitate to steal a railroad bond, Leela decided. Anyone as hateful and bitter as she must have a lot of things to feel guilty about. Leela always felt there was more to Hattie's past than anyone in Mexia ever knew. Maybe her lies were catching up with her, Leela concluded. She didn't care how old or how frail Hattie was supposed to be, she wasn't leaving her house until she got some answers.

"Oh, God," Leela moaned aloud as she hurried on. "What I'm thinking cannot possibly be true. It just can't."

A spring rain had left black water in the gutters, and the oil-soaked streets were sodden and slick. Early blooming azaleas burst pink and red along the esplanade, but she smelled nothing but the thick odor of gas that continued to hang over the town.

A fast-moving Buick rumbled through the street, splashing mud in its path as it barreled toward town. Leela jumped from the pine-board walk to avoid the oily spray and tore her silk stocking on the splintered railing fronting the street.

Dashing down Belknap, past Mildred's Cafe, she kept her eyes straight ahead, determined not to look over at Victor's Model T parked in front of his office. So, he's back, she thought, knowing he had left his car at the train station when he departed for Dallas. She hoped he would not see her.

She took longer steps and hurried across Commerce toward Main, feeling slimy water seep into her shoes as she pressed on. At Bowie Avenue she turned left, nearly ran the length of the block, then stopped in front of Elvina Hopper's house to stand trembling on the sidewalk, now unsure about her mission. She assessed the darkened windows as if they would tell her what to do. What to say. How to begin this impossible conversation.

Leela squinted her eyes nearly closed, clamped both hands into fists and mounted the short flight of steps to knock boldly on the weather-beaten door. Within seconds, Elvina Hopper appeared.

Leela stood defiantly before the woman she had not seen since ordering her out of the kitchen at T.J.'s wake.

"Hello, Elvina."

She nodded at Leela and did not reply.

"I'd like to see Hattie," Leela said, surprised at her own calm tone. Elvina Hopper surveyed the woman on her doorstep icily.

"Does Hattie Wilder still live here with you?" Leela asked, wondering what was wrong with the stupid old woman.

Elvina nodded again and looked straight ahead.

"Well, I need to speak to her. Right away. Will you please tell her I'm here?"

Elvina reached into the pocket of her starched blue apron and pulled out a handkerchief, then slowly wiped her wrinkled forehead, her chin, her faltering eyes. She shook her head and stepped back into the house.

"What's wrong?" Leela did not move. "Is Hattie here?"

Elvina nodded.

"Go tell her I'm here to see her," Leela insisted, tired of standing on the porch. If Hattie was inside she wanted to see her.

"She can't talk," Elvina finally muttered. "She can't talk," she repeated backing farther into the dank old house.

"What do you mean?" Leela asked.

Elvina motioned for Leela to follow her. "Come, see for yourself."

Leela followed Elvina through the tiny parlor into a small cubicle in the back. On a narrow low bed lay Hattie Wilder, eyes fixed on the ceiling, double chins sagging, the left side of her face grotesquely twisted.

"Go on, talk to her," Elvina urged. "She ain't gonna say nothing back." She walked to the bedside and looked down at her longtime friend. "Found her like this late last night when I come back from visiting my sister. Can't get her to say a word."

Leela remained at the foot of the bed. Hattie was transfixed. Rigid and immobile. Her wiry gray hair stood out about her face like the stiff iron spokes of a bicycle wheel. The wrinkled lids of her hooded eyes were thrown back, exposing two dark circles that had no life. The bed covers hardly moved with each breath.

"Did you send for Doc White?"

"He came out early this morning. Said she's had some kind of shock . . . some powerful scare. He says she's gonna need a whole lot of nursing care. Hattie's my cousin, Miz Leela, but I can't take care of her. Not by myself. Somebody's got to do for her. I'm not able. Not me."

Leela sank down onto a chair at the side of the bed. This is my son's grandmother, she told herself. No matter what happens, that will never change. "Perhaps I can help out, Elvina. I'll talk to Doc White. Maybe there's someplace we can send her where she can get the kind of care she'll need." Leela was quiet for a moment, then asked, "Would you leave me alone with her for a moment?"

"Suit yourself. Doc White says he don't even know if she can hear what you say. But go on and talk to her, maybe she'll come 'round."

After Elvina left the room, Leela pulled the chair closer and looked over at the disfigured woman.

"Hattie, I believe you can hear me. And I believe you have the answers to the questions I came here to ask. And even though you can't speak, I want you to hear me out." Leela saw no sign that her words had been understood.

"Did you know my father, Ed Brannon?" Again, no sign of recognition. "He worked for the MK and T and used to pass through Waco. Did you ever meet him? Please try to make a sign, Hattie. Blink your eyes. Something!"

The woman lay perfectly still.

"Where is Carey?" Leela demanded. "Do you know what he has done? To me? To your grandson? I can see what he's done to you. I must find him, Hattie. Maybe he can answer my questions. Is he still in the city? In the county?"

Hattie lay like a wax figure, hardly breathing.

"Try to make a sign, Hattie. Please. This is very important. Carey is in a lot of trouble. You know that, don't you? I'm not the only one looking for him, but I've got to find him before the men he cheated catch up with him. They may not let him live, even to go to jail. If you can, give me a sign that you know where he is. I must talk to Carey, Hattie. I must!"

No response.

Leela sat back in the chair and watched Hattie's grotesque face. Saliva dripped from the corner of the old woman's mouth. Leela picked up a towel and gently wiped it away. "You know what I'm after, don't you Hattie? Is Carey my half-brother? Is he, Hattie? You're the only one who can tell me the truth."

The already pale skin of Hattie Wilder's face went almost white. Her motionless form appeared frozen, though the room was stifling hot. Two black flies circled the woman's head and one even landed in her hair. Leela waved the insects from the bed and leaned closer, searching for any sign of recognition.

Disappointed and saddened by Hattie's crippled state, Leela sat at her bedside for another twenty minutes. As the afternoon sun began to disappear, Elvina stuck her head back into the room.

"She ain't said a word, has she?" She came closer. "Miz Leela, I know we done had our differences, but if you can do anything to help out with Hattie, I'd be most thankful." She came more fully into the room and lit a candle to disperse the rapidly advancing shadows. "I been probably Hattie's only friend, since we was girls together. I just hate to see her like this. But I blame that no-count son of hers for bringing this on. I been seeing it coming, ever since he come back to Mexia. Hattie took to the drink more heavy than usual, and been a bundle of nerves and worries ever since he first showed up."

"Do you have any idea where Carey might be?" Leela asked.

"Might try asking over at Mildred's Cafe, that's where I heard he was living."

* * *

"He'd be angrier 'n a hornet being run outa his nest if he had any notion I'd let you in here." Mildred carefully unlocked the door to Carey's room and pushed it open. "But if you got reason to believe he's done run out on his rent, I guess I better check and see if his belongings is still here." She pocketed her heavy ring of keys. "Now that you mention it, I ain't seen Mr. Logan since last Friday afternoon."

Leela remained behind Mildred, standing in the dark hallway as the landlady walked cautiously into the room. She raised a thin bony arm and held up her lamp.

"Don't look like nothing's missing," she sniffed smugly at Leela, shining the bright light into the shadows. She eased open the carved door on the tall armoire. Carey's collection of suits, vests, shirts and shoes were still arranged neatly inside. "He ain't gone nowhere. Nowhere far, that is. Not with all he's left behind."

Leela followed Mildred into the room to see for herself, fascinated by the precise way Carey had arranged his extensive wardrobe.

"Do you know where he might be?" Leela asked. "It's very important that I find him." She drew out her words while pulling a ten-dollar bill from her purse. She held it under the lamp.

Mildred looked at Leela, then down at the money, her face relaxing as she opened her palm.

"Claude Varnet's been hanging around. I heard him say he's supposed to meet Carey at some bootleg joint on Denton Street. One of them places where all the regulars go to buy their likker. Go to the last house on the right, before you cross Sumpter."

Chapter Thirty-One

Josephine's place, Leela thought, hesitating for a moment, then boldly squeezing past prickly hedges to enter the weed-filled sidewalk. Parker had described it precisely: two stately bur oaks on either side of the porch, overgrown flower beds struggling to put forth blooms at the foot of the steps. The porch sagging drunkenly in the middle. There was no other house on the street quite like it.

A dim light shone through a partially shaded window where a scrawny gray kitten sat purring on the sill. It jumped down and disappeared under the porch as Leela raised her hand to knock. She waited and listened. No answer. She knocked again, more loudly, then pressed her ear to the door. She could definitely hear movement inside.

The door whined on rusty hinges as someone cracked it open. Josephine peered outside.

"What do *you* want?" Josephine hissed lowly, gathering her open blouse closed around her breasts. She fumbled with the row of buttons with one hand, glaring at her cousin.

"I want to talk to you, Josephine." Leela cringed at the hateful scowl the young woman sent her way.

"Well, I don't want to talk to you." Josephine slurred her words together and began to close the door. Leela put her hand out to stop it.

"Don't you shut this door! This is important, Josephine. If you don't let me in, I'll come back with the sheriff. You don't want any trouble, now, do you?"

In the silence that followed, Leela could hear the kitten crying under her feet. She did not take her eyes off Josephine's sullen face.

When the door opened wider Leela slipped in, uninvited, and stood in the dingy hallway facing her cousin. The two women stared uncomfortably at one another. Leela watched Josephine put her hand against the wall to steady herself, while straining to focus her heavy-lidded eyes.

"Why did you come here? What do you want? Did Momma send you? Parker? What do you want?" Obviously intoxicated, she struggled to pronounce each word.

Leela looked around the trash-filled hallway. The cloying smell of fermenting grapes and distilled corn penetrated every corner of the house.

"Is someone here with you?" Leela started, unable to say anything else.

"What business is it of yours?" Josephine barked, slamming the heavy door shut. The aging house shook and trembled with the assault.

"Do you know a man named Carey Logan? It's very important that I find him."

"Why come here, to my house?"

"Because I was told Carey Logan would be here and I've got to talk to him. Tonight." Leela watched Josephine carefully as she talked.

"You better go," Josephine ordered, fastening the buttons on her thin cotton blouse. "There's no one here but me. I was sleeping. Go on, Leela. Get out of my house."

"I don't believe you," Leela snapped. "You weren't sleeping

when I arrived. What's going on, Josephine?" Leela looked toward the ragged bit of crocheted fabric separating the dim hallway from the kitchen. She could see a tall shadowy figure on the other side. "Is he in there, Josephine? I told you, if you don't cooperate, I'll come back with the sheriff."

Before Josephine could answer, the curtain was flung aside and Carey Logan stood there, filling the doorway. Naked to the waist. Smooth olive skin shining golden in the lamplight. His muscular arms crossed against his broad hairless chest. Dark wavy hair slicked back.

Shocked at the sight of him, Leela caught her breath, and her stomach fluttered and tumbled into spasms.

"You looking for me?" he asked calmly, the hint of a smile playing over his lips. He stepped back into the kitchen and let the curtain fall behind him. Leela snatched it back and followed.

"Yes, I am," she answered in a voice just below a scream, trying to control herself, hoping the confrontation would not turn into an ugly, bitter scene. There was too much she had to find out. With great effort Leela went on. "You and I have a few things to settle. You know exactly why I'm here, so don't play the innocent! You've got a lot to answer for, Carey Logan!"

Carey threw back his head and roared with laughter. The childish gleam in his eyes appalled Leela; he obviously found the whole affair amusing, like a game of chance where he'd come out the winner.

"Answer to you? Who are you kidding?" He shrugged his well-built shoulders, dismissing Leela as he sat back down at the table and filled his glass full of whiskey. He knocked down half of it in one gulp. "What'd you come here for, Leela? Changed your mind about marrying me? Or maybe you need to borrow some money? Things getting a little tight out on the farm?" He grinned, slamming his glass loudly on the table.

"How could you forge that lease and sell all those worthless shares? How could you, Carey?"

"Nothing to it," he replied flippantly. "A skill I acquired as a kid and have profited from handsomely as a man. Rather like an artist, you know? Takes talent and patience to do it." He smirked at her and licked his lips.

"Don't you see what you've done? You've ruined everything."

"Me? I don't think that's fair. Have you spoken to Mr. Beaufort? Seems he's had a hand in this also."

"There's nothing left for anyone now. Even if your letter from T.J. held up in court, there's nothing left of Rioluces. Everything has been burned to the ground."

"What a pity," Carey said sarcastically. "Everything's burned down, you say? Any idea who the culprit was? Such vandalism. A real problem for Beaufort, I'd imagine."

"Stop it, Carey. You know exactly what happened. You're the one behind all this destruction. And just what have you proven with your worthless, hateful scheme?"

"That Beaufort is as stupid as a horse's ass, for one thing. And Carey Logan gets what he wants, for another."

Josephine shrank back into a corner as the two raged on.

"Did you really get what you wanted this time, Carey?" Leela asked. "I think not. Maybe this time you overplayed your hand."

"Shut up!" Carey yelled, veins bulging in his neck. "You and Beaufort. What a pair! You should thank me for showing you just what kind of man he is. Thought you'd outsmart me? I showed you. Both of you. Where's your lover boy now, Leela? Where's this dream man you trusted and gave yourself to? Why isn't he here with you now? Could it be there's trouble in paradise? What happened, Leela? Have you cast him aside? Like you did me?"

Leela wanted to slap his face. "All your highfalutin' talk about loving me. Wanting to marry me. You've been scheming to get your hands on my land and my money since the day you came back to Mexia. And if you think destroying Victor will force me into your arms, you're just as crazy as I thought."

Carey got up from the table and circled it, stopping inches from where Leela stood.

"Force you into my arms?" He let out an ugly snort of a laugh. "I don't ever remember forcing you, Leela. You came willingly once and you'd have come willingly again." He grabbed her by the shoulders and pulled her face to his. "But I don't want you now!" He squeezed her until she winced with pain. "Do you hear me? I don't want you!" He dug his fingers into her flesh. Leela bit her lip to keep from screaming as Carey tightened his grip.

"Am I hurting you, Leela?" He mocked her expression. "Oh, I'm sorry." Quickly he let her go. "I'm very sorry. I'd never want to hurt you. Not you."

Leela rubbed her arms and glared at him, suddenly regretting she'd come here alone.

"I went to see your mother this afternoon," Leela started, trying to judge how far she could go. Carey was obviously drunk and not at all concerned with what he'd done, but she'd come too far to back down now. She watched as his bloodshot eyes flew open.

"What'd you go see Ma about? What'd she tell you?"

"Nothing," Leela said calmly, feeling a little more in control. She waited for him to speak. He walked away, sat down again and poured himself two fingers more, tossing them down before talking.

"I didn't think she would," he said. "She ain't got the guts to tell you."

"To tell me what?" Leela could feel her knees beginning to weaken, her mouth go dry. As much as she dreaded it, she had to hear the truth. "What?" she prompted again, watching rivulets of perspiration drip down Carey's smooth chest. His handsome physique no longer thrilled her; in fact, it made her so uncomfortable waves of nausea rose up. She could hardly bear to look at him.

Carey raised one eyebrow, then calmly reached under the table and brought out a small pearl-handled gun, slightly bigger than the spread of his open hand. He laid it gently on the table.

Leela froze. She never dreamed he'd have a gun. Carey was a hustler, a gambler, a liar and a cheat, but she never figured him to carry a weapon.

"Do you like it?" He ran his index finger over the nickel-plated barrel. "It's a Colt automatic, thirty-two caliber. You know, I was told bullets from this pistol can penetrate five one-inch pine boards at fifteen feet. It's true. I tried it myself the other day." His face had no emotion. "Never had a gun till I came to Mexia. In this town . . . if you ain't carrying a piece, you're fair game. Never seen so much shooting and killing and carrying on as I've seen since I came to this place." He pulled out the magazine to check the bullets. Leela could see it was loaded. She didn't dare try to move.

"So, you talked to Ma, huh? Good for you . . . I ain't got nothing to say to her." He snapped the magazine back into place. "Ma ruined my life," Carey muttered. "I'm sure she didn't tell you that. Did she? She would never tell a soul how her lies and her silence kept me from having the kinda life I deserved." He stared at the gun, then laid it back down.

Leela remained standing at the table. Josephine moved farther back into the shadows.

"Your mother is very ill." Leela's voice quivered. She paused, hoping Carey would come to his senses and put the gun away.

"She's always been ill," he said bluntly. "I don't ever remember her feeling well. Drank too much of that moonshine and dandelion wine. I always thought that stuff would kill her one day, but I never said nothing—she'd never listen to me. Why should she? Nothing I said ever mattered. Did you know that, Leela? I never mattered that much to anybody. I grew up a nobody. Never did know just where I came from." He raised tormented eyes to Leela. "Not 'til just a day or two ago."

"What do you mean?"

He gazed past her now, as if avoiding her question, and a far-off look came over his face. "You were the one I thought would make me happy. We could of been, Leela, you know that."

"Please, Carey, don't bring that up. I was lonely, confused, desperate for attention. You came along and flattered me. Told me I was pretty. Said all those things T.J. never could. You knew what you were doing and did not care about the consequences. That was so long ago. I was young. I made a mistake, poor judgment, that's what it was. We had no future. Never. Not for a minute. You should have realized that."

"Oh, no. You should have run off with me—left my dull, miserly brother. We'd of had a grand life together, you and me. For eight long years I thought of nothing but you, coming back to you, having you for myself."

"It was all wrong, Carey. I was married to T.J. I never should have encouraged you at all."

"And I should have confronted old T.J. back then. But, no, I ran away instead."

"It was the only thing to do. You knew it. We both knew it."

"You're the only woman I ever truly wanted to be around, Leela.

You know that? Women crowd me. Hang all over me. And I can take 'em or leave 'em, that's the truth." He lifted his eyes to Josephine. "Even this one here." He half stood at the table, pointing his glass toward the shadows. "You wanted me, didn't you? Didn't you? You fat freakish whore."

Josephine screamed and covered her ears.

"Don't!" Leela shrieked.

"Don't what? Tell the truth?" Carey threw his glass at Josephine, laughing perversely as it crashed at her feet. He picked up the gun and sauntered toward Leela. "You don't want to hear me tell how I dreamed of making love to you? Only you! You don't want me to bring back memories of those long, hot afternoons at T.J.'s farm?" He stood before Leela, his hand hanging loosely at his side. He fiddled with the gun as he spoke. "Well, I got a whole lot more to tell you, lady. So you better be quiet and listen."

Leela's breath was coming in gulps. The room was stifling hot, and all of a sudden she felt the dampness of her shoes, the mud and grit on her face, the slimy oil on her skirt, now tangled around her legs.

I've got to get out of here, she thought, realizing she had made a grave mistake confronting Carey like this. He was drunk, raging mad, drifting in and out of reality and Leela wanted only to leave.

"Forget about the past," she pleaded, pushing her hands toward Carey to keep him at a distance. "You've ruined my farm. My life. My son's future. And you're going to pay for this. The sheriff will find you and put you in jail."

"I doubt that," Carey threw back. "That hayseed sheriff's not looking for me. He's been paid well enough to leave me alone." He reached out and grabbed Leela by the wrist. "You wouldn't turn me in to the law, would you, *sister*?" He narrowed his watering eyes and pursed his thin lips together in a mirthless challenge. "Would you turn your only brother over to the sheriff?" He twisted her arm until she screamed aloud and begged him to let her free.

Leela felt as if her heart stopped beating. Her eyes widened in horror and a great tremor swept through her body. The room shimmered and swayed, tilting and pitching the distorted figure before her. She felt as if she would faint.

It's true! she cried to herself, sinking inside as fiery pains shot up her arm. Aunt Effie had figured it right. Carey Logan is my half-brother.

His angry eyes pierced her. Leela tried not to look at him but it was impossible. The agony contorting his face overwhelmed her, sending shivers of dread to the center of her soul.

Leela pulled back toward the table, straining to free herself from Carey's hold. But the two remained locked together, his hand burning into her wrist, their souls slammed together in anguish. A numbness crept through Leela, draining her, washing her, stripping her senses away. She watched in horror as Carey waved the gun above her head.

"What do you think of that, Leela? Having me for a brother?" The words slurred into a low, even growl. The sound of his voice seemed to revive her own.

"Put down that gun, Carey! You're scaring me!"

Abruptly, he lowered his hand. "Scaring you?" He lifted his chin and laughed. "Ha! Scared of your brother? Well, don't be. I won't hurt you, Leela. But you better listen to what I have to say."

She stood tensed, rooted to the spot. Wondering what more there could possibly be.

Carey went on. "That was hard news to take, I'll admit. But Ma had her reasons for keeping quiet . . . if you let her tell it. What the hell? So now I know who my daddy really was—too late to make much difference." He loosened the grip on Leela's wrist. "So I been hankering after my sister . . . all these years!" He laughed ruefully, scornfully, and raised the gun again, brandishing it as he yelled, "My sister!" Then squeezing his dark eyes shut, he screamed, "I hope Ma burns in hell for this!"

Leela covered her mouth with her free hand and struggled to pull away.

"Don't go," Carey said lowly, tugging her closer, almost as if he wanted to kiss her. She pushed against the slick warm flesh of his chest.

"Put the gun down, Carey." Leela began to cry. "I'll stay. We'll talk. Just put the gun away."

"Quit telling me what to do," he snapped, stroking the pearl handle with his thumb. "You're acting just like Ma, always telling me what to do. Never a good thing to say." He narrowed his eyes at her and leaned closer. Leela shied away, but he tightened his hold on her arm.

"Let me go!" Leela pleaded in a shaky voice, words strained with fear. "Why don't you put the gun on the table? There's no need for this, Carey. Can't we just sit and talk?"

"Don't think there's much left to say," he began, pulling her fully against his perspiring body as he moved the pistol along her back.

Leela clamped her lips together, bit down hard and when the gun appeared at the side of her face, she jerked away. In one swift movement, a blur of desperate motion, she yanked her arm free and tried to knock the gun from his hand. She missed.

The twisted agony on Carey's face pierced Leela just as the pistol exploded. His eyes widened in surprise, his mouth dropped open, but no sound came out. The gun fell onto Leela's chest, leaving a trail of dark red blood to her waist before it clattered with a thud onto the scarred wooden floor.

As Carey slumped onto the table, blood dripping down his chin, Josephine emerged screaming from the shadows and fled barefoot into the street.

Everything happened so quickly. Leela heard the front door slam shut behind Josephine and from a distance heard her shouts of terror in the street. Too stunned to move, Leela remained rooted to the spot where Carey had held her, staring in horror at the side of his head: the gaping hole where his ear had been, the dark thick blood dripping down his neck, across his golden shoulders, onto his gray woolen trousers. She noticed, numbly, that his eyes remained open.

Leela sank down onto a chair across from her brother and covered her eyes with both hands. Her sobs came quickly and painfully from deep inside her body, and she trembled so violently the table began to shake.

Within minutes, she heard the door open, footsteps in the hallway, people coming into the room.

"There she is!" Josephine cried out to the sheriff, who stood alongside her, taking in the scene. "She's killed him! I saw it. She shot him in the head!" Josephine stepped up to Leela and pointed at the gun. "There, on the floor, is the gun she used. In cold blood, I tell you. I saw everything!"

As Leela lifted her head and looked up at Josephine, she saw a perverse glow of triumph illuminating her cousin's blotched, bloated face.

Chapter Thirty-Two

The sheriff's heavy touring car rolled slowly through the wet brick streets. Leela edged forward on her seat, peering through the gloomy drizzle to catch a glimpse of the familiar clock tower rising up in the center of Groesbeck. Like a stalwart protector of the official county seat, the redbrick shaft, crowned with a regal, turreted roof, was set with two round clocks, one facing west, the other toward the south. The luminous dials, like two owlish eyes in the overcast sky, watched over Leela as she approached the Groesbeck County Jail.

The trip from Mexia had taken nearly an hour, and when the sheriff and his deputy shoved her from the stuffy car, Leela recoiled from their touch, glaring at them in humiliation. Iron handcuffs bound her hands so unmercifully tight, the tender skin on the inside of her wrists chafed and burned.

How dare they bind her with chains? Shove her around? Treat her like a painted trollop picked up off of Belknap Street? Couldn't they see that Josephine Alexander was insane, that her twisted self-pity had scarred her and driven her beyond all reason? How maddening it had been to stand by and listen to her hysterical stream of accusations. And Sheriff Thompson! So anxious for an arrest he would have taken the word of a child!

The sound of her own damp shoes scraping the uneven bricks echoed through the night, growing louder and more irritating the closer she came to the imposing courthouse. Leela shuddered and blinked back tears, terrified of entering the tall carved door that would seal her inside the official court of Limestone County.

Haltingly, Leela climbed the steep granite steps, passed beneath the towering limestone arches fronting the courthouse entrance and followed the deputy sheriff to her small, dark cell.

A deluge of unanswerable questions engulfed her, nearly distracting her from the smell of mold, urine and rotting straw that pervaded the dungeonlike space. What would happen to Carey's body? she wondered as the long key turned in the lock and the heavy iron door slammed shut. Hattie couldn't tend to her son's funeral arrangements, and who else even cared about placing him to rest? Would her brother be shoved into a common pauper's grave, with no marker to signify his presence in the world? The thought sickened her, as did the image of Carey's bleeding body, slumped over Josephine's kitchen table, that would not leave her mind. The smell of his blood still filled her nostrils.

How odd the way this man, her brother, wove his tragic past through her life. There were still so many questions to be answered. Would Hattie ever recover enough to explain how this had happened?

Leela eased herself stiffly onto the low, sagging cot, lay down on her side and fixed her eyes on the floor. Tears slipped over her cheeks and dampened the mildewed pillow.

How would she clear herself of this charge? she worried, absently tracing the network of cracks and spaces in the cold brick floor of her cell. She began counting bricks to still her soul, to keep from shattering the numb resolve so shallowly holding her world together. Would word get to Parker? Effie? Would anyone come to help her? She needed a lawyer. Arrangements must be made to secure cash. Even her beautiful ruby-and-diamond ring was gone, confiscated by the sheriff. She doubted she'd ever see it again.

Money, she thought, a smirk coming over her face. At one time she had more than she could spend, now she didn't even have funds to hire legal counsel.

The sheriff had refused Leela's plea to send a message to her aunt, but many curious onlookers had crowded up to the porch, watching intently as she was handcuffed and pushed into the police car. They had heard her cries of protest. Surely someone would get word to Parker at the *Banner*; all news reached him in time.

She pushed herself up from the cot and swung both feet to the floor. It was difficult to even think about Victor. Her heart crowded into her throat and she could hardly breathe. Blood pounded through her neck, rushing into her head, making the room swim in circles before her eyes. Leela placed her head in both hands and lowered her face to her lap.

Here she was, charged with murder. Murder! It was impossible to accept. She pressed her fingers into her temples, then murmured to herself, "If only Victor were here . . ."

Victor! In anguished confusion she yearned for him, would rush into his arms if he appeared, would place her face into the warm, soft curve of his neck and let him stroke her flaming hair. But he wasn't here and their love was dead.

The wrenching sobs that flowed through Leela came from the deepest, rawest part of her soul. How could she face the future alone again? Isolated once more in the backwoods of Limestone County, struggling to make a life for herself? She fought to swallow the painful lump in her throat, wiped her face with the hem of her muddy skirt and resolved to push thoughts of Victor Beaufort aside.

She couldn't spend her time fretting over his betrayal. She had to pull herself together and prove Josephine a liar. She had to save her own life now.

He had spent the past day and a half clearing his name. From the county lease office, to the offices of Starr Oil, to a meeting with each one of the men from East Texas. Victor Beaufort had proven he'd been swindled. He was a victim just like the others.

Reluctantly, the oilmen had agreed that there would be no legal charges against Victor, but by the end of the day one thing was clear: Victor Beaufort and the Beaufort Drilling Company were blacklisted in Mexia, financially ruined. Victor would never get the money to sink another well, at least not in Limestone County. No one wanted any dealings with him.

Victor sighed and slumped in his chair, his mud-splattered boots making puddles on the floor. Exhaustion claimed him, yet he knew the most difficult task still lay ahead. After nearly forty-eight hours of nonstop work, the oil field fires were extinguished, but the rigging, the equipment, the storage tanks and pipelines were all totally destroyed. Without a major infusion of capital, Rioluces could never be opened up again. Even Starr Oil had quickly released Victor from their contract, moving on to more productive fields. No one wanted to bother with his burned-out lease; it would cost too much to start up again.

Yesterday, he had gone searching for Leela at Effie Alexander's house, but was told she had left suddenly, gone off to visit someone. Effie had refused to tell him who or where. His attempts to find Carey Logan had been equally fruitless. Seemed no one had seen the scoundrel since Friday night.

Victor rose from his desk, going to stand at the window overlooking the busy street. He shook his head as if clearing it, trying to decide what to do next.

He felt the weight of his betrayal grow heavier, crushing his shoulders like an unwelcome embrace. He had been foolish to trust Carey Logan and more foolish to believe he could make such a deal without Leela finding out. The entire affair had backfired. Exploded. Everything was lost: his company, his lease, the woman he loved.

I've got to find her. Today, he vowed. She must hear him out. Leela wouldn't throw their future away so quickly. She loved him, he knew it. And if he found her, he wouldn't rest until he convinced her to forgive him.

Victor turned from the window and let out a startled cry. He hadn't heard her come in, hadn't felt her presence in his office. Effie Alexander stood looking directly at him, and she appeared to have been there for quite some time.

"Victor," she started. "Something awful has happened."

"Leela?"

Effie nodded, wiping red-rimmed eyes.

"What is it? Where is she?"

"She's in the county jail in Groesbeck. She was arrested last night for the murder of Carey Logan."

Victor stared at Effie in disbelief, refusing to absorb what she had just said.

"Go to her, Victor. She needs you," Effie urged. "Forget about those angry words you two threw at each other. She's in real trouble now. You've got to go see her. Help her. She's innocent. I know she never killed that man."

Victor snatched up his Stetson and pulled on his jacket.

"Do you want to ride over with me?"

"No, you go on alone. Kenny needs me here."

Without looking back, Victor bolted out the door, down the steps and leapt into his car.

Parker arrived at daybreak, coming in with his briefcase and notebook, looking very capable but worried.

Leela tugged at the hem of the stiff gray chemise she'd been forced to put on, embarrassed by her dowdy appearance.

"They took away my clothes in the middle of the night," she told him. "They even confiscated my ruby-and-diamond ring . . . the one Victor gave me. They said the clothes were evidence for the hearing, and I guess I've seen the last of my ring."

Parker nodded. "Probably so. But you still look beautiful, Cousin Leela. Don't worry, we'll get you out."

"How?" was all Leela could utter.

"I'll make arrangements for a lawyer. As soon as I can locate one to take the case. I hope Daniel Riley from Dallas is available. I met him in Washington. He'd be a good man to defend you." Parker reached over to take Leela's hand.

"I have no money to retain him."

"You still own the farm, don't you?"

Leela nodded.

"We can use it as collateral for his fee. Leave it to me. It will all work out."

"Where's Effie? How is Kenny? Do you know what's happened to Carey's body?"

"Hold on, Leela, one question at a time." He gave her a puzzled look. "Why should you care what happens to Carey Logan's body?"

She took a deep breath and looked away.

Because he was my brother, she thought, my flesh and blood. We shared the same father, whom neither of us knew. And, unbidden, the awful thought arose: Because I may have caused the accident. I lunged for the gun. I startled him. The surprise on his face. Oh, God, what did I do?

"I don't know," she finally said, hesitating to gather her thoughts. "He was drunk, talking out of his mind, confused. Oh, Parker. It was an accident. Carey was just fooling around with that gun. Trying to scare me, impress me. Oh God, I was scared. And just before the gun exploded, he looked at me as if he could see directly into my soul." She shuddered and lowered her head.

Parker settled down to the business of asking a few questions. "Let's go over exactly what happened in that house. Have you said anything to anyone?"

Leela didn't answer right away. Then she wiped her tear-streaked face with the back of one hand and told him of Carey's painful rambling, avoiding any mention of Hattie's confession.

Parker moved closer and repeated his question. "What did you tell the sheriff, Leela?"

"I told him the truth. Carey Logan shot himself by accident. That's all there is to tell." Her indignant words echoed through the cell.

"And Josephine is lying?"

"Yes. Yes," Leela replied desperately, the strain of reliving the incident taking its toll. She reached out and grabbed Parker's arm. "Josephine's been waiting for a chance like this: a chance to hurt me, humiliate me and get her revenge. She was laughing when the sheriff took me away, Parker. Laughing!"

Parker put his arm around Leela's shoulder. "I understand . . . and I believe you, Leela. I know you didn't shoot Carey Logan. But how Josephine could try to pin this on you, I just don't get it."

Leela turned to her cousin and said sharply, "Then you really don't know Josephine."

Thirty minutes after Parker left to make arrangements with the lawyer, Victor appeared at the iron bars separating Leela from the rest of the jail.

"Stay outside the cell and you got fifteen minutes," the deputy barked, turning his back on the visitor.

Victor stepped forward, appalled at this ugly turn of events.

"How are you?"

Leela raised angry eyes at Victor and ran a hand over her dirty, tangled curls. She lifted her chin slightly, unable to bring herself to speak.

Victor was stunned at how drawn and fatigued Leela appeared.

"Leela, please, don't shut me out. We need to talk."

She remained silent, watching him through half-closed eyes, remembering the last time she'd seen him. At the train station in Dallas, where he had kissed her good-bye, knowing what he was sending her back to. Knowing his betrayal could destroy their love. Now all she wanted was for him to go away. It hurt too much to look at him.

"I was wrong to sell part of my lease to Carey Logan without telling you," Victor started, a frantic edge to his voice. "I admit my mistake. And I'm sorry, but I was desperate to keep the lease from falling into Thornton Welch's greedy hands, so I made a pact with an even greedier man. My mistake. I see now I should have come to you."

Leela's heart raced. Yes, she thought, you should have come to me. Wasn't our relationship strong enough to weather that? A matter of money! Nothing else! Money, she thought bitterly, wondering if having so much of it was really worth the pain.

Yet for all her anger, her heart broke for Victor. His shoulders were slumped in humility, giving him an air of defeat. She could see how devastated he was. But the events of the past two days had sapped her. Confused her. She was not able to talk of forgiveness. Too much had happened too quickly. Everything was changed. Victor had initiated the chain of events that led her to this cell. She glared at him, unyielding.

"We can overcome this, Leela, if we work together. I've settled everything with Starr and the men Logan cheated. They're out of the picture now. The lease is free again. It may take some time, but you'll see. We'll bring Rioluces back." He paused, distraught. Leela's hostile expression had not changed. "I met with a possible investor in Dallas. I know I can get the money to bring everything back. We can start up . . ."

"Not *we*," Leela cut him off. "I plan to sue you and break my lease with you. I want full control of my oil reserves. If there is anything left to salvage of Rioluces, I'll be the one to bring it in. You taught me well, Victor. I think I can read the fine print on any lease ever written . . . and understand exactly what it means, too."

Victor winced. Her words struck home.

"I guess I deserved that remark, but I wish you could understand my feelings."

"I understand how you feel," Leela shouted, "but right now, how you feel is not important! Look at me, Victor! Look at me!" She jabbed her fingers into her chest. "Do you see what your pride has done to me? I may never get out of this place. How dare you talk of forgiveness? How dare you even think about coming back onto my land! I am surprised that you had the nerve to even come here and face me!"

Victor had no response. He gripped the iron bars between them and riveted Leela with a troubled gaze, determined to stay and work things out.

Leela went on. "I think I could manage to sink a few wells—all I need is the capital. Yes," her voice rose higher with nervous excitement. "Rioluces will produce oil again. Just watch me, Victor. Derricks will rise from the land, pipes will crisscross the fields, huge storage tanks will line the creek. But you will not be anywhere near it, let alone be the head of production!"

Victor pressed himself against the bars, not flinching in his resolve. "You don't have to sue me to break our lease. It's your land, Leela. I'll give up my rights. If that is what you want."

"It is," Leela said coldly. "I'll find the money to bring Rioluces back. And I can do it without your help." She turned her back to him. "Just go away, Victor. Please."

He continued to stare at her. The gray prison chemise did not conceal her elegant posture, the determination and pride that were part of her. He loved her so. If only he hadn't been so proud! He could have gone to her! Victor yearned to reach out and take her in his arms.

"Don't shut me out so quickly, Leela. I admit my actions were misguided, but my love for you has never changed."

She turned around.

He watched her closely as he spoke. "You're right. Pride kept me from coming to you. How do you think I felt? Misreading that lease like I did? Then, to ask you to come up with that money? Never!"

"A man who believes in the woman he loves would rather let her help him than risk losing her forever."

Victor nodded slowly. "You're right." Suddenly, he smiled. "But you know something? You are most always right. That's what I love about you. You're about the smartest woman I know." He stepped back from the bars. "I had hoped you'd forgive me, Leela. I want nothing more than to make up for the pain I've caused and help you get out of this mess."

Leela remained immobile, afraid to speak. Her throat closed painfully. There were no words to say. Inwardly, she cringed at the torment she was causing Victor.

"You know, we all take chances," he said in a solemn, almost reverent tone. "Now and then we make mistakes. You ever made a mistake, Leela? Have you ever done something you later regretted?"

They looked at each other across a river of misery.

"Guess I played my hand as best I could. . . ." His words drifted with despair. "Maybe you're right. You might just be better off without me."

Leela watched Victor's face fall in resignation. As he backed away from the cell and turned to leave, she opened her mouth to stop him. But the words she needed were not there.

Leela stood rigidly in the center of her cell and listened to his footsteps echo down the corridor. Would he return for the hearing? she wondered. Would he be there to hear Josephine tell the judge of the passion she unknowingly shared with her brother? She hoped he was gone for good. After such a shocking revelation, Victor would never want her back.

Reverend Pearson pulled his chair as close to the bed as his bulky frame allowed, then opened his Bible to the Twenty-third Psalm. He read it lowly to Hattie, looking over the rim of his glasses to watch for any response. There was a definite change in her expression. Her wide, staring eyes flickered shut for a moment, and a tear slid from beneath her lashes. Reverend Pearson felt encouraged and plunged ahead with his message.

"This is the same verse I read over Carey, Miz Hattie. I thought you'd like to hear it. He's placed at rest now, in the Woodlands cemetery, in a shady spot next to T.J."

The Reverend was certain Hattie Wilder could hear him, and it seemed only fitting that he let her know what had happened to her son.

Reverend Pearson had been shocked by Effie Alexander's visit, asking him to please see that Hattie's son got a proper burial. But even more shocking had been Hattie's condition, changed very little since the night Elvina found her.

Poor woman, he thought, reaching over to pick up a towel to wipe saliva from her cheeks. Both sons dead and she's left like this. Such a shame, the tragedy this family has had, and now with Leela in jail for murder. He shook his head solemnly, making a mental note to drive over to Groesbeck tomorrow to see her.

Perhaps I'm the one to blame, he chastised himself. If he had listened to T.J. Wilder and respected his wishes, maybe Carey Logan would never have returned. This terrible state of affairs might have been avoided. He sighed and turned his mind from such thoughts. There was nothing he could do except pray.

"I told Elvina that some of the ladies from the church gonna be coming by, checking on you, helping you eat. You gotta try to eat more, Miz Hattie, but things will get better, you'll see. And I'll be here myself, as often as I can. Don't you worry about a thing. Your boy's with the Lord now. And you know what? Mr. McBay at the funeral parlor did a real good job on Carey. When we laid him to rest, he had a right peaceful look on his face."

Chapter Thirty-Three

"Hear ye. Hear ye. Hear ye. The Honorable Circuit Court of the tenth judicial circuit of the state of Texas, in and for Limestone County, is now open. All persons having business before this court draw nigh. Give attention and ye shall be heard. God save the state of Texas and this honorable court." The bailiff finished his declaration, moved quickly to one side and fixed his eyes on the bench, waiting for the judge's arrival.

Like the hammer blow of the steel maker's mark, the formal declaration brought the full weight of the law down upon Leela. She bit her lip and nervously turned to her lawyer. "I'm so frightened," she breathed, feeling her hands begin to sweat.

"Don't be," Daniel Riley reassured her. "Just relax."

It had taken three days for Parker to find Daniel Riley, but for Leela the agonizing delay had been worth it. The young lawyer from Dallas who had just won a case very similar to hers was enthusiastic, patient and polite. She just hoped his decision to have her case heard by a judge, without a jury, was indeed the right way to go. She took a deep breath and surveyed the courtroom.

She watched the nervous twitch of the bailiff's lips as he eyed the court, waiting for the unusual crush of people to find seats in the small wood-paneled room. Every bench under the high square windows was filled and overflowing. Spectators lined the wall in the back of the room, peering around the ornate plaster columns in their way. The hum of buzzing voices rang in Leela's ears. She eased her head to one side, anxious to see who had arrived.

Effie and Parker sat together on the first long bench in the courtroom. Effie gave Leela a reassuring nod, smiled with her eyes and nudged Parker. He raised his head and looked over at his cousin, mouthing the words "Don't worry" before taking out his familiar notepad to begin taking notes for the paper.

Josephine, sitting apart from her family, stared straight ahead, her plump cheeks pulled into a deep scowl, bitterness radiating from her face.

Behind them, Victor surveyed the proceedings with an air of detachment, his body turned sideways in his seat, his back turned toward Leela.

Riley touched Leela on the shoulder. "It's about to begin. Remember, Leela. Stay calm and tell the truth."

Leela smiled weakly at her attorney, who, in her opinion, looked entirely too young to be a real lawyer. The fine sprinkling of freckles across his ruddy cheeks and his thick unruly red hair gave him a boyish appearance that made her feel old.

She was tired. Nervous exhaustion had seeped into her bones. After eight days in the county jail, she wanted nothing more than to be done with it.

"All rise," the bailiff called out. "The Honorable Judge Andrew Black, presiding."

A serious man with a pinched red nose stepped up to the bench and took his seat. Those in the room sat down.

Leela looked behind her again, trying to catch Victor's eye. Daniel Riley nudged her, shaking his head. "Eyes on the judge," he admonished. Leela straightened her back, took a deep breath, and willed herself to concentrate on the hearing.

"Will the defendant please stand?" Judge Black tapped his fingers on the large podium as he stared down at Leela. She and Daniel Riley rose together.

"Leela Brannon Wilder," the judge began, "you are present before this court to answer questions related to the death of Carey Logan on the fourteenth of May, 1921. You have been arraigned and formally charged with first-degree murder. How do you plead?"

"Not guilty, Your Honor," Daniel Riley answered for his client.

"Take your seats," the judge instructed.

Leela sat quietly, trying not to let herself get so nervous she'd start to shake. As the opening statements were read, she began to feel as if she had floated away, had removed herself from the proceedings and someone else was really sitting in the chair before the judge.

Words from Mr. Pollem, the prosecutor, drifted over her.

". . . and the state of Texas expects the evidence to show that after a violent argument, Leela Brannon Wilder shot Carey Logan in cold blood, on the night of May fourteenth. Her motive was revenge. Vicious, calculated revenge for the deceased's role in the destruction of her oil wells and her home through his unsuccessful attempt to profit from her land. As the witnesses will demonstrate, Leela Wilder and Carey Logan had a long-standing relationship, which, when ultimately unveiled by the state, will prove beyond a shadow of a doubt that this act of murder of which Mrs. Wilder is charged was a desperate attempt on her part to remove Mr. Logan from her life."

Leela shrank deeper into her seat, wanting to disappear completely. Her fear that the prosecution would confuse and distort her naive infatuation with Carey Logan was now confirmed.

Cautiously, she glanced over her shoulder again.

Victor Beaufort's solemn eyes caught hers and remained riveted to her face. She had never seen him look so much like a stranger.

The prosecutor droned on. Leela drifted in and out of the proceedings, coming to attention when the first witness was called: Sheriff Thompson.

"Did you question Mrs. Wilder on the evening of May fourteenth at the Denton Street address referred to in this case?" the prosecutor asked.

"Yes, I did," Sheriff Thompson replied.

"In what condition did you find Mrs. Wilder?"

"Nervous. Scared."

Leela listened to the testimony, thankful that the sheriff was prone to one-syllable answers with no elaboration and that Mr. Pollem confined his questions to the procedural aspects of the lawman's behavior. She was relieved when the witness was turned over to Daniel Riley for questioning.

"Would it be fair to say that Mrs. Wilder's condition bordered on hysteria?" the defense attorney probed.

"Hysteria?" Sheriff Thompson scratched his chin and thought for a moment, then answered. "No. I never thought she was hysterical."

"How would you describe her condition?"

"Well, in my opinion, I thought she was kinda actin'. You know, making it up to look like she was so upset."

"I'm not interested in your opinion, Sheriff!" Riley quickly interrupted his witness. "I want to know how Mrs. Wilder appeared."

"Well," the sheriff mumbled, "I didn't see a whole lot of tears."

"Did you immediately consider her a suspect?" Riley drew closer to the sheriff and leaned over him.

"Why, sure. I had an eyewitness who said she saw everything. Yeah, I considered her a prime suspect. She had blood all over her dress."

Victor Beaufort took his seat, raised one hand and swore to tell the truth, without once looking in Leela's direction. As a hostile witness he appeared before the judge only because he was summoned. His answers were curt, to the point of being rude, and he cautiously refrained from saying anything that might be damaging to Leela.

He gave them the details of the contract, his reason for selling to Carey Logan and admitted his mistake in going against Leela's advice.

At those words Leela leaned forward, elbows on the table, trying to get Victor's attention. It was no use, he avoided her gaze, focusing on the far back wall or looking down at his hands as he spoke.

I've hurt him deeply, Leela thought. And now he has admitted, right here in court, before a roomful of strangers, that he lost the woman he loved as a result of his dealings with Carey Logan.

She sat and watched him testify, thinking how far apart they remained. It's all my fault, Leela told herself, I was the one to push him away, and now I hate that he's accepted my decision. She listened to him flounder for words to explain his behavior while trying to avoid discussing their relationship.

And suddenly she no longer wanted to be apart from him. She wanted Victor's love; she needed him at her side. No good could come of their suffering alone.

As Victor described the agony of his decision to sign over five percent of his lease to Carey Logan, Leela relived his torment and understood his rationale: He was desperate to prove himself, and his love for her had spurred him into the ill-fated agreement. He had not acted as hastily as she had accused him. He had considered his options and gone ahead with the deal, paying dearly for his bad gamble. Now, what was left for him to do?

He was too proud! Too stubborn! she lamented. If only he had come to me!

She sat rigidly as he described the damage done by the mob to the oil fields, the farmhouse, the barns and the land. Shuddering at the memory of the explosions, Leela silently pleaded for him to look at her. But still Victor steadfastly ignored her. An icy chill swept over Leela and her resolve to punish Victor began to soften, her hunger for revenge evaporated. She'd hurt him enough and now she was sorry.

By the time Victor stepped down from the stand, Leela's head was pounding, split in half with pain. But she sat tensely upright, dreading the next witness: Josephine Alexander.

With Josephine's testimony, Leela thought, my future with Victor Beaufort will be determined.

The sullen scowl on her face had melted, transforming Josephine into a vision of innocent composure. After settling her plump frame into the high-backed chair, she smiled sweetly at the judge, calmly surveyed the curious visitors filling the courtroom, then blinked her eyes at the prosecutor. Josephine Alexander was thrilled to be on the stand.

At the prosecutor's request, Leela's first cousin began to relate what she witnessed on the night of May 14.

". . . and I wondered right away why she had come to my house. Leela's never been one to visit."

"Is it true that you and your cousin were on unfriendly terms at the time of Mr. Logan's death?"

"Yes, sir. Cousin Leela is a selfish, wicked person, and I will never forgive her for the way she treated me when we were younger. She took over my room, my friends, my dolls; whatever was mine, she just took it. She's still taking things that don't belong to her out of my momma's house. Just plain greedy, she is, just greedy. I hated the way she walked all over my family to get whatever she wanted. She even convinced my brother—my only brother—to leave Mexia." Josephine fixed Leela with a blank stare. "We never got along. Not from the first day she came to live at my house."

"Did she ever threaten you or a member of your family?"

"Not really, but she always said awful things about me and especially about my husband, Johnny Ray. She turned my mother against Johnny Ray so bad, we had to run away to get married. They argued all the time. That's why she stayed away. My husband never liked having her around."

Leela grabbed her attorney's arm. "That's a lie," she hissed into his ear. "They were never married, and I was the one who stayed away from her."

"Don't worry," Daniel Riley said calmly. "You'll get your chance to respond."

"On the night that Carey Logan was murdered," the prosecutor continued, "what did you overhear the defendant say to the deceased?"

"It was terrible the things they said to each other. Frightening, too. I know I heard things never been told before."

"Go on," the state's attorney urged.

"Well, Leela was spitting fire when she got inside the house, screaming about all the damage that had been done to her place. Told Mr. Logan he was gonna pay. Not in money, I thought, but pay with his life or something like that."

"Objection!" Riley stood and called out. "Conjecture!"

"Sustained," the judge ruled. "Miss Alexander, we don't want your thoughts, only exactly what you saw and overheard."

"Oh, yes, Your Honor."

"What was Mr. Logan's response to the defendant's allegations?"

"He laughed at her. He said she was crazy. Said it wasn't his fault those men got all riled up and burned her oil fields that night."

"Who produced the gun which was used to kill Carey Logan? Did the defendant bring the gun with her?"

"No, no," Josephine said quickly. "It was Mr. Logan's gun, all right. I knew 'cause I had asked him not to leave it in the kitchen table drawer. But he never did anything when I asked him to move it."

"Why did Mr. Logan have a gun? Was he suicidal, despondent? Did he talk about taking his life?"

"He never said a word about killing himself." She grunted disdainfully. "He only had that gun for his own protection. Lived over on Belknap Street, you know. Pretty rough over there. He told me he never even had a gun 'til he moved over there."

The prosecutor faced the courtroom as he asked the next question. "You say he never talked about taking his own life. Did he talk of taking someone else's life?"

Josephine looked perplexed. "No, not that I remember."

"Did you actually see how Mr. Logan got shot?"

"Yes, sir. I did. I was standing in the same room, behind Leela."

"Please tell the court exactly what you saw."

"They had been arguing for a spell when Mr. Logan grabbed Leela by the wrist. She got angry and pushed him away. He went to the table and took out his gun."

The prosecutor interrupted. "Did he point the gun at the defendant?"

"Not really, he just kind of held on to it like it might make her stop screaming at him. I think he wanted to scare her."

"Go on."

"He walked over close to her. She said something about calling the sheriff. He told her it would not do any good . . . she tried to grab the gun from him."

"Tried?"

"Yes, sir. She missed the first time. Then, when she grabbed at it again, she got it and shot him in the head. Real fast. It all happened real fast."

Leela clamped her hands together to keep from screaming, digging her fingernails painfully into her palms. You liar! she wanted to call out. You spiteful selfish liar!

"Had Mr. Logan been drinking on the evening of his death?"

"Yeah, he drank a little too much, but he wasn't violent or anything like that."

"Was he intoxicated when the defendant arrived?"

"Well, he'd been drinking for most of the day. I guess he musta been pretty tight."

"Did you ever see Carey Logan behave in a violent, dangerous manner?"

"Never."

"Let's go back to their argument, please, before the actual shooting occurred. What did the defendant do when Mr. Logan laughed at her accusations?"

"Well . . . that's when things got all mixed up." Josephine waited to be asked a specific question.

"What do you mean, all mixed up?"

"Leela said something about Mr. Logan wanting to marry her and because she refused him, that's why she said he forged those papers and caused all this trouble."

"Marry him? To your knowledge, did the defendant and the deceased have a close relationship?"

A low murmur of surprised voices rumbled through the courtroom. Leela began to shake. Her hands felt clammy.

"I never thought so at first, but from what Mr. Logan said, they were once lovers, a while back . . ."

An audible gasp rose up from the crowd.

"Lovers? How long ago?"

"I gathered they musta been carryin' on while she was still married to Mr. Logan's brother." Josephine peeped down smugly at Leela. "I was shocked to hear Cousin Leela had been unfaithful to her husband. But you see? You never can tell about women like her. They'll do anything to get what they want."

Voices rose to such an excited level, the judge rapped his gavel three times and ordered silence.

Leela's hand flew to her mouth as she jerked around. Through a blur of tears she could see Effie sitting on the edge of the bench, a pained expression on her face. Parker rubbed his forehead with one hand, keeping his eyes downcast on his notepad. But Victor's blazing eyes fastened on hers, and Leela saw that all was lost.

She swung around and faced the judge, her breathing rapid and uneven.

". . . but I don't see how they coulda done that," Josephine continued.

"Why?" the prosecutor probed.

" 'Cause Mr. Logan called Leela his sister. Said once she had come to him willingly, but now he didn't want her 'cause he found out she was his sister." Josephine shrugged her big shoulders and let a smirk touch her lips. "Can you imagine that? I'm telling you, you can't believe a word that woman says. Would you believe a woman who would carry on with her brother? While she was already married? She's an evil, greedy woman, Judge. That's the way I see it . . . any decent person would."

The uproar from the courtroom was deafening. Leela jumped to her feet and yelled, "She's the one who's lying, Your Honor! She's the one who's not telling the truth. There's more you need to know. Please, Your Honor."

Leela yanked away from Daniel Riley's sharp tug. "I can explain it!" Leela begged for the judge's attention. "She's not telling the whole truth. Let me explain."

"Sit down, Mrs. Wilder! You are out of order," Judge Black barked. He slammed his gavel down three more times. "Sit down and remain quiet. You will have your turn to speak."

Leela gripped the back of her chair to steady herself, and as she began to sit, some movement in the crowd caught her eye. She turned to see Victor walking toward the high carved door. She never saw his face, only the back of his jacket, fringe swaying from his broad rigid shoulders as he strode out of the courtroom.

Victor! she called silently. Come back! You must listen to what I have to say. Oh, God, please.

The heavy paneled door swung shut behind him.

"Visitor!" the deputy sheriff announced. Leela blew her nose into the lace handkerchief Effie had given her and looked up to see Parker.

"Oh, Parker." She rushed into her cousin's arms and let him hold her tightly, the feel of his solid, familiar shoulders bringing a semblance of relief. "It's all gone so badly," she managed to whisper against his jacket.

"Hush, Leela. It's not over." His own voice trembled with anxiety.

"I don't think I can stand it any longer." An air of panic infused her words. "What if I'm convicted? Parker! What am I going to do?"

He could feel the tension in her body winding tighter. "Don't lose control now, Leela. I know the situation seems hopeless, but you've got to hold on." He sensed her relax a little. "Remember when I was in jail?"

"But you weren't accused of murder!" she countered.

"No. But for a seventeen-year-old boy, it was pretty frightening." He eased her off his shoulder. "You stood by me then. Now it's my turn to stand by you. I'll do what I can to get you out of this."

The muffled sound of voices in the hallway filtered into the cell.

"You'll have your chance to set everything straight," Parker said reassuringly. "Just use this time to pull yourself together. You've been through a lot, but hold on."

Pulling back, Leela searched Parker's face, knowing she could tell him anything and his love for her would not change. "You know it's true." Her words were bitterly spoken.

"What?" Parker prompted, hoping Leela would unburden herself to him. "What's true, Leela? The things Josephine said?"

Turning from Parker, Leela sat on the cot, her eyes averted. "Partially true. Yes, it is." The admission took all of her strength.

"Tell me, Leela. It's all right."

In the fifteen-minute recess granted by the judge, Leela told Parker of her ill-fated encounter with Carey and how she learned he was her half-brother.

"Put it behind you, Leela," was all Parker said, stroking her hair to comfort her.

Leela blew her nose, wiped her eyes and managed to give him a weak smile.

Chapter Thirty-Four

The hearing was scheduled to resume the next morning at ten o'clock sharp, but by nine, when Parker and Margaret entered the noisy courtroom, guards were already turning people away.

Victor did not come back, Leela noticed with despair. The memory of his angry stride from the courtroom made her flinch.

Effie, who was scheduled to testify, sat with Parker. Josephine, already cross-examined by the defense and not required to return, had smugly shown up again.

The defense soon called Effie Alexander to testify on Leela's character. With her loyalty split, she avoided the damaging testimony of her daughter while adamantly defending her niece. Effie portrayed Leela as a sober, generous woman who often went out of her way to help others. A woman who, in her opinion, could never have taken another person's life and certainly would never lie.

Johnny Ray Mosley took the stand next, delighted to have a

forum from which to criticize Josephine. Daniel Riley probed his relationship with the woman who called herself his wife.

"Are you currently married to Josephine Alexander?"

"No," Johnny Ray said quickly, smirking at the crowd.

"Were you ever married to her?"

"Never."

"Please explain to the court why she considers you her husband, as indicated in her testimony yesterday."

"She moved herself out to my pa's farm when she found out she was pregnant."

"When was that?"

"Oh, some time back. The boy's close to fourteen now."

"The boy? Is he your son?"

Johnny Ray contorted his mouth, squirmed in his seat and looked past Josephine. "She says so, but I never was real sure. She was always slipping off, you know? I didn't wanna cause no fuss, so I just went along with her. She's the one who moved in on me. I ain't even sure if the baby girl's mine either. With a woman like Josephine, a man can be tricked. That's the way she operates. Tricks and lies." He picked at his fingernails as he continued. "Now that the oil's come in on my daddy's farm, she says the kids is due their shares. Even filed a lawsuit against me. But she ain't gonna win it. She's just trying to get my money for herself; she don't care nothing 'bout them kids."

"You lying bastard!" Josephine shot to her feet and screamed at Johnny Ray. "You know damn well Oliver's your child. So is Penny. Looks just like him, Judge. You oughta see the boy. Looks just like his daddy."

Judge Black rapped his gavel to regain order in the court. "You sit down and be quiet. You are completely out of order. Sit down!"

"Next time I see you in court I'm gonna have them kids with me! You can't deny 'em, Johnny Ray. You know them kids is yours!"

"Sit down and be quiet, Miss Alexander! This is not a paternity hearing." Judge Black beat the desk with his gavel and frowned menacingly at Josephine.

She flopped down heavily in her seat.

Daniel Riley went on. "Why would Josephine Alexander lie about the marriage and the children?"

"To get her hands on my money. She knows I wasn't never her

husband and never wanted to be. She just dreamed up this marriage stuff. There wasn't never no legal papers between us."

"To your knowledge, were Miss Alexander and the defendant, Leela Wilder, on unfriendly terms?"

Now Johnny Ray turned his deep-set eyes on Leela. She flinched and tensed her jaw.

"Oh, they never were on real speaking terms. Seemed to tolerate each other for family sake, you know? They never spent much time together, kinda went their separate ways."

"Are you and Josephine Alexander still living together?"

"No. She got up one day and told me she was going to visit her momma."

"Did she?"

"Naw. She was lying. She stole some things what belonged to my daddy and went to live in the house over on Denton Street. Didn't do nothing but start selling bootleg whiskey outa that house. I stayed away from her after that."

When Johnny Ray stepped down, the judge ordered a short recess. Leela and her attorney took advantage of the break to review her impending testimony.

"Leela, you've got to tell me everything you know about Carey Logan. Were you two related? Was there reason to believe he'd shoot himself? All this must be clear to me or I cannot adequately defend you."

Leela paced the cell in a panic. Riley kept the pressure on.

"There is a very, very weak point in the case, you know," he said, continuing his probing.

"What?" Leela asked, stopping abruptly, eyeing Riley cautiously.

"It's not likely that a man who had Carey's reputation for cheating and running schemes against people and high living would be so despondent he'd attempt suicide." Riley paused, giving Leela the opportunity to speak. She said nothing.

"The prosecution will infer that Carey Logan never planned on killing himself—or you, for that matter . . . and that you had a hand in his eventual death." Riley gave Leela an inquisitive stare. "Is there something else I should know? Perhaps there was more to Carey Logan's despondent state that night than you've told me?"

Leela stiffened, then strode closer to Riley. "All right!" She yelled at him. "Yes! Yes! There was more!" She didn't stop until she was inches in front of Riley. "He told me he had just learned from his mother that he and I were fathered by the same man!" Her shoulders heaved and trembled as she let him absorb her confession. "Carey was my half-brother. And, yes! He did seduce me, but I never had sex with him. Never!" The words tumbled out as Leela agitatedly smeared tears from her cheeks.

An awkward silence descended over the cell; then Riley reached out to touch Leela's shoulder.

"I needed to hear you say that," he comforted. "Now I know which way to proceed." He offered her his handkerchief and stepped back. "There's no way to substantiate Carey's allegation . . . he's dead . . . his mother cannot speak. I won't bring the issue up. But when you are cross-examined, speak the truth, Leela, and only give information that has a bearing on the case. Understand?"

Miserably afraid to reenter the courtroom, she nodded.

"All right then. Let's go back in and get this hearing over." He stepped back and let Leela pass in front of him. She turned and said, "Thank you, Mr. Riley. I know I hadn't been entirely honest. Now I feel much better about this. I only hope the judge will understand."

Back in the courtroom, Lydia Grey, an aging spinster who occupied her time sitting on her porch watching people come and go on Denton Street, lifted her pointed chin, adjusted her spectacles, and repeated her oath.

"Where do you live, Miss Grey?" Riley asked in a brisk, rushed tone. He had told Leela that Miss Grey's mind tended to wander and he'd have to be direct, clear and swift to get her to relate in court what she saw that night.

"Six-eight-five Denton, near Sumpter." Her words were clipped, clear, and properly spoken.

"And where is your home in relation to the house where Josephine Alexander lives?"

"Right next door," the elderly woman replied, sniffing loudly as she picked at the side of her mouth with one finger.

"And were you at home on the evening of May fourteenth?"

"Yes, I certainly was. I'm always at home. I don't even go to market anymore. My neighbor brings me groceries and anything I need." She sounded more smug about that than disappointed by her homebound state.

"Please tell the court what you saw and heard on the evening in question."

"Well . . . can I back up a bit?"

"If it's relevant."

"I think so, because Miss Alexander's had such a crowd of folks traipsing through that house since she's been there. A shame, it is, the things that go on over there."

The judge glanced down through hooded eyes, unsuppressed irritation on his face. "Please be specific, Miss Grey."

"On Friday night before the shooting, Mr. Logan showed up. I saw him coming down the street, all frantic, talking to himself, no coat or tie, very disheveled. He seemed rather crazed. He was clutching a brown satchel and talking up a storm, out of his mind, as if there was somebody right there beside him. Went straight up to Miss Alexander's door, knocked and went in. Never came out 'til I saw the sheriff bring out his body. Stayed in there three days."

"Is that unusual?"

"I certainly thought so . . . everybody on the block knows what goes on in that house. Folks just come there to buy their hooch and get on out. I thought it strange this one never came out. So I figured he must be somebody she knew real well."

"You said you did not see Mr. Logan after he went inside?"

"Not exactly. I saw him through the windows—she does not even have curtains over her windows—but I did not see him on the street."

Daniel Riley raised his eyebrows in acceptance of her observations. "What else did you see?"

"The two of them, Mr. Logan and Josephine Alexander, carried on something awful. Drinking, shouting, playing cards. For money. He had a pile of money on the kitchen table. They'd be arguing, then laughing, then throwing money around. Half-dressed, too. It went on like that for three days. I had a feeling something awful was going to happen. You can't live wild like that very long before something awful happens."

"Did you see anything specific on the night of May fourteenth?"

"Yes. When Mrs. Wilder entered the kitchen, I could see everything." Lydia Grey paused to explain. "You see, Your Honor, my kitchen window faces directly onto hers. And if I'm cleaning or fixing my supper, I can't help but see what's going on over there. She ought of had curtains."

"Go on."

"They argued. I couldn't hear exactly what was said, but I saw Mr. Logan take a gun from the kitchen table drawer. He never pointed it at anybody but himself. At his head. I saw him do it and it was a terrifying thing to see."

People in the courtroom began to whisper, their voices like a muted chorus beneath the witness's convincing words.

"Order in the court!" Judge Black cracked his gavel for silence. "What happened next?"

Miss Grey smiled at the interest she had stirred among the crowd, gingerly straightened her delicate lace collar, and went on. "I saw Mrs. Wilder try to take the gun away. One time. She couldn't get it. Next thing I knew it went off."

"You heard a shot?"

"Yes. Then Mr. Logan fell down on the table and Josephine went screaming into the street. I let her come in and use my telephone. I'm the only one on Denton with a telephone—that's why I keep such a keen eye on things. I can call for help if it's needed." She nodded vigorously, as if reassuring herself that she was indeed a very good neighbor. "Anyway, Josephine came in hollering about a murder and called the sheriff."

Leela fell back in her chair in relief, grateful for this truthful rendition of Carey Logan's death. Now she would be acquitted, she told herself. Now she would be believed.

The cross-examination of Miss Grey was short and uneventful. She did not waver from her story, and the prosecutor soon relented and excused her.

It was late afternoon when Leela took the stand. Feeling hopeful but terrified, she wanted only to get through her testimony and put the ordeal behind her. Daniel Riley had whispered that Miss Grey's statements were very supportive and things were looking up.

The questions put to Leela by her attorney were those they had rehearsed and she knew would be asked. True to his word, feeling there was no way to corroborate Josephine's allegation that Leela and Carey were brother and sister, Daniel Riley avoided the issue entirely.

He restricted his questions to the sequence of events on May 14, introducing a copy of the forged lease papers, not denying the fact that Carey Logan had been instrumental in the destruction of Leela's property, presenting his client as a woman angered but not capable of murder. And based on the statements of both Josephine Alexander and Lydia Grey, Carey Logan had been drinking heavily that night and had possession of the gun.

"And what happened when you tried to take the gun away?" Riley asked Leela.

"I missed it. I think he may have jerked slightly. It all happened so fast . . . but I remember the look of shock . . . surprise on his face before the gun went off. It was horrible." Leela could feel tears running down her cheeks. "I refused to believe the pistol had gone off, but it had."

"And after he was shot, what happened?"

Judge Black leaned forward to hear better.

"He fell toward me," Leela said huskily. "The gun slipped from his hand and hit me on the chest. That's when the blood got on my dress. Then he fell onto the table." She choked back tears. "He lay there bleeding, and Josephine ran out, to get help, I supposed."

"And when Josephine Alexander returned?"

"She was out of control. Screaming that I had killed Carey Logan. That I had pulled the trigger!" Leela slightly rose from her seat. "She was wrong! She just wanted to blame me. Besides, she was in the shadows, she could not have seen exactly what happened."

"Did you shoot Carey Logan?" Daniel Riley asked his client.

"No, I did not," Leela answered, her voice low, unemotional.

"How did Mr. Logan die?"

"It was an accident. He killed himself by mistake."

"Thank you, Mrs. Wilder."

The prosecutor took over. Harold Pollem, a middle-aged attorney who had been born and raised in Limestone County, was not considered an aggressive man, but he was thorough. He had a low-key approach that started out very smoothly, but as he probed and probed he would dig so deeply into his witnesses' stories, they would often break down and give him much more information than even he ever expected. Such was the case in his approach to Leela Wilder.

As the methodical prosecutor moved forward with his case, many spectators in the courtroom grew weary of the plodding questions and began talking under their breath. The judge had to order silence several times during her testimony.

After an hour and thirty-five minutes, Leela began to wish that he would get to the actual shooting. Her attention wandered slightly and she looked up to see Victor slip through the door and scan the room until he connected with Parker. The two men nodded discreetly at one another.

Victor did not sit down. He remained standing alone in the back, seeming to glower at Leela, a dark shadow cast over his face. Leela shifted in her chair, sitting taller, lifting her head, determined to make it through the final stage of this hearing without breaking down.

So he's back, she thought, the pain of his rejection still stinging the sides of her face. Well, he could have stayed away. She'd finish with this testimony and walk out of here. A free woman. And she'd never speak to him again.

As much as she wanted to ignore his presence, Leela could not help shifting her eyes to his. The sight of him weakened her. Everything around her faded and rippled into shadows. She stared, transfixed, at Victor, realizing his dark, gloomy mood was not anger. He looked miserable, contrite, standing with his Stetson in his hands, bent at the shoulders as if the burden of his unhappiness had conquered him.

Pollem droned on, covering the same questions Leela had already answered for Daniel Riley. Nothing differed in her responses, little differed in his line of questioning. Until he asked her:

"How were you related to the deceased?"

Throwing back her shoulders, Leela remembered Daniel Riley's words of caution: "Do not admit to anything that cannot be proven. Do not complicate your situation."

"Would you clarify that question, please?" she asked politely, feeling her stomach begin to tighten. Now it has begun, she thought.

Pollem let out an exasperated sigh. "Were you related in any way to the deceased?"

"Carey Logan was my deceased husband's half-brother," she carefully replied.

"What I mean, Mrs. Wilder, is, were you related by blood to Carey Logan?"

"I'm not sure," she said evenly, drawing out her words.

"What do you mean, you're not sure? What is it that you don't know?"

"I don't know if Carey Logan was telling the truth when he said I was his half-sister."

"Had you ever been told that before? That Carey Logan and you were related by blood?"

"No, sir."

"Then where do you think he got that information?"

"He said his mother, Hattie Wilder, told him."

"Did you ask his mother about this?"

"I tried, but she was unable to speak. She's had a stroke and cannot talk."

"Did you have an intimate relationship with Carey Logan?"

"Intimate? What do you mean?"

"Intimate! You know exactly what I mean. Were you and Mr. Logan involved in an affair? At any time? Past or present!" Pollem faced the judge as he bellowed, "I remind you that you are under oath to tell the complete truth, Mrs. Wilder. Did you and Carey Logan have an affair?"

The silence that descended over the courtroom bordered on reverence. Mouths hung open, breathing stopped, necks stretched forward, waiting to hear her reply.

Leela clasped her hands together and looked down at Daniel Riley. He nodded for her to go ahead and answer the question.

"I mistakenly allowed myself to be captivated by Carey Logan's charm eight years ago."

"You were married when this 'captivation' took place?"

Leela nodded.

"Speak up, please!"

"Yes," came her weak reply. "He set out to seduce me. I was lonely and vulnerable. We embraced . . . he tried to take advantage of the situation." Locking eyes with Victor, she added, "But I never had a sexual relationship with Carey Logan. There was *never* a physical consummation."

The gasp rising up in the courtroom sounded like a choral refrain.

"At the time you visited Mr. Logan on Denton Street, what was your relationship to a Mr. Victor Beaufort?"

Leela did not answer.

"Mrs. Wilder, didn't you have an ongoing relationship with both Mr. Beaufort and Mr. Logan at the same time?"

Shocked spectators murmured in surprise, their voices growing louder and louder as Leela sat there, trying to gather her thoughts.

"Isn't that the truth, Mrs. Wilder? Please answer the question."

"No! That is not the truth. At the time I met Mr. Beaufort, I had not seen Carey Logan for seven years."

"But isn't it true that Logan's actions against you were the reason you terminated your engagement to Victor Beaufort?"

Leela could hardly utter the word. "Yes, but—"

"And so on the night of May fourteenth, when you sought out Carey Logan, you took revenge on him . . . not only for destroying your oil fields, but also for destroying your relationship with Mr. Beaufort. Isn't that right? Isn't that why you became so enraged you shot the deceased?"

"No!" Leela looked directly at Victor, so agitated she stood up, leaning over the wooden railing before her, imploring Victor to believe what she said. "I did not kill Carey Logan. He was frightened, despondent, and drunk. He said he loved me, but had been told by his mother that I was his half-sister, that we shared the same father. The news had devastated him. He was out of control!"

"Please, sit down, Mrs. Wilder!" Judge Black ordered.

Leela eased down into her chair and lowered her eyes, unable to stand the torment on Victor's face. "That's the truth—that's what Carey Logan said before the gun was fired. I don't know if what he said is true. I don't know for certain that Carey was my half-brother, and until Hattie Logan is well enough to talk, no one will know the truth. But you are right about one thing." Now she addressed Victor directly, the briefest flicker of disgust sweeping over her face. "I despised Carey Logan. Beneath his smooth talk and handsome face was an ugly twisted soul. His infatuation with me and the tragic relationship he had with his mother fueled his scheme to get my land and to drive Victor Beaufort out of my life. He nearly succeeded. Victor Beaufort and I were *both* victims of Carey Logan's greed." Leela lowered her head into her hands and wept.

"I have no more questions," Harold Pollem said in his deep, resonant voice.

Leela wiped her eyes and rose to leave the witness stand, searching the crowd for Victor. She did not see him. Had he left? A slow burn of humiliation stung her. Didn't he understand what she had been trying to tell him? She was sorry! She was wrong! She wanted him back. How could he disappear like that? Impatiently, she scanned the packed courtroom. How dare he walk out in the middle of her plea to regain his love? He doesn't even care about the verdict, she realized. Leela gripped the back of her chair and slumped down in exhaustion.

Daniel Riley patted her on the arm and whispered, "Don't worry. It's almost over."

Judge Andrew Black called for a ten-minute recess, stepped down from the bench and disappeared behind a door. Leela sat with her attorney in silence, her knees trembling beneath the table. Riley drew pictures of animals on the back of a long white envelope, calmly awaiting the verdict. There was nothing more to be said at this point. They had done the best they could.

The bailiff announced the judge's return and everyone rose in expectation. When all were seated once more, Judge Black cleared his throat and peered over his glasses at Leela.

"Will the defendant please rise?"

This time Leela stood alone.

"I have listened to all the testimony and examined the evidence offered by the prosecution, and I am now ready to render my decision."

Leela stood paralyzed before the man who was about to determine her fate. The room darkened slightly, the stale heat in the stifling space threatening to overcome her. She clutched the edge of the table and waited.

"With the conflicting testimony of two eyewitnesses to the events leading up to the shooting death of Carey Logan, I must believe that neither clearly saw what actually happened. Whether the defendant was or was not related to the deceased cannot be determined and is immaterial to these proceedings. Therefore, based on the testimony given here, I find that Carey Logan died of an accidental shooting. All charges against the defendant are dismissed." He banged his big gavel with three loud cracks, got up and left the courtroom.

There were jubilant cries from the agitated crowd, and many well-wishers thronged forward with congratulations. Leela was hugged and touched and kissed on the cheek by many who had believed in her innocence. Effie and Parker rushed to her side and crushed her with embraces of happiness. Yet as Leela searched the crowd for Victor she was devastated not to find him.

EPILOGUE

Leela took the half-finished glass of lemonade from Kenny's hand and placed her fingers lightly on his shoulders.

"Time we got started," she addressed Parker. "Better get going before it gets too late."

"Kenny," Effie began, kneeling to put her arms around her nephew. "It's not a pretty sight at the farm, but your momma's right . . . you need to see it."

Parker put on his hat and kissed Margaret on the cheek. "We won't be long. I'm kind of anxious myself to see how things look."

Effie watched them leave, thanking God that Leela's acquittal yesterday had brought her back to her son. Going back to Rioluces would be difficult, but it was the beginning of the future.

During the ride to the farm, Leela held her son tightly as he asked her a thousand questions about jail. Had she been afraid? Did the sheriff scare her? Did she have to eat bread and water? Were there lots of rats? As best she could, Leela tried to answer him, while struggling to put the entire incident out of her mind.

She was nervous about Kenny's returning home; he had not seen the devastated landscape or the skeletal remains of their house. She hoped it would not frighten him, for everything was charred and ugly.

They soon rounded a curve in the lane and Rioluces rose up: blackened, ash-covered acreage. The stark sight of the shattered farmhouse shocked Leela and memories of that terrifying night engulfed her. Cautiously, she glanced at Parker, who took his eyes off the road to give her an understanding nod.

As they drew closer, the blast of the explosions and smell of the thick oily smoke flashed into memory. We were lucky to get out alive, she thought.

As they swung through the broken gate, the sight of Victor Beaufort's black Model T parked by the side of the house jarred Leela. She gasped slightly, leaning forward, her hand tightening on Kenny's shoulder.

"It looks like you have a visitor on the place," Parker mused aloud.

"Oh, that's just Victor," Kenny piped up, smiling as he hunched closer to the window. "Wow, the place is all burned out, isn't it, Ma? It's worse than I thought. Do you think Victor can fix it?"

Leela did not know what to say. The boy knew nothing of their troubles. "It may be too much for Victor to fix," she finally replied, her heart racing at the thought of his presence.

The car rolled to a stop and Kenny jumped out.

"You be careful, son," Leela called. "Don't go into the house, it's not safe." Her words fell on empty space, for Kenny had already rounded the house, chasing a small gray kitten.

Parker helped Leela from the car. "Don't worry about the boy, I'll keep an eye on him. Go on. Go see what's on Beaufort's mind."

Leela could see that Victor was facing her. At the bottom of the hill he stood immobile and tall, his shadow stretching thin and black into the dusty barnyard, marking the land with his image. She started down the hill. He made no move to come to her.

Pushing back her hat, shaking loose her hair, she drew closer and stopped within two feet of Victor's silent form.

"Hello," he said, shattering the wall of silence between them.

"Why are you here?" was all Leela could manage.

"I hoped you would come. Parker said you might."

She moved back slightly. "He told you I would be here? On Rioluces? You and Parker arranged this?" She felt cornered, trapped into a childish attempt to bring them together.

"We talked," Victor admitted. "Several times," he added, a sheepish expression sweeping over his face. He hesitated, filled with confusion—the embarrassment that comes with a difficult confession. "I told him the truth, Leela. I am very much in love with you, and I'm not at all concerned with what came out at the hearing. I know what kind of man Carey Logan really was. He used you! He used all of us!" The suffering in his voice, the tension in his face, and the urgency of his plea cut straight to Leela's heart. "I love you. Nothing will ever change that. The pain I've caused you will haunt me for the rest of my life, and I don't have the words to tell you how miserable and lost I feel."

Leela swayed at the onslaught of his confession. Tilting her head back, she struggled to remain composed. Victor's words convinced her that his love was unconditional, his commitment unshakable.

"I don't know how else to say it," he went on. "I need you in my life." His words rushed out in an agonizing stream. "Damn the land! Damn the oil! All I want is a future with you. I love you, Leela."

Leela opened her mouth to speak, but very gently, as if calming a child, Victor placed his fingertips over her lips.

"But if there is no hope for us," he said tenderly, "tell me now, my love, tell me the truth, and I'll be on the evening train back to Oklahoma."

Leela removed his fingers, thrilling to the feel of his hand in hers. It's been so long since I've touched him, she thought, remembering his hands roaming the length of her body, making her soul sing with joy.

"This is very difficult, Victor. So much has happened."

"Yes," he agreed. "I understand your anger, I do. But I won't leave Texas unless you tell me to go," he finished, his voice husky. Victor turned his face away for a moment, then pierced her with an expectant stare.

Leela felt the sincerity in Victor's voice creeping into her heart. Her eyes traveled from his wide Stetson to his rugged jaw, to the fringe swaying gently from his broad shoulders. She thought of loving him again, holding him close, stroking the smooth satin skin of his back. She took a deep breath and sighed aloud.

"I've been through hell, Victor. A hell you helped bring down on me. It's not so easy to forget . . . to forgive."

Victor moved closer and put his arms around her waist. She did not pull away.

"Yes," he whispered, his breath warm and delicate on her cheek, "and I also know that anything worth having is not easy to claim."

His words stirred her. She moved nearer and allowed him to press her head onto his shoulder. He ran his fingers through the blazing tangle of her hair, gently caressing the warm spot at the nape of her neck.

"I do love you, Victor. I do," she admitted. "I'm just not sure we . . ."

"Love is all we will ever need," he murmured. "With love, the forgiving and forgetting will come . . . in time." He felt her stir beneath his hands. "Please, don't say another word," he cautioned. "Let this do the talking for both of us."

Leela raised her head from his shoulder and saw he held his hand out to her. In the center of his palm lay her ruby-and-diamond ring.

"My ring," she cried. "You got it back!"

Victor laughed and slipped it on her finger. Then he kissed her with all the passion and fire Leela knew would be hers forever.

AFTERWORD

Many of the African Americans who became wealthy from the discovery of oil in Mexia (pronounced Ma-hay-a) owed thanks to Mexican general Jose Antonio Mexia. In the mid-1870s, he purchased thousands of acres of land and laid out the town at the headwaters of the Navasota River. The acreage was then divided among the white settlers, ex-slaves and the freed black men and women who flocked to the western edge of the city to build their homes. None realized that they had settled on the most valuable oil-rich land of the Balcones fault.

Nestled between Spindletop, America's first and most famous gusher, and the dusty windblown boomtowns of the Permian Basin fields, Mexia was at the crossroads of Texas's oil discovery trail. As black gold gushed forth from the rich crescent-shaped fault, all oil production records of the era were shattered. Headlines across the nation blazed with staggering production figures from the Mexia area fields, which peaked in 1924 at 59,325,876 barrels—one-tenth of the total production in the nation and twice as much oil as had been produced in the country so far.

Tragically, a frenzy of unregulated, wasteful exploration swept through the Mexia area, exhausting the reserves and devastating the land. By 1940, most of the boomers, wildcatters and major oil companies had moved on to other discovery sites, leaving the tired pumps circling Mexia belching forth a few dozen barrels a day.

Looking back, production experts believe that if properly regulated, the oil fields of Limestone County could have lasted for one hundred years.